Clive Ashman

LAWYERS OF LUGVALIO

VOREDA BOOKS

First published by Voreda Books 2021
Copyright © Clive Ashman 2020-21
www.voredabooks.com
enquiries@voredabooks.com

ISBN 978-0-9556398-4-5

A **CIP Record** for this book is available from the **British Cataloguing in Publication Data Office**
Printed & bound in Gt. Britain by **Biddles Books Ltd.**
Castle House, East Winch Road, Blackborough End, Kings Lynn PE32 1SF

iv

Dedicated to the team of archaeologists & volunteers who unearthed the Edenside bathhouse together.

And their hope it might one day be displayed.

With special thanks to the team of pre-readers who so patiently reviewed my early drafts.

Including not least, nor in order of effort:
Charlotte Alcock
Douglas Thomas
Helen Byass
Julie Husband
Marcus Alcock

And also acknowledging:

The quotation at page 297 by Robert Graves is from his "*I, Claudius*" and reprinted by kind permission of the Carcanet Press, 30 Cross Street Manchester M2 7AQ

v

NUMBERED KEY TO LOCATIONS – MAP OF BRITANNIA INFERIOR

(Showing 'ITER II' the main road-route from EBORACUM *to* LUGVALIO)

I.	EBORACUM	- CITY, COLONIA & LEGIONARY BASE
II.	ISURIUM BRIGANTUM	- TOWN & OFFICIAL TRIBAL CAPITAL
III.	CATARACTONIUM	- A TOWN, FORT & BRIDGEHEAD
IV.	'STANWICK'	- TRADITIONAL TRIBAL CENTRE OF BRIGANTES
V.	MAGLONA	- A COHORT FORT
VI.	LAVATRIS	- COHORT FORT - 'THE SUMMIT FORT'
VII.	'MAI-DUN'	- SMALL FORT/CASTELLUM ON THE STONE MOOR
VIII.	VERTERIS	- A FORT (OTHERWISE 'VERTERAE')
IX.	BRAVONIACUM	- A FORT & SETTLEMENT
X.	BROCAVUM	- A FORT & SETTLEMENT
XI.	VOREDA	- A FORT & SETTLEMENT
XII.	LUGUVALIUM	- A CITY & TRIBAL CAPITAL (OR 'LUGVALIO')
XIII.	UXELLODUNUM	- 'THE HIGH FORT' - BASE TO ALA PETRIANA
XIV.	VALLUM AELIUS	- 'THE ENTRENCHMENTS' (HADRIAN'S WALL)
XV.	VINDOLANDA	- 'WHITE LAWNS' – A FORT & SETTLEMENT
XVI.	CORIA	- MILITARY DEPOT & TOWN (OR 'CORSTOPITUM')
XVII.	ARBEIA	- 'FORT OF THE ARABS' – A SEASIDE SUPPLY DEPOT
XVIII.	EPIACVM	- ISOLATED COHORT FORT, GUARDING LEAD MINES
XIX.	TRIMONTIUM	- THE ROMAN FORWARD BASE AT NEWSTEAD
XX.	LIMES ANTONINUS PIUS	- ANTONINE WALL FRONTIER SYSTEM
XXI.	'THE OCHRE FORT'	- AN ANTONINE WALL FORT
XXII.	CLOTA	- THE FIRTH OF CLYDE, SCOTLAND – A SEA ESTUARY

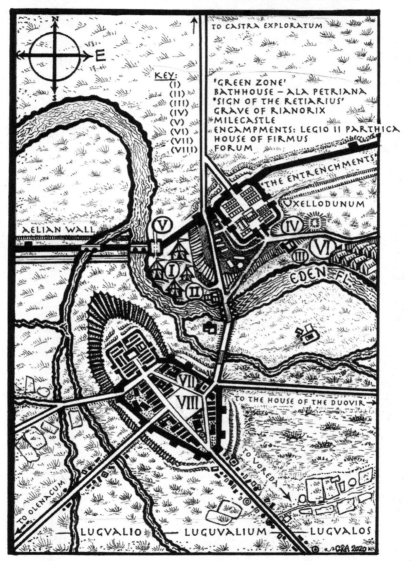

KEY:
(I) 'GREEN ZONE'
(II) BATHHOUSE – ALA PETRIANA
(III) 'SIGN OF THE RETIARIUS'
(IV) GRAVE OF RIANORIX
(V) MILECASTLE
(VI) ENCAMPMENTS: LEGIO II PARTHICA
(VII) HOUSE OF FIRMUS
(VIII) FORUM

'LAWYERS OF LUGVALIO' © Clive Ashman 2020

THIS STORY IS BASED ON REAL-LIFE EVENTS

Clive Ashman

Prologue

The Ochre Fort, Limes of Antoninus Pius, edge of Caledonia: AD 161-2

The centurion Marcus Firmus stood alone on the slumping turf rampart of his Ochre Fort and looked out onto endless sheets of rain. The best defence they had these days would seem to be the weather. If ever the clouds parted and the sun came out for longer than a week, then he feared for their safety, knew the tribes would come down. Marooned by an emperor's order on this fortified border to malign wilderness, he and his men were sworn to defend a civilisation too many days' march away to rescue them, for all its promising that one day they'll withdraw.

Till then they must hold the line, await their fate with patience. Imagining that when his own nemesis appeared - as for anyone it must – then it would be swift and soon, arriving from the north.

When in reality she came later - from the south and slowly.

Burdened with unspoken tensions like these, while still looking outwards and north, he unconsciously grabbed a merlon off their timber battlement. A large piece of it came away in his hands - wet wood crumbling between his fingers like rotting flesh to snag on Apollo, engraved in his signet ring.

Firmus turned away in disgust. He nodded to a nearby sentry, shrouded in his soaking cloak, exchanged passwords, and then half-walked, half-slid down some slimy steps in the rampart-backing to rejoin the inner road. His dedicated suite of rooms were no less damp and disintegrating than any other barrack block where auxiliaries keep warm beside horses, but the difference here was privacy. He could get away from the men.

Soon he was comfortably settled beside a warming charcoal brazier, with an oil lamp for light, but his interlude of peace didn't last for very long:

"What are you doing?" she said in a vexed voice, walking through the door.

"I'm reading."

"Reading...?"

"Yes. A book."

"It looks more like a rolled-up tent, to me."

"It's a scroll."

"Oh, a 'scroll'. What's that?"

"It's writing – marks, words made on vellum. A calfskin – you unroll it."

"What's it about – what do they say?"

"It's Tacitus."

"A Roman?"

"Of course. He's writing about his father-in-law. A famous general called Agricola, who conquered these lands, long ago."

"Well, he didn't do a very good job of that, did he? Just look around you now."

"It's history, written about his father-in-law. With us, that means his wife's father."

"Is family important to you Romans?"

"Only when we're dead. While you're alive, they always let you down. But Tacitus was very proud of his relative. He was a great man, a great soldier. The tribes up here would tremble at his name."

"Was?"

"Oh, yes. Agricola's been dead a long time."

"How long?"

"Must be sixty-five years at least, maybe more. Peacefully at home, in the reign of Domitian. But he campaigned all over Britannia once – and conquered Caledonia."

"You said. And much good it's done the lot of you."

Clive Ashman

He'd never seen a tattooed woman before. It was something barbarians did. But here he was, entertaining one in his room: there'd be a scandal at home, if they knew. It was Epiclitus, the slaver, who'd brought her. The men had clubbed together with what pay they'd otherwise waste on gambling and bling to get themselves a whore for the fort. While away the winter nights. Epiclitus duly brought her up from the coast on a mule in fulfilment of their order, but from the very moment Firmus saw her, he couldn't let it happen.

The men weren't happy about it and there might have been a mutiny, except they had more sense, fearing the penalties. Humiliation, flogging, and death. So their centurion, Firmus, bought her for himself by paying a little more to the men, who despite making a tidy profit on the deal as a result still went away muttering, while Epiclitus didn't mind one bit because he knew he'd got his price.

She remained his slave but, in the privacy of his room, that didn't seem to matter, didn't seem to count. As far as Firmus was concerned, and whatever others might think about slaves, she was a human being to him. And – by the light of his oil lamp - a very beautiful one, if difficult to grasp.

They had sex on a sheepskin in front of the brazier. He couldn't call it 'making love' because her outlook on the matter was unknown, but it meant a lot to him and he needed the intimacy anyway, whatever she thought about that.

"*Legum servi sumus ut liberi esse possimus*" he'd whispered gently to her afterwards, breathing in her ear.

"So what does that pretty piece of Roman rubbish mean?" she said, stretching-out on her forearms like a puma he once saw in the Colosseum. It had just killed a convict, condemned to be tied to the stake. A man tethered like he is - unable to leave his post.

He smiled back: "We are slaves to the law, that we may be free…"

Lawyers of Lugvalio

Clive Ashman

Chapter I

Insula XIII of the Colonia Eboracensis - Britannia Inferior - AD 208

Hey, you!" a coarse voice rang out, echoing across the width of an empty street. Rude and peremptory - interrupting my happy recollection of cutting a witness off at the knees.

"What, me…?" I said, half-turning towards rooftops but reluctant to look back.

"Yes, you. Don't turn away from me!"

"I beg your pardon?" Adjusting the satchel strap over my shoulder, but striding jauntily on. Hoping that he'll go.

"I know who you are…." he said, sounding nearer now.

"Eh? What are you on about?"

"Me - I know who you are. That lawyer".

"What lawyer?" Reverting to rhetoric, as if to prove his point.

"You know very well *'what lawyer'*. Him what did me and me brother out of our inheritances. Like the rest of your kind – nothing better than a crook!"

"I really don't know what you're talking about…. what it is you mean." (Gathering speed). "But, I don't want any trouble…" I'd added, hoping it might help.

"Don't you dare walk away from me. Talk to me like that - like I amount to nothing. When this time it's me what's doing the talking, and you're that bastard who…"

Lawyers of Lugvalio

He paused briefly to look up and down the street, satisfy himself no-one else would hear some pretty personal disclosures he only wants sharing with me. Including - as my inkling had it - the very thorough kicking that's likely to be part.

Normally, at this time of day and during the working week, the scene of our encounter was a popular thoroughfare. A busy cut-through into one of the main shopping streets - meaning plenty of people about. But not today, as my luck and the Fates have it, because now it's completely deserted.

Not a single, living soul around to come to my aid, as my pursuer can easily see. My foolishness in not keeping to the rules – walking publicly abroad, alone and unescorted – gifting him the certainty I can suffer his attentions, whether kindly or not.

Now I really felt worried.

"That bastard what diddled us, stole our inheritance. So come back here and face me like a man…"

I wasn't sure if the gap between us gave time or he'd have the legs on me, but absent anyone else intervening, waiting around politely to see if blows (*or maybe just words of advice?*) were what my antagonist had in mind should be the last thing on mine.

Left no other option for me.

Awkward, unwieldy and unmanageable enough as formal wear; the heavy folds of a toga are an even greater hindrance when you need to run, I can tell you. But turn and run I did, scooping its woollen mass into one shapeless ball out of which my valiant limbs emerged to pummel the paving, propel me up the road. And I'd thought I was getting away with it too, until hearing his breath close behind me was followed by a pain in one ear.

He'd hit me. The swine had hit me – an actionable assault!

Hurt and indignity gave the Wings of Mercury, speeded me up. So I ducked under the red-and-white striped canopy of a roadside stall then weaved across the road into a covered side alley - my thudding steps echoing in a brick tunnel before emerging into the courtyard of some impenetrable slum.

Its ammoniac stink what hit me next – nearly made me retch.

Clive Ashman

Those vats of yellow urine which advertise the premises of a fuller: his customers' cloaks and clothing, out stewing in the sun. Flags of cloth hung outside to dry, but adding fresh obstacles for me to dart around and under. Help confuse a pursuer whose angry shouts and panting I could now hear right behind me:

"Bloodsuckers, the lot of you – nothing of a conscience…!"

Entering a part of the city – of my own dear city, Eboracum - which I've frankly never seen nor smelled before, and that right gladly till now. Confronted with a choice of four or five inscrutable alleyways for exit – any one of which could prove a fatal dead-end, or else grant me an escape from a fuller's foetid yard. Faced with this dilemma, I chose the least imposing, the very darkest and dingiest - offering silent prayers to Themis as I did so. Because if I ran into the proverbial brick-wall down here, then it's hard to imagine any more tawdry locale in which to bleed to death alone, end a bumpy career.

Blood pounded in my head as my feet did the ground. Above me, ancient boundary walls built out of red brick or yellow stone twisted and turned, blocking the view. With no roof to its route but only the sky, there's no overlooking building and no protective oversight available, either - whether from strangers or gawpers. While the empty alleyway I followed swerved suddenly at some random corner, leading at right-angles into another short, straight section that's bounded on its left by a cheap industrial building of wattle-and-daub, a single rickety door ajar in its wall. Hoping its entry might offer me refuge before my pursuer rounds the bend, I paused to breathe-in sharply - forcing my body, clothing and satchel together through a narrow gap.

Four labourers in filthy, sweat-stained smocks looked-up in stunned astonishment when I burst into their world. A free man in the toga of a citizen inserted into the repetitious labours of men almost certainly slaves. Save for the red glare of a furnace-mouth in one corner and that sliver of daylight I'd slid through, their workshop stood as completely in the dark as they did.

Petrified in every sense - frozen into whatever position I'd caught them in: whether clutching pincer, hammer, or a set of long tongs. A cast of stunned statues captured forever mid-stroke, inside their hellish murk.

"Help!" I begged them, but all they could do was look back at me. Goggle like idiots.

There was a roar from the door and a black shape burst howling into the room. Only the man with the long-handled tongs came to life, laying them directly across its path. There was a bang and a crash as they brought his target down in a pile of iron bars, stock from the works.

"Out!" shouted his colleague, pincer-man, pointing emphatically to the far end of their long, narrow workshop. Adjusting to the lack of light, a flight of irregular stone steps leading upwards to the other door indicated could just be discerned. I needed no further encouragement: a hop, skip, and a jump resolving their three bumpy slabs before I emerged through a door-frame, blinking in daylight.

Now I realised where I was - back in the land of the living, the new Temple of Serapis straight ahead of me. Familiar local territory: my own personal patch. Crowds filled the street and its flanking colonnades - white-linened flocks of women who might include my wife - out shopping with children and slaves. But whether she's present or willing - let alone quick enough on the uptake - I couldn't expect much by way of protection from these few detachments of women. Making my appeal to a cohort of soldiers marching up towards their fortress might have been a better bet, but they're too far away to hear.

The next possibility of rescue appeared in the shape of a line of merchants' wagons, heavy goods moving along for their next customer. Crowding a busy scene as they mingle with the usual pedlars or street-hawkers shouting-out their wares; several stray dogs and that one, foraging pig. Typical town-centre traffic and a chaos which may - together - deliver me fresh diversion: a log-jam of vehicles and vagrants in which I can safely disappear?

No, not if I'd assessed my pursuer's character correctly: a relentless, dangerous maniac. Oblivious to third parties.

Fixated on vengeance or violence - and focussed only on me.

So with no chance of safety left me outdoors, then - much like my chaser – the solution's inescapable. Why I should hide inside another building and this time *not* be found...

Reaching a set of stone steps up to the Temple of Serapis, I dodged a water-carrier and tucked myself tightly below its pediment to grab another glance along the street. I'd hardly managed a proper look at my assailant but, if I hardly recalled him, he clearly remembered me - hence the grudge, I suppose?

What definitely registered was his ruddy complexion – born of farming stock? Face framed by a curly black beard and that set of matching eyebrows which merge on his forehead, reflect ingrained resentment. Features to match the red-faced, angry man in a dark grey tunic currently patrolling an open colonnade down the south side of the highway. Stopping briefly to check inside each shop-cubicle like he's hunting for something - *or someone*.

Someone like me?

Realising my best chances of safety lay here, I bounced up its steep steps to go looking for the temple guard. Distinguishable by the large brooch of office fastening his cloak, I found him standing inside the main chamber beside a life-size statue of the eponymous, seated god - their image so lifelike, you'd believe.

Where I breathlessly announced myself as: "Justinus the advocate... in mortal danger from a stranger! From a stalker... someone who's following me now. A maniac, in short... outside on the street as we speak... I claim sanctuary here, seek protection from the god. In the Sacred Name of Serapis, please help me!"

The sort of people who do this sort of job can vary enormously in calibre, intelligence, and integrity. Why my safety lay literally in the lap of the gods – one of whose temple guards looked me up-and-down the once and then smiled:

"I'm sure The Great God will care for and save you. Just as a successful advocate like your grace will generously reward His Kindness, donate to the fabric..."

Fact is, I've never been that keen on exotic or Egyptian cults - and as for *'successful'*, well... I ask you! How can you call a self-respecting professional *that* and then expect him to survive on less than your average legionary gets paid in a year? Because, I can tell you, that's where the effects of inflation and the edicts of a long-gone emperor – the Divine Claudius, it was - have capped our fees for cases. As if my honourable profession was a calling fit only for rich men! Intended more to provide intellectual stimulation than a reliable source of income, even of food...

And I can imagine whole generations of jurists whose wealthy fathers' advice always amounted to just this: *"By all means have an occupation, my boy, but never let it assume the character of work."*

Too luxurious a philosophy for someone like me! No, with a humbler background like mine, does anyone seriously believe an antique edict dating back to Claudius represents a fair reward for all those years spent in study and practice, or gives me enough to make a decent living on? *Oh, please - don't make me spit!*

When there's always been my clerk and the witnesses to pay off - not to mention our travel costs, or else the client's supporters club massed down there, at the back of court. Plus other expenses necessary to the practice of law – including, just sometimes, the judge. Why it's a hard enough job budgeting for these expected costs without additional calls on my revenue account – like some deserving charity, money-grubbing official. Because in my line of work, working out who and what you owe then being sure to pay them back - whether for promises made on the way up, or favours done on the way down – is fundamental to how well you play the legal game. To your personal survival.

Or as our great jurist, Marcus Fabius Quintilianus, generously allows: *"...if an advocate's domestic circumstances mean he needs an extra income to meet the usual essential demands on his purse, then there's no philosopher who'd forbid him from accepting some recompense for his services. Not when even Socrates and Zeno, Cleanthes or Chrysippus, took a collection for fees from their pupils."*

Quite right – I couldn't put it better myself. With authorities like these on my side and however others see it, if we hard-working men of the law stuck to the official charging structure, then none of us would get by, earn enough to live on. Although it's a rule not easily got around, whose penalties can be swingeing. No, if I do get paid for a case – and I do mean '*if*' – then for a jobbing lawyer like me; stuck in the north of Britannia, our province at the end of the world; half the time I think myself lucky if the client's paid me off with some measly joint of meat, a thin pot of stew…

"You may hide in here, and meditate on The Divinity. While I keep watch for you and report back, once the coast is clear…" said the guard, pointing to the actual statue itself.

He seemed a genuine type, and gestured to the side of a plinth supporting the stone throne upon which this blackened likeness of Serapis sat; a cornucopia gripped in one hand, the rudder of a ship in the other. In fact, although convincingly rendered, this stone throne of His was really painted wood, with a hidden door-opening in the side panel I assume they use for miracles. The guard pressed firmly on a small piece of architrave to operate a concealed mechanism causing it to open, then gestured for me to climb through into the tiny recess now exposed. Once I had and the secret panel closed on me again, I found myself all alone in the dark, hugging my knees and satchel.

This small space beneath the plinth felt dusty, rather smelly and unpleasantly claustrophobic – not enjoyable at all. However, as my eyesight became accustomed to its gloom, a few chinks of daylight piercing some scattered gaps or knotholes helped brighten my mood, if not also illuminate a serious predicament.

It really was all down to the guard. If he betrayed me, then I'd be dead meat and soon. Dead or at least pulverised - thoroughly tenderised. Without a weapon to defend myself, there'd be no fighting back possible from inside this confined space. Not when carrying such items in a public place is illegal anyway, under the urban law, and me the lawyer who knows it.

No, all I could do was sit things out in this hole, trust to the guard and his god - contemplate the status of Serapis. Of an eastern god much favoured by our emperor – and a deity whose consort, Isis, is thought to be the mistress of our fates. *Including, on that day, of mine.* And also of visitations foreseen, including this

11

particular one that's due – once I hear, through the crack, a familiar voice by the plinth meet the calm tones of my guardian:

"Are you here for worship?"

"Yeah, well, I… honour The God…" blurted a man whose coarser tones I instantly recognised, in from the street.

"Why a donation is conventional. So tell me, do you have any specific requests of our Great Deity?"

"Yeah – I do! Has he seen the lying lawyer, Justinus? Pompous little man in a dirty toga. I hate him, you know, I curse him…"

"Ah! *Does Great Serapis see…?* My word - how deep a question is that, friend! No, I cannot speak for The God - only for myself, who does not recall your donation…?"

"Bugger your donation, mate. I just popped-in to look for someone, but see no-one else is here. So, thanks for that, mate. Yeah, thanks for nothing – 'cos I'm off!"

At least he was right about the dirty toga. With all I'd endured while wearing it, my courtroom best would need a proper trip to the fullers, sometime very soon. Once I'm safely back home that is - then there it would be sent. Or should I say *'if'*…?

The only thing to follow that final remark was a long silence, but I knew better than to move, remaining absolutely still and quiet until I heard a kinder voice I'd come to know for the guard's:

"Don't worry, Justinus. He's gone now – walking away up the street, looking in every shop while he does so. I don't think he's likely to return here or trouble us again, but all the same I'd suggest it's best you sit tight for a wee-while longer. Not a nice man, I can assure your grace – he seemed very cross. So I'll just let you know once I'm fully satisfied it's safe to climb out."

A time for thought also affording me the opportunity to hunt through my pockets, toga, and satchel in search of small change. The chance to establish how much of a donation to the temple I could actually afford. Unfortunately - and meaning no disrespect to The Deity – it turned out to be not very much at all. Since it also represented everything I had in the world, it would have to do for my expression of gratitude. Be sufficient for Serapis.

Clive Ashman

On re-entering our everyday world of daylight and obligations, the guard was polite - though less than impressed by these humble offerings of mine. At least the warm words of thanks and appreciation I accompanied them with were fulsome and generous. They were also sincere. However, for our mutual safety and to spare further embarassment, I lingered no longer in his sacred temple but made haste homewards in the opposite direction to my assailant's trajectory.

An unpleasant episode, overall - not to say a little demeaning, which was why it hurt a little. While some might think me pompous, I would chalk it down to experience. Accept how an unfortunate street confrontation gave my reminder of some enduring truths to the rough-and-tumble of law. Its salutary refresher on the nature of everyday legal practice in this tough northern town I choose to call home. A clear illustration of classic urban dangers which everyone should know about - even me. Firstly the usual one, about walking home from court alone. Its second in accountability. About being more responsible, I suppose - more circumspect in what litigation I take on.

Because if cases like these seem to myself and fellow practitioners no more than abstract intellectual exercises, our jurisprudential games, then for some of the parties involved I guess they're more significant. Nearer life and death perhaps – maybe graver yet than that? Like Marcus Aurelius says:

"The first rule is to keep an untroubled spirit. The second is to look things in the face and know them for what they are."

And if nothing else, although not always a reliable income, at least my modest legal practice has always offered me an interesting education in other peoples' lives. Life as she's lived and harsher truths that go with it - including how brief it may be.

But for someone like me, who if only for the sake of a quiet life, deliberately chose to specialise in wills and estates - a dull field of practice perhaps not figuring too highly in my more-driven rivals' ambitions, despite its one key advantage:

That whatever trouble I encountered that day down the alleyway was a pretty unusual event. Or else it had been, till then.

Lawyers of Lugvalio

An ugly confrontation hardly representing the kind of physicality a respectable practitioner like me usually encounters - considering most of my clients are dead, less prone to be demanding. Even less so once prone, once gone across the Styx.

But if being chased around the stygian back-alleys of Eboracum gave my personal preview of Hades, it's hardly what I signed-up for, as a gentlemen-at-law. That preference for the quiet life probably also behind my refusal to believe whoever it was who tried to warn me later – weeks after escaping an angry pursuer – that soon I'd be facing far greater threats. For rather longer too.

So much for circumspection. Difficult to credit but true – that fresh from one narrow escape, I should let myself be entrapped in what would soon become any cautious lawyer's idea of the *'Twelve Labours of Hercules'* as re-enacted.

Even without mentioning the awful journey itself, mired in what shortly became our most arduous case yet. All of whose ordeals I would incur as if a willing volunteer. Every torment arguably the direct result of my own, personal self-delivery into the yawning maws of danger. Heedless and desperate for work.

Stuck inside a horrid litigation whose every stage seemed twenty-times worse than its predecessor but offered no escape. No respite till its end. So who in their right mind would have volunteered for that – or this bruising contact sport from which I try to claw a living? As my wife will insist on pointing out, it seems incredible that a lawyer of my experience should have been so thoughtless – reckless even - about what I agree to take on.

But the fact is, I was, and take it on I did. All of it for a lady…

Accepting the enduring truth – as my senior clerk, the wise and thoughtful Tiro, so often likes to mention – that *"hindsight's a wonderful thing."*

And if he and I would choose to carve a modest private living from the false hopes, bitter vendettas, and ruined expectations of some various wounded others, then we gentlemen of the law should accept another truth. One inherent to our calling:

How there'll always be that element of risk.

Chapter II

Back in the *officium*, it was touching to find them so concerned: "Master, how are you?".... "Where in the world have you been? We were all so worried"... "What's been going on? They said you left the court of the Praeses many hours ago – went out the front door quite alone – completely unescorted!" babbled Tiro and the others, almost as one.

'*Tiro*', my law clerk, is not in fact his original name - although to be fair, it's so long ago, I cannot honestly remember the real one. *I must ask him sometime.* He is of course a slave, but Tiro – whom I named many years ago upon purchase, after the famous Republican lawyer, Caius Tullius Cicero's legendary secretary – is also my indispensable friend and helpmate, without whom I could not maintain the professional practice I do. Or get in the fees.

"My dear Tiro, I am perfectly well, thank you – just a little shaken."

"And your best toga looks like it's been dragged across a field..."

"Nothing the fullers can't remedy."

15

Lawyers of Lugvalio

"I'll see to it at once. But how did it end up looking like that, Master, presumably with you still inside?"

"An unfortunate incident on the way back from court. Quite unexpected, but all my own fault. That's right, I accept it, for walking on my own. Ambushed in broad daylight on the public highway by a wild-looking well-wisher. And with nobody around to help me, then if there'd been a well handy, I'm sure he'd have thrown me straight down it. Lacking a well, he chased me round the rougher end of town instead – through a fullers and a working foundry, then into that new Temple of Serapis they've built beside the river. Where a quick-witted guard bravely hid me beneath The God Himself. *Thanks be to Serapis!*"

"Zeus, you really have been in the wars! So who was your assailant, Master?"

"To be frank, I haven't got the faintest. I didn't recognise him, while he didn't introduce himself to me. Looked a bit rustic, is all I can say. Complaining that he and his brother were '*diddled out of their inheritance*' – or at least that's how he put it. What he said."

Since pleading contested wills or disputes about the administration of deceased estates forms such a big chunk of my practice (*No, I never said it was exciting…*) and will always cause disenchantment for someone, then this was hardly a description to distinguish my pursuer's case from all our dreary others.

"Mmm…" said Tiro "Him and his brother. '*Diddled*', eh? That doesn't give us too much to go on, Master, I'll have to think back. Assuming it was one of our cases…"

That was the trouble. Each case generally contained at least one scrap of interest – maybe a unique point of law, some intriguing fact or titillating scandal. But while things were going well and the work kept flowing-in, they and the client were as instantly forgotten once the next case arrived. A fresh set of facts for me to concentrate-on while Tiro cranks out the bills on our old ones. Chases up the debts.

No wonder I was so hopeless at remembering most of my former cases – a tired brain can only hold so much information, and I tended to discard whatever had gone before. Including - most especially - their names.

"I still think we need to try and identify who this man was..." piped-up our new lad. *Rianorix, his name.* Only recently enlisted as Tiro's junior assistant and hence keener to contribute: "As a precaution. Because what if he doesn't give up and manages to trace you - then comes snooping round here? What if he found his way to the *officium*, my lord, broke-in to cause you trouble?"

Now there was a thought. Rianorix might be barely old enough to understand the specialist work we do here, but the boy had a point and my inner voice agreed. We certainly needed to know.

Tiro waved his arm to indicate the ordered racks of old scrolls and wooden writing tablets stacked neatly behind him:

"The answer will be up there somewhere, I'm sure. It's just a question of us taking the time to go through them all, Master." *'Domine' he says - always in the vocative, respectful to a fault.* "Looking-out for similar facts and a name or names to go with them. We'll get on with it straightaway, Master, this afternoon."

A response typical of his efficiency but begging the bigger question: *'How come there's time?'* And with this concern in mind but trying to raise the general mood, I jauntily enquired instead:

"So tell me what's next, dear Tiro, tell me what I'll be up to tomorrow? Pleading in court, or else some boring advice work? Just tell me the truth, man - are we *BUSY*?"

Tiro pursed his lips, wrinkled his brow and made an arch from his elbows up to his fingertips, like I'd posed an impossible riddle. "Well..." he said, eventually. "Apart from the singular possibility I'll mention shortly, it's fair to say that – overall - things do seem to have gone a bit *quiet* recently. A little less movement on the ledger."

"Oh! That's unhappy news. Though you mention an interesting possibility...?"

"Yes, Master. I don't know too much yet about what their fees might amount to, or how much we could charge, but the existence of some – shall I say, rather unusual - circumstances suggests it might be the making of you, of your reputation. Not to mention

17

the creation of precedent, your name engraved on the record in perpetuity as its trailblazer."

Precedent, eh? Now there's a word to set a lawyer's pulse-rate racing. Imagining the giddy pride at becoming what Tiro calls a 'pathfinder'. Forever associated by one's peers in the profession with some novel-but-enduring piece of caselaw: *Thinking of briefing Justinus of Eboracum, you say? Oh, yes, he's THE MAN on wills and estates.*

"Trailblazer, you say?"

"Indeed, Master. In every sense of the word."

"Every?"

"There'd be a degree of travel involved. Outside the jurisdiction."

"I'm only registered for practice here…"

"Indeed. But if the claim originates here and the court which must hear it can only sit elsewhere, then elsewhere we must go and you can still be heard."

"Elsewhere?"

"To Luguvalium, Master, or *"Lugvalos"*… Or even *"Lugvalio"*, as the Carvetii will style it. Their strong place… the walls of Lugh, I'm told it means… some sort of local war-god or suchlike. Can be spelled with one or two 'l's, depending on your preference."

The Strong Place of Lugh? Some sort of native war-god – oh, yeugh!

No, never mind how anyone says it, none of it met my preference - to be frank. Because the fact was, I'd already decided that I didn't like the sound of what any of this implied for the quality of life likely to be enjoyed up there, at Tiro's venue for this suggested litigation.

No, not one bit of it, but since a thrusting man of ambition like myself should never turn his back once opportunity comes a-knocking, I tried to show a modicum of interest:

"*Lugvalio*, you say, Tiro? Stuck in a permanent westerly-gale and always dark in winter - the town that's spelled with two 'l's to ensure it matches '*Hell*'? Civilisation's final *civitas* before the barbarians close-in. Marooned beyond help at the World's End there, below Hadrian's doomed entrenchments?"

"Er, yes, Master - sort of. Located more towards their western end, I'd think. Though it claims the status of a city and - were our case to be heard – is also where we're likely to run the provincial governor to ground. Could expect to find his tribunal sitting in session, up there on assize."

"In a garrison town and military depot, clinging with frozen fingers to the outer edge of empire? Forever facing-down our implacable northern enemies. While beyond it there begins... just a nothingness, Tiro, a nothing. The trackless, Caledonian waste."

"Maybe you're right, Master, although I suspect it's hardly as bad as you paint it. But if the *legatus* makes it his business to lodge there and it's good enough for him, then it should be more than good enough for us. Might I tell you about the case itself?'

"I salivate at the thought, good Tiro. Tell me more."

"We've recently been approached by a local lady, resident in the Colonia. A female person of high birth and impeccable virtue, married to a man of praetorian rank. Her instructions to us rejoice in reporting her aged father as alive and in good health. An elderly man with a long and distinguished career in the military. As a youth, she says he was lucky - selected for service in the *Equites Singulares* in Rome, the emperor's mounted Life Guards. But now he must confront his own mortality in the office of Regional Centurion - overseeing good governance around Lugvalio and the Wall."

"Elderly, you say, but still in harness to the end – that's splendid! But how old exactly?"

"Tough as old army boots, I'd guess, since – believe it or not, Master - this old gentleman of Britannia has surpassed his eightieth winter! And as you shall hear, has still not lost his vigour."

"Quite an achievement. Though I hope he's made a will?"

"You are ahead of me, as ever, Master. Yes, *he has*, and precisely the reason why a noble lady now wonders if a man with your breadth of experience might agree to act for her."

Lawyers of Lugvalio

"So what's her problem, Tiro? He's head of the household, after all – their *paterfamilias*. Until he dies, she knows she can't own anything - all the power rests with him. The property likewise. But presumably the will of a loving father can be relied on to take the necessary steps. Provide for her afterwards, if need be?"

"Ah, well, there's the rub..." he said, stroking his beard.

"The rub?"

"Tragically widowed and via a chain of circumstances happening on-or-around the time of his unfortunate bereavement – possibly slightly before that, the client is willing to concede – it appears that the Regional Centurion of Lugvalio was driven in his grief to seek consolation in the arms of a young woman of twenty. A female person of tender years with whom he fell violently in love and then as promptly married."

"No, he didn't, did he? The old devil! So is that our intended client's complaint?"

"Not as such, no. Something more grievous than that, because - within eleven days of his happy nuptials granting our client a new step-mother young enough to be her daughter - the Regional Centurion also took the necessary steps to make a new will. One which disinherits his daughter in favour of this unknown female half her age."

"By all that's sacred, what a rotten trick. To whom does he leave the estate instead?"

"To the new step-mother, as I say. Herself now accompanied by a child, the infant daughter fathered by a common soldier, who as promptly made off. Hence the *centurio regionarius* has taken additional legal steps to adopt this infant of hers as his own..."

"We are looking at a suit for patrimony." I said. "It would require a lot of work. There would be witnesses to be found and interviewed, proofs of evidence to be taken. Having to travel such a long way makes everything more difficult too, but I'm sure we could cope, if required. Although it would certainly cost her, be expensive. Does this lady have means? Could she pay?"

Clive Ashman

"I believe so, Master. Her husband is a man of Praetorian rank, an important personage in the life of this province, whose official status at the Treasury means we could reasonably expect he'd help her out with our various costs and expenses. Which to be blunt - and since your own purse is so empty - means she's become our only hope of rescue, to be honest. Frankly, Master, I'm just about worn-out from fending-off final demands. Only today it was your vintners, and then there's the ink-makers - while neither were first. Never mind the *'Disappointed Beneficiary Brothers'*, our absence from town should spare us from any further embarassing street confrontations with your creditors. So taking these extra considerations into account, Master - what do you think? Will you act for her... please?"

I paused briefly for effect before responding, while my staff looked up at me expectantly, awaiting a judgement with reasons:
"For me, this unfortunate lady's case might epitomise the ideal noble cause. Invoking the spirit of Quintilian, she offers us the rare opportunity of achieving moral good. Because if we could all stand together, confront these regrettable circumstances in which she finds herself – hoping on her behalf to oppose their imposition – then her's could be a cause more than honourable to plead. *Before any court.* What's more, as a case containing such unusual facts and promising finer points of law, it's likely only to *enhance* my personal reputation for advocacy. Considering good Tiro, as you know, how often it is said - and wisely - that a pleader should only undertake the causes of his friends. Or else deliberately choose to act in that very class of case which he knows most of his peers would *refuse* to take on..."
Tiro looked alarmed at that prospect, but I continued apace:
"A category to which we should add a third kind – one prescribed by the late, great Pliny himself – by which I mean those special causes or claims most likely to become quoted before the courts by our fellow jurists. Cited within their pleadings - both now and into the future. Those rarest of cases which can go on to earn an afterlife - metamorphose into glorious

precedent - so earning an illustrious mention from our greatest philosophers of jurisprudence for many generations to come. Long after we're gone…"

I paused to judge reactions, then viewed my audience sternly:

"Because if ever I met a litigation promising us most of these features – and I look forward to meeting the noble lady, so adding another, and her to my circle of friends – then, surely, my dear and loyal Tiro, this is *that one!*"

"Oh, my! What on earth did all that mean, Tiro? Does our master accept – will he agree to take it on?" asked red-headed Rianorix, innocently breaking a stunned silence with the classic mistake of too many a courtroom novice. Assuming a stage whisper won't be heard, under their breath.

"Yes, boy, I think it does – that he will…" shushed Tiro back. *A little crossly, I thought.* "Just so long as she pays."

"The road to Lugvalio beckons!" I added with a wave, extending the wool-wrapped fold of my left arm for emphasis, as if in a court.

"Then we'd better get that toga of yours off to the cleaners, straightaway…" replied Tiro, putting his bronze pen down onto the surface of his desk with elaborate care.

Chapter III

The home of she whom we hoped would become our next client, Lydia Firma, was a good-class, two-storey dwelling house located in a better part of the Colonia, the settlement for retiring veterans of the Ninth Hispana legion founded a century-and-a-half ago on the opposite river-bank to their enormous fortress. On the basis gods must go to a mountain, if the mountain will not come to them, Tiro and I had been obliged to cross town in order to take her instructions.

In her middle years, Lydia remained an attractive woman, with lively eyes the colour of periwinkle and dark, curly hair piled-up atop her forehead according to the latest fashion. Emulating the empress, as seen on coins. While her long, dangly earrings appeared made from gold decorated with red garnets, and should therefore be expensive. Another good sign, how I took it.

Silently admiring the fineness of her facial features, a woman well-preserved by wealth, I found the overall effect only slightly marred by her mildly protruding chin. A feature which the study of physiognomy has taught me, via long years spent in the courts, may offer reliable signpost towards the quality of determination within a subject's character.

Obstinacy, even?

Lawyers of Lugvalio

Feminine perfection of appearance - within my incomplete experience – always needing one diagnosable flaw, for it to reach any sort of zenith.

She had received us in the open, in the peristile - a square, sunlit garden located to the centre of her house, where rosemary grew in terracotta pots and a pair of pet sparrows tweeted in a cage. Calmly seated in a high-backed wicker chair placed decoratively between apple trees, and holding a fan to waft the humid air around, any last wasps of September, we found her waited on by an old man in yellow uniform. A retainer of hers whom I was somewhat unsettled to see appeared to be taking notes.

"You will find my father a difficult man, as I have, and a fierce opponent few dare to cross. It's all about him. Everything he does must have him as the focus."

Tiro and I looked wonderingly across at each other, as she continued: "Now that Aurelia, my mother, is but ashes - and what portion of them we could recover from the pyre are sealed into a rough pot my father buried in his garden - he considers himself free of all other obligation. Without even taking time to observe the usual period for mourning, he took that woman from the town who's living with him anyway and made her his wife. After this, and only eleven days after their wedding was publicly formalised, he summonsed to attend on their house in Luguvalium an ignorant local notary. An uneducated man, barely literate himself, whom he orders to create a new will for my father, revoking his old one. By whose generous terms my new step-mother and her bastard child are set to inherit everything which he owns and – as he did not flinch from telling me directly in this letter I received in Eboracum, only three nights ago - I am to get nothing myself. Nothing at all!"

"My clerk, Tiro, has told me of your wretched predicament. He says you came to our *officium* only the other day, requesting I act on your behalf. Is that still your wish, lady?"

"Yes. I am his daughter, his own flesh and blood, his only surviving child, but now my new step-mother walks over the self-same garden land he's placed my mother's ashes in. At least my mother is spared knowing how badly I'm served by her widower, my father, but this dreadful state of affairs cannot be right - not in any family. That's why I called you here, Justinus. It's a matter of principle, an awful situation that simply cannot be allowed!"

"I understand you, lady. Although you're yet to share with us the wrongdoer's name…?"

"His full name is Marcus Cocceius Firmus – which as you will learn, belongs to the most notorious litigant in all Britannia."

"A litigant already, eh? I see. Well, it's my advice, lady, that we should be the litigants now. I would therefore propose issuing a suit for patrimony in your name which he will find himself summonsed before a competent court to answer…" I announced in my gravest courtroom tone - after the usual respectful pause, appropriate to client revelations.

"This case of yours, assembled and pleaded by me, will aim to make the biggest possible impact upon your father and the court of trial, alike. Shock them into acting in your favour. We will say that your father has failed completely in his moral duty to make proper provision for you, and the court of trial should make a binding order that he does."

Lydia looked up and smiled, like a cat spotting a mouse: "Yes, Justinus – exactly what I thought."

How often does this happen, I ask myself inwardly. The client who comes to you hot-foot in desperate need of advice, while you're as desperate for their fee. Then no sooner have you offered it (*carefully, mind…*) than they lean back in their chair (*usually it's my own…*) to concede as condescendingly as they please, that they'd "…*thought so all along.*" As if Justinus's only useful contribution to the whole piece is merely to confirm their sage assessment - all those prior assumptions which a clever client never mentions in opening - but '*Thanks for that, anyway…*'

My twenty years of diligent legal labour and hard-fought courtroom practice exposed for superfluous gloss by good old common sense - as if law and justice even mean the same thing!

Lawyers of Lugvalio

Girding my metaphorical loins, I smile graciously at her innocent complacency and resume my explanations anyway:

"This case will require a lot of work from us all to prepare. It will be like a military campaign. There will be other witnesses to be found and interviewed, proofs of evidence to be taken. While having to travel so far to be heard makes everything that bit more difficult too, as I'm sure you will realise, m'lady. But I'm convinced that we'd cope. And I hope you also understand why it will require your attendance at trial in person, as well."

"You can rest content there, Justinus. Not a prospect to cause me concern either, since I've travelled to Luguvalium often enough for my household to know the way. No, we're familiar with the route and its hardships. Eight days on the road should do it... weather permitting."

"Good! Because if not the journey itself, then a court's pre-trial procedures contain as much in hard going. Although I genuinely believe we can help, you must understand why I never promise a successful outcome to anyone. What you can be sure about is that myself and my assistants will do everything humanly possible to achieve a win. If we respect the gods and their ritual, follow the correct steps in law and conduct ourselves properly, then maybe the gods will smile on us. Not recovering everything, but..."

"It's only a shame I can't do all this for myself. Life's taught me never to rely on men..." she said, as if distracted by memory, looking upwards to the sky (*while Tiro and I could only gaze at each other, eye-roll in unison*) "... let alone the gods!"

"Yes, it must be frustrating for you, madam. I sympathise. Unfortunately, I'm afraid it's well-settled old law that leaves you hobbled by your sex. You'll find no women lawyers here, just us two men to make do with instead... "

"So what happens next?" she said briskly, any hint of self-pity as immediately gone.

"The way it works is this, ma'am: I go in front of a suitable court and, in co-operation with the judge hearing it, formulate a case. Put flesh on the bones. With a civil claim of this value, involving persons of your own and your father's significant social status, we would need a senior judge. And in this situation, I'd imagine that would either be the provincial governor himself, or else maybe what they call a judicial legate."

"Mmm, I understand the basic processes, Justinus, but where on earth would you go to unearth major players like these?"

"Well, in normal times it'd either be here or Londinium, I'd guess. Unfortunately, we no longer live in normal times. What with all the kerfuffle and upheaval of the last few months, there's no doubt in my mind that we've little option left us but to hit the road. Go out and look. Because once Emperor Severus arrived in Britain this spring, began assembling an army to recover Caledonia, then it's likely that most of the important judicial figures we'll need for your case won't be very far behind him. Trailing in his wake."

"So how do you discover where they'll be, at that exact point when you need them?"

"Mainly by educated guesswork, I suppose, a process of elimination. That, and asking about. At least we know for certain that your father, the Regional Centurion and intended respondent to our claim, is permanently based in Lugvalio. Which helps us. At the very least establishing our need to pop over there and summons him in person. Turn up one day at his house."

"He won't like that."

"No, m'lady, no-one does. The key thing to remember is the emperor's publicly stated intention to re-invade Caledonia - for which objective every other business of state is currently sacrificed. So we'll examine reports and gossip about the latest movements of his household, plan our own to match. Although it's safe to assume that, barring any late-season crises, they'll be back in barracks by mid-October for the Festival of Armilustrium. After the usual march-pasts and torchlit processions, animals sacrificed to Mars *etcetera*, everyone should be settled down nicely in time for our arrival. The valiant soldiery tucked-up warmly in camp. Although the army's weapons get ritually purified and symbolically put-away, their logistical preparations will continue over winter at pace. Which means that's where and how we'll find them, as these important public figures we need for your case get easier to pin down. Because whether it's the provincial governor or his *legatus iuridicatus*, either one's competent to preside over – to help formulate - your intended claim. But until Armilustrium comes and so long as they're absent from Eboracum – out in the field with the emperor, say, inspecting the Aelian Wall with his staff – then I think we should treat neither official as readily available to us now."

"So if I understand what you're saying, it's that once the military campaigning season formally finishes for the year, it's all down to us successfully guessing where these key men finally end up? Then tracking them down to wherever – so that you can make an application on my behalf before them, in person?"

"Yes, ma'am, precisely how it works. But if you wanted to place bets, then – from what I've heard in the courts, and after they left Eboracum for the frontier this summer - my money's on the main imperial party stopping at Lugvalio. And fairly soon, too. First of all and if only for a while, before returning here. And if I'm right, another piece of symmetry that would be helpful to your cause, convenient to confronting your father."

"I see…" she said, at that thought sounding less keen.

"Although we shouldn't discount alternative possibilities, either…" I added. "Like the emperor calling-in at one of his main supply-depots, for instance. Whether that's Coria in the middle of the Wall system or Arbeia at its end. Well if he does, then that's no problem either, no issue for us. Because neither location is impossibly far from your respondent or those witnesses-as-to-fact I expect we'll need to find and draw-on. Although - as I've said before, ma'am – I'd put money on Lugvalio."

At which Tiro chipped-in, his remarks directed towards me:

"But, Master, I thought his second son – Geta – remained in Eboracum? While the emperor himself, along with the elder one and most of their palace officials, are surely bound to end-up back here anyway. If only eventually, before midwinter comes. So wouldn't it be a whole lot better and easier for us just to stay-put till they return? Rather than go chasing up and down the length of the Aelian Wall, hunting imperial officials in the rain?"

"Yes, Tiro, right in principle, wrong in practice!" I replied. "Likely they will and yes, it could be. But with no guarantee our eighty year-old respondent could survive another British winter, I think we hardly dare wait so long for his case to be up and running. No, I'm afraid m'lady here wants her claim resolved urgently. By which I mean before her father dies and departs for the Styx - so activating his current, unjust will."

"I see...." she smiled. "Some interesting considerations there, gentlemen, most of which leave me entirely in your hands. Reliant on you both to make whatever arrangements you think necessary to our achieving successful conclusions. The only kind I'm interested in, by the way. But since it's so urgent and already mid-September, how soon can you start?"

"Subject to one or two minor formalities – straightaway, madam" I confirmed, offering her my best in winning smiles.

"That's good news - but *'formalities'*, you say? What else would you need from me?" she asked, observing me daintily. Tilting her head to one side like a bird's.

"Or maybe from your husband...?" I countered.

"Oh, no, Justinus, you needn't worry about my husband!" she added briskly, almost scornfully. "I'll deal with him – there'll be no problems there. What else remains outstanding?"

Tiro glanced at me, eyes rolling yet again, and I nodded encouragingly before he lowered his lids to speak: "Well, there's one other little thing, lady. Another delicate issue, additional to what we've already canvassed. The question of our likely expenses, incurred from running this case."

"Oh, yes" she said. "I know you lawyers don't come cheap."

"It's not so much that, m'lady..." intoned Tiro, suitably glum in that practised way of his. "More the longstanding convention in law that those who act as advocate for the benefit of others may only do so for that category of person whom they would class as friends. Why we would need to call you our *'client'* and – ever since an ancient edict of Claudius - the most we may charge such a *'friend'* in fees is modest in the extreme."

"Why I'd be grateful, ma'am, if your minute-taker could rest his pen for a while…" I interjected firmly, glancing across at the old chap in the yellow tunic.

Lydia took the hint: "You may leave us now, Silenus…" she sighed heavily. Wheezing as he went, we watched his vivid saffron shoulders go bobbing back through the garden and into the house, before Tiro resumed:

"Yes, we may provide your friends at law, at court - but only on the basis you show us your gratitude, lady, whatever the Deified Claudius says."

"I think I've got the message - thanking you both! So, yes, I'll meet the main expenses involved: accommodation, food, and tolls. Deal with the court fees and scribes. Make both my carriages and two sets of draught animals available to us, as transport for the journey. Plus a team of pack-mules and those of my servants my husband says he can spare. But as for the rest – well, that must depend on outcome."

"On outcome, lady?" I gasped, at even the merest whiff of her suggestion coming.

"If you don't win, I won't pay. It's as simple as that, Justinus."

"Hrrummmph…" I blustered. "No win, no fee! I don't think that's been tried before."

"Take it or leave it, Justinus. Don't forget this case could be the making of you, set an important precedent in law. You may never get another chance like it, ever again – I know you'll never get to meet anyone like my father again, that's for sure….."

There was a long silence during which Tiro and I were probably stuck for words – it was hardly satisfactory, but we were hardly overrun with clients either. *I wonder if she knew?*

He looked at me and I looked at him.

Already I had an inkling of what dealing with her father might be like - but I had no work; we had no money; and there were no better, alternative cases available to us anyway.

She drummed long henna-ed fingernails on the iron table we sat around and looked at me with penetrating blue eyes: "So, if you're not both '*too busy*' - can I take it that's agreed?" she added.

"Well, provided your reward is proportionate to our victory, when it comes… " I muttered ungraciously.

"I am a Roman lady and know how to show gratitude to my friends. Is there anything else you'll be needing from me today?"

"Err… well, yes. One other thing, madam. Do you have children?"

"I'm pleased to say we do – two fine sons, Flavius and Julianus. Aged eight and ten years, too young for the broad stripe."

"That's good, because they'll need to come along with us, on our little expedition."

"I understand. Then you will find them by my side throughout. Anything else?"

"Ensure no-one cuts their hair."

Lawyers of Lugvalio

Chapter IV

It took two weeks to gather everyone together, along with their equipments, then get our baggage train ready for the road. Presiding in person over these complicated arrangements was the instructing client, Lydia Firma herself, with whom my managing clerk, Tiro, found himself obliged to make regular and respectful consultations, scuttling back and forth across town with wooden notebook in hand.

"Your main responsibility on this mission, Tiro, is to keep the client happy" I'd tell him with mock sternness, the several times he complained.

A client who'd been right about her husband, as well. Quintus Curius Aculeo, a procurator of sorts, worked for the Treasury – for the *Fiscus* - an overpowerful public institution with which that minority of my clients wittingly known to the tax system were too often prone to clash. Dragging me into some of their spats.

Aculeo himself I knew for a tetchy old accountant whose gloomy temperament seemed at odds with that permanent truth about senior public officials - how money from the exchequer will always stick to their fingers, if only in passing.

Whatever the reasons for this, or his general air of dissatisfaction - as if rank or opportunity rarely made him happy - at least Aculeo's successful career had provided many of the other compensations more usually associated with wealth: not least a decorative but troublesome wife, a nice house in the better part of the city, and that impressive set of wheeled transporters which Lydia Firma made available to us for our impending trip.

A handsome pair of four-wheeled carriages as much designed for making explicit statements about status as any conveyance, their enclosed wooden bodies were clad in embossed red hide and hung on matching straps to absorb the worst jolts off the highway. Each of them drawn by a strong team of mules sourced from the better army breeders, their coachwork and roofs decorated with miniature bronze statuettes of those gods known to specialise in guarding travellers on the road.

Lydia Firma and her two sons, Flavius and Julianus, plus the old man in saffron - Silenus, her steward - and two twittering female attendants would travel in the first carriage, leaving her crack legal team to cram into the second. As well as myself and Tiro, that would therefore include the new office-boy, Rianorix, plus Tiro's clerical assistants, Sennovarus and Sulio (*even a slave like Tiro may own slaves*). And all of us required to share the interior of this second wagon with the looming bulk of Decimus Ascanius.

Lately retired ornament to the Sixth Victorious Legion, Ascanius was the ex-soldier I'd recently recruited for my own protection and that more physical work - like serving writs in person - which Tiro tends to shrink from. My '*Outdoor clerk*' as I dubbed him would soon find himself far busier than I think he imagined.

To these should be added Tocitanus and Trenico, her carriage-drivers at the front - also our baggage-handlers, as and when required. While a further half-dozen spare mules were ridden by supernumerary staff - including Aulus Equitius, a proper ostler and farrier - until draught animals tired. The good news being in how this meant - to begin with at least – that there'll be no-one in our fifteen-strong *equipe* who is left needing to walk.

While we milled around beneath the city's red-striped grey and whitestone walls, waiting to set off - and after my own private goodbyes to wife and household made earlier - I thought it only courteous for me to inquire about our patron-cum-sponsor's:

Clive Ashman

"Tell me, madam, how did your noble husband take it when you bid farewell this morning? What did good Aculeo say - because I most sincerely hope he wished you and indeed all of your supporters the very best of luck in this enterprise?"

"No, Justinus, that's none of your business – although, no, he did not. More bothered about who'll run his household while we're gone than the success of my case. His Parthian shot about ensuring I bring both of his carriages back safely, intact...."

"Look, madam, are you still certain you want to go through with all this?" I asked her directly, for one final time. "You know we've a long way to travel. And if a week on the roads in autumn can be tough enough, then the mental pressure from formal procedures we'll undergo in court together, right from arrival, is likely to be of another order of magnitude altogether. So I should ask you once again, lady - can you do this thing?"

"Oh, yes!" she said brightly, nodding a curl-bedecked head with such emphasis, gold and garnet earrings danced entrancingly in the red light of dawn: "It's a matter of principle."

"Excellent!" I said, and meant it most sincerely. Because there is nothing more calculated to gladden a lawyer's heart than enjoying the clear instructions of a well-off client bent on litigating over principle. When nothing could be more reliable in offsetting that financial insecurity haunting my adventures in law to date - or in generating those fees over which an advocate nightly dreams - than becoming briefed by a client of means. A person as fixated on confronting some perceived slight or injustice in need of righting, as their lawyer must be on fees.

So that as the Unconquered Sun God drew over the orange rooftops of Eboracum - and armed by this growing confidence in my client's commitment to her cause - I leapt aboard our transport with a real spring in my step. Without shedding any sensible awareness of what risks we probably ran, the danger of falling victim to what Tiro and the Greeks call *'hubris'* - or otherwise losing the case - I felt more ready for battle and optimistic about the future than I think I had in years.

Lawyers of Lugvalio

And after much toing-and-froing - including the usual minor panic over someone's missing cloak - and with our dutiful execution of traditional roadside offerings made to Mercury, or the Gods of Safe-Homecoming, it seemed everyone was ready. Assuming the gods were satisfied too, their peace duly obtained, it appeared our little expedition could quit the Colonia of Eboracum via its westernmost gateway without any further fuss.

Leaning back gratefully as it did so, a convenient window available on my left from which to inspect that pleasant countryside which unrolls beyond a city's walls, I must have retained some lingering need for reassurance. Because, turning to my senior clerk beside me, I would ask him once again:

"Tell me truly, Tiro – will we make money from this caper?"

"No enterprise can be certain, Master, although I remain of the opinion that it represents our very best chance in ages. Such a big case! And since we travel there all-expenses paid; surely - this time at least - we cannot turn an actual loss?"

Of course, the sensible Tiro was right - as usual. If me and mine were to be returned to solvency, I knew we had to take its challenge on - we had no other choice. Encouraged by his words, I raised my arms in the traditional supplicant's gesture and stageily intoned: "Let justice be done, though the heavens fall..."

Without me imagining for one moment that they might. Another early assumption at risk of offending the Fates?

However, what this remark of mine most certainly did not mean was that I felt any happier about effectively working for nothing, without guarantees of payment. But beggars, as they say...

If a Roman mile runs out at a thousand paces for proper soldiers on the march, then it was seventeen miles from the City of The Legion to the small tribal capital known as Isurium Brigantum. The location which, that evening, would provide our first stop.

And despite its three lanes of hard-packed gravel being among the widest and best maintained we would encounter on the journey, they were enough of a jaunt to occupy us and the mule-teams all day. Bowling along them at a pretty pacey rate, I'd say.

Clive Ashman

With a week to kill, the journey itself would be what granted most their opportunity for getting introduced to a diverse range of fellow travellers. For establishing early on what allocations of time and activity - whether social, domestic or pleasure - best suit an individual's routine, when out on the road.

Not intending to waste time on chat, I'd brought along plenty of reading matter to occupy me. Another part of the process of limbering myself up for the case. Riding in the suspended luxury of our patron's carriage also promising me useful time-out from the hurly-burly of town. A breathing space where I could carefully research the important legal and technical points I'd be relying on come trial, whilst also avoiding creditors.

Tiro and I were agreed our week-long journey to Lugvalio could also be helpful in its opportunities to take a more detailed set of instructions from the client herself, en route. Including extracting better information about her wayward parent, his general character as a testator, or whatever else motivated these fiscal unfairnesses the regional centurion seemed determined to inflict on an unfortunate daughter. Or indeed any other material which we could use to discredit him in front of a jury.

Hence, taking time to ride with Lydia in her own carriage would enable Tiro and myself to identify certain key points of evidence useful in formulating those specialised legal pleadings which could become the very core of how her case would be fought out in court, blow for blow.

The weather was fine and the countryside charming, everyone in high spirits and the animals pulling well, so that when we rolled into town - that small but well appointed *civitas* of Isurium Brigantum, regional capital to the Brigantes tribe - there was already a sense among us that things could only go right.

Originally chosen a century–and-a-half ago by invading Roman armies to site a small fort, the name "*Isurium*" represents our Latinisation of the nearby River Ure. The old fort is of course long gone, but the modern town's rectangular defences, a fifteen-foot wide bank and palisade, enclose about fifty acres, I'd say.

Lawyers of Lugvalio

Our coaches crossed the six foot-deep, flat-bottomed ditch fronting them via a tidy wooden bridge beside the amphitheatre, before we made formal entrance into the town beneath its southern gateway. Substantial administrative buildings rose to greet us as we did, plus some rather fine houses. Our overnight inn not quite so - its fleas the biggest distraction, not decor.

This miniature *civitas*, if not its tinier parasites, was familiar territory for me as the home to some of my more rural clientele, within the recent past. Where I'm called in to resolve disputes about the disposal on death of minor country houses, those glorifed native farms whose uncouth proprietors will insist on calling '*villas*' despite their valuation to the lower end of any local property market. Where I remember spending a particularly dreary week stuck in lodgings there, while arbitrating an impenetrable argument about title to its brick and tileworks between two competing claimants, each as thick as their product.

The same semi-itinerant, low-grade legal work keeping the wolf from my door also tending to devalue one's professional standing in the eyes of more picky rivals confined to the Colonia. But at least my last visit here gave useful local knowledge about where, or where not, to eat-out in Isurium. Plus a few humorous experiences to share with companions and lighten their mood?

"Yeah, it seems a nice enough little town..." said Ascanius, my ex-army bodyguard, while he sat there, scratching, outside the simple wineshop I'd chosen that night for its oysters: "...but don't be fooled. Everyone here knows the natives can't be trusted."

As long-time residents of nearby Eboracum, neither Tiro nor I need to be reminded how indigenous Brigantes remain the largest tribe in Britannia - more numerous than fleas but just as troublesome to Romans. Although it was their more recent offending which I was annoyed to hear my new minder tactlessly evoke, right in front of local drinkers:

"When Clodius Albinus pulled the legions out of Britannia, took them off to Gaul opposing Severus, and Brigantes rose, it was my brilliant mates who took the punishment. Them what died..."

Clive Ashman

"Be careful what you say, Ascanius!" hissed Tiro – ever the master of discretion, even in a wineshop. "No-one mentions Albinus anymore, as if you didn't know. He's *persona non grata* now and not to mention, dead…"

Although Tiro's already too late, because Ascanius has taken drink and this whispered warning barely breaks his stride:

"Yeah, Tiro, don't I know it, mate! 'Cos once our army's gone to Gaul – but before *that man I'm not allowed to mention* lost his head at Lyons, got it sent in a bag by Severus to the Senate so they knew he'd won - these stupid Brigantes mistook our absence for their final chance. Raised rebellion right across the north, starting-off in Stanwick, their ancient stamping ground. How we nearly lost the lot, not a dozen years gone-by. *So that's why I say it.*"

My head was in my hands but Ascanius took no notice of the message, merely dropping his voice towards a slurring whisper:

"Why I've always said you should *never* trust Brigantes. No, boss, because they've got no time for towns, have they; while this Isurium of theirs… Well, it's just a Roman joke, ain't it, boss? A walled sanctuary for tax-farmers – for Aculeo and his ilk. No, boss, we'll never win them over. Not never, I'd say… *Hic!*" he burped, halting unexpectedly.

If I quickly told Ascanius to shut-up there and then, I remained privately obliged to grant some truths in his rant. Concede how in their pomp - once upon a time and a very long time ago, before we imposed Isurium on them instead - the Brigantian nation had enjoyed a primitive statehood of their own.

Only a few miles further along the Great North Road from where we sat now. That place they call Stanwick: *'The Stone Wick'.* Their one-time Celtic fortress and trading post with Rome, once girdled by fully six miles of looping rampart. By fortifications whose needless length would far exceed the capacity of even this most populous of barbarian nations to wall with willing warriors.

So that when our legions arrived to smash their armoured way in through gaps occurring, one hot summer's afternoon a century or more ago, there was no going back for Brigantia. Not when Rome prefers its client tribes obedient, and good at paying taxes.

Lawyers of Lugvalio

"I don't know too much about Stanwick...." Tiro remarked quietly, to soothe an embarrassed silence. "Though I've read plenty of what Tacitus says about their queen: about Cartimandua, the legend! That woman the Brigantes took for their queen, Rome for its ally: *'Cleopatra of The North'* what your Roman soldiers called her. Who fell out with the king, her husband Venutius; then went off with her chariot-driver, so they say. Maybe with your general too, poor old Petilius Cerialis; who had to do a midnight dash cross-country with cavalry just to rescue her. She certainly led Rome a merry dance, that's for sure."

"And here we are in Isurium, boss, on our way to rescue yet another woman..." added Ascanius, bouncing-back into the conversation with a swagger from the shoulders like he's already forgotten my recent telling-off. Only adding to the harm:

"Just like we did with Cartimandua – despite all the trouble she caused! Honestly, boss, you do begin to wonder why we let it happen – maybe you can say? Why do we men always get ourselves into so much bother, always over women? When I thought they're not allowed to own land and property, anyway?"

"In the name of all the gods, Ascanius, don't go announcing our mission to the whole bar! And our latest client is the father's only natural-born child, his only one left. Why ever should she *not*?"

Another ignorant intervention from him to set me wondering too. Only mine was about why exactly I'd agreed to add this loud-mouthed former soldier to our party in the first place?

One thing was for sure, he was well down the road to getting me annoyed. Which was not a good start.

Chapter V

From Isurium to the next staging post, Cataractonium, was twenty-four miles north on a good road across fairly level plain, but a major hike all the same. It meant us getting deeper into Brigantian territory all the time.

For this leg of the journey, Tiro and I arranged to swap seats with Silenus and Lydia's two female attendants, so we could travel together in their mistress's coach, take our client's more detailed instructions in private. Placing the asthmatic Silenus above, clinging onto her sons, who recklessly insist they'll ride on the roof despite their mother's misgivings. At least they had plenty of bronze gods available there for passengers to hang onto.

This left Rianorix, Sennovarus and Sulio barely able to contain their joy as both her young women squeezed, squealing, into our second carriage for the entire day; Ascanius folding his arms.

But since I was never an owner or employer who treated moral guidance as any part of my remit, these were arrangements I usually left for my staff to sort out among themselves. Because the likely scale of discomfort or danger in whatever else we might encounter during this trip was something uncertain, and I don't begrudge my boys their fleeting bit of fun.

When the work starts, it's different.

As we bounced along and Tiro took notes, I began by taking Lydia back to the very beginning of her story.

Lawyers of Lugvalio

I found her dignified but articulate about her grievance and the character of her father; open and honest about her fears:

"I am someone used to money, why I stand most frightened of losing it. My husband is unpredictable and mean, while my father cuts me off. As a woman, I know I could be left with nothing, destitute in fact. And to be honest, I do not want to find myself a beggar, Justinus. It's a prospect to terrify me, quite frankly!"

Since I believe in being thorough and we had time on our side, I aimed to begin our discussion with the client's early years, before exploring her parents' personal circumstances – including financial, of course. This approach follows my usual practice and, on this trip for once, I found a willing interviewee.

The son of a soldier himself, she confirmed that Marcus C. Firmus, her centurion father, was born eighty years ago: a remarkable if not unprecedented achievement. Whether it was the Fates who decreed his entry into the world should occur in the province of Lower Moesia beside the mighty River Danube, nearer the Black Sea, she portrayed it more as the result of his father, her paternal grandfather's decision to enlist in Rome's auxiliary cavalry. And then to settle his small, illegitimate family - whose existence standard Army Regulations will deny, for mere *auxilia* like him - as close as possible outside the gates of his first front-line posting. In Moesia.

Long-lived as his new baby son, our Marcus, would also become; the client's grandfather had himself survived twenty-five years military service on the Danube frontier to earn an honourable discharge and the award of Roman citizenship. This during the reign of then-emperor Nerva, the imperial sponsor whose personal family name - *'Cocceius'* – is proudly held by all of the grandfather's descendants, into the modern day.

"Both my father and my grandfather were born horsemen, you see. From grandpa's side, he's born into a long line of Thracians - a race who live and breathe horses. Virtually live with their animals, love them quite literally. When my father walks into a room you'll know him as a horseman straightaway by his bowed stance and posture, unbowed spirit. Weathered by life's storms, but unbroken. There's nothing left can break him."

"He sounds splendid. A man following his father into the *auxilia*, the native cavalry?"

"Yes, into exactly the same kind of regiment as my grandfather's - a Thracian cohort."

"That's nice to hear of - family continuity. But I also hear your father was later drafted to Rome and served in the emperor's mounted bodyguard. Quite an honour?"

"Yes, that's correct – you've clearly done your homework. They only take the very best and his prowess in the saddle was noticed by those higher up. How he got sent."

"Though Rome is a long way from the Danube."

"It is. As are those glory days of his, when he served with the *equites singulares augusti* back in Rome, a long time before I even came along. Times long gone-by, even then."

"So where did you make your entrance, and - dare I ask it of a lady - when?"

"Forty-four years ago, here in Britannia – so now you know! Pater was thirty-six years-old by then, and a senior officer. Following his period of service in Rome, his next promotion from the *auxilia* called him to serve with the legions. This was fairly unusual, but with his distinguished career history to date, they immediately appointed him to the centurionate. To a vacant post with the Second Augusta legion in darkest Britannia, initially based at Isca Silurum, the legion's nominal home. Their depot."

"Down in the south-west?" I ask, gratified to be younger than a client - if only slightly.

"Yes. He'd done really well, but the price of all that success was being posted out here, a long way from home. Sent to our island at the end of the world, this strange land of mist and mysteries. Somewhere which doesn't seem to want to let *any of us* go."

"You've not told us about your mother...?"

Just as I spoke, the carriage must have hit a pothole or similar in the roadway, for there was a terrible crash which shot through its wooden frame with an awful shudder. Everyone reached out for something to hold onto, if only the person riding beside them. Despite the bang, and even before it, I'd grasped something else – a different sort of shudder going through my client, her reaction to what I'd thought an innocent question. Momentary as it was, she as quickly collected herself then continued:

"So, in a relatively short period of time, my father has gone from being an ordinary cavalry trooper out there on the Danube, to becoming a senior commander of heavy infantry across here in Britain. Since he was always so professional, so very good at his job, it seemed he'd manage this latest transition as successfully as all the others."

Obviously, I'd noticed her adroit diversion of subject away from the mother and back to the father, not to mention her closing note of doubt about him. However, I decided not to do anything, other than making mental note about the mother being a point to make sure of following-up on later. Once a better opportunity presented, when it felt right. Why I asked her instead: "You say *'seemed'*…?"

"With hindsight, I expect there were signs. Things he did back then which no-one at the time thought important but, with hindsight, loom large in retrospect. Things happening long before I was born which relatives alive at the time thought harmless, even amusing, and still retell within the family. Like they don't matter. Actions assuming a greater significance for me now, now that I know what I know…"

As a man who deals in hard facts but enjoys the company of women, I deprecate the compulsion common to their sex when testifying about family rupture or affairs - of letting themselves be side-tracked by nebulous emotion. Roving off the point. In too many will-related cases I'm asked to run, all this *"he said…she said…"* stuff lacks real relevance; leading myself and the court into evidential dead-ends. Why most of the judges I know will firmly stamp on it at trial, from the very start.

However, I viewed the circumstances of this current case as potentially something different. If only because, through careful mining of this vein, I hoped to extract the shining ore of fact. And since those whom the gods would destroy, they first make proud, my deployment of the kind of emotionally-charged material which I've got in mind and she's already hinting at - as part of my piece by piece dismantling of the Regional Centurion and his intimidating reputation, inside a public courtroom - might this time win us the day.

"Let's try and take it steady, m'lady. Try and recapture these events as they occur, both in his story and yours. Because Tiro here will be turning your verbal account of today into a proper witness statement. A document we might later rely on in court. So let's keep things in order, shall we? Now that we know your father's posted to the depot of the Second Legion at Isca Silurum: tell us how things went for him down there?"

"Pretty well, I'd say – or at least to start with. The Second Augusta when he joined it, had served in Britain for a hundred and twenty years, arriving with the invasion. He was proud to find himself part of its continuing history. A typical soldier, my father loved hearing about his new regiment's glorious record and its long list of battle honours, their campaigns in Spain, Germany, and then Britain. But by the time he and his teenage wife from Moesia arrived at Isca Silurum, he said they found its regimental-depot virtually derelict. The vast garrison running on a care and maintenance regime and most of its barrack blocks empty, roofs falling-in. Because the Second Legion had already spent most of the past forty years elsewhere. In multiple outpostings, split-up into detachments along the Aelian Wall before being sent north into Caledonia again."

"Yes, m'lady. People often say of our Northern Entrenchments - whether they mean Hadrian's more enduring works, or whatever Antoninus Pius tried replacing them with later - that they're nothing more than monuments to human sweat. To the sweat of the legions. And I expect the far north is where your father's comrades had gone to, by the time he arrived in Isca to find it empty. But what about you, where were you in all this?"

Lawyers of Lugvalio

"Oh, we're still talking about the time before I came along. He was a serving soldier after all, and I expect a new, young wife – never mind begetting a baby - were the very last things he'd want with him on campaign. So he left my mother far behind, because no sooner had Dad arrived at Isca than he's sent urgently north. Sent away on horseback to find the scattered detachments of his once mighty legion hanging-on across the rim of Caledonia. Holding off the tribes from a set of worn-out fortifications - the *limes* of Antoninus. Works decreed by Pius to mark the start of his new reign some twenty-five or so years before, but now in drastic need of replacement. Where my father found himself allocated to command one of these broken-down forts towards the centre of what – in those days - was still Rome's northernmost frontier. Put in charge of low grade auxiliary cavalry, not that tight legionary cohort he probably expected - and this pathetic collection of indefensible defences they're corralled inside. Hunkered down behind a set of sagging turf ramparts and worm-eaten walls, waiting for the enemy to attack them, again…"

"At least he'd be happier running horses?"

"I suppose there'd be that in it for him, Justinus, though I've good reason to believe he wasn't."

"Happy, you mean?"

"My father was – sorry, is – an unusually superstitious man. Fearful of the gods and desperate to please them, he lived through that great pestilence which took Marcus Aurelius. You know, the philosopher emperor who believed that if only he deferred to the oracle of the Clarian Apollo in far-away Asia – got all his armies to engrave their appeals to the gods, put their trust in Apollo's magic arrows – then he'd save them from a plague."

"Oh, yes, the Antonine Plague! Did he not notice, that not one of those oracular remedies actually worked for us?"

"I think that, much like Aurelius, my father's a typical Marcus. Defined by rigid attitudes long-ingrained. Why he was always so anxious about preserving his personal *Pax Deorum*, placating gods' demands. A serving soldier, obedient to orders from the centre but also coming armed with unshakeable private beliefs in a whole set of gods. Gods who'd brought him safe across an empire but, so far from home in Caledonia, now seem a long way away indeed. So distant from the Danube that he fears they might desert him, if he's inattentive. With good reason too, if you think about it, because by then he's probably realised that he'll never see the plains of Moesia again. Not alive anyway - maybe in a pot. Nor as he guessed it, would my mother, Aurelia, either. The young wife, sixteen years his junior, who waits alone at Isca..."

"Where do you think these growing feelings of isolation might have taken him, m'lady?"

"To a dark place, I shouldn't wonder. Though it's more a case of where events took him, because – if it wasn't pretty obvious to him straightaway - he couldn't have arrived on the northern frontier at a worse time."

"Which was?"

"I'm not sure exactly – maybe a year or two before I'm born? Around that critical time when Antoninus Pius dies and Marcus Aurelius succeeds him; our armies abandon Caledonia. A distant period of crises and retreats where my father committed a series of... made some personal misjudgements, I'd say. An unfortunate set of actions of which he's oddly proud. What they were exactly, I'm not sure we fully know, but they've haunted him and the rest of his family ever since. From that day to this, I'm certain."

"I see..."

"You do, do you, Justinus... do you really? Why we're stuck in this coach, making this miserable journey? Because the main reason why I'm all the way out here, dragging myself and my household through the middle of nowhere, forty-odd years later, is finally to hold him to account - at last. Enduring the rigours of the road with you, but absolutely *longing* for judgement day!"

Lawyers of Lugvalio

Clive Ashman

Chapter VI

It was nearly dark when our little convoy arrived at the southern gatehouse of Cataractonium. Dangerously close to that hour when – the credulous believe - evil spirits stalk abroad. If that's true, then we were fortunate to arrive inside its ring of defensive walls and guttering oil-lamps before any got chance. Finding our night-time shelter behind the built safety of ramparts, curtain walls invisible in darkness, we could still hear those foaming rapids of the River Swale which give the town its name.

Roaring away madly, somewhere nearby and northwards.

All the more disappointing also to discover that the Cataractonium you'll find behind crenellations belies any romance in the name with a day-long bang of hammers from more than fifty roaring foundries and as many stinking tanneries. Less of a town and more an industrial estate, there must be several hundred metal-bashers here, who conspire by day to create that veil of smell and smoke which lingers all night like a shroud over its shabby sheds and even meaner private houses.

Ascanius, showing an initiative I thought went to his credit (for a change) immediately took it upon himself to set off through this man-made fug and find us the highways office. Gone to get some permits issued, transit-tokens fit to cover our party over the next stage of the journey, starting first thing tomorrow.

49

Lawyers of Lugvalio

With an army background and new to the team, but after a pretty poor start, he now appeared over-anxious to demonstrate how useful his former military experiences might prove for us.

Whatever credit he deserved or his experience amounted to, annoyance and hindsight reminded me that perhaps our pre-appointment interview of him lacked rigour in detail. But after knowledgeably pointing-out how Cataractonium was the last proper town we'd encounter before entering the military zone, an inhospitable area where the country only gets emptier, respectable travellers fewer (*the danger from wild animals, maybe even bandits, correspondingly-greater*) Ascanius had set off down the street on his errand. Leaving me alone with this cheerful reminder of risk to rattle around in my ears.

It did not stay there long, because I had more important things to worry about than banditry or bears, wolves or wild boar. Not for the first time finding myself preoccupied with much darker thoughts - about my adversary, this antagonist I'm yet to meet.

("*Most notorious litigant in all Britannia....*" what she'd said).

Envisaging the metaphorical clash of arms to come – this formalised struggle between two intellects, two competing personalities - who would become the eventual winner of this most primal contest? Well, if me and mine were to eat this winter, then I knew it had to be m'lady; the law aligning with her claim.

It had to.

Because any alternative outcome – the court finding against us, my client losing her inheritance – bore no contemplation. This great, technical set-piece battle between us would be fought-out over fundamental questions that allow only one side to survive.

Within a short time, Ascanius was back and wanting money. There were fees and tolls to be paid for, up at the highway office - if we wanted to travel further along the road, that is.

Since I had none, I sent Tiro off to join him and request funding from our principal client in the expectation she'd see us right, as agreed – which of course she graciously did. Lydia, on the basis of her husband's treasury status, had somehow wangled two rooms for herself at the official *mansio*, where she was comfortably lodged with both sons and her three attendants.

For moral support while my staff went there and asked, I had decided to accompany Tiro and Ascanius part of the way along the main street, and at this late time of day was surprised to notice another woman, dressed in scarlet and limping painfully, veer across the empty carriageway towards us. Out alone at this hour in the fading light, I put two and two together to reach an obvious conclusion but was quickly proved wrong, because this phantom of evening was no prostitute, but a celebrant priest.

A minister of religion - of sorts.

"What in Hades' name is this that's coming our way?" wondered Ascanius, out loud.

Dressed as a woman, this mediator with the gods was in fact a slightly-built young man, although sheathed in a dress and quite blanched around the face. The white of mercury, as I guessed it.

An officiate as much weighed down by his jewellery as the spiritual demands of his role, he wore a chunky necklace of jet beads, two shale armlets, and one anklet cast in bronze. All of the clinking regalia thought necessary for his curious calling.

"It's a *gallus* – a eunuch priest in the mystic cult of Cybele" whispered Tiro. "The reputed mother of all gods and a great goddess herself – or at least for those who'd choose her. Who will claim her capabilities extend into every field of human action. From peace to war, fertility to nature. Not to mention law or disease, so they say."

"Law or disease, eh?" I laughed grimly, knowing full well the background but acting like it's news. "Here's the cult for us, eh, boys?" I sneer, so they know I don't mean it.

Our security detail, Ascanius, who - like most soldiers and veterans - was a thorough-going adherent to Mithras and could contemplate no other, just stood there appalled.

As well he might, since we could tell this pitiful phantom, approaching us crab-like thorough the dusk, was in considerable pain as he dragged himself along. Holding his arms out in the usual gesture, all this limping priest could manage - if but hoarsely – was to beg us desperately for alms:

"Give to the Great Mother Goddess, give to Great Cybele!" he exhorted. "Only believe, and your every enterprise shall meet with success, for She will know why you're here. Only gift The Goddess and Her temple, then your success becomes certain… in all your endeavours!" he gasped, his eyes shadowed by pain, not by the ash that I'd thought.

I consider myself among the least superstitious of men and more an Epicurean, but in the darkness of that unfamiliar street and the light of everything still preying on my mind, his appeal cut me to the quick. And this time, that too familiar reality of *yet again* owning nothing of value, no offering I could make – certainly not coin – had gone beyond embarrassing. My personal inability now verged on the frightening. Because what if I – what if we - couldn't give anything at all? Could the Great Goddess Cybele really ensure I'd lose my client's case? Would '*She…*' leave me penniless for ever? The unfairness made me angry:

"What sort of bargain is this, you offer?" I shouted furiously back – to my own surprise as much as anyone else's - but something inside me just snapped. I'd had my fill of religion framed by donations: "What benefit can poor folk like us hope for from transacting with your goddess, we men without money?

And why should we care, I thought to myself – why should we be struck dumb by his begging, by the sight of a pathetic, wounded priest prancing about before us in this tawdry dance of death? On an ordinary grimy street in another northern town, what relevance could it hold, what philosophies could it amount to? My own firm answer was nothing at all – just another eastern myth, another outlandish creed peddled to gullible masses.

Its grisly tale of Attis, the youth stricken with guilt after betraying that classic older woman whose sexual powers haunt him – Cybele herself. Betrayed for a younger replacement. The eternal triangle as Anatolian fairytale, one as old as the hills. Until you reach its unexpected bit where Attis goes mad and, for a form of penitence, decides on self-castration….

Unsurprisingly, soon dies.

The ritual recently re-enacted by this dismal spectre staggering about before us, or that's how I guessed it. This local fanatic who, judging by the signs, has really gone and done it - sacrificed more than blood. So I looked at Tiro, and Tiro looked at Ascanius, who simply looked sick. The priest himself looking back, blanched by loss of blood in fact - not mercury, as I realised. Viewing us with such an obvious despair and disappointment, poor soul, that he decided to turn his tortured legs and frame around. Started dragging himself slowly away, back up the road.

"That's tragic…" said Tiro, as we watched him sidle off. "On the promise of immortality, they work themselves into a trance through howling, dancing, and drink - then cut their testicles off, using something sharp. Their temples keep a special tool on the premises, you know, like you'd use for gelding horses. It's supposed to staunch the blood…"

"Urrgh!" I said. ""It didn't work in his case, did it, poor devil?"

Suddenly and to my personal surprise, Ascanius broke away from our group without a word and followed this unlikely figure up the street. Tiro and I watching from a distance as Ascanius reached into his arm-purse to bring something out and hand it to the priest. Once he'd rejoined us, I quietly asked him:

"So what was all that about?"

"I felt sorry for him, sir. And besides, like you always tell us, it's about assessing risk. And we daren't take any. Not with no gods, nowhere. Not on this mission. So we try them all, in my book."

"Thank you for that, Ascanius, you're right. It's appreciated. But I thought you didn't have any money left either? Or at least, not till the end of our trip, when you're due to be paid?"

"Yeah, well… you know, boss. I found some. A bit I had left."

"There's one important thing I forgot to ask you, Ascanius, when you got this job. What exactly did you *do* in the Sixth Victorious Legion, Decimus Ascanius?"

"Well… I, err, I… err… ran the burial club, sir."

Lawyers of Lugvalio

"The burial club?"

"Yeah, the burial club for the fourth cohort."

"Is that it?"

"Well, that and the usual army stuff, you know."

"We never saw your discharge diploma..."

"You never asked."

"If so, that was my fault. But I'm definitely asking you now. Have you got one?"

As Ascanius was perfectly well aware, I was referring to the inscribed bronze sheet awarded on retirement to all soldiers who successfully complete twenty-five years' honourable service with the eagles. Assuming that they do - and they're honourable.

"Err... no, boss. I haven't got one, to be honest."

"Why is that?"

"A bit of a misunderstanding, that's all."

"A misunderstanding?"

"Yeah... "

"Involving the burial club, by any chance? Funds from the burial club?"

"Yeah... as it happens, sir, it did. Yeah, something like that."

"Well, let me make it very clear to you, Decimus Ascanius. If there's anything else like that occurs on this trip - anything like that at all – if any money goes astray, for instance, while you're working for me, then you need to be very clear indeed about what will happen to you."

"To me?"

"Yes, Ascanius, to you. Because – if anything does - it will be your balls nailed up for decoration on the whitened walls of the Temple of Cybele. No question, believe me!'

Chapter VII

The Ochre Fort, Limes of Antoninus Pius - edge of Caledonia: AD 163

Say I did it!" she said, looking down at the trooper Nectovilius stretched out in a scarlet spatter of his own blood. Spreadeagled and lifeless on the stone floor of the centurion's private quarters, laid in a blood so dark it's almost black.

Like a black lake, spreading wider. Soaking into stone.

"Say that when he touched me, and wouldn't take no for an answer, it was me that stabbed him - not you, when you arrived and caught him."

Firmus was appalled, yet - even in the utter horror of it - still felt touched to the core by her naked loyalty to him: "No, you cannot! They would crucify you, or send you to the mines. No, I'll stand by you – we can sort this out, bury him under the floor…"

"Firmus, are you mad? His comrades will come looking, and you are his chief."

"He's not even a proper Thracian…!"

The enormity of it was appalling: that an infantry centurion, their commander, had killed one of his own cavalrymen in cold blood. That their decorated centurion, M.C. Firmus of the Second Augusta Legion; once an ordinary horse-trooper himself until he joined the emperor's *Equites Singulares* at Rome; that someone distinguished like him could manage to plunge a military dagger – a *pugio* - into the thorax of a drunken auxiliary he found messing with his woman.

Lawyers of Lugvalio

One of his own men.

There was nothing written into military regulations which could vindicate that type of behaviour. Yes, there are plenty of centurions who half-beat their men to death with vine-sticks on the march, on the parade ground - but killing them outright, using a blade? No, that was something different and completely out of order - why Firmus knew he must pay.

His career would soon be over, unless they came up with a plan, but only she could think of one, and a half-baked one at that:

"Yes, I shall say that I did it…" she insisted. "Let the law take its course. And then afterwards you can come in and rescue me, Firmus. Ride in like the wind, like the crazy Thracian horseman I know you to be, then spirit me away! Ride away together forever, far into the west. I know some good places we can hide, live happily ever after. What do you think?"

Firmus didn't know what to think, but wept anyway. He wept for his glittering military career. He wept for his dead father, who'd be appalled if he knew. He wept for this slave woman and their unborn child. He even wept for his child-bride, Aurelia, stuck hundreds of miles away in empty Isca; or the dead trooper in front of him; but eventually pulled himself together. Enough at least, *to try and think of some way out… like she'd said…*

It was true what he'd said before, though:

Trooper Nectovilius of *Cohors II Thracorum* wasn't even a proper Thracian – so what right did a man like him have to serve in a regiment like this one, anyway?

No, it was worse than that.

Trooper Nectovilius was a bloody Brigantian, and by killing him like this, the Centurion Firmus had just created an endless blood feud with the entire Brigantian nation.

One to last a generation.

Chapter VIII

We pulled out of Catractonium for another twenty-four mile trek – aiming for Lavatris - on the Kalends of October. This was the beginning to our Roman tenth month and we were glad to go.

Not planning on looking back the once while we did so - not after that uncomfortable overnight stay my team had endured in spartan accommodation claiming virtue through an absence of luxury. Its whiff of drains or our curious encounter with a priest of Cybele equally disconcerting, leaving us to board our transports and quit this place with nothing better to remember it by than perhaps a bad smell, a bad dream. Or a few more fleabites to increase our collections with – extra redspots to decorate the thigh.

Except our decision to leave seems to have prompted the old place into making a final effort – knowing it should have made more of itself before these last moments in town. As if those cussed souls who comprise its council are loathe to impress, but once we're seen rolling-out early from their northern gatehouse, suddenly come over all keen to display what public works they can sometimes commission, when the fancy takes them.

"Great bridge!" said Tiro, who loves this sort of thing. "Impressive piece of work!"

Lawyers of Lugvalio

And what a sight it was, this over-engineered civic achievement launching our departure across the Swale. Sprung from the town's stone gateway, a huge timber bridge soared outwards and upwards to carry the main road over cataracts below. Supported by a steeply revetted embankment - its glacis studded with a million river cobbles, mortared into place as an armour against erosion – it's braced by stone piers. Whoever ordained it - whether military or magistrate - no human construction could better display what drama and scale our Roman engineers can bring to a landscape, once we decide to. Like the fort adjacent, it's built to tame a native river, convey an empire's travellers in safety upon their Great North Road, but delivering stronger messages yet about the reach of Rome's power.

Crossing by this magnificent construction, it's only a shame what awaits us on the far bank. Waiting and wanting, the soaring sublime carrying us directly across into the shabby and ridiculous. No better than a shantytown: that continuous line of narrow-fronted sheds set on both sides of the road as it exits the town. Little better than stalls: each with one oven, a chimney to the rear and – however hungry - surely your obvious last resort?

Yes, the food was fast and cheap - but you get what you pay for, don't you? Victuals of the very lowest quality, and who could fancy that? Yet for those souls who do, a disreputable collection of grubby chefs wait patiently on the roadside. Ready to ambush the hungry with their choice of undercooked, overcooked, or else completely-uncooked meals. Set out for sale beside an open, filthy street - *and let's not mention the sewer...*

Whatever I personally thought, it seems these sights and smells were sufficient to stop our whole convoy. There and then in their tracks, like they're transfixed. Including, as we inevitably did, the weak-willed and short-sighted - not to mention certain other persons lacking common-sense - our carriages and crew came together in the one immediate, grinding halt. Almost colliding, so keen were some on board to inspect this roadside offer.

As if anything available here was even attractive...?

Clive Ashman

Chief among those surrendering to self-inflicted ambush was my bodyguard, Ascanius. Harbouring no such doubts, he was the first - jumping out of our coach while it's still moving with a soldier's cry of glee: "Hey-up, lads – it's *thermopolia* time! Your one last chance to get some decent grub inside you before we hit the road. Pile-in, boys, and fill your boots!"

Left alone to guard my own health, I think I was the only one in our party not buying *anything* – save for me and m'lady, of course. And if I consider my body a temple, then that's where it will hide itself once circumstance requires: 'Praise Be To Serapis!'

The name of another god gone-up in my estimation. Compared with all his competitors - especially that cruel one, the cursed cult of Cybele.

Leaving we abstemious few to wait politely until the self-indulgent many tear themselves away from this kerbside cornucopia of cookery, its dubious delights. But once the ramshackle buildings that hawk them have finally petered-out *(braver friends with stronger stomachs taken their fill)* then perhaps the rest of us might resume the route? Which, happily, we do.

Finding our route northwards more of a boulevard but mainly lined by tombs, the occasional chapel or temple. That long, linear, and melancholy domain beyond any town where its cemeteries – by sensible Roman law – can only be placed. And if a little further-out, but further down the same road, too many inhumations seem no better than lumps and bumps – burials identifiable only by their one, flat stone or perhaps a wormy timber sign, faded epitaphs in paint - the bigger memorials we passed on first leaving town contain the great and the good. Those fortunate few whose ashes enjoy their final resting place inside a professionally-built monument, often many feet high.

How many of those inside died from something they ate is probably the last thing you're told. Surprising really, since it ought to be a matter of wider public record and their inscriptions seem to report just about everything else. Copious information including the deceased's name and social status; their trade or profession; and whatever lifespan they achieved. All of it in abbreviated Latin, plus a closing nod to whichever relative or beneficiary under the will took on the responsibility and expense of raising these memorials to lives well-lived. Legal duties and obligations I'm familiar with from my own field of law – and probably enhancing my personal fascination for other people's choice of epitaph, what words they put on their tombstones. Why they make such compulsive reading for me and there's barely one we passed that morning which I didn't try and read, calling out to our driver to slow down if necessary, so I could.

Indeed, the more I succumbed to this morbid curiosity, the more it felt like the dead of Cataractonium spoke to me directly. Although to qualify that effect, and in this mortal's humble opinion, their conversations too often tend to the one-sided. Are too self-absorbed for my liking, too-frequently ending in wistful rebuke or tendentious phrases like: *"Think of me as you pass by, traveller...."* or even *"That's my last word, now go on your way."*

Well, thanks! Others invite the passing wayfarer to make libation in their memory - which was more touching - or else that memorably-tragic one, lamenting the incompetence of their physician. Both of our carriages stopped to read that one - before we made a long face to each other then discreetly resumed. Because everyone knows what usually happens to the kind of well-off people unlucky enough to afford the intervention of doctors – as even Ascanius does, from his service in the army.

And since these memorials are raised in open countryside, upon what's hardly sanctified ground, there were several more carrying an additional exhortation to treat the tomb with respect. Not to damage it nor add other interments (*whether family or not*) or otherwise to disrespect the deceased and his burial plot. Now - so far as these official-looking notices go - it's my settled jurist's opinion that the dead are quite frankly wasting their time here, since requests like these are in practice unenforceable at law.

Especially when you're dead.

However the notice which rocked me most – which felt so personally offensive - appeared unexpectedly on the side of a big,

Clive Ashman

brick-built tomb housing a dealer in textiles and dyes. On whose side in large letters, I read this charming endorsement:

"Lawyers and the Evil-Eyed - Keep Away from My Tomb".

I don't know why those two particular categories were singled-out, but this was certainly the inscription which offended me most here, and that's what it actually said. So who was it who'd rattled *his* cage, then – this dealer in textiles and dyes?

Now as a lawyer and up to a point, I'm mature enough to realise this is something you've just got to accept - like being chased down the odd alleyway. Getting used to hostility, I mean - though it's rarely received from beyond the grave. But if I had a gold solidus for every crashing bore who ever approached me at a dinner party and then condescendingly sneers, like they were the first thinker to devise this brilliant question of theirs:

"What I've always wanted to know, Justinus, about an occupation like yours - is how can you defend someone, when you know they're really guilty?' Then they tap the side of their nose and stand there expectantly - like you'll think they're Aristotle, rather than a fool.

Fortunately, Cicero's rather good on this, so I generally defer to him. Usually quoting that bit in *"De Officiis"* about an advocate's duty - *'Trial of Sextus Roscius before Sulla'* where it's easily found. My citation of him normally followed by me heading straight for the furthermost wine-waiter, opposite side of the room.

But while we're on the subject of disreputable professions – the textile-dealer's jibe still rankling - what I find more unseemly and disturbing than some posthumous insult from a buried tradesman is to see their tomb's more-enduring role, as a workplace for whores. Like we noticed on leaving Cataractonium that cold October morning - though I'm told the same occurs in Rome, along the Appian Way and even to this day.

Their sordid trade dignified – if dignified it may be - by a theatrical roadside backdrop of stone pediments and cornices, portrait busts and pinecones. All those carved recitals of morality, reminders of mortality. Their engraved assertions of virtue and lifetime achievement from our dear departed - beneath whose mausolea, the uncouth will screw.

Lawyers of Lugvalio

Despising carved requests that they should kindly please refrain, shadowy figures drift listlessly between funereal structures. Their pimps ensconced in brazen supervision on a folding-stool or battered campaign-chair, touts for the passing trade. Holding court like shabby kings over wretched subjects in this kingdom of the damned. Filthy and despised the whole lot of them, but at least they're alive. Or at least for the moment – and better them than robbers, or worse scoundrels of the highway.

Though it seemed most of our fellow travellers thought the sight of these characters little less than amusing – nudging each other in the ribs and guffawing - I tend to view them more grimly. But never - I hope – as primly. Whilst Tiro for his part, a man better versed in matters historical than I'll ever be, spoke up to draw an unexpected parallel while we passed them:

"You know, Master, whenever I see a common whore wandering among roadside tombs like these do, it's always a sight to put me in mind of Alexander...."

"Of Alexander, eh, Tiro...? Errr, which one do you mean exactly... and how would that work?"

"It's Alexander the Great, I mean, Master. The legendary Macedonian who historians say once conquered half the globe, killing nearly as many. Yet never coupled with courtesan nor princess, not to mention the odd hoplite, without sensing in his action some redolence of death, a foreshadowing of his own..."

If that sounded pretty extravagant a remark, I still thought I understood the basic point which Tiro was making here. Even I am aware of how the great Alexander managed to die so young. Sex and death what did for him - that same human cycle keeping a specialist in Wills and Probate like myself in a steady stream of work, if not so much in funds.

And, as if to underline Tiro's point, only a bit further out of town on a road still lined by these morbid monuments to the dead, we finally found the temple dedicated to Cybele herself – the only cult I've known to generate its own.

Clive Ashman

Of her unfortunate priest there was today no sign and, suffering some serious self-inflicted injuries, I would doubt he survived the month. You could only hope his adherents had buried him well.

"The most important thing you'll need to do with my father..." Lydia Firma said firmly, as I rode in her carriage and the last of these wayside tombs went rolling-by us "...is to understand his past in detail. Fill in the gaps. Understand it without excusing him. The chain of events which has created this present unhappy situation in which we all find ourselves. Because out of that level of detail, Justinus, I'm convinced a clever man like you will work out what should happen next – including at trial."

"Do you think he might change, and save us all the bother?" I asked, hoping against hope. "People can, you know, whatever they've done in the past?"

"Oh, no! In theory he could - of course he could, but people never do. *'Leopards and their spots...'* And I'm certain my father won't - no matter how hard the rest of us try to persuade him - because he's always done what suits him best, always! Living in the moment, because that's what's most important to him. His approach to life. The here and now - nothing else comes close. Tomorrow can look after itself. No, not even this final chance at obtaining some redemption in our eyes, come the time of trial, will make him change his ways..."

"All these epitaphs for the dear departed, ma'am, rolling past our window..." I said. "And here we are, m'lady, writing your father's - before he's even dead?"

"No, Justinus, you're wrong!" she sighed. "He's writing his own already, even as we ride towards him. And he'll be its true author, you can be sure of it - there'll be no-one else to blame."

At our next stop for water - after a new road westwards to Luguvalium had split from the principal, northern one - our ostler, Aulus Equitius, put his cheery face in through a window to mention a diversion: "Stanwick and its open-air market is, I'm told, handy for bargains. Good quality horse or mule fodder, available very cheaply. So how's about we call in? Not too far off the main road, and since the going's flat today, what do you say?"

Lawyers of Lugvalio

Tiro expressed himself as keen – as mentioned, he'd read all about Cartimandua in Tacitus and Cassius Dio, so was dying to see the spot. The very place where his *'Cleopatra of The North'* once held court. This unusual point of feminine connection - and her liking for public markets - perhaps what also encouraged Lydia, our patron and paymaster, to cast her deciding vote. To admit that she, too *"wouldn't mind"* if we made a slight diversion.

The only dissenting voice we heard came from Ascanius - typically complaining that the only time you'll meet civil Brigantes is when they want to sell you something - but he was heavily outvoted. So whoever's fault it was, a democratic decision. Although, with hindsight, one probably mistaken.

Our client had been given to understand by Equitius that *'The Stone Wick'* – its *vicus* or market - was only about three or four Roman miles off the main Imperial highway. Which is presumably how he sold it to her and the rest of us as a minor departure only, from the day's agreed itinerary.

Meaning that when we arrived at that point on the route where these paths diverge, the native from Roman, it was make-your-mind-up time. At which point neither of our two drivers hesitated up front, but did exactly as they're told - obediently setting the nodding heads of both carriage teams onto the minor road.

And straight into ruts.

While slotting the iron tyres of our carriages into the deep wheel-tracks of this lesser lane might have seemed easy enough at the time, it would be getting ourselves safely out of them afterwards which became the big issue. How we'd escape from here already become that thing which grew to bother me most.

Before we'd even got there.

Chapter IX

Having - rightly or wrongly - made the decision to abandon our chosen itinerary and the official Roman route, we now found ourselves taking a very different path. Because there were no official signposts out here. No imperial milestone, nor anything else to confirm or deny that this alternative destination might prove a very different world. Another world altogether.

Just a rougher surface and a lot fewer signs of maintenance to hint what differences in culture or ways of life this older road might lead us into - how quickly things can change. Yet almost immediately the trees around us grew taller and bolder, crowding-in upon this sunken lane as if to take a closer look, examine us as strangers. Soon it felt like we were falling steeply downhill through a tunnel of foliage, sunlight flashing less frequently through fewer gaps in the green canopy that thickened above us, while rogue branches reached out to scrape their prehensile fingers down the sides of our carriage.

I am a city dweller and wilder places like these are for me an unwelcome and an unfamiliar experience, but I would hardly have been the only person in our party acquiring a profound and disturbing sense of being secretly watched by others – by spirits of place, ancient gods of the forest, whatever's in those trees.

But still we pressed on, regardless...

Lawyers of Lugvalio

This route adopted became a deeper green lane, semicircular in section; our carriages, mules and horses struggling along in the bottom where water drains and rocks fall, pieces of broken tree and other debris end-up. The going got increasingly more difficult by the mile, more dried-up river bed than a proper road.

Eventually not so dry, when we encountered several wet and boggy places where the wheels on each wagon became so densely clogged with mud that it took the combined efforts of our two drivers, Tocitanus and Trenico, plus Aulus Equitius and Decimus Ascanius, bodily to turn their spokes and drag both carriages out of the clinging mire, one after the other.

"Is this really a good idea?" asked Ascanius pithily - now being covered in clay, yet neatly illustrating the principal fault with democracy. How the losing side will never accept its outcomes.

He might well have voted against it, but returning the way we'd come could be as tedious as getting this far, so there's no better answer than continuing. At least it coincided with the first positive development, where the impenetrable tree cover began to thin-out and, between the trunks of individual oaks, we first saw open fields - some of them cultivated. That point when I realised we were entering the beating heart of Brigantia itself.

On fully emerging from the trees, we made our arrival before what anyone would still class as a proper *oppidum*. One whose great, looping earthworks once embraced the fortified royal centre and an unassailable citadel for the whole Brigantian nation.

Or else they did - until Rome arrived, imposed on them Isurium.

Defensively and practically speaking, Stanwick still seems pretty hard to make sense of and, I'd guess, equally so to defend. Because this was no hilltop eyrie or cragbound fortress, but a fortified '*town*' sprawled across rolling fields, prime agricultural land. While what its five or six miles (*that's no under-estimation*) of ditches enclose must easily exceed seven hundred acres of ground. Painstakingly dug-down deep to the bedrock, these same ditches probably producing enough stone to frame the matching ring of ramparts, fifteen-foot high, which crowns them above.

Clive Ashman

Leaving us heading straight for their centre, immersing even the least sensitive of our party in a growing sense of *'The Other'*.

Only Aulus Equitius appeared unpeturbed - and maybe he was, having perhaps been here before - hence his request. While I kept my misgivings to myself and Ascanius was openly unhappy, Tiro seemed beside himself with excitement:

"Most impressive…" he kept on saying "…most impressive!"

As our coaches lumbered ever deeper inside this encircling maze of high earthern banks topped-off with white drystone walls, the outside world disappeared to sight amongst a labyrinth of defensive dykes or livestock enclosures, studded with circular huts. A huge labyrinth which stank like one giant great byre. From now-on, our way back to the metalled Roman road, to Lavatris and safety, felt not just unattainable but irrecoverable.

For me, if no-one else.

"Impressive, you say, Tiro?" I asked, the contempt in my voice deliberately unconcealed, my fears less so.

"Maybe not by your lights, Master, but it certainly is by theirs. And historically – yes, most interesting. Most interesting, I'd say. Holding such powerful associations."

"Associations?" I asked, when the only ones I'd managed so far were between cattle and dung.

"Yes, Master. When your armies first arrived in Britannia, the Brigantes were the largest tribal group – and willing to be friends. So Rome formally recognised their queen, Cartimandua, knowing she'd maintain a useful buffer state against the other northern tribes, whilst the legions concentrate on conquering the south."

"She must have been quite a girl, eh, Tiro?"

"I think so, Master, because, for the next twenty-five years, Cartimandua stayed in control, hung onto power - right here in Stanwick. That's why I find this place so fascinating, Master. Why I'm so glad we've got this chance to visit here today. It's all in Tacitus, his 'Histories' you see. That Cartimandua was probably as cynical as you Romans, in herself. Using you for her power base, knowing that she could call on Roman military support whenever it's wanted, whenever she felt like she needs to. And so long as her Brigantes were paying your taxes in kind – delivered living things of value, like hunting dogs, slaves and horses – then everyone was happy with the deal."

"So you're telling me that I should treat this place like it's the melting-pot, where Rome met Brigantia and trade deals were done? Our ambassadors came and went?"

"Indeed. And to be fair, Master, I'd expect things not to look that much different today."

At first I'd scanned the scene for positive signs evidencing Tiro was right, but as we neared the centre of this huge fortified enclosure, it more resembled a ranch. Countless stockades and fenced-off corrals full of black cattle or brown sheep – the native peoples' wealth. Stinking, unmade lanes between them swarmed with shepherds and farmers, horse-dealers and hangers-on: all the personalities, trades and callings of an agricultural market. I knew it would be busier since we were approaching the time of their great Celtic festival – Samhain – marking the end of harvest and approach of winter. When their markets get swollen by every buyer and seller off-loading animals for slaughter, or stocking-up on supplies to get them through darker times coming.

Suddenly we were forced to a stop as the lane we followed through this mercantile chaos narrowed ahead. Its width filled by one native woman and her two ragged boys driving a flock of geese through what had been another gateway in this curving complex of sinuous fortifications. Waiting for her flock to pass, I put my head out of the side-window and looked up to inspect a wooden-walled gatehouse above. Applying the new spirit of intelligent enquiry I'd consciously modelled on Tiro's, I noticed above its crossbeam - silhouetted against the light and arrayed across its width - a row of wooden posts raised as decoration.

Their tops were crudely carved to approximate spheres and as our carriage moved forward again, the angle of the light changed and I got a better view. What kept me looking I can only guess but, no, they weren't carved at all, these decorative '*spheres*'.

Clive Ashman

In fact they were heads, severed heads. Human heads, mounted on spikes or spears then left in the sun to dry, and – eventually, I suppose – to shrink. If only meant for domestic ornament, they still left me sick, and it was I alone in our party who'd bought nothing at all from the food-vendors of Cataractonium.

No, these people were nothing like us. There was not a Roman anywhere – or at least none I could see, in the multitude that pressed round us. Not one thing that's familiar. Our carriage rocked as the throng pushed past it, trying to squeeze through and enter the gateway ahead, following the woman with geese.

I looked out of my side window one more time, only to become eyeball-to-eyeball with some sort of warrior. A man with a flowing moustache and missing, broken teeth, his hair white and solid, pulled up into spikes. The man's face was covered with tiny blue dots, tattooed in concentric circles onto his skin, and I noticed he carried some type of weapon, maybe even a spear.

Although perhaps I'm mistaken, and it was only a staff?

Whatever, but in that frozen moment, he looked directly at me and I looked directly at him, and I think it is fair to say that his personal distaste for me was - quite evidently - a great many times more than what little ill-will I might have felt towards someone like him. So much so that I immediately retreated from the window and his bare-faced hostility laid bare, just outside our carriage. Looking inwards to my clerk instead, and seeking his aid:

"I don't like this place, Tiro, not one little bit. There's a man outside who I don't like the look of - the atmosphere's bad, and it's been a big mistake coming. So how soon can we leave?"

"That'll be down to Aulus Equitius and whether they've found some feed - I understand he's off with Rianorix, arranging it now. We'll just have to stay patient and wait for their return..." he soothed. "I'm sure they won't keep us waiting long."

"Do the people here hate us?"

"The Brigantes? No, of course not, Master - or at least they didn't when your armies first arrived. So long as Cartimandua was their queen, her people believed she enjoyed a special relationship with Rome. Or else that's what she told them…"

"Special in what way?"

"Let me give you an instance from Tacitus. In the ninth year from Claudius's troops first landing in Britain, there came a hero in the Britons' eyes: a singular man who coordinated resistance against Rome. Eventually, this war leader – Caratacus was his name - felt forced to flee north. Seeking sanctuary in Brigantia, he arrived here in Stanwick, where Queen Cartimandua immediately had him arrested, chained-up, then handed-over to the conquerors. Writing in far away Rome, Tacitus believed that these events were important – why I brought that volume with me: *"Her authority had lately increased, since she betrayed King Caratacus into the hands of the Romans and was thus considered to have provided the Emperor Claudius with his triumph."*

"He's a rebel and a terrorist, so she did the right thing. I hope we rewarded her handsomely?"

"Of course you did. With gold and silver, weaponry and wine; but in the end all Cartimandua was doing was helping the Romans appropriate her kingdom, one step at a time - at leisure. Though she believed that loyalty to Rome would always secure her authority and her throne; long term, she couldn't have been more wrong. When it only led to an inevitable downfall instead, because it was not long after she surrendered Caratacus to them – with all the bitter resentment *that* caused - that the first civil war broke out amongst her people and their federated tribes."

"First?"

"Yes, and this first time it happened, your general just sent in some troops. They successfully rescued Cartimandua and took a few hostages for good measure from the kinsmen of her consort - Venutius, the king, who'd led this first revolt against Rome and his queen. And I suppose as a plan to improve her king's behaviour, it probably worked for several years."

"But wasn't there something similar later, involving a chariot-driver…?"

Clive Ashman

"Yes, Master, it seems there was - a second civil war. Over a shield-bearer, not a driver in fact - as I read it now. Because when the Queen decided enough was enough, she divorced her ageing husband, Venutius. Left him for good - mainly because of his anti-Roman views, I suspect - then took up with one of his younger retainers. So, yes, this Vellocatus she married next might well have been her husband's armour-bearer, have held a similar job. But isn't that sort of carry-on not untypical of more than a few royal dynasties - even Rome's wealthier families?"

"There's often similar gossip from the Palatine, it's true, but let's avoid dangerous talk like that, eh, Tiro? Just tell me what the histories say her old Brigantian cuckold, Venutius, did next?"

"One thing's certain, Master, apart from rallying his people against Rome and their lawful queen, he's sure to have reinforced Brigantian defences here. So this final form we see today is probably his work. Though maybe that's another job he never quite finished before your legions arrived. What's for sure is that - inside the space of one bloody afternoon - Rome's soldiers will have showed Venutius and his warriors just how much time and effort they'd all wasted, restoring its walling and ditches."

"Final cue for us properly to conquer the rest of the north, I suppose? Impose direct rule at last?"

"Eventually, Master, yes, it was. Once the long-lasting love-feud between their Queen and Venutius met its inevitable end – that was the political outcome. But hardly so neat nor so certain to begin with. Nor won anything like so easily as you imply."

"They caught us on the hop?"

"To start with, yes again - I think so. This second time around, your soldiers were too thin on the ground – what with other crises in the empire; rebellions in Germania or Judaea. Or simply none nearby. Anyway, when the Brigantes rose a second time, all that's available to face them was one single regiment of cavalry. *'Our auxiliaries, on both horse and foot, then fought several engagements with varying success, but eventually rescued the Queen. While the kingdom was left in Venutius' hands – and the war in ours....'* is how Tacitus more tactfully describes it."

Lawyers of Lugvalio

Tiro gestured to the book he had in his hand, like I do in court.

I laughed: "Wonderful stuff, Tiro - you seem to know it all by heart! Old Venutius won, and his naughty wife got chucked out?"

"Up to a point and only for a while, Master, but I guess that's essentially it. At least until your imperial governor, Petilius Cerialis, managed to return here in strength. Brought a full legion to finish-off the king. And Rome could raise her brick basilicas in Isurium Brigantum at last, to govern them from for good..."

"Then in relation to the original question I made of you, good Tiro – 'Do they hate us?' – then surely Ascanius is right. The correct answer, nowadays, is unfortunately still 'Yes'...?"

"I'm afraid that's probably true, Master. Though perhaps you'll understand why a keen student of Tacitus feels so thrilled to find himself standing here today, correct volume in hand. Standing upon the very soil and beside ancient ramparts once a mute witness to dramatic events. A veritable northern Troy."

"Like that city south of Thrace. And maybe why native Brigantians still swarm over its ruins, like somehow they matter?"

Tiro nodded and pointed to a gap in a mound near the carriage:

"You can still see where Cerialis slighted its walls and ramparts at regular intervals to ensure no-one would raise rebellion against Rome from here, not ever again. Though these natives defy Rome's restrictions to this day with their assemblies and trade – an unlawful breach which customers like ourselves only help to condone. And speaking of which, here's our own animal-man, Aulus Equitius, come back from the market."

His red face and bald head stood framed at our window, glowing with pleasure: "Yes indeed, gents, and I can report us getting m'lady a really good deal here. Twenty sacks of bargain oats bought for the price of ten, and loaded-up for free."

"Then can we go now?" I asked him. "*Please!*"

"No problem, Justinus!" said Aulus, like he wondered why all the fuss. "We're putting them on the mules right now, then it'll be straight back onto the main road for everyone. No problem..."

Clive Ashman

Aulus Equitius might have believed there was no problem but I was not convinced. Not when we'd diverted from the normal route into a furnace of tribal resentments, their sleeping volcano.

Surrendering ourselves to the care of somewhere notorious in our island's history for fomenting rebellion against Rome. Unnecessarily parading ourselves in the face of a defeated people who – in breach of prohibition – hang around to this day among the wreckage of lost glories they still blame us for losing.

From the time of our obvious first arrival, we must - by any waterclock - have spent at least an hour there. Very publicly parked, right at its ruinous heart. Waiting - however quietly or discreetly in ourselves - inside a pair of bright-red, leather and bronze-bedecked coaches pulled by matching, glossy teams.

While the scrapings of Brigantia slowly file past us, noting every detail. Hating us more with each one.

No, the main problem to my mind was in how much we'd done to draw attention to ourselves. To our pair of fancy wagons, carrying a small group of well-to-do Romans - several of whom were women and none of whom seemed armed.

A long way off the road.

Whilst there'd been no problem before, my greatest fear now was that we might have created one. That somehow – in ways I couldn't yet begin to define – we might be bringing all the bitterness of Brigantia right along with us. Back onto the road.

That could be too high a price, for twenty sacks of feed.

Chapter X

The muddy struggle we had getting out; along the long green lane up from Stanwick then back onto the main road; meant we never made Lavatris that night as originally planned. Whilst the worst thing that happened – or so it seemed at the time – was when a nearby farmstead overlooking the lane unleashed a pack of guard dogs onto us - for reasons unexplained, but without one hint of apology either. Country folk can be like that, but it only added to my private sense of darker times coming…

Instead of Lavatris, that evening we felt more than grateful to make do for our lighting, shelter, and security with the lesser fort and smaller civil settlement - plus decent timber *mansio* – we discovered at Maglona. Whilst for readers' future reference, or anyone thinking of emulating our journey, I should confirm how this fort and its useful facilities stand nicely sited together on a convenient river terrace. Put there to guard an important road-bridge across the boisterous River Greta, not far from Stanwick.

Neatly aligned with its riverside terrace is the fort's impressive eastern rampart – not only enhancing the overall defensive capabilities and angled fields of fire available in that quarter, but also adding a few extra degrees of personal reassurance for me personally, after stranger events that day.

Clive Ashman

Beside the riverside terrace, that eastern rampart needs no ditch, but I felt relieved to note how all other angles of Maglona's defences in depth benefit from the well-cut, double-ditch system ringing its walls. Not to mention a regulation earth rampart supporting curtain walls in stone, and the narrow causeway leading to a gateway overlooked by several of the latest design in mechanical, bolt-firing guns, set high on her towers.

Why, for a change, I felt safer.

All of which point to recent restoration works only underlined by seeing the name of our illustrious governor - Lucius Alfenius Senecio himself - engraved in fresh, red paint above the stone lintel that greets you on arrival. Four from our group passing directly under its portal and through the north gate of the fort, in order to present our compliments and travel-permits to the commander in person, as legally required.

The latter officer's name was Valerius Restitutus, a thin man who listened with what I suspected was a polite interest only to our – *well, mine in particular* – trenchant accounts of what offending we witnessed at Stanwick.

In theory, he was an infantry cohort commander, but of his theoretical five hundred soldiers, approximately three hundred or so had been abstracted north to support the emperor's intended efforts in Caledonia - while another hundred or more were either on leave; on the sicklist; dead; listed as deserters; or else non-existent in the first place. In reality, he had very few men left to do anything with, about anything - his fort virtually empty.

In the privacy of their remote *oppidum* nearby, it seemed to me that those native Brigantes could get up to pretty much whatever tricks they fancied. But at least Restitutus had soldiery enough to paint-up inscriptions, keep the couch grass down…

"Any man who's never been a soldier always thinks the less of himself, Restitutus - and I include myself in that category…" I'd conceded. "But when you've got soldiers listed by name: easily-traceable individuals from your own roster who've gone missing through desertion, then that's another thing altogether. Where I feel entitled to comment, as a concerned citizen - to confirm what I know – that the law is unflinching, its penalty usually death."

I don't suppose the commander at Maglona much appreciated being lectured on military law by a mere civilian, one who's briefly passing through, but Valerius Restitutus simply sat there. Blinked two owlish eyes and helplessly shrugged a set of hunched and rounded shoulders at me, like it wasn't his problem.

In my inexpert opinion, the man was unfit for command, but I knew he didn't care and both of us expected me gone by the morning - as would be the case. However, I still decided to give him a piece of my mind, although it was hardly my business and - knowing the soldiery - I was probably lucky not to have been thrown off their base, there and then. The fact that I wasn't, perhaps another illustration of essential moral weakness?

What Restitutus could not have known was that I'd been making the study of military law a major feature of my journey. Swotting-up its sources while travelling in the carriage. Because there's more to life than the Will of the Dead and a successful lawyer needs more than one string to his bow. So I'd been carefully looking-up the penalties for misbehaving soldiers - on a whim maybe, but also seeking to add another useful strand to our developing case?

"The second book in Arrius Menander's *'Of Military Matters'* very clearly states" I'd continued, like a dog with a bone: "*When a deserter is found in a city, it is usual for him to be punished with death; if he is caught elsewhere, he can be reinstated after a first desertion, but if he deserts a second time, then he must be punished capitally.*"

"Yes, very interesting, Justinus, though I suspect you won't find too many cities around here..." he said, looking down and tugging at the serrated edges of his scale armour like they're a new discovery. "But if you're really so bothered about deserters, why don't you get out there and hunt some down for yourself?"

Despite him, we left Maglona in brilliant sunshine and began the gradual climb westwards up to Lavatris in good spirits. For this leg of the journey, Ascanius had taken-up a vantage point on the roof of our patron's carriage, and it was the diagonal strap across his chest for its scabbard which led me to notice he appeared to be carrying a sword. Another souvenir from his military career, I supposed, but this one more useful, if unlawful in town. At least we would not be entirely defenceless, should any of the Brigantes seen yesterday decide to come after us.

About thirty-foot wide, it was a good, well maintained road that we followed, and it drove for the far horizon with utter directness, unflinching in purpose. Never deviating but remaining absolutely straight for mile after mile, its subtle gradient and smoothly engineered embankments never varying, taking us gradually higher all the time. Fortunately, scattered along its length - whether in vehicles or on horseback - there seemed more traffic about than you'd expect to find out there. Mostly military and plenty going west. This gave a sense of safety in numbers which also helped our mood.

I'd begun to look forward to our little consultations with the client and on this day too, we resumed in her carriage, in the usual way. In particular, I wanted to start this session by discovering more about some generalities she'd ended with: "Last time we spoke in detail, m'lady, you'd mentioned to me about what you'd called *'some personal misjudgements'* of your father. *'An unfortunate set of actions'*, how you put them to me then. Might they be relevant to our case?"

She bit her lip and, although she wasn't sitting opposite, I'd swear a tear came into her eye. Then she collected herself and said: "There was something happened at his fort – when we still held the *limes*."

"Of the Deified Antoninus Pius?"

"Yes, them. On the edge of Caledonia, before the army pulled out."

"Something unfortunate, ma'am?"

"Yes, quite!"

"Go on…"

Lawyers of Lugvalio

"One of his soldiers got killed. There was a scandal. A slave girl belonging to my father managed to stab this soldier to death, right inside the officers' quarters."

"He had a slave girl?"

"Yes! It's hardly unusual, you know. Lots of soldiers keep slaves…"

"Yes, of course - I do realise. That's fine, ma'am, it's fine."

"She probably cleaned and cooked for him, a domestic, that's all. There's nothing wrong with that, is there?"

"Yes, I expect she probably did… no, of course there isn't."

"Anyway, Justinus, the thing is that somehow or other this slave woman of his got her hands on a knife…"

"Quite possibly from the kitchens where she cooked?"

"Indeed, quite possibly. Anyway, the thing is, this kitchen knife, or whatever it was, ended-up jammed into the trooper's chest. Right in. While my father was off out somewhere… hunting or something."

"Oh dear!"

"Quite. Anyway, it all got sorted out, eventually. An examining magistrate came up to the fort, there was some sort of trial, and she was sentenced to the mines. Salt mines."

"Not sentenced to death?"

"No, I don't know about that, Justinus, I don't understand why she wasn't."

This is where I hesitated, because it is well established law that a *mulier* – a low status woman like the sort we were obviously talking about – may only avoid the inevitable execution, or hardest of hard labour, which together represent the only possible penalties for a serious capital offence like murder, if she's with child. In these delicate circumstances, a question I thought it wiser not to press. Instead, I simply stated: "So the girl's not dead and she remained his lawful property?"

"Exactly."

"Oh, well. These things happen - especially on the edge, out on the *limes*. It's another world out there. Another world altogether."

"...And we're talking about a long time ago. But what's it got to do with our case?" I added.

"Because when she later got kidnapped by pirates from the government salt-pits they'd only just sent her to - and then he somehow bought her back, paid money for her release - it led directly to my father's legal case about her. The one he went and won! You see, my father's litigation over this stupid, stupid girl is become infamous. Notorious! He's mentioned personally by name in the law reports, cited by jurists, because he won against the government. Against the government! Why my father thinks he's untouchable, can do whatever he wants, and I find him so completely embarassing. Because my father still believes that - if he can defeat the government - then there's no-one left in this world alive who'll dare to take him on."

"Until we come along and try?"

"Yes..." she said faintly, and now she really was crying.

Of course I knew about his case – did she really think I'm the sort of advocate who doesn't do his homework? Didn't know what I'm taking on here? Only I wasn't going to tell Lydia that - much better it should come from her.

Another reason why, on the principle of '*Know-Thine-Enemy*', I'd already written-out for myself - in longhand on a piece of smooth bark - a copy of the commentary published about it by that great Roman jurist, Sextus Pomponius. Keeping it close to my chest on a cord, like a talisman for luck. My amulet against an adversary - that bit in his Twenty-Seventh Book, where Pomponius states:

"The right of post-liminium exists both in war and in peace.... So that where a woman who - on account of some offence - had been sentenced to labour in the salt-pits, was then afterwards captured by bandits belonging to a foreign nation; sold by the right of commerce and then ransomed, restored to her former condition; the price of her ransom should be paid by the Treasury to the Centurion M.Cocceius Firmus."

"That case is in the past, it's history. Is history going to stop you today, lady?" She looked up at me defiantly, and blinked back her tears: "No, Justinus, it's not!"

Lawyers of Lugvalio

I'd expected nothing less from this most determined of women, but tried diplomatically to change the subject by asking her instead: "So, tell me about your mother..." just at the very moment our carriage lurched to a violent halt and unknown voices started shouting loudly outside: "Lavatris, Lavatris; everyone off for Lavatris!" I looked out of the window, and there we were - parked right beneath its outer walls. Barely midday and already we're here, our little audience over.

A bluff, intimidating fortress in grey, Lavatris – *'The Summit Fort'* - is strategically important because of where it stands: controlling a vital crossroads high in the hills. Built on a raised earth platform where four separate trunk roads converge to meet its matching entrance gates; these ways arrive from several points of the sun but also other Roman forts, each a day's march away.

For our part, we'd come in from the east, via Maglona and the Great North Road; while over to the south stands Virosidum; to the north, Vinovia; and finally that long drag west of it, across The Stone Moor to Verterae itself - or Verteris. The one I guessed we'd be tackling tomorrow. Each of them a hard way on foot to encounter yet another identically-square, stone Roman fort: squatting astride yet another river valley like a gigantic grey toad. Stopping-up the mouth of one more hidden dale and all those native people it's been put there to control. Because Lavatris fort itself is just another component in Rome's great enduring plan. In a spider's web of roads and iron grid of garrisons, laid to keep Brigantia cowed.

Stepping outside, you could feel by how much the temperature dropped. As I climbed backwards, down the steps from the carriage, a bird-call went gurgling up above me, high into the sky. A unique and gorgeous, bubbling cry that seemed to trill with utter joy and ecstasy, over all that terrible majesty and empty grandeur of the northern fells surrounding it below, to send a sympathetic shiver shooting down my spine.

Clive Ashman

"That's a curlew, that is. Wonderful call..." said Ascanius, climbing nimbly down to join me from his seat atop the carriage.

We watched a plain brown bird with a curved bill go flapping quickly over the fort's tiled roofs, and it seemed incredible to me that a creature so quick but ordinary could produce a song that's so sublime: "Last of the season – I doubt you'll hear another one like it, not 'til next spring."

We were gathered in the wagon park, a low-walled open annexe set beside the fort, amongst several other travellers' wheeled vehicles, but unsure whether to continue our journey any further that afternoon. Since she was the person who's funding this trip, a decision requiring Lydia's casting vote: "No, I think we should stay put, Justinus - Verterae is too far away today, and there's things to do here. While we get that wheel fixed, you can speak to the commandant about people he might know."

The usual garrison at Lavatris is a *cohors equitata* – one of those mixed units of part-cavalry, part-infantry, whose patrols are ideal for rougher country. Like that peat-coloured monotony of moorland and bog which, even on a good day, stretches away in all directions from Lavatris, as far as the eye can see. But more important to our sponsor's keynote decision to hang about this afternoon was the fact that – whether through serendipity, coincidence, or the beneficence of gods – the unit of soldiers that's based here are officially classified as 'Thracians'.

How I ended-up drawing the short straw: nominated as our party's ambassador and heading over to the headquarters building with a collection of travel permits (scrawled-out in ink on flatter bits of amphorae) rattling around in my bag. Carrying them up for an official inspection before we paid the tolls, but also as a pretext for that 'casual' enquiry into *Cohors I Thracorum*, its history and veterans, which my instructing client is now suggesting I should make, while we stay here.

Unlike his counterpart at Maglona, Quintus Calpurnius Concessinus, commander of The Summit Fort, seemed a man at the height of his powers. Including his grasp of perspective:

Lawyers of Lugvalio

"There's a Big Push coming, you know...." he'd said to me almost immediately, after a few perfunctory pleasantries: "A Big Push is due and everything's prepared – Severus did the same thing in Syria and now it's our turn."

"Our turn?" I said.

"Oh, yes. No coincidence, I think, and you can't blame Lucius Septimius Severus Pertinax for doubting us still. Or wanting his revenge. After all that Severus went through to become our emperor in a bloody civil war, there's bound to be prices to pay."

"*Prices* – in plural?"

"I think so. When he's had to fight his way to power against the military governors of not one, but *two* Imperial provinces – and one of them was ours. Pescennius Niger in Syria, then Clodius Albinus over here. Why the armies of both provinces can expect to see their loyalty put to some sort of test. So the legions of Syria get marched off into open desert to confront the Parthian hordes; and now our British legions can expect the same treatment. Ordered off next spring into the arse-end of Caledonia, carrying one simple instruction: '*Kill anyone or anything that breathes, torch anything that burns.*' I've been up there, Justinus, so I know what it's like. Another sort of desert, another sort of hell – somewhere you'll as easily die of cold as be eaten alive by midges. Maybe even both, within the same season."

"Though some say Severus intends his Great Invasion to be no more than a stage to the ultimate character-building exercise for two troublesome sons. His hope they'll grow together."

"Antoninus and Geta? Well, I expect there's a grain of truth in that story, too. Certainly I've met the first one, only this year, when the whole Imperial family came travelling through here. '*Caracalla*' he's nicknamed - it's after his cloak. Accompanied by two Danube legions on the road outside and all of them heading north. What an incredible sight that made for, Justinus, I'll tell you! On a hot summer's day, their columns ran for miles. Though I doubt that cold Lavatris, or even Caledonia, could draw a hot youth like our Caracalla is, from the fleshpots of Rome..."

"You are a Thracian cohort here?"

"Historically, you're right - we were. Though that's become more a matter of military tradition, since most recruits we accept nowadays will be local Brigantes."

"Tell me, do you hold any earlier records, *praefectus*, about where else this unit might have served? Or else those men who retired? Let's say forty years ago - maybe more, maybe less?"

"We might, though I'd be surprised at anything so ancient. But why are you asking?"

"I travel with a fine lady…"

Concessinus crooked an elegant eyebrow.

"She is *clarissima femina*, a woman of the utmost virtue and distinction who – for sentimental reasons only – demands I make enquiry of any Thracians we meet on the way. Simply because her late father served in one of their regiments. Based in The Ochre Fort on the now-abandoned *limes* of our Deified Antoninus Pius, where she'd like to track his service. Respect an ancestor's deeds, as done for the country."

"I see, Justinus – an enquiry not unknown."

"Why I wondered if you'd help?"

"No, I cannot, although our standard bearer may. He's the keeper of records, guardian of pay. I'll give him your name, mention the particular locations which interest you, and let's see what he can find out for you by the morning."

"You have been beyond kind, Concessinus. If not tomorrow, maybe I'll catch-up with you on our way back, let you know how we got on?"

"Oh, you won't see me here again, Justinus. Got a promotion to command Caesarian cavalry. Going north and onto the Wall. A little local difficulty with the Corionototae they want me to sort out. It won't take me long."

Lawyers of Lugvalio

Chapter XI

The Ochre Fort, Limes of Antoninus Pius - edge of Caledonia: AD 163

The centurion-commander and his four trusted companions - a complete *comitatus* of culpable collaboration - rode silently out of the old fort's decrepit south-facing gateway just one hour before sunset, heading straight for the Firth. In both theory and law, they were in fact deserting, save that no-one else had watched them go. And any who said they did, would most surely have to die.

The stakes were increased by that much.

On a cloudless night, they rode down to the great estuary of Clota. Down to where, on a sandy beach beneath a gigantic dome of black volcanic rock sticking out over the water, they met Epiclitus and his mule. To Firmus's mind, two horses of a similar colour - but needs must, when necessity drives the carriage.

Out on the water, an alien vessel moved slowly towards them, its sail furled and cloth-bound oars dipping and rising silently in the moonlight. Secretive and sinister.

"Here come the lads! My lovely boys, centurion, come all this way to rescue you your treasure!" said Epiclitus, as the black curragh glided onto the beach.

Lawyers of Lugvalio

Followed by sixteen bare feet, all padding on sand.

The eight men aboard were either Attacotti or Scotti – Firmus found it impossible to tell them apart – and although they lived in Hibernia, it had long been their habit to treat Caledonia as if a personal stamping ground. Their convenient cockpit to a uniquely grim trade.

Because while it was always their job to take the captives, then afterwards they must resort to Epiclitus – rely on him for the retail and detail. Together, the very worst of men, the sort centurions should suppress - yet here he was out with them on a joint mission together. Fellow creatures of night.

Almost brothers in arms?

So the sooner this fleeting 'friendship' was over and done with, forgotten, the better - but first they must talk terms:

"A thousand denarii and three talents of torn silver, measured purely by weight. My maximum and my final price for recovering her intact. No more and no less. Paid out to Epiclitus at the fort gate, including your share, two days after delivery. No earlier and no quibbling. So long as – with your help - I do receive the girl. Intact and tonight. Complete and unharmed - because she's carrying a child. Without her, you'll get nothing."

"If you must have the girl, Roman, then we will want the rest. Take anyone we choose from the salt-works, no questions asked. No quibbling. And by the way, while we're over there – who can we kill?"

"The girl you will be bringing out for me is the one they call Caria. She'll be delivered unhurt, do you understand me?"

The Attacotti and their Greek fixer looked back at him blankly, so Firmus continued anyway:

"And don't forget, either: I'll be wanting a proper receipt."

Chapter XII

As *vexillarius* or standard-bearer to the First Cohort of Thracians, based at Lavatris fort, Rufus Sita would spend most of his days quite quietly - in book-keeping maybe, or counting piles of cash.

Thanks to his important desk-job as both regimental paymaster and archivist – conveniently avoiding the callousing of sword-drill, also practice camps - his bony fingers instead became ink-stained, from their forever holding pens. Permanent battle-scars and a truer testament to his more genuine vocation.

It was therefore only occasionally - and once the payroll's complete, both columns balancing - that Rufus Sita the *vexillarius* would be called upon to ride at their head. Bravely carrying his regiment's embroidered flag into battle for yet another pointless bloody skirmish, out there on the moors. And much like handling other people's pay, here was another high profile role too prone to attracting attention. Probably why Sita had therefore resolved to reconcile these unwelcome drawbacks to an otherwise satisfactory career by cultivating the most self-effacing of styles.

To the point of a shyness unusual in military service – and my explanation for why, when he sidled-up to me in the wagonpark at Lavatris that morning we left, I didn't even realise who he was.

Lawyers of Lugvalio

"You're the man who's been asking about The Ochre Fort?" this unknown and anonymous soldier, dressed in a plain brown tunic without even a belt, had crept along to our carriage to ask me.

"Yes, soldier... and you are?" I said.

"I am Rufus Sita, sir, the *vexillarius*. The prefect has asked me to look through the records on your behalf. To see how far back they go. So I have."

"I'm sorry? Oh, yes, of course! Yes indeed, Rufus, good to meet you and thanks very much for looking... so what did you find?"

"Not a lot, sir, I'm afraid. The lady who's asking seems to have got mixed-up - between our boys in the First and another, Second Cohort. We've nothing on file about them."

"I see."

"But I did find a link, sir, nonetheless. Just the one, mind you - between us Thracians in the First and them over in that unit what you're talking about, up at the Ochre Fort."

"A link?"

"Bit of a local tragedy, more like. It was a long time ago, but around the time she's interested in. One letter only, surviving in our archive."

"Go on..."

"A local lad, recruited at Lavatris and doing nine years, before he was transferred to that unit you said, the Second Cohort. Sent away full of optimism to go away north, up to the *limes*, but he only came back dead."

"You say there's a letter?"

"More of a polite note on a tablet. Wooden-bound and sealed – why it's survived. Ours is just a copy. From a centurion in the Second Augusta Legion but commanding auxiliaries - the Second Cohort of Thracians in that same fort you've been talking about, at around the time you mention. Writing here to his father or parents, and the village elders, with condolences and that."

"His parents?"

"Yes, sir. Of a local tribesman called Nectovilius, who enlisted in our cohort here as a volunteer before he later got transferred.

Clive Ashman

Sent off to Caledonia, though he didn't last long out there. Ironic, really - not killed by the enemy, but murdered in cold blood by a slave, inside his new commanding officer's quarters. Bit of a local legend, the crime still unforgiven, because they don't forget their grudges that easily round here. No, Brigantes are like that: kick one and they all limp – even forty-odd years later."

"Well, I hope they punished the offender, Rufus, whoever they were - but who was it who wrote this letter to the parents, the one you've just found?"

"He signed himself off as '*M.C. Firmus*' and claimed to be a centurion, seconded from the legions, but that's all we know. I only hope they got the guy that did it in the first place."

"Do you think there's anyone left around here now who was alive at the time, might remember it in person? The crime and the victim?"

"After that number of years?"

"Is it even possible?"

"It might be. Not here, but where you're headed, there's a dedicated veterans' club for ex-Thracians over in Luguvalium which our unit keeps some contact with – run from the Temple of Mithras."

"The kind of man I'm thinking of could easily be in their mid-sixties by now, but there's few who reach that age. You'll know better, Rufus, but maybe the army takes too much out of you - for who in the ranks survives that long?"

"Ha, you'd be surprised - it's hardly unknown! Their head man, the one you'll need to speak to, is called Longinus Matigus. He lives on his own in the *vicus* at Voreda, last waystation on the main road in, before you get to Luguvalium."

"Perhaps we could call in?"

"Well, I'll happily give you his details. And of course veterans like him are always glad of a visitor – assuming the old codger's still breathing, by the time you actually get there...."

Lawyers of Lugvalio

Chapter XIII

Outward-bound from Lavatris fort and en-route for Verterae, during the morning of our fifth consecutive day on the road since Eboracum, we found ourselves travelling towards a complete wall of weather, rolling eastwards to hit us. While the highway we followed climbed gradually higher and higher westwards to meet it head-on, we could see what was coming for ages.

Heading straight towards us was a mighty, aethereal barrier built out of slatey-blue cloud. A wall which grew ever taller as it blew-in from that quarter. And once it finally fell upon us to do its very worst, our poor mules nearly lost all momentum. Leaving their unfortunate drivers and outriders fully exposed, doubled-down in flapping oilskin as they all bent to the storm.

Even inside the carriages things were bad enough, with everyone squeezed in, seeking refuge from weather. We'd shuttered both side-windows to keep the rain out and, if it was gloomy outside, inside the compartment was so dark we could barely see one another. The noise from the rain falling outside, rattling onto then bouncing off the stretched skin of our wagons; the howl of the wind and the shouts of the drivers; all of it made conversation impossible but left no light to read with.

Lawyers of Lugvalio

All I could do was close my eyes and think, but for everyone it was the same ordeal. Just a case of knuckling-down, putting-up with it and keeping-on going. Keeping-on slogging on.

Easier said than done. Water streamed off the metalled roadway into deep drainage ditches either side, washing parts of the surface away. Our pace had slowed to a crawl just at the very point where we reached the highest part of the route, where the most effort would be needed and the least shelter available. In every direction the land extended limitless away - empty, heartless, and featureless. A useless wilderness of rain-lashed bracken and heather fit to rival Caledonia. And Ascanius was right about the curlew, because we never saw another.

Winter was coming and we were in its way.

Through a slit in the window-shutter, I noticed the outline of a wooden tower right beside the road, the silhouette of some sort of watch or signal station, although lacking signs of life. No military purpose could be served by being up here in this sort of weather anyway - no mortal being could stand it - and I hoped we wouldn't linger long either. No, the only course was to continue fighting our way forwards and westwards, straight into the unremitting heart of a strong, developing storm. Upwards and over, onto the Pass of the Stone Moor itself. Our only comfort in the knowledge that tonight's destination – the fort at Verterae – stood on sheltered, lower ground.

Far below this godlike fury from the skies.

At the very top of the Pass, we were forced to stop - physically unable to continue. The animals were exhausted, their drivers chilled to the core. There's a vast marching camp sited up here whose earthen banks, ditches, and gateways once in the past provided tactical defence - if not actual shelter - for larger military units passing through these mountains. Over many generations.

A good place to die for a soldier, if only from exposure, but we didn't plan to stay because Ascanius insisted that we'd find an active military post nearby. Somewhere just around the corner and lower down the road, whose physical protection from rain, wind, cloud, and cold would be more real. Persuaded by his veteran's promise, we staggered off blindly again.

Out into unrelenting mist and bone-soaking rain we lurched, heading north-westwards in one last, desperate effort to escape the worst this weather can throw at us. How we found ourselves and our carriage teams gratefully joining a broad *agger* or engineered embankment which veered right-ways and northwards over horribly broken ground. Following the overall curve of this route, but bordered by a dangerous margin of steeply tumbled rocks, we were disturbed to see the land fall away sharply to our left into apparent empty space. Westwards it fell, black rock giving way to nothing more substantial than cloud, while we all struggled on beside it. Scared and utterly lost.

The official *'Itinerary II'* which we'd been working from describes the modern road as keeping to the north-west of a small, stone fort which Ascanius assured us remains operational, somewhere near the summit of the Pass. However, while everyone keenly kept watch, hoping for its sudden appearance from the mist, nothing did. And it was only after several of our party passed a further while missing, gone on foot to wander about amongst countless crags and black boulders littering a benighted hillside, that someone fortunately found – no, fell into, I'd say – a narrow hollow-way. Another man-made lane, one we prayed would lead us directly toward an invisible fortlet's gate.

Before it could, an unexpected fork in a road we'd only discovered through bumbling-about amongst this low cloud sweeping over the moor helped to aggravate our predicament. But happily – and without even tossing a coin – the navigational choice we made at this junction would turn out correct.

Calculating that the rougher of these trackways would eventually divert to go around the fortlet, its paved equivalent more likely to lead us straight to its gate, we were delighted and relieved to be proved right. Shouts of glee rang out through the fog as our missing searchers were reunited with us - with m'lady, our carriages and the mule train - where we waited patiently on the hill, before guiding us confidently over yet another rock-strewn brow towards the lost fort.

A purely military installation, this important fortlet guards the last known summit before The Pass of the Stone Moor ends by dropping away westwards. Supervising the main road where it comes up to the Pass, but unlike the old marching camps above, it retains a skeleton garrison of some dozen unfortunate men. A garrison of military castaways cooped-up in one barrack block, complete with stabling for a few beasts they have to run errands.

Adequately defended from attack by a masonry wall six-feet thick and fifteen-foot high, it's ringed by a ditch and supposed to overlook – or else does in good weather – the vast panorama they claim unfolds below. That isolated hill station whose commanding location is well known to the local tribesmen – if we revert to their tongue – as the fort of *"Mai-Dun"*.

Measuring only about a hundred-and-fifty by one-hundred feet externally, the paved road passing through what's a small enclosure anyway further reduces the space inside for buildings. So more important to us than than its naming or strength would be the quality of roofing - what respite it offers from weather. Suffcient shelter for visitors to see out a storm?

As we emerged through shrieking winds and flying water to discover, present our bedraggled selves before their gates, men from the fort rushed out to receive us with the most genuine demonstrations of hospitality I've ever met with from military.

"In here, this way… get yourselves out of the rain!" they insisted.

Posted up here to this lonely, god-forsaken spot, I could guess they were glad of company, of anyone who called. But whatever their motivation, it was wonderful how these kindest of soldiers surrendered their largest rooms to the ladies before cramming everyone else into the rest of the building. The glowing charcoal braziers they brought in turned the atmosphere warmish, not to say a bit damp and headachey, but any sort of shelter was preferable to the deluge without. While we were only grateful not to have died out there from cold, in that awful wilderness.

Clive Ashman

While the rest of us slowly warmed-up, Aulus Equitius busied himself with our animals, fitting as many into the fort's small stable as possible without them biting or kicking. Talking kindly to his charges like they were difficult children - *"Oh, you would, would you...?"* - he calmed them by walking round the stalls and distributing as much of his bargain feed from Stanwick as hadn't been waterlogged in the downpour.

It was barely midday, but the sky outside resembled dusk, with no sign of let-up, no encouraging hints of blue. Leaving us with nothing better to do than wait and rest - to pause and sit out the storm with patience while gods made up their minds and a gale blew itself out. Drying-out slowly, we stayed grateful of shelter, but it was hard to imagine being crammed in here overnight, knowing Verterae wasn't that far away.

By late afternoon, the possibility of resuming began to look more feasible, so that by common consent we agreed to make a dash for it. From the gates of Mai-Dun everything was downhill, which would definitely help. Although instead of hauling, the main job for the mules and their drivers would now become braking - preventing a pair of heavy carriages and occupants with luggage, from running away out of control down an endless hill. An effort likely to lessen as gradients eased and the roadway levelled-out, during a lengthy descent where the corner towers of our next fort, Verterae, became increasingly visible ahead, peering over trees.

A welcome sight, indeed, though it was still raining slightly down there too, below the cloud-base, if not so heavily. The wind also abated, whilst having our destination in view throughout a careful, gradual, four-mile descent encouraged team morale.

A time which passed quickly and before long we'd arrived.

This latest Roman station - where we definitely would spend the night - comprised a securely walled compound of about three acres set defiantly on the widest part of a narrow, bumpy ridge whose principal curiousity is its resemblance to a hog's back.

Beyond the fort astride a distinctively shaped ridge, land falls steeply away to the north and down to a beck, while its southern

95

flank overlooks a narrow marsh. Together, natural features which work together to provide a formidable vantage for the fortress we'd rely on overnight for ensuring our stay would be safe.

To the east of Verterae fort is a small *vicus* or civil settlement, where we had further hopes for a hot bath and some half-decent accommodation - while to its east is a cemetery, somewhere we hoped not to need. I said that half in jest, but only because poor old Silenus had been suffering terribly with a fever of sorts ever since we left Maglona, and that dreadful weather up on the moors round Mai-Dun had hardly helped. But his mistress Lydia and her assistants were doing their level best, while what little the rest of us could do was to hope and pray to the relevant gods. Including, in my case, to pray it wasn't catching.

Adhering to a settled ritual established over the course of our journey for presenting route-passes and tolls on behalf of friends, staff, and fellow travellers, I was once again deputed to make myself known to the fort commander in his headquarters. In practice, I'd come to appreciate what interesting opportunities this minor representative role gave me - if only for comparing what manner of men our government entrusts with travellers' safety on the road, the security of arms.

Good, bad or indifferent, in which camp should I place this one?

Lacking the spinal curvature of a Restitutus, yet never less like a soldier than I've seen, Probius Agendus greeted me at his office inside the headquarters building with the distracted air of a man who's more occupied by re-arranging his desk than hearing the latest intelligence off the road. Only his belt to show him an officer, while everywhere around him you looked there were boxes and parcels, sacks and pottery jars. Organised chaos.

Overflowing from desks and tables, piled up around the walls, each one was strung with a strong, red cord whose knot is affixed with a shiny, silvered seal embossed with unit emblems.

"What with the emperor's pending *'Big Push'* and that, we're almost run off our feet..." how he freely admitted it to me.

Clive Ashman

Astride the main road from Eboracum, Verterae was more a centre for receiving and distributing the post or other military supplies, than a first-line combat outpost. Army couriers, wagons, and mule-trains came flying up the Via Decumana then out again, all day long – even in bad weather, like we'd just had.

"Oh, no, not *bad*…" said Agendus "…the weather's always like this here. Always raining. Nothing unusual about today's offering – just you're not dressed for it. Why it pays to wrap-up."

Ex officio another 'Thracian', if only by virtue of his appointment to command their Seventh Cohort as run from out here - but even if he was, Probius Agendus had somehow in the course of it metamorphosed from fierce Balkan warrior into pedantic postal worker.

Sensing a captive audience, he was quick to show me a waxed wooden wall-plaque on which numerous tin seals were mounted for display, before proceeding to tell me in detail which military unit each example represented:

"They're all done in hot-moulded lead – it's very malleable, so you get lovely levels of definition, as anyone can see. So each seal carries the unique emblem of the particular unit sending out the consignment. Its stamp, you might say…"

"Right. So you know exactly where they've come from, but how do you know where they're going?"

Agendus paused and gave me a baffled look, as if I was slow, then continued: "Obviously we require the destination to be clearly written-out - *in words* - on the outside of the package. Like on this one you can see here. Where it says '*At Luguvalium: or if not there, Trimontium*'. But if it's not, then we simply send it back."

I could imagine what pleasure that gave him.

"Look, they're all here…" he insisted, thrusting the wooden plaque into my hands for closer inspection:

"Those are official seals for the Second Augusta and Sixth Victorious Legions along the top row – a capricorn for the Second, charging bull for the Sixth. And here's my own Seventh Cohort, in pride of place adjacent. Right next to them you'll find the Sixth Thracians too; and a seal from our First Cohort, come all the way

97

from Lavatris, like you are. Then there's the First Cohort of Batavians, Fifth Pannonians beside them. Second of Lingones are next, then a rather rare one from the Sixth Raetians. And for special mention of a cavalry wing, then I think the famous Ala Sebosiana will do us rather nicely – don't you love their little horse? While sent from the same location where the lead these seals are made from is mined in the first place – and, yes, if you thought the weather's bad down here - well, let me present you with the Second Cohort of Nervians. Marooned in the wilderness, stuck out there forever, up at windy Epiacum..."

"Lovely" I said, gripping the plaque for dear life, like I cared.

Chapter XIV

For one reason or another, the waystation at Verterae got itself added to a travellers' shortlist of certain stopping-points on *Itinerary II* which myself and like-minded others were always desperate to leave. Places best avoided, on any future trip.

A sentiment not helped by the resident unit and its prefect – someone I was interested to hear his own troops refer to in private as *'The Collector'*. Together they'd created such an obsessive atmosphere of nit-picking, fuss and fault-finding, that their whole approach to daily business felt too reminiscent of particular practitioners I sometimes cross swords with in court.

Why our small group had assembled outside the *vicus* next morning a little earlier, and with rather more enthusiasm than usual, planning a get-away for first light.

Knowing there's fourteen miles of hard-packed gravel to cover before the next fort, Bravoniacum, where we hoped a small settlement beside it would provide better comforts or facilities than we'd enjoyed for a while. So off we went into a light drizzle but all in good heart, anticipating our arrival by-and-by.

The going we encountered felt much easier for our animals, while the undulating countryside which we passed-through was rich and well-cultivated, nice and easy on the eye.

Lawyers of Lugvalio

Just the occasional unkempt stretch of moor, or that continuous backdrop of blue mountainside and grey cliff unravelling away to our right to remind us of upland horrors we felt lucky to survive.

"Oh, how I wish this rain would stop!" I groaned aloud to no-one in particular, my companions closing their eyes in sympathy.

On this side of the country, away from the high ground and at this early time of day, any other traffic we shared the highway with was few and intermittent. Perhaps the penetrating mizzle puts less-urgent travellers off, but it was during one of those quieter spells that I glanced out of the right-hand window, eastward to the mountains, to see a long line of men.

Half-running, half-walking in single file, and nearly parallel to us, they were at that moment crossing open land. A dozen at least, loping along nearly as quick as our wagons could roll, and each one carrying a set of spears like they knew how to use them.

I stuck my head and shoulders out of the same window and looked upwards to where Ascanius rode sword-point above me, sitting on the roof. "Who are those men?" I asked him straight.

"Only tribesmen, Justinus, local tribesmen. You need not be concerned. A hunting party, I'd guess, no need to fret."

"By tribesmen, Ascanius – do you mean *Brigantes*?" I'd said, affecting a casual interest. Like ethnographic curiosity drove my diffident enquiry, not a congenital nervousness grown more active since Stanwick.

He thought for a moment and then looked away in the other direction, down towards the river, as if my question wasn't interesting enough: "It's hard to say, boss - out here and at this distance. They might be, might not…"

"And if it's only a hunting party, Ascanius, who or what would they be hunting?" says I, pursuing my ignorant townsman's enquiry. Ridiculous to him, but borne of anxiety. With no oracle let down from the roof, I withdrew from the window and sank into my seat. Perhaps I'd leave my adviser alone awhile, let him stew on this question while he monitors the band. See how long this group stays with us, or whether they peel off?

Clive Ashman

In the meantime, I turned towards Tiro beside me again: "Just two days left to Luguvalium, m'lady's staff are saying. So how do you feel about that – looking forward to our arrival, eh?"

I'd swear he made a face: "Yes, of course, Master. Although it will only be then that our real work begins…"

"Don't worry, Tiro, I've got an agenda in mind. A whole list of jobs, ready to tick off."

"As I do, Master, as I do. Of that you may be sure." And I was sure. Because Tiro and I always worked confidently together, functioned well as a team, which was the secret of our success - even if I've heard some say (*my wife in particular*) that I let him be overfamiliar. Overlook his status as slave. Either way, we knew that this unusual case could be our greatest test, the making of us both, for which none of that would matter.

"Tell me, Tiro, how long have you worked for me, now?"

He scratched his brown beard, recently sprinkled with grey, as if he had to think: "Well according to the ledger, Master, your purchase was made twenty years ago, and I've been with you ever since."

"Forgive me, yes, of course - is it really so long ago? And I've been meaning to ask you for a while – only because it's slipped my mind, not that I don't really know – what name you joined us under? Remind me…"

"I was once Namatobogius, son of Colinagius, from the Votadini tribe - taken hostage at the age of twelve. But now I am just '*Tiro*' and that's good enough for me."

Which was good to hear. Because I've always felt that, as a name, Tiro is honourable and short enough - while having been a hostage pre-sale might explain his excellent Latin and Greek.

Because as I often say, my senior clerk '*Tiro*' is a well-read man, and knowledgeable in law. Someone who's learned enough to appreciate the lofty reference in his newer name, whilst at the same time also wise enough to recognise his master is no '*Cicero*'.

Nevertheless, and with all my admitted shortcomings, we'd rubbed along well enough together till now, and I'd been thinking carefully:

"Of course you were – now I remember! But at least '*Tiro*' is easier to say. And this time we've spent in the carriage together has given me chances to think."

"To think? About the case, Master?"

"Yes, Tiro – well, yes, and also no. Because I've also been thinking about you."

"About me, Master?"

"Indeed. I've been thinking about all that you've done. How hard you work and how good you are at your job."

"Thank you, Master, I'm glad you think that. Very glad, it's nice to be appreciated."

"And I've been thinking about your liberty."

"About my liberty?" he exclaimed, his face lighting up.

"Yes, about granting manumission."

"Master! But what would I do as a freedman? How ever could I live?"

"I hope you'd continue to work for me as before. Except I would pay you."

"Pay me, Master? But you haven't any money!"

"No, which is why it would have to depend…"

"Depend?" he asked, features still flushed, if not so animated now.

"On us winning this case. That's how it will happen – once she pays her fee."

It was only when I saw the colour go out of his face and his deflated features fall, that I realised how little faith my experienced managing clerk had in our achieving a successful outcome to Lydia's unusual claim. Or even getting paid.

The point in our journey when I suddenly understood that the ever-reliable Tiro did not himself believe that we were going to win.

It came as quite a blow, I can tell you.

Chapter XV

In the end, we did get to Bravoniacum alright, but I remained bothered about that hunting band which – at a distance – still kept pace with us beside the road. There was nothing that they actively did to threaten us, but just their presence felt uncanny and generally had me spooked – I don't know about the others.

Anyway, at one of our regular stops to rest and water the animals and in order to propitiate my anxieties, Equitius had taken a faster mule and ridden-off ahead. There is a cavalry garrison based at our destination and eventually he returned with six mounted troopers, who were happy to ride along with us for the final run into town, provide reassurance.

Ascanius never did reach a decision about whether they'd been Brigantes, or else some other lot, but either way the question became academic when these spearmen disappeared - melting silently into the brush as suddenly, once cavalry arrived. But if Fortuna smiled on us in that way, by the following morning it seemed that Her Outlook had changed.

Bravoniacum itself is only a small place, but I can report it as a properly equipped way-station offering a reasonable standard of inns and stabling for the respectable traveller, so that every member of our party would be well-housed that night.

Lawyers of Lugvalio

From which slumber and my dreams of scrolls unrolling, I was woken most abruptly in the morning by the sound of women howling and keening, right within the yard.

Silenus had gone to bed cheerful, but by morning he was dead.

Quite what he died from, no-one could say - whether it be the sweating fever, or else a shortage of breath. My lady was distraught – he'd been a pillar in her service. "*My rock...*" is what she said but her two sons, Flavius and Julianus – whose hair, I was glad to note, had grown pleasingly floppy – were equally badly affected. Her servant had been like a grandfather to them.

This left us with a funeral to organise and much potential for delay, but at least it happened in a proper town where the necessary facilities and equipment could be organised and bought within a small radius. Lydia may have stated her personal determination to strike the right balance - between doing justice to the deceased and maintaining progress on our journey - but it was still going to cost us a day.

With the help of local undertakers, Silenus was prepared and anointed, then installed on a wooden bier, where he lay surrounded by floral garlands and one of those cheap, pottery dinner-sets you buy-in especially for the occasion. Tiro's own clerks, Sennovarus and Sulio, helped Tocitanus and Trenico, the baggage handlers, to carry it all while a couple of musicians we'd borrowed from the inn set off before us in front. This left we survivors more than sufficient to provide an adequate cadre of mourners without the expense of recruiting professionals. So, to the accompaniment of flutes, that evening we all made our melancholy procession together down to the town cemetery a mile away, beside the main road.

Where I'm glad to say that the lady's maids in particular did a tremendous job, what with their tearing of clothing and ritual weeping. Since they'd probably known poor old Silenus best, had cared for him in his final illness, then these contributions of theirs seemed especially appropriate. Sincere.

Meaning no-one can say we didn't give him a proper send-off.

Clive Ashman

With a coin in the mouth to fund the ferryman and his bier mounted over a pit full of branches and charcoal, the local priest of Belatocadrus (*Yes, hardly ideal, I know, but all we could get at short notice…*) intoning some suitable words in the background, the fire below was duly ignited and away Silenus went. He and his little, wandering soul, gone in smoke and floating particles.

With what ashes and bits of bone were left behind gathered into a small pot and then buried, the funeral feast was held back at the inn. After a few jugs of wine, things didn't seem half so bad…

Those who knew him swapped stories about what a larger-than-life character Silenus had been, while I thought it particularly admirable how m'lady circulated within our ill-assorted party, considering what a range of social statuses it contained. Gracious to a fault, she'd also paid for the ceremony.

Later that evening in the inn, I watched the light from a chain-mounted candelabra on the ceiling flicker over her piled-up jewellery, irridescent hair, while privately reflecting on what an uncommonly handsome woman Lydia Firma was.

According to the dog-eared copy of '*Itinerary II*' we carried, it would be another fourteen miles from Bravoniacum to Voreda, with a rest-halt due halfway, so I realised we couldn't start this latest leg until the following morning, our eighth on the road. Nor could we begin so early, not with some in the party still suffering from last night's wake.

While when we did finally set off, it stayed dry at first, but in no time at all began to rain again. Just for a change.

The route we followed now was fairly level and pretty well-drained, covering a mainly agricultural landscape to which spinal mountains we'd crossed two days ago provided a backdrop to our right as a river developed its strength to our left.

We relied on our carriage-drivers and Ascanius up on the roof to look out for the next military base we'd visit - '*Brocavum*' as it's known. Placed as Rome's guardian beside a vital road bridge over that river I mentioned – the locals call it '*Eden*' – its oak planks would be essential if we were to get ourselves dry across, before aiming northwards to Voreda.

Lawyers of Lugvalio

But if Brocavum and its useful bridge were what everyone else looked-out for, what I personally felt the most preoccupied about was spotting stray Brigantes: 'hunting-parties' in particular.

One of several good reasons why we deliberately avoided a well-known short-cut in the shape of that high level route which cuts the corner, going straight towards Voreda and missing out Brocavum. Because as far as I was concerned – I can't speak for anyone else – Rome's forts feel like your mother.

You need to keep them close.

Fortunately Brocavum itself wasn't hard to find, while no war bands appeared that day, or none so far as I'm aware. From this point on I felt much happier, if only from my sudden understanding – thanks to Tiro's patient explanation – that we were now officially within what he calls the '*Respublica Carvetii*'.

Safely inside the confines of their separate tribal area, a canton which would extend all the way north to our final destination. Which in terms of taxation or the Roman local government - and also what it says on those fresh movement-passes with which we were issued at Verterae – is a modern administrative concept. Albeit used to describe the traditional territories of a tribe - in this case, the quaintly styled '*Deer People*'.

An invisible boundary then, but still an important legal status. And once I realised we'd crossed it, the development that prompted me to press Ascanius again about the risk of seeing any more Brigantes, now we've descended from the mountains into another tribal realm. Unfortunately, I found him annoyingly vague around certain geographical and ethnological topics over which – despite his oft-voiced dislike for them – he probably thought I'd become needlessly over-sensitive. While I just thought him stupid and evasive, because he clearly didn't know:

"I dunno', sir – the Carvetii, eh? Yeah, I think they probably were a small… thingy. A-what's-its-name? '*Federated tribe*'? Back in Cartimandua's day, I mean, like Tiro keeps on about. But subservient to Brigantia - actually part of it? Well, that's a different question, boss, where I've not got the foggiest. Really not my field. Though what sticks most in my craw is what them Brigantes did recently, during our civil war. So maybe you could ask around, once we arrive in the city. Begging your pardon – it's their Carvetii *civitas* after all. No, I'm only sorry not to be more helpful, boss, but I think you realise, I still don't like them much."

If Ascanius was out of his depth, then I knew I should accept his limitations with good grace, seek answers elsewhere. Or else forget about Brigantes completely, concentrate more on our case?

According to an antique inscription Tiro spotted above the southern gatehouse at Brocavum, its water-worn lettering on red sandstone decipherable to this day, the original construction in wood of the very first fort here was overseen by Tacitus's famous father-in-law - in person.

"Yes, by Gnaeus Julius Agricola himself...!" he beamed.

An epigraphic discovery and direct link with history delighting Tiro beyond measure, once we arrived and he'd found it. Yes, I think it made his whole trip, while we others only felt hungry.

Sited on the south bank of one river but near its confluence with another, Brocavum commands not only an important role in history but also the junction of two Roman roads. One our current north-south choice, and another going east-west. Both of them intersect here before crossing the river by a single wooden bridge.

And the principal reason why we'd come, not wanting wet feet.

About three and half acres in extent, we requisitioned the grassy frontage to its modern, stone-built fort for an impromptu rest halt – over a couple of hours only. Nestling beside the stream, I personally consider the site of Brocavum to be one of the most attractive settings for a military base seen on the whole journey to date. That it stopped raining once we arrived there will undoubtedly also have helped.

So that sitting on a green bank carpeting an eastern rampart to the fort, I could nibble contentedly away at a few slices of bread, apple, and cheese, while we watched the river rush madly over countless dark rocks in its bed, protruding above water.

This welcome break from a long journey also balm for the soul.

How the latest garrison gets theirs might be a different matter.

Lawyers of Lugvalio

Recently transferred from Asia Minor to support the emperor's coming *'Big Push'* - never mind how cold or wet they find it - I can scarcely imagine what any newly-arrived horse-soldier from the *Numerus Equitium Stratoniciano* must make of their new home.

Especially all those stone altars dedicated to Belatocadrus they will have discovered littering their parade ground at various drunken angles. Residue from the predecessor garrison's approach to military piety, and a native deity similar to Mars, Belatocadrus might have furnished the only priest willing and able to take funerals in Bravoniacum – enhancing my knowledge of creeds - but I cannot imagine what his horned head and nasty goggle-eyes; that squat body and little, squared-off shield; must do for the men of Stratonicaea. If not to simply frighten them?

Although you could say it's their perfect introduction to the underlying weirdness of Britannia, that secret sense of the *'Other'*.

Or else its 'post-liminal' quality, as we Roman jurists like to say.

Reluctantly leaving Belatocadrus and Brocavum's pretty riverside behind us, our highway north bridged the rapids then a water meadow or two before hauling itself up - then over - a huge shoulder of land. One our itinerary simply refers to as *'The Red Hill'*. Reaching its crest, the main road widens here into three separate lanes before driving north again, so we thought we'd pause to give our hard-working animals another breather.

Everyone climbed off or out of their carriages once again. Standing around to absorb an astonishing panorama appearing to the west, where a mighty range of impenetrable mountains rose up before us as if they'd fill the sky. Block access to the sea.

It was true to say that few in our party had ever seen anything like it - not this side of the Alps – so no wonder we gasped.

From here, the road's highest point, it was nearly downhill all the way and a short way at that. Five miles north at most, I'd say, before we'd arrive at Voreda, nearly too late in the day.

Just another cohort fort and just another *vicus*, laid at one more junction for two arterial roads – including that important one, emerging from those mountains. Arriving from the west.

Clive Ashman

An unassuming settlement not unlike most others, any visitor to Voreda might reasonably decide. Except that here there was someone potentially capable of making a unique contribution towards our own impending case, and I dared not miss that chance. Nor this man I had in mind.

Before anyone else died, I needed to find him in time.

"Excuse me, lady…" I said to Lydia Firma, while we chatted on arrival near the official *mansio* by the road, watching as Tocitanus and Trenico unloaded both our wagons.

"There's an old man up there in the village whose name I've been given. He's a senior veteran, someone I think I should see."

And Fortuna be praised – I was lucky.

Lucky at finding him in.

Lawyers of Lugvalio

Chapter XVI

When Longinus finished speaking, I sat silently for a while with the ancient Thracian veteran on the steps of his unpretentious wooden shack behind the *vicus* at Voreda, the army's final roadside station before you arrive in the city.

Looking back towards the looming blue fells, digesting the enormity of what this old soldier had just confided in me, we sat quietly together. Almost in a state of shock.

Sitting in unspoken friendship like we were two comrades who'd known each other all our careers, been through a lot. Our joint gaze going westwards over the empty carriageway of the main road for Luguvalium and across the serried rooftops of the cohort fort beyond. Watching a molten sun slide down behind the unmistakeable profile and curved summit of that unique mountain which locals call '*Saddleback*' - turning its distant slopes from orange to lilac, lilac to black, in the space of what probably were only moments but seemed like eternity.

Seeing the Unconquered Sun God making His nightly disappearance like this – gone in flames behind the Mountains of the West with no promise of return - felt horribly similar in practice to that mortal god whose final destruction we – myself, a fine lady and her loyal entourage - have travelled so far together to achieve.

Lawyers of Lugvalio

And if we can handle this freshly-disclosed but forty year-old set of facts more adroitly, then we might bring Firmus down in flames to crash and burn like Icarus. Litigiously speaking…

But never mind my own ideas for how we'd handle an oncoming case, what Longinus Matigus had just described to me must have seemed at the time to his fellow conspirators like a brilliant, daring plan. *Or maybe total madness?*

To rescue his girl for Firmus, they would aim to exploit the Ochre Fort's existing links with the slaver Epiclitus - invoking the latter's role as a business professional and broker to add a few contacts or associates of his own to their whole, developing plan.

His usual offshore suppliers - only this time persuaded to tackle the latest job with less of their thuggish method. In reality, a rescue: no kidnapping by force here, please, but a proper precision extraction. Whereby certain valuable property of Firmus – the imprisoned slave-girl, his Caria – would be recovered intact and complete. From inside a government salt-works.

The woman who - despite their pantomime of mad Hibernian violence - would be dragged away unhurt, then safely restored to her owner and lover. To an officer deserting his duty, and this in time of war. A man whose loyal companions – including the young Longinus - barely understand what motives drive him, yet commit the same crime. Abandoning their posts to ride out at night, joining-in with pirates to rescue the centurion's woman.

What would be presented to the *Fiscus* as a ransom, as monies paid-out to wrong-doers by a reluctant property owner acting under duress, would in fact be their generous performance fee, pre-agreed by Firmus with the gang. While their plan's eventual success would boil-down to a number of factors, only one of which was how good they were as actors.

And best of all, once the deed was done, Firmus could use the courts to sue our government for its negligent lack of care, its careless neglect of his valuable property. Claiming back from the state whatever he'd paid-out to Epiclitus and those seafaring rogues to recover her, shared with the *comitatus*.

Clive Ashman

As if they were unimpeachable expenses, modestly incurred through the principled restoration of an owner's lawful rights.

So that through robbing the Treasury then charging them for the privilege, Firmus could bravely restore the Glorious Supremacy of Law – earning himself a mention in the law reports into the bargain. A form of legal immortality obtained by illegality - you had to admire their nerve, its utter immorality.

And sitting here beside me - apart only from Firmus - was the last survivor of their gang. The only member of the centurion's *comitatus* who's left to us living.

My witness as to fact - provided he's willing to testify and I can persuade a court to allow him. Not to mention drag Longinus before one, keep him alive until he's needed.

But just when I was about to ask him directly if he would go along with all this, the sun disappeared. At which eclipse, leathery old Longinus turned to face me in the darkness and said:

"I think there's one more thing you should know, Justinus."

"Something else as well, you say, Longinus – on top of all this?"

"Yes, sir, and something you'll probably think to be worse. Because you see, Justinus, it wasn't actually his girl that stabbed the trooper, Nectovilius..."

"Not the girl?"

"No, sir - not her. No way. Because it was Firmus himself - using his officer's dagger."

Suddenly I remembered bitter, round-shouldered Restitutus and his sour, parting shot upon our leaving of Maglona, never imagining for one moment how right he'd soon be proved. *Nor so accurately either – another of life's little tricks?*

Because here I was, just like he'd recommended: out in the field and busy. Hunting down deserters.

Another rotten job I'd never really wanted.

Lawyers of Lugvalio

Chapter XVII

It is fourteen level miles from Voreda to Luguvalium and we managed them quite easily, long before dark. While that line of nine or ten men with hunting spears I'd spotted again to the east - loping along some higher ground, across to our right – achieved a similar pace. Whether or not they were the same gang of tribesmen I'd noticed previously, or else a completely different lot, this time I didn't trouble Ascanius for an opinion. Whether on destination or ethnicity. No, not this time – not when he didn't seem to know or care too much about either issue, whether it was Carvetii or Brigantes. Only old grudges, and whatever they did in the war.

And knowing there'd soon be far bigger issues for everyone to worry about than these few, faint echoes from a long-defeated people, I guess he was probably right.

As for that Great City towards which we'd laboured for so long - on arriving there ourselves, the immediate surprise was at how unlike the expected civic form of a *civitas* it turned-out. Not to mention – to our condescending eyes - small and remote. Because in its rough frontier ways, Luguvalium seemed a whole world away from more metropolitan forms of life to be had in that Imperial Colonia we'd only quit some nine days before.

Lawyers of Lugvalio

Right from our arrival, the narrow streets, dirty alleyways, and linear lanes we found at Luguvalium seemed to seethe and churn in a permanent state of flux. Boiling in ceaseless turmoil, now that the military equivalent to three times the usual population had suddenly marched in.

Arrived here come winter, come looking for some temporary form of home in a liminal city sited on the outer edge of darkness. In a so-called 'city' that's one of only three places along the Aelian Wall where we non-military - or else the natives - are officially allowed to pass through the frontier in any number.

Aside from our little party, most of the other new arrivals would be soldiery of some kind. Hardbitten legionaries on leave from ongoing renovation and rebuilding works, quarries by the Wall. Labouring under the direction of L. Alfenius Senecio, imperial governor, and busy making good more mindless damage caused by enemy attacks. Or those elite bands of mounted escorts to our Imperial family, imports from Italia, to whom you might add the men from northern British garrisons - ordered to assemble here before winter arrives. Directed to prepare; to re-arm and re-equip before the emperor's offensive takes everyone north into the far killing-grounds of Caledonia, from early next spring.

Matching similar preparations occurring along the whole Wall, each individual man comprising one more tiny piece in a great emperor's plan for revenge on his enemies, raider or Roman.

Every one of them come in armour and in search of any sort of shelter: come to claim a private place – *somewhere, anywhere would do* - for their own winter quarters. Somewhere to see-out the wait.

So that by the time we arrive ourselves, not so long after, there is not a single bed nor private room to be found unclaimed, not anywhere in town. No space at the inn. Not when there seem to be armoured legionaries on the move or billeted, just about everywhere – like rabbits in a warren.

Soldiers cursing and swearing, stamping about, carting heavy equipment up-and-down stairs inside every loft and cowhouse.

Half an empire's army.

Clive Ashman

Why the question of our own accommodation became first and foremost among many intractable problems which Luguvalium - *or Lugvalio, Lugvalos, whatever you call it, however it's spelled* - soon came to set us, over as many days. Nor the only thorny decision we needed to make immediately, meaning now and at once:

"I intend going straight to my father's house, to make myself known..." Lydia had stated, once we'd parked-up in a busy street outside the Temple of Venus and Mars.

"Is that a good idea, m'lady?"

"In a town this size, the *centurio regionarius* would hear of my arrival pretty soon, even if I didn't announce it myself. So there's no point in hiding, Justinus, because his servants would tell him anyway. Whatever else happens, I will go and stay there in the normal way – he'll think it odd if I don't. I will make a virtue of necessity and show the old tyrant his grandsons, for perhaps the final time."

"And attempt a reconciliation?"

"No, Justinus, there's no question of that, because he expects his own way. And as our *paterfamilias*, that is his legal right. Something that's never going to change. So that what we've got in mind doing here won't even occur to him, though you lawyers should aim to lie low. Avoid his attention, until the time for action comes."

Why the whole legal team in her second carriage had no choice but to go back: our patron had spoken. All the way back to Voreda, where we thought there'd be more space. Space for the six of us in a bit of a dump, more a hostel than inn, but still open at sunset. After all that we'd been through, somewhere else whose poor facilities won't much impress my bunch of boys.

"Never mind, lads..." I said boldly, sensing disappointment:

"We'll go back in again tomorrow, find somewhere better, and then get right on with the case. Once proceedings are issued, there'll be no need to hide."

Driven by that determination and anxiety we had about our client - upon what Tiro privately insisted we should treat for billing purposes as representing the *tenth* day of our expedition –

117

Lawyers of Lugvalio

by the following morning Tiro, Ascanius, and I were riding the same fourteen miles back into Lugvalio, this time on mules.

We were accompanied by Aulus Equitius, who would hold the reins in town and see to their livery and feeding, while we three went off to make our initial reconnaissance of the city. Not my preferred means of travel, these mules - no, not by any means, but as transport much less prone to draw unwelcome attention. Why we decided to leave Lydia's bright red carriage parked under cover at Voreda. Hidden inside a barn behind that elaborately decorated four-wheel wedding-car our innkeeper hires-out for local nuptials, providing a nice little sideline.

Along with her carriage, I left our three clerks - holding my firm instructions to guard it and our luggage with their very lives.

"I thought she said you lawyers should lie low?" Decimus Ascanius muttered - as an infantryman, never fond of mules.

"Maybe she did, Ascanius, maybe she did. But she won't know the first rule of business, for Tiro and I…" I gasped.

"First rule of business, boss?" he asked, bouncing along beside.

"Yes, it's to look after the client, Ascanius, look after the client. That's why we're going back in - I don't want to find her being bullied by her father. Put off taking things further."

The city we re-entered had barely calmed down since we first saw it last night. After relinquishing our rides to Equitius and stretching our legs with a walk between the usual line of tombs, up the final stretch of Londinium road where you see its southern gatehouse, we found ourselves part of a much larger crowd. An excitable mob, pressing noisily forwards as one toward the centre.

Viewing it properly in daylight that morning, I suppose I'd best describe Luguvalium as resembling a ship. A ship sailing proudly northwards into oblivion along a naturally-defensible plateau, bordered by water to its north, west, and east. Sited where two rivers meet beside a freshwater marsh, but within easy reach of an estuary widening to sea, and her entrance for real ships.

Though this city we entered seemed relatively small, its elevated plateau was strongly defended by high walls and towers.

Defences we found completed by the newly-reconstructed stone fort now mounted at its 'bows' to look north - a southern, civic gatehouse guarding those rearward parts suggestive of a 'stern'. Whilst in terms of our own intentions upon that morning, I suppose you'd say we were planned on heading for the bows.

"What in the name of the immortal gods do you think is going on?" asked Ascanius - travelling without his sword again, in obedience to urban law - as we found ourselves swept helplessly along the Londinium road and in through its southern gateway by a cheering, good-humoured crowd. And although their mood might easily change, for now it was only *"Ave... Ave... Ave Imperator!"* that the mob was currently chanting.

Once within its circuit of walls, a mob pushing us nearer to the centre of town, until finally we squeezed into an open space where a single fountain stood, ringed by yet more crowds. Their market place or forum, where we anticipated answers to Ascanius's not-unreasonable question. Where what it was they rushed towards resolved itself into a triumphal procession; into serried ranks of unarmed soldiers in full parade dress marching into this ship-shaped city through a pair of eastern portals.

For any ordinary citizen who lives on the outer edge of empire - and I include ourselves in that number, that day - it felt utterly extraordinary to meet a living emperor. Right here in Lugvalio. To put human face to an exceptional being, otherwise seen only on coins. Come here upon his *adventus* and deigning - willing even - to present himself before us in person; upon what for most of us present would be the very first, and probably the only time, in all our hard lives. A man – almost a god - whose curly hair and twin-forked beard were yet so instantly recognisable. No wonder the crowd must cheer him like mad, and we three joined in.

Dressed in a magnificent military uniform as our commander-in-chief and standing before us on his *quadriga*, a superb four-horse chariot – whilst holding a gold sceptre in the one hand, olive branch in the other; a praetorian soldier beside him holding its reins - the great Septimius Severus looked down upon us cheering northerners with so serene an expression of placidity and benevolence that it seemed impossible to square this *'Father of His Country'* with whatever else we may have heard...

Staged today in Luguvalium, right here in front of us, would be a series of scenes or set-pieces so spectacular, so grandiose, as to be more than appropriate in Rome – at even the Mother City herself. Never mind way out here, behind *'The Walls of Lugh'*.

Yet standing behind the emperor, and following the settled rituals of ceremony, we saw a Parthian slave crouch to crown him with laurel, such a simple symbol to evoke his many victories.

While only paces behind, an enormous, muscular bull with a tiny head - the finest found on the frontier - was slowly being dragged on a plaited, white rope towards the Temple of Jupiter. This huge, unwitting beast lumbering towards a bloody end. Towards sacrifice closed by searches for augury, by the usual anxious rifle through coiled, steaming entrails in the hope of finding meaning. Ancient procedures in which few believe but where our emperor officiates in person as *pontifex maximus*. Eternal Rome's ultimate priest, announcing his findings as omen - whether for good or for ill. And a set of omens which (I guessed already) would surely turn out well: May the Gods be Praised!

"Ave... Ave... Ave Imperator!" went the mob again, in reckless anticipation of bloodshed to come. Wild with joy at the prospect.

Since earlier that spring, when Severus and his vast entourage first arrived in Britain - then my home city of Eboracum - it's true to say that myself and fellow-citizens had become privileged to witness quite a bit of this sort of state ceremonial or military display. Ceremonies which never cease to fascinate and impress – although by now familiar, never viewed with contempt.

Because and despite whatever private emotions I may entertain - *would never dare express* - about our current emperor, or how so many people had to die for him to reach this powerful position, the fact remains that we presently enjoyed the company of the ruler of the greatest empire our world has ever known. Come among us in the Island of Britain, even to this *'Strong Place of Lugh'*. That I, with friends and colleagues, should be witness to such events - could watch him live and walk among us - was indisputable. Remains utterly remarkable, unforgettable but true.

So remarkable in fact that, in the face of all this shouting and pageantry, I briefly forgot the reason why we'd come. All that way over mountain and river to the frontier *civitas* of Lugvalio - nearly as far as our emperor had himself. So why was it, again?

"Come on, lads!" I said to Tiro and Ascanius as soon as I did remember, pulling them away like fascinated schoolboys from the edge of watching crowds. "We've got better things to do today than stand around gawping like the unemployed and idle. Let's make a start by reconnoitring the layout of this place. Find out if those law officers we're looking-for have actually arrived. Because I want to see this new case of ours up on its legs and running, boys, and I want it done soon."

Northwards and eastwards, from a market-place packed with spectators and soldiers, go the two principal streets of this city. Forking away in each direction, so we disengaged from the mob to take the first one - going leftish or north-ish. In no time at all this first street led us past the narrow frontages of shops, the clawing paws of beggars, directly towards a stone fort mounted on the city's bows. Where we encounter further scenes of power – only less choreographed, though still shaped by human effort.

The crenellated walls and turrets of the latest fort ahead were so new that its fresh-cut stonework glowed primrose yellow, scaffolding still in place. Labourers swarming everywhere, ox-carts delivering more stone. Where we noticed a bareheaded optio of infantry, gripping his swagger-stick while he supervised a line of men in soldiers' undress dismantling a framework of ladders and walkways, throwing pieces down. He looked up in mild disinterest as Ascanius strolled across towards him to ask:

"Good morning, optio, looks like your men have done well - a fabulous job! So what unit are you from?"

The optio acknowledged this compliment with barely a nod, but responded: "And what's it to you – who wants to know?"

Lawyers of Lugvalio

"Excuse me! My name is Decimus Ascanius, a veteran, sir – who's not long left the Sixth. And I've never seen such works, optio, nor so much going on…?"

Mollified by praise and a professional link, the optio mellowed enough to admit: "We're from the 'Lucky Twentieth', and as the emperor will say, blessed to be selected to support his 'Big Push'. Come the start of next season, its western supply-chain will be run from out here, these new granaries and weapon-stores of Luguvalium. In the space of eight months, we demolished the old timber fort that stood here and replaced it with this brand-new depot you can see. So, yes, like you say, old comrade - a massive effort, but we did it! Let's hope our commander-in-chief is as pleased…" The optio sighed, his sense of exhaustion palpable.

Ascanius shook the optio's broad hand, then clasped his chain-mailed shoulder in another gesture of brotherly solidarity before crossing the road to rejoin us, a troubled look on his face:

"You've got to feel sorry for these lads from the British legions. They know and I know what they're going into, what awaits them next spring. Caledonia's a dark and dreadful place – I know it, boss, having been there myself. A living green hell, a wasteland of moorland and mountain. Stagnant waters that breed biting flies and blue-painted warriors who all want to hurt you. No, I don't envy what these guys will find themselves facing up there, but I suppose an angry emperor must have his revenge…"

"Yes, but who's he taking revenge *on*?" asked Tiro. "Who does he want to punish the most? Is it the Maetae and Caledones, for breaking their treaties by invading during the civil war – for wrecking the Wall? Or else your British legions – those men who dared support Albinus, went across with him to Gaul?"

"That's a fair question, Tiro, though the answer's probably both…" I replied. "Because our Severus is the genuine article: a truly hard man. How he got the top job, I guess, once the *'Year of Five Emperors'* ended in his favour. And don't forget he'll be going north himself next spring: setting out along with his men into that same green hell friend Decimus describes. No, it's not like he

122

won't share in their suffering – you can't fault Severus for that. A tough old soldier who's never known defeat. Much how the current client describes our latest opponent: her litigating father."

They both took the point and went quiet, thinking of that.

In the meantime, we walked along together behind the city ramparts - seeing so much smoke, hearing as much hammering from this depot of the Twentieth, that you'd think us back in Cataractonium. The army was forging and tempering quality steel on an industrial scale here, because they'd need javelins and swords aplenty to replace weaponry likely to get lost or stolen in the glens of Caledonia. While soldiers, by contrast, are more easily replaced – as the trooper Nectovilius himself was, I assume.

Viewing his case now, from the distance of years.

Our walk brought us onto an eastern circuit and, eventually, to the city's double-arched gateway. It faces onto a marsh and the road from Uxellodunum which Severus and his entourage used to enter town. Here, on a corner inside the walls and only a few strides away from us, directly over the road, stood a large house. Two storeys tall to its terracotta-tiled rooftops, with a row of rented shops inserted into the outer wall that bring income to the householder. Advertised by graffiti as the official domicile to a *regionarius*, the lair of our opponent, it brought me up short.

Because now I knew that we'd really arrived. That our journey is over and the real war begins. Our own metaphorical invasion of Caledonia, but - if it's to be fought out in a courtroom instead - no less bitter for that. No quarter to be given, no mercy.

"What do you wish us to do now, Master? Shall we check on the client?" said Tiro.

"Knock on the door? asked Ascanius.

By the look of it, there were plenty of his own clients or hangers-on lingering around Firmus' bronze-plated doors who'd tried that gambit already, awaiting their patron, but I certainly wasn't going to add us to the queue or share in their dejection. No, none of us would stand out here until there was a proper summons in our fist, ready to be served.

Lawyers of Lugvalio

"No, boys, we'd be stirring up a hornet's nest today, and do more harm than good. We need some other way of renewing contact with milady. So let's explore a bit more of the town while I think, then maybe we'll return."

In pursuit of imperial law-officers instead, we went out through the arches of eastgate to follow the main road as it dropped down onto low-lying land - mainly marsh, reeds, and shallow water - before it heads over a sandy island in the middle. Aiming towards a high bluff occupied by yet another Roman fort, but one whose commanding views over a city and its flood plain put its sentries within shouting distance of the Twentieth's new-build.

It's unusual to find two military bases placed so close together, but I can confirm that here a visitor will. By which I mean the elite cavalry garrison of Uxellodunum - "*The High Fort*' as it's known. Enjoying an unusual proximity to the original fort and *civitas* of Lugvalio, Uxellodunum remains a relatively recent addition to this interesting local landscape.

About ninety years ago, I'd say - when the Aelian Wall of which it forms part was devised by the Divine Hadrian himself. The frontier whose construction he ordered "*to divide the Romans from the barbarians*" as Hadrian's biographer - and Tiro's favourite living historian - the bestselling Cassius Dio, neatly puts it.

"If we're to run the guys we're after to ground, then first we need to find out where the imperial court is billeted. When my best hunch is, it will be somewhere over there." I pointed north.

So Tiro, Ascanius, and I went for another casual saunter along the river bank together, looking like a set of layabouts.

Crossing the stream via an island and two bridges, we saw to its left a deep hollow of grassy sward whose natural depression was filled by numerous large marquees. Disclosed by waving flags and triangulated by military structures mentioned, this natural arena backs onto the Aelian Wall itself, so creating what must surely be the ideal location for an Emperor and Master of The World, for Lucius Septimius Severus Pertinax Parthicus Maximus himself, to lodge his family in purple pavilions and safety. This veritable tented *Roma* of vast imperial suites, pegged-out in temporary lines inside a hidden dip, just beyond Lugvalio.

"Incredible!" said Ascanius and he's right. No other word for it.

The landform they occupied might be a natural product of river erosion, but I could quickly imagine how its topographical relationships - between this city on its plateau, that cavalry fort on a headland nearby, the tented green between – could be practically important to our day-to-day management of my client's planned litigation. How these places might shape it.

Especially now that the emperor had decided to house his Imperial household down there in the bowl during their brief stay at Luguvallio, within controlled conditions of the utmost physical security. Which, at the very least, could require much to-ing and fro-ing from us - between whatever temporary accomodation we found for ourselves and wherever my client's case came to be tried, before whichever judge. Something else to factor in.

Admiring it all, we'd not walked much further along the river bank before being confronted by a soldier, followed by another and another. Found the whole riverside to be crawling with them.

"Praetorians!" gasped Ascanius.

He was right - and what popinjays they were. Every buckle and badge, binding or breastplate, decked-out with polished bronze. Every fixture or fitting done in gold and enamel it seemed. Even the lowest of them helmed-out with scarlet, in nodding horsehair crests - including this one now standing across our way, no older than eighteen and still spotty with it:

"Halt, in the Emperor's Name - who dares enter the Green Zone? Who are you, citizens, and what is your business?" he shouted, like it took him weeks to learn.

"My name is Justinus, the advocate, and I'm come in search of the *legatus iuridicus*. Or failing that, an appointment with the governor…"

"Lucius Alfenius Senecio is our imperial governor, citizen, though I doubt he's time for you!"

The praetorian held a javelin at the port, his large, rectangular shield resting on the path and blocking us from moving further along the riverbank. Which seemed the appropriate time for me to deploy that technique of which we lawyers justly feel proud – what we modestly describe as our '*Skills of Persuasion*':

"Now look here, my good fellow..." I began, intending to oil his inner wheel, obtain a brutish cooperation through reason.

Quick as a flash and simultaneously, Ascanius stepped forward, too – I'd not registered till then how tall he is – and thrust his crumpled, battered features into the unfortunate Praetorian's face:

"Now listen good, you limping, overdressed Daughter of Cybele: this gentleman here is Justinus of Eboracum, the famous trial lawyer, and if you don't play ball with him, then he'll be suing the pants off you - in the nearest court what's sitting. Why I suggest you get yourself and your toy armour straight across to your nearest Decurion. Where you ask him nice and polite-like for the very latest location of them-there gents what my boss says he wants seeing. Now... *so move your arse, sonny!*" he snarled.

Incredibly it appeared to work, because the young soldier scuttled off back down the path to consult as directed, although Tiro seemed horrified:

"By all the gods, Decimus Ascanius, you cannot be serious! These are the Praetorian Guard! People who can assassinate an emperor one morning, auction-off an empire the next. No one messes with them, Ascanius - you'll get us all killed!"

In a perverse sort of way I was suddenly proud of him, but Ascanius had well and truly blown our cover. Now everyone at court would know we'd arrived, but he only smirked anyway:

"Nah, Tiro, you needn't fret about him - Severus sacked all of the last lot. Them what murdered Pertinax in the palace, ran the auction you describe. Why the very first thing Severus did once he marched into Rome was parade and sack Praetorians. Replacing the whole palace guard with men he could trust, direct from Danubian legions. Didn't you hear this one's dense accent – it's a dead giveaway! Might hardly speak Latin and be as thick as pigshit, but they're good, reliable foot-sloggers, these ponderous Pannonians. Oh, yeah, always respond well to a proper telling-off, in my humble experience. And look out, here's the proof – his decurion's coming over…"

Indeed an officer was and, while we might have braced ourselves for his reaction, he couldn't have been more helpful:

"Good evening, gentlemen, I understand there's a lawyer present, wanting an appointment at court?"

Perhaps this latest helmeted Praetorian's courtesy and co-operation had been wrung out of him by something more complex than fear, since I've lately grown more aware of a widespread awe for the law. Something more observable within the common people, but maybe a deferential attitude nowadays also communicating itself among our common soldiery?

You can only hope.

Either way, this particular decurion of Praetorians seemed most agreeably polite, while I realised that I needed to capitalise on an unexpected opportunity. One which we'd only won – as I'm forced to admit to you now - thanks to Decimus Ascanius's abrasive approach on the day.

"Take me to speak with the Clerk to The Lists…" I demanded.

Like there's no-one else I'm willing to see.

Lawyers of Lugvalio

Chapter XVIII

We met-up with the lady Lydia the following day, in her scarlet, four-wheeled carriage. Our rendezvous made by appointment in the *vicus* of Voreda - below the main road through the village and within the courtyard of this latest fleabitten hostel where we, her obedient lawyers, find ourselves reluctantly required to be stuck.

"How did it go when you saw your father this time, on arrival at the house?" I asked her, gently.

"It didn't take long for us to fall out again, I'm afraid, Justinus..." she sighed, stroking a stray lock of hair away from red lips. "And he's not going to change his will, either. That man is incorrigible and I don't know what annoys me most – him calling that strumpet my mother, or else promoting her little soldier's bastard to the world like she's my latest lovely sister."

"What else did he say?"

"He says his new wife is more important to him than my boys – than his grandsons!"

"Oh, how unfortunate! What was your response to *that*?"

"Well, of course I had to point out they're actually his own flesh and blood. Whereas the new strumpet most definitely is not. And that a child is forever – a spouse only temporary. None of which went down well with him either, I can tell you."

Lawyers of Lugvalio

"Oh, dear! So how do you feel about your latest experiences with him, milady? Are they likely to change your plan, I mean?"

"No, but I'm still raw, Justinus… I still feel bereaved."

"Over your mother?"

"Yes, of course, simply because I am. And I've lost them both now. As you know, I've not been back to this city since before my mother Aurelia died. Why, almost on arrival at my father's household in Luguvalium, I went straight through the open atrium into the square garden at the centre of his house. My father's told me he buried her ashes there in a simple pot, beneath two almond trees. They're not in bloom at this time of year, October, but that's where he says she's resting now. So I kneeled down there beside their empty, withered branches, Justinus, and I prayed. Made a respectful sacrifice to the gods, my humble offerings of wine, hoping it might ease her path across the Styx, give some respite for her soul."

"Did it help? Do you feel any better for doing all that?"

"Not really, Justinus, to be quite honest. Especially not with his new wife – the latest replacement – skipping about the garden in her dainty leather sandals even while I'm doing all this. Like she hasn't a care - the sacreligious little minx!"

"So it's made things more difficult for you, then, as I take it, ma'am – for you to be staying up there at his house?"

"Difficult?" she almost yelled. "You can say that again, Justinus! Oddly enough and most of all, because of its memories. Its reminders of sitting on my mother's lap when I was small while she spun wool in the garden. The number of times she'll have said to me: 'Trust No Mortal'. Poor little me imagining it's the more obvious baddies from Greek fable she's warning about. Never for one moment supposing that the day might arrive when abstract examples of human weakness or treachery my mother drummed into me as a child would ever come about for me. Or apply to a relative. To our nearest and dearest, not some malevolent stranger – my own flesh and blood. Let alone that it should be my own beloved father, the great war-hero himself, who would come to betray us. In so many unexpected ways…"

My response was more measured, but considerate:

"I'm truly sorry to hear you speak like this, ma'am, but unfortunately it's quite often the case. That family can - in my professional experience - too often let you down. Like some old people seem to grow more devious and selfish with age."

"Hmmm, maybe so, Justinus - but at least they serve a useful purpose, help keep lawyers like you in work. And on that subject - what developments can you report from your side?"

"I'm pleased to confirm, ma'am, that we successfully made contact on your behalf with the Clerk to the Lists inside the imperial encampment. Who's graciously made an appointment for me to meet out there with the *legatus iuridicus* in just over a week's time. Where if all goes well, milady, out of our audience with him should come a formulated version of your claim. A short set of words sufficient to pin-down the key issues we'll end-up contesting at trial. And as part of this process, there'll be a summons issued shortly for us to serve on your father in person, requiring his attendance before a court there. Where, maybe for the first time, he'll find himself having to answer for his actions."

"Then we need to have you gentlemen accommodated back in the city as soon as possible, if this thing of mine is to be done efficiently and well?"

"Exactly, milady, we do."

"Leave it to me, Justinus. There are influential people I know in town we can speak to - men not in thrall to my father but married to my friends. Yes, I know the city's full to overflowing but don't worry, I'll get something suitable organised for you and your team, just as soon as we can."

Lydia was as good as her word. Two days later, Tiro, Ascanius, and I, plus the three law clerks, had removed from Voreda and were comfortably housed in a converted stables set high on the headland of Uxellodunum, beside its famous fort.

Our cosy billet there might have been just the sort of accommodation to attract rats, but happily they seemed diverted by richer pickings at the cavalry fort and its granaries next door, so we didn't suffer too much on that score. And if it was a little smelly, better warm and rodent-free. Somewhere, seated on its doorstep, we could enjoy a view of the river's curves below and, as Ascanius was impressed to find, see a large detachment from Severus's new *Legio II Parthica* arrive to set-up camp down there.

This being late October, temperatures plummet at night, so we didn't envy his Parthian legion their unhealthy location, just grateful our client hadn't acted an evening too soon for us. Providing an ideal location from which we could access the Green Zone - a short walk down the hill and in my view increasingly likely to be the venue where her litigation played out to trial. Whilst in my privately expressed opinion, the further we resided from the house of the *regionarius*, the better for everyone's health.

Priorities as relevant to my client – why I strongly advised her she should be prevailing on friends and acquaintances in the town to make her own household safer too, decamping very soon.

The following morning she'd arranged it herself, moving out to become housed with her sons and ladies' maids on the first floor of a sprawling farm-cum-villa, located on flat ploughland to the south-east of town. Accommodated there thanks to another useful friend, the middle-aged wife of a local magistrate: the *duovir*, one of two serving on the city council. And a country husband not inhibited from describing the influential *regionarius* in his own inimitable words as: '*no better than a plausible rogue*'.

Whatever caused his unusual readiness to house a colleague's errant daughter, or criticise the centurion, I took it for the first sign that there might be influential personalities within this town who would be willing to align with our cause against a significant local figure. But whatever the private opinions of the magistrate, once Lydia and her staff had done their moonlit '*flit*' then Firmus would know the hunt was up - that something was afoot.

Which was what she announced later, when we convene in her newest rural lodgings for an update on progress: "He knows about it now, you know, Justinus. I'm sure my father's guessed."

Clive Ashman

"Don't trouble yourself, ma'am, because soon he'll know for certain. Once we've been before the court and Ascanius serves the writ on him, your father will have it in writing."

"How difficult is that? And who shall form the court?"

I realised the time had come to warn her of some harsher truths:

"You need to understand, milady, that never mind your father, or whatever standard of advocate he wheels-out to act, the downside to running this litigation of yours at Lugvalio is its potential for finding ourselves arguing your case before some of the brightest legal minds in the whole Roman empire. I mention this possibility not to worry you, but only so you know the risk."

If Lydia looked concerned, then I'll grant it's quite a thought to grapple with. For anyone - including me. You see, we'd already suffered one run-in with the Praetorian Guard during that unfortunate confrontation on the river bank where Ascanius bawled-out the sentry. But if a loud-mouthed bodyguard's public announcement of my legal status had rendered the duty-decurion strangely deferential, you wouldn't imagine a man like him met too many jurists like me, during his average day. *Err, except...*

Because with hindsight I might be completely wrong about this. When there could have been a more significant reason for the decurion's peculiar politeness. And, if I'm right, one we should exploit – assuming we planned-on crossing the width of this northern river or the glittering sentry-lines which guard it, more often. Because such officers are no longer merely soldiers - and no sensible lawyer on the make should ignore a remarkable recent shift in our leader's policy and expectations; about the character and professional background required from those men he chooses to command his bodyguard of troublesome Praetorians.

Modern appointment criteria shifting from the career-soldier towards certain, softer skills more commonly found among legally-qualified courtiers, in administrators and jurists. Meaning no more hard-bitten 'grunts' and now some proper *praetors*?

All a direct consequence - as I explained to the client - of Severus's last Praetorian prefect (*and trusted former friend*) Gaius Fulvius Plautianus unwisely misjudging those powers and privileges inherent to his office. Leaving our noble Emperor reluctant - *but immediately obliged, it's accepted, there's no argument -* to have Plautianus murdered. So creating a job vacancy, but for a new kind of man – one who is now more praetor, than 'grunt'.

The first in a whole chain of palace events making this shift in emphasis which I'm gently introducing to my client almost inevitable. Events prompting an emperor who once trained in law under Scaevola to replace his head of Praetorians with a fellow former law-student - the legendary jurist, Papinianus himself.

Why I felt obliged to explain to Lydia that it's about time we also faced up to a new risk – namely that the most famous lawyer in all Rome might be another resident of the Green Zone. Commanding the emperor's imperial bodyguard instead of drafting pleadings, but obliged to follow him all the way out here for the privilege. Conscripted to far Britannia and the freezing lip of Caledonia but, for light relief, asked to intervene in our own little case - if only to keep his hand in?

Either way - as she was gracious enough to admit, had to agree: *"What a small world we inhabit!"* When the emperor's patronage of his latest Praetorian prefect, not to mention of another brilliant jurist just as likely to benefit (*It's the great Ulpianus, I mean...*) leaves our modern era sure to go down in history as a veritable golden age for the Roman jurisprudence.

And whatever the risks to my client, even if nothing else good comes out of her case, it still left a knock-about Eboracum lawyer amazed to find himself in an era graced by so many legal shooting-stars. Any of whom might be present in Britannia today - among a whole host of famous names slumming it this winter, here on the frontier, up the road at Lugvalio?

'Names' I felt as nervous about bumping into in person - or else encountering as a judge in our modest little case - as I already did about another formidable adversary, who stood as yet unmet.

By which I mean Marcus C. Firmus himself - our notorious *regionarius*. The Litigator of Lugvalio: my client's aged father.

Clive Ashman

And if an unspoken sense of inadequacy is common enough in any profession; the fear of being shown up as some kind of imposter no different to doubts probably stalking every performer; then these are personal insecurities I'd never dream of sharing with clients. Oh, no - although this one's not daft, since she quickly gets my drift:

"Brightest legal minds, eh, Justinus? So who've you got in mind?" Lydia quizzed, pursing her lips in that way she has.

"On your behalf, m'lady, we've braved the highest mountain passes to chase the imperial court, and soon we'll face a judge. Who he'll be, I really cannot guess - although it appears there's a pretty exotic collection of world figures available round here to choose from. All of them resident in the Green Zone, inside a tented city. Any of these men and, yes, I'm afraid it will be men, ma'am, as we discussed before – so unfortunately not the empress - could *walk* a judicial role, Which includes them hearing our case. Because most of them are - or else have been - proper, practising lawyers at some point during their career."

"Isn't that a good thing, Justinus?" she posed.

"Possibly, but not if it adds-up to arrogance or impatience. Contempt for little folk like us. What's for certain is that they're all highly-confident individuals - men used to exerting power on a world stage, living remarkable lives. Known to the turning page of history, never mind we minnows. And whether it's the Syrian *praefectus* of Praetorians, learned Papinianus - or maybe Ulpianus himself, another famous '*name*' – the only sure outcome for you and I is that we'll have a tough job on our hands."

"Tough?" she sighed.

"No, I won't hide things from you, m'lady, because it will be. Even without us adding this other element of risk. Facing-up to whoever they select from a collection of clever, powerful men - none of them strong on patience – just to hear our case."

"Oh, yes, Justinus - men!" she scoffed. "Is my whole life to be ruined by men?"

"All I can say, m'lady, is that this particular one will do his very best for you. His utmost…."

Lawyers of Lugvalio

Chapter XIX

On the morning of my first appointment with the judicial legate, Tiro, Ascanius, and I marched smartly out of our cosy billet by the High Fort and downhill through a lofty stand of pine trees - heading for this important road bridge we've used before to cross the wide river which locals call *'Eden'*. Where a top-grade highway up from Lugvalio town traverses a set of six stone piers before passing through a single archway within the Aelian Wall.

Preface to its spearing-off into that trackless infinity of uncharted desert and darkness we all know for Caledonia. A major invasion route, this road will doubtless be vital in next season's rendition – that terrifying *expeditio* we're so grateful to be spared – although the campaign of litigation I'm triggering today could easily be as brutal, in its shades of human conflict. We lawyers' forms of combat may be fought-out using only words, but they're no less vicious and fatal for some folk - believe me.

Why we three paused by the threshold of our lodgings on leaving, mumbling private prayers to whichever god or gods would have us or help us. Making the briefest of offerings to the household's own *Lares* before we swung out into the weather and a common fate together. Oh, yes, the weather - because the usual rain clouds hung low over Lugvalio, soaking the rooftops again.

Lawyers of Lugvalio

I looked across to the wet watermeadows of the Eden - beneath Uxellodunum and its cliff - towards the tent-lines of half the Severan army, where the best part of two Roman legions were spread-out across a floodplain. Shrouded in the damp wood smoke of a thousand camp-fires, they seemed to run for miles - though I wouldn't want to spend a winter down there myself, not if the river rose. And if this rainfall continues, here's another local disaster that's just as conceivable – like the fears I hold for us.

As we reached the mossy decking of its timber road-bridge, we stopped and loitered by a criss-cross parapet, awaiting our client and entourage. Our pause also enabling Rianorix, aided by Sennovarus and Sulio, finally to catch-up with us in a faithful pursuit of their principals. The three of them struggling manfully towards us under the combined weight of all my boxed notebooks and writing materials - plus any legal authorities, the '*Institutes*' of turgid Roman jurists, which I might find myself needing to cite in full before a *legatus* who turns awkward.

From occasional bitter experience of standing on my hind legs before a tribunal unwilling to accept arguments I've spent half the week in drafting, I'd learned to treat these frustrations as just another occupational hazard. One to always plan-for. Why '*Be Prepared*' is my watchword when it comes to courtroom practice, and my clerks end-up carrying so much:

"Master, master…" panted poor, wee Rianorix, putting down a bulky load. "I'm sorry to be slow… but I was getting worried about your more valuable stuff being ruined. Because I know you won't want *any* of your lovely latin *codices* getting wet!"

I do like staff that worry, because there's plenty needs worrying-about in our line of work; and that's even before our more usual problem - that of getting paid. However on this occasion we were more fortunate, as a practical solution hove into sight:

"You're a good lad, Rianorix, but don't fret about the rain…" I said, kindly: "Here's milady's carriages, coming up the road. You can load our baggage into the back. Keep them nice and dry for the last part of our way there, down into the zone."

Clive Ashman

A distinctive pair of scarlet coaches were toiling up the gradual incline from Lugvalio's eastern gate towards us, crossing over one bridge onto that large island or sandbar in the middle of the river, before they enter the second bridge, by whose parapet we lolled. Affecting a relaxed unconcern, if only for her benefit, I greeted my client loudly from the moment she rolled-up:

"Good morning, ma'am! May we hope your representatives find you in good spirits today - ready for the fray?"

"Good enough, Justinus, though surely it's the spirit of the gods and their luck - not your much-vaunted judges – we'll have more need of today?"

I'd already told her that I didn't know whom we would face, nor which *legatus* I'd find myself pushed in front of. That he might be a Papinianus – even perhaps, Ulpianus – was more than enough.

My doubts over the identity of our likely judge is located towards the edge of that limited set of legal uncertainties I'm usually willing to share with a client – especially one who acts like she's more of a patron. But very shortly, and for better or worse, we'd find out soon anyway. Even if I still believed privately that both her luck and mine would come to be defined by what character of chairman we met. Our nemesis, indeed?

But once my lawyer's legal luggage had been loaded onto her second carriage, my staff embarked inside, we forgot about all that and bowled along happily. Just a short distance it was to the riverbank, where we found the usual line of gilded Praetorians waiting to greet us, their officers sheltering inside something new.

Since we'd been last, they'd constructed an impromptu guardhouse or checkpoint at that point where the track leads down into the Green Zone. A roofed timber structure to keep the rain off shiny armour, oblige every driver to stop.

Since this was a routine I could see being repeated daily, it was important to take control. Get it right first time, whilst keeping Ascanius in check. Hence I was quick to jump out alone and '*advocate*' our safe entry, so to speak – wanting to cut to the chase:

"My name is Justinus and I am the lawyer for a great lady in whose carriages we ride. We hold an urgent legal appointment at noon with the judicial legate himself, and I'm sure he'll be as glad as I'd be if you could take us there directly, escorted of course."

This seemed to be the thing. Rather than accede to whatever made-up rules or random regulation palace guards might invent, if left to their own devices, I thought it better to take the initiative myself, pander to their sense of self-importance.

Give them a walk-on role in a process we're going to follow anyway, something useful to do. Like those apocryphal stories where soldiers spend an entire career carrying a single message over a series of empty parade grounds, useless and unchallenged.

So they can bore each other in the tent-lines with a story about that time they acted as escort for the famous lawyer, Justinus, when he pleaded in the courts at Luguvalium. How familiar he'd been - how freely they'd joshed with the great man as he strode confidently through the imperial pavilions with them, on the way to winning his latest brilliant case. What witticisms he'd shared!

Either way, an approach seeming to do the trick with that morning's rota for the guard. Following a perfunctory visual check made through carriage doorways; their narrow-eyed scan of occupants or luggage; a pair of Pannonians were deputed by their peers as fit and proper men to guide a toga-ed lawyer through Praetorian encampments, en route to meet a legate.

"That's great, gentlemen, and I must thank you for your help - a proper credit to the Guard! We'll follow you in our carriages..."

Yes, it's not as if I was going to walk there in the rain, was I?

So I climbed back into the second carriage and we all set off after these two crested Praetorians, who – I have to say - marched ahead of us in grand style, shields tight to the arm and javelins to the shoulder, down the metalled track which leads to the bowl of the Green Zone. Showing such impeccable dignity as they did so that you could imagine the very next pedestrian we came across - face-to-face and casually strolling the other way - might as well be an emperor, or maybe just the son of an emperor?

Either would do. And any of which encounters (*as historians would later confirm...*) at this exact hour of that particular day;

during this consulship and that calendar month of this very year; not to mention this unique location upon the surface of our globe; were each of them equally feasible. A sobering thought, indeed.

This slope we followed had been surfaced with timber for ease of access, a corrugated roadway offering horses greater grip. At the point where it gently dips to enter the bowl, I put my head out of the window to capture a unique and fleeting panorama. My eyes recording a spectacular sight never to be forgotten by anyone who saw it – one I'll remember to the end of my days.

Higher-up and away to my left, on a north-facing terrace level with the bridgehead, the first sight was its only permanent building. A long rectangular structure constructed from red sandstone whose domed roofs were whitewashed like sepulchres.

Here, within walking distance of our own crummy lodgings was a brand-new bathhouse. *(If only we'd known!)* Intended, I assume, for our present horsey neighbours – for Uxellodunum's resident garrison, the Ala Petriana. My assumption it's new only reinforced by a prominent dedication to Severus's current wife, to the Empress Julia Domna, freshly picked-out in in white lettering above the building's main, front door. And since I assumed her to be present in camp with us today, it must have been quite a *coup* for the local *Ala* to have their heated ablutions for one thousand sweaty troopers decoratively blessed by her own endorsement.

But beyond it – there's more. In the bowl ahead an entire village has grown up - no, almost a town! A temporary city made from huge pavilions, each the length of a basilica and mostly clothed with purple, embroidered in gold thread.

Yes, purple! The rarest and most expensive textile dye in the world, extracted from a million minute sea-creatures off the coast of Carthage. If you're the most powerful man in the world, ruling its richest empire, I suppose you're entitled to have your marquees and tenting made from whatever takes your fancy, and here there were yards of it. The finest threads and most precious dyes in the world, pegged-out in countless soaking panels to keep Lugvalio's drizzle off an emperor and his family.

At least today's prevailing wind would keep the flags straight.

Lawyers of Lugvalio

And though I hoped their expensive dyes don't run, it left me moved to wonder what a wealthy, lawyer-hating textile-dealer of Cataractonium, laid-out in his tomb by the road, might make of this extravaganza in gold cloth? (*I'm almost sad that he missed it*).

And if that thought sparked another (*"Maybe I followed the wrong career?"*) it later prompts my quip about this vast green bowl and all its contents being better dubbed the *'Purple Zone"*...

But however it's known and even if it's wealth in textiles which protects our imperial masters from the grisly weather, then it's the grey stone of our Aelian Wall which bears the more significant responsibility – that of shielding their magnificent encampment from the north, or northmen. The Divine Hadrian's work descending quite steeply here: down from Uxellodunum's crested headland and scar before heading across a grassy backdrop - this bowl - towards the banks of Eden. Beside them a milecastle, guarding the crenellated footbridge which carries the Wall across that same river. All of them lit by flaming torches and punctuated with Praetorians, appointed and charged to ensure our revered imperial family can rest easy, all hours. For the duration of their stay, by night and by day.

With additional military support and oversight available from that new depot-fort up at Lugvalio – not to mention the glorious Ala Petriana itself, barracked where we stay. Encircled also by Eden and its bridges, together these works enclose a ring of steel that leaves this *"Purple Zone"* surrounded. Could there be a more suitable or secure a location for an emperor; for his family and household - along the whole length of Rome's final frontier?

Truly impressive.

Led there by two Praetorians, here's the dramatic landscape setting where we discover the tent of the *legatus iuridicus* located towards the front of this imperial village. Disappointingly (*but much like its occupant*) appearing old and ex-army, made mainly from leather. Brown leather at that - reflecting his relative status?

Although there's precious little else there to reflect anything. Outside the legate's tent, at noon, it may have been grey and overcast, but inside it's almost dark. Only a few guttering oil-lamps left lit within to illuminate his obscure legal proceedings.

However, as my eyes became used to the gloom and our porters carried in the necessary kit, I realised we were not alone. Rows of wooden benches and folding chairs along each side of the marquee disclosed applicants, supplicants, and litigants with their families, lawyers, and supporters. Plus six reluctant candidates from the local panel of jurymen, kicking their heels.

Nor were we first in the queue.

At the far end of the tent, I could just make out a raised wooden dais supporting a long folding table and several campaign chairs. The middle one was fully filled by a hunched, almost crouching figure, writing rapidly on parchment with a pen. Because of the limited lighting, he appeared no more than bulky silhouette, but I soon realised that this must be the presiding legate, the men beside him clerks.

They all looked pretty busy.

Lydia came by and joined me, sliding onto a chair kindly vacated for her by a considerate young man I hardly saw. It might have been dark but I sensed her disappointment at the scene - not her idea of a court, I suppose. Clients often report their disappointment with our court system, but for me it was just another venue, somewhere else to play the usual games.

"What's going on?" she hissed. "Who are all these people?"

"The man seated to the middle of the dais is the judicial legate, ma'am, and those people waiting down the sides are here for his appointments. Don't worry, he'll get to us in time."

A tall, thin figure whose name I'd forgotten but could recognise from their distinctive white surplice, a sign of senior civil service, took shape in the shadows, approaching us from the side:

"We spoke the other day, Justinus, and I believe you're here to represent this lady?" the apparition enquired of me in a low tone, while others spoke more loudly at the front.

"Yes, indeed, we were supposed to be on at noon…"

"I'm sorry about that…" sighed the Clerk to the Lists, "but as you can see, we're rather busy. Expect some slight delay."

Lawyers of Lugvalio

Lydia made a face, so I thanked him politely and tapped her silken arm: "If there's one thing you'll learn from attending on the courts, m'lady, it's the virtue of patience. Because there'll always be some hanging about…" I reassured. Though I could see how agitated it made her – for more than one reason.

"When it comes to the law, Justinus, it seems to me that all your vaunted patience does is to wear us down and cost me yet more money. Why must everything legal take so long?"

"If the law grinds slow, ma'am, it grinds exceeding fine…"

"Well it feels like a terrible waste of everyone's time to me. Like you lawyers spin it out deliberately – want to use-up our funds. Knowing it's clients like me who have to stump-up for it all."

All I could do was grimace – she probably had a point. Almost certainly did, if Tiro was anything to do with it, as my personal costs draughtsman-in-chief. Considering that *"nothing comes for nothing…"* as Tiro likes to say, and even lawyers must be fed.

So to cover her and my embarrassment, I started sorting through a pile of notebooks instead – not that I could read them - until I saw the white shape of the Clerk to the Lists floating past again.

"Who's the legate that's sitting?" I leaned across and asked him.

"Tiberius Claudius Paulinus. Ex-army and a friend of the emperor. Cosy with his son. Tread carefully, Justinus, he's not in too good a mood today…"

So that was encouraging, only increasing my growing sense of trepidation. Something I couldn't communicate to my client, notwithstanding – it's important they should always feel your confidence, even if the outcome to their case is the only thing you don't feel confident about. Leaving everyone in the dark.

Eventually our turn came around when the Clerk to the Lists reappeared and gestured towards the front. Myself in turn indicating to the client that she should follow us, Tiro marching alongside. The legate, an older man of about fifty, looked up from his pen work once we assembled there, to glower from his plinth:

"And you are…?"

Clive Ashman

"My name, sir, is Gaius Januarius Justinus, the advocate. Here to represent my noble client, Lydia Firma, in her application for due process."

I drew my right hand from the folds of my toga to show where she stood demurely beside me, eyes suitably downcast.

Paulinus looked her appreciatively up-and-down the first, then me a late second (with rather less interest) before asking:

"I see. So where do you hail from?"

"From Eboracum, sir, the *Colonia Eboracensis*."

"I know it well. And your intended application?"

"You might think it a little unusual, sir - a suit for patrimony against her father, to be brought in the name of my client, his daughter. She will affirm in due course that he has failed to make proper provision for her in his will."

"I see. And you are registered at the bar of the courts in Eboracum?"

"Yes, sir, I am."

"Then I see you, Justinus, but I cannot hear you…"

"YES, SIR, I AM REGISTERED ….in Eboracum, I mean… I AM REGISTERED THERE!" I answered, in my loudest courtroom bellow.

"THEN I CAN SEE YOU, BUT I CANNOT HEAR YOU!" the legate shouted back.

Lydia looked completely shocked by this sudden explosion of bawling and looked across to Tiro for an explanation, but then I realised what he meant and responded more quietly:

"I think, with respect, sir, you will find that you can. And, what's more, that you *should* hear me… Hear us both, in fact. Because this court is a moveable feast, and we have travelled over the mountains to find you."

"Why should I hear an Eboracum-registered lawyer here in Luguvalium, when I am being told that the emperor's other son, Geta, was left behind in your city, along with trained advisers, specifically to attend to civil justice and government over there?"

"Because – if I may say so, sir - the aged person who'd be the respondent to any summons issued from your honourable court

145

lives right here in this city. Less than a mile from us now. While our cause of action against him only became understood in Eboracum once my client received her eighty year-old father's unwelcome notification of her disinheritance. Via a formal letter which her father created and then sent to her personally, *from Luguvalium*. Saying she's now cut out of his will, where a twenty year-old new wife takes her place. So originating our cause. And as far as your final question goes, I can assure you, sir, that – for whatever reason - the emperor's second son, Geta, currently resides even further away from us all, in the city of Londinium. Which would take both sets of parties several *weeks* to reach…"

Tiro grinned at me and nodded his approval, but there came a long silence from Paulinus while he considered my arguments, fiddled with his pen and jotted down some notes of what I'd just said. Leaving us looking up at him in the lamplight while we awaited his decision. On tenterhooks, as some of you might say.

If so, an unfortunate analogy, because our contemplative hiatus in proceedings was rudely interrupted from elsewhere by a bout of animal screaming. Though the source was most definitely human and I knew exactly what it meant - of course:

The rack and hot tools.

"Vero, vero, vero…!" some poor unfortunate kept on shrieking-out, in a whole series of blood-curdling cries. One after another.

Yet despite his crescendo, then that increasingly desperate set of heart-rending pleas for mercy with which they're followed-up, our presiding legate appeared oblivious, sitting calmly on the bench. As if all's well with the world. But not so my client, for whom here's another feature of our life in the courts to upset her:

"What in the name of all the gods is that terrible noise going on behind us?" whispered Lydia, all the colour gone from her face.

I patted her forearm kindly and whispered softly back: "Don't worry about that, m'lady, it's quite common in the courts…"

"Common?" she said.

"Yes - routine even, I'd say. You see, it's a long-standing requirement of the law, ma'am, before we admit any witness evidence, that the oral testimony of a non-citizen - or a slave - can't be given in court without them being *tested* properly first."

"Tested?" she asked. "Properly, you say...?"

"Yes, ma'am, '*tested*'. Or tortured, to be more precise..."

"Tortured!"

"That's right – it's only common sense, after all: the application of heated instruments. How else do you think it could be done, m'lady? How else could you expect a reasonable court to feel satisfied that the verbal testimony of any low-grade witness present before it was truthful... reliable even?"

"How else, indeed...?" she whispered.

Happily for us - and whoever they were - the unseen wretch in question stopped screaming as abruptly as they'd first begun.

Paulinus leant forward to address us like he never even heard it. Just another of those everyday distractions you tend to filter out, as he kept a beady eye on my client while really addressing me:

"I've heard what you say, Justinus, and applying this court's residual discretion, I'm prepared to agree that your client's case can be heard here. In Luguvalium. And I'm also willing to entertain your personal appearance before it as her advocate..."

"Thank you very much indeed, sir. That's appreciated. So does it mean we can proceed to formulate a claim now?"

"Not today; no, it doesn't, Justinus. You'll find I very much operate on the jurist's principle of '*audi alterem partem*'..."

"*Audi alterem partem*?"

"Yes, advocate – '*hear both sides*' is among my keynote mottoes. And in permitting this lady's case to proceed to the next stage, she needs it clearly understood that I'm only allowing her that opportunity without any prejudice whatsoever to the greater question of whether this claim of hers actually has merit or not."

Then he looked away from fondly regarding her to address me directly: "I don't know whether you as her representative had expected something different from me today, Justinus, or believe it differs from what other legates or praetors do in similar cases?"

He continued: "Unfortunately, what others may or may not do will not affect my decision today one bit. Because if we are to formulate, together, the terms on which your client's claim for patrimony is to be tried to judgement here, then – in the interests of fairness – it's always been my practice to involve the respondent or the defendant in that initial process. Hearing both sides. A practice you will not persuade me to change."

"I understand that, sir, and appreciate your frankness, respect the policy. But can you confirm we've got the court's consent to our side summonsing my client's father to appear before it on a given day, in relation to this matter?"

"Yes, Justinus, you do and - as you've said yourself - because of its temporary location and our peripatetic nature, this court is something of a moveable feast. Even I don't know how much longer we'll remain camped-out down here. So, yes, I'll grant you three days in which to bring him before us, by whatever legitimate means the '*Law of The Twelve Tables*' envisages a claimant using to force an intended defendant – or indeed defendants – to appear in answer to a suit."

"Only three days, sir?"

"Three days – no more and no less. I look forward to seeing you all then. Next case!"

Lydia, Tiro, and I scooped up our draped clothing then bowed respectfully towards the tribunal, before walking briskly off. Followed by the rest of our boys, labouring under the weight of my boxed writing gear and books to scuttle away after us.

"Did we come all this way just for that?" demanded my client crossly on the wet grass outside, the very moment we'd ducked through an entrance flap and been returned to soft grey daylight:

"I thought you said we'd do the formulation thing today?"

"Yes, ma'am, but you heard the man. That's not how he does it. But I'm still pleased with the progress we've made. Concessions he granted. What's more, he did us a favour – dropped us a hint."

"A hint, Master?" enquired Tiro, intrigued by this idea.

"Yes, Tiro, I felt there was a clear hint from him that we should have more than one defendant – and I think he's absolutely right. Technically-speaking…"

"About another defendant?" my client asked, visibly perking-up despite her experiences in the tent.

"Yes, ma'am, because – as the legate himself implied – I've realised we should be adding your new so-called '*stepmother*' to our intended claim. Because if his latest wife really believes that she's going to become the main beneficiary to your father's will when he dies, then that's something we should specifically challenge. Making her someone else we should add to the summons, disabuse of that idea."

"So you don't think he took against us?" she continued, looking more encouraged.

"The legate? No, milady, not at all. Though it shouldn't be like that. Not with a judge, anyway. They're supposed to be unbiased, impartial, and that's how I felt he was. After all, he did agree we can run your case over here, and that I can act for you. Both of which are good results, concessions not to be taken for granted. Neither of them might have been achieved had we found ourselves appearing in front of a wrong 'un…"

All in all, I was feeling decidedly chipper about the prospects and already planning our next move. Had more hope for the case. To help clear our heads afterwards and maintain this conversation, myself and the team were chatting in a cheerful group that walked behind the coaches, rather than climbing in.

Walking to beyond the rows of purple pavilions and lines of streaming pennants, until we reached that point where a wooden roadway rises to lead traffic out of the bowl beside the Ala's brand-new bathhouse. That point where Ascanius arrived in step beside me to very discreetly mention:

"I think the time has come when we ought to have a private word together, boss. Especially about Paulinus. Because there's things I think you should know…"

Lawyers of Lugvalio

Chapter XX

As the largest cavalry fort in Britannia, Uxellodunum is home to one of only six double-strength cavalry wings in the entire empire and the only one posted to our province. Making it unique.

Statistical facts I mention mainly to reflect its strategic importance as a military base. But also to explain why it should come as no surprise to learn how we found the fuller's stink of a thousand-plus horses came to permeate the whole fabric of our daily life there. *Much like the stink of cattle-coping does at Stanwick of the Brigantes.* And having lived up there beside 'The High Fort' for about a week by now, some people I knew were beginning to pass similar remarks about me. Including - rather hurtfully - an especially-fragrant client who most often smells of roses.

The fort accommodating these malodorous beasts and their highly-trained riders might be unusually big, its position astride the Aelian Wall imposing, but there's little else to commend it. Or attract the casual visitor, beyond them. And if this lingering smell of horse manure isn't enough to put you off, then the random collection of civilian barns and broken buildings which share a windy headland with the fort in question would hardly merit the status of *'vicus'* and you'll find little else inviting.

Lawyers of Lugvalio

Why it's no wonder – saving whatever limited facilities are available in their new-build bathhouse down the hill – your typical off-duty trooper from *Ala Gallorum Petriana Milliaria Civium Romanorum Bis Torquata* is unlikely to linger too near his fort for too long. Not if he's after those forms of rest and recreation more interesting to soldiers. When a short walk involving two bridges and a sandy island, in crossing one river, can deliver him - via Lugvalio's eastern portals - to the hidden pleasures of town. Well away from officers and oversight.

Though the only exception to this dearth of local entertainment we found at Uxellodunum occurred beneath a painted sign. That of *'The Retiarius'* - a tiny bolthole of a wineshop clinging to existence and a cliff-edge below the Ala's southern gatehouse.

Purportedly run by a retired gladiator (*'a contradiction in terms…'* snorts Tiro) and dedicated to his former category of combatant within the Roman arena, the inn's interior walls were decorated with genuine net-and-trident sets. Exhibits allegedly rescued from the scene of some of our landlord's better fights. And even if only half of it were true, the atmosphere they'd created was great.

But whatever their authenticity, it was to these premises and the sporting trophies which adorn them that Tiro and I had repaired with our ex-army clerk on the evening of my first appointment with the legate. At the head of our unwritten agenda, receiving certain newer points of information which Decimus Ascanius had promised me, on us exiting the zone.

With a jug of white Falernian on the table to set off some bowls of lightly baked fish, garnished with garum, we huddled in a gloomy corner to review today's events:

"You said a thing about Paulinus…?" I opened, leaving the rest to Ascanius and looking him in the eye.

"Yes, boss – Tiberius Claudius Paulinus."

"The judicial legate I appeared in front of today?"

"Yes, boss, him - I just wondered if you knew his background?"

"Well, he carries himself like a soldier – an old one, at that. While as a judge, he's definitely not one you'd get very far with, at pulling wool over his eyes. But that's about as much as I can say. So do you know any different?"

"He's a soldier alright, boss, or he was. Top man of a legion in his time - you know, a legionary commander: *legatus legionis*. In charge of a battle group – there's few rise higher than that."

"It doesn't surprise me, Decimus. That's an imperial appointment but his career's not over yet, not by the look of him. Nor judging by what the Clerk of the Lists had to say: a friend of the emperor and still on the *cursus honorum*, the ladder for progression. With further yet to go, I shouldn't wonder. Friendly with his son, too, or so the Clerk said. Although he didn't say which one - the mad one or the bad one - Paulinus seems sharp enough to me. But how's that relevant to our case?"

"Since we've been staying here, boss, I sometimes go down to the Temple of Mithras in town."

"That's no problem, Decimus, if you find it helps..."

"Because I'm a former soldier – and it's a good place to bump into similar-minded guys. With Mithras our Lord of the Sun."

"Absolutely."

"Which is where I've seen him, boss, though he wouldn't talk to an ordinary grunt like me."

"No?"

"No, boss, of course he wouldn't. Though I bet he'd talk to a regional centurion - if they found themselves together in the cave, say, or worshipping at the temple..."

"Well, has he? What are you actually saying, Decimus?"

"I don't know, boss. Maybe I've not been there enough times. I know I've not seen him with Firmus yet, but that don't mean our centurion doesn't go..."

"So?"

"Tiberius Claudius Paulinus was until recently the commander of the Second Augusta Legion. The same regiment you told me our client's father once served with..."

"That's true, he did, Decimus, but their service must be thirty, maybe forty years apart? It's not as if they overlap."

153

"Maybe so, boss, but if they ever met-up in the Mithraeum, got to compare notes…"

"I understand what you're saying and you're right to warn me."

"Yes, Master, Decimus *is*!" interjected Tiro. "Who's to say this link might not cause Paulinus bias? Work to undo our claim?"

"I understand the point. But he was perfectly fair with us this afternoon, surely. Don't you think?"

"Maybe so. But that's not to say he'll stay that way, Master, once Firmus appears in front of him. A fellow officer from the same legion - the legion Paulinus once ran, led from the front? Its name and battle-honours must be carved onto his heart. So if a man with that background comes before him, in whose favour will the noble legate decide? Favouring his brother veteran: the so-called hero of ancient campaigns, stricken in the dignity of years? Or else some middle-aged woman: an ingrate entitled by her sex to own nothing at all, but cushioned from penury anyway by a wealthy husband in the *fiscus*?"

I was shocked to hear Tiro speak with such force. Maybe it was the Falernian talking, or maybe my wife is right when she says I let him be too forward, to verge on impertinent. As she will frequently remind me, privately at home: *"He is just a slave!"*

Or perhaps Tiro is simply anxious that we won't win the case and none of us get paid – that he won't win his precious freedom, either? Whichever it was, for the moment I stayed willing to allow my loyal senior clerk a little leeway, some balance of the doubt.

Because if I do not, then who is left me whom I can trust in this fight - amongst any of these mortals?

At least our discussions had achieved something – renewing my sense of foreboding. Their nagging suggestion that when we met Paulinus next for the Formulary procedure – a process intended to give shape to litigation, limit its technical scope through an agreed choice of words – then Tiro might be proved right? That old legionary loyalties could conspire against us to leave my client's claim trussed-up, like a hen for market.

Clive Ashman

Helpless against these two old foxes from the Second Augusta, secretly making joint cause together, between judge and defendant. Hunting together through our insecure hen-house to leave me cold outside, nothing left of my client but feathers?

Whilst I gnawed my lower lip imagining all this, the shaven-headed landlord came around and collected our bowls, brusquely persuading us to accept another jug of wine.

"Why not?' is what I said, and it was then I noticed the knitted scar running down from an ear to his chest. Seeing my inner cynic confounded yet again (*he's a genuine gladiator after all?*) it made me relent, knowing his wine would only go on the slate. By now everyone would know who I was, so there's no chance we'd escape without paying. And after this afternoon's performance in that tented green hollow, down by the river, everyone in town would know why we'd come here as well?

Word of which mission had probably also reached the centurion Firmus, by now. And even if it hadn't, our next job tomorrow was to make sure that it did, by sending Ascanius out across the valley to announce us. To bang on those bronze-plated double-doors of the *regionarius* and demand his attendance upon Paulinus at the date and time ordained. Our very next mission, for which my man would need some briefing:

"Never mind whatever secret prejudices you or Tiro suspect the legate of harbouring, Decimus, I'm happy that he handed out a proper edict requiring Firmus to come before his tribunal the day after tomorrow. A court order that's legit'. And if we appointed you to our team without first checking on diplomas, then maybe you can compensate for that oversight, first thing tomorrow. If you can present yourself at the centurion's door and demand he complies with this order, maybe that might engrave your credentials afresh, prove your worth to us through action."

Ascanius winced at this barb but I continued anyway:

"Listen, boys, we're going to have to be ruthless about this job. Yes, we can force him to come – and it will be you, Decimus, who'll be the herald for this unwelcome announcement. Although what happens when we get him before the tribunal is another

155

story, a separate battle for later. But first we need to summons him as the initial step in our campaign. And if he says he won't come, then we'll drag him there directly, physically if need be. As the law says we can – so maybe another job for our Decimus?"

"But don't forget the other option, Master…" Tiro commented. "Instead of going immediately to court, you know Firmus could offer it a *vadimonium* - his monetary promise to appear in court on a certain day, on pain of losing his deposit?"

"I'm not too worried about that option, Tiro, because our opponent won't try it. He's a public office-holder with a reputation to lose – Firmus is the last man in this city to try and skip a court appearance. Besides, his curiosity will be piqued – he'll want to know what our line is. And I'm told he's a very arrogant man, one who believes he never loses. If we play this right, that overconfidence might be his undoing…"

I could see Tiro wasn't convinced, but our stylised world of formalised legal conflict was a whole new form of warfare for Decimus Ascanius. A brand-new experience. One which made him the more willing to believe in me, to take my promises at face value and aim to recoup his own reputation in the process. At least we comprised between the three of us a pretty determined bunch. Men prepared to shape our destiny for ourselves, rather than leave it to the soothsayers like too many brother lawyers seem to. A cohesive quality I worked hard to reinforce:

"Whilst if Firmus doesn't come - and don't get me wrong, boys, because I'm sure that he will – then as plaintiff, our client can go back and ask the court for official permission to take legal possession of the defendant's whole estate, maybe sell it on later."

None of these alternative outcomes were likely, but I was pleased to detect a returning confidence in my lay colleagues' demeanour. As to be a winning team, you must first believe that you'll win - the theme to which I returned:

"Look, lads, we've got a lot in our favour here, the gods on our side. At this stage in proceedings, the power and initiative pretty much rest with us. And unlike a game of '*Little Pirates*', it's not all down to how the dice rolls down a tower or the random whim of gods. Because I – you, we – have done a lot of work between us to prepare this particular case. Since it's my general experience as a lawyer that the more cases I do - the more I practice my art and the more carefully I draft my pleadings - then the more it pleases the gods. And the luckier I get."

Neither of them were blessed with attractive features, but I was gratified to see something approaching sunshine traverse their honest faces.

"Excellent. So let's finish off the Falernian and then it's early to bed. Tomorrow's another big day."

"Let's just hope it's a good one…" said Tiro, draining the jug.

Lawyers of Lugvalio

Chapter XXI

By this time we knew the ropes and our way round Lugvalio pretty well, however you choose to spell it. That familiar gradual descent from the High Fort at Uxellodunum, then another leisurely stroll across Eden bridges under the supervision of regularly spaced sentries from the Praetorian Guard, posted at intervals along the riverbank's footpath to our right. Day and night, they scrupulously monitor any human attempt at approaching the Green Zone, if only lit by flares. On a morning however, we tend to find them more friendly and definitely less aggressive, while most by now would seem to have learned our names – their goodwill important to us.

Between the two bridges there's a large island, almost without buildings save the odd barn, a vast grassy sandbar used only for grazing cattle; and then finally the second pontoon, which leads the traveller upwards to a gateway in the city walls.

Their eastern portal, where our heart-rates rise as we tackle a slight approach ramp - not because of any effort in the gradient but because we know that just around the corner lies one of the largest houses in town. Home to her father and scene to much of our client's later childhood, whether happy or otherwise. An evocative location I know she'll forever associate with these formal acts of litigation we're about to commit on her behalf.

Of which the next move will be ours, announcing her first.

Lawyers of Lugvalio

At the mansion of M.C. Firmus, there's a pilaster-framed entrance porch inset on his boundary. In width and depth it almost matches the adjoining shops, but unlike these cubes of commerce, it penetrates the wall. Around whose doors a cloud of his clients hang, waiting like scavengers for their patron to emerge or acknowledge their existence in any useful way. How it's usually done – although less so at Luguvalio, I'd assume. More commonly in the rest of the world, especially so in Rome.

Awaiting their patron, who drops the odd scrap of food, help, or consideration to his social subordinates – men he relies on to return favours with allegiance. Who guard his doors or cheer his speeches; vote for him come election-time and exhort others to do likewise; carry any bags. Heckle his enemies or turn them over, as-and-when required. Symbiotic obligations and benefits consistent with an ancient social system now adopted here. And if Firmus's example was an outlier, I'm sure it's hardly the only example of Roman habits faithfully followed, this far to the north.

More traditional yet are lawyerly processes we're about to activate in the street outside his house - summonsing the defendant to court within the Roman formulary system. Where Ascanius walks ahead of us to be their standard-bearer, while Tiro and I are like his generals, watching safely from the rear.

He goes across to the porch where clients wait and joins their motley queue. Some look questioningly up at him, but get no response because the stranger ignores them completely. There's a wooden bench across one sidewall to the porch and Ascanius takes a commanding seated position there, crossing his legs like he's a man perfectly at ease. Gifted with fixity of purpose.

Everyone gives him space and gets the basic message – that when these double doors open, he's to be the primary visitor. The one their patron's porters should be seeing-to, first.

Tiro and I had adopted a pair of woollen hooded cloaks – mainly for anonymity but also for the weather, because it's raining again. From beneath their deep cowls we could each pass for Caracalla, but pretend more interest in the outdoor stall set opposite, selling wildlife and poultry in ramshackle cages. Meanwhile we are kept busy keeping observation on the opponent's house over the road, across a foetid, filthy highway.

Watching Ascanius at rest, reclined on another man's porch.

Naturally for this time of day, the whole length of the street was buzzing with activity, which sometimes blocked our view. Since the entire city had effectively become an armed camp for the duration, there were columns of unarmed soldiers coming and going all the time, in every direction. On their way to one building project or another before winter gets a grip.

These weren't the only columns of humanity passing through, since we also witnessed long lines of men fastened together by chain around their necks. Captives on their way to market, no better than merchandise. Who or what they once were - or where it was they came from, what brought them to this pass - were each, as facts, impossible to tell. So common a sight in our everyday world, but also too frequent - why most of us free folk don't even notice, even fewer care.

Too busy looking out for ourselves.

Right behind these slaves but prevented from overtaking by their awkward, staggering gait, came a succession of heavy wagons laden with construction materials, from the city's eastern gate. Drawn by oxen or mules, their ill-tempered drivers did not hesitate to demonstrate how inconvenient it was for them and their cargo to be held up by nothing more worthless than this walking convoy ahead. Shouting and cursing at delay, the wagonneers whip their animals for outlet instead - as if to decry what unfairness and obstruction the world puts in their way.

But then a cockerel in one of the cages crowed unexpectedly, its shimmering display of green tail-feathers briefly dragging Tiro and my attention away from man's inhumanity to man. To a fleeting distraction as quickly interrupted by further shouting and hulla-baloo, only this time from across the street, not down it.

We looked up to realise the crowd outside Firmus's porch had suddenly grown. Swollen by a fresh batch of roughnecks, pushing and shoving. The focus of their boisterous attention apparently a tall, upright fellow in formal dress now emerging onto the stone threshold of the regional centurion's house.

He stood towards the centre of a widening ring of onlookers, his demeanour so proud and dignified that I nudged Tiro in the ribs like our job's been sorted, but his response was different:

"No, Master, that's not Firmus. Only his head porter, as you can see by the bands on his tunic. No, our man's yet to show and when he does, expect a *very* old soldier. Although perhaps there's a chance the employer will be following his porter outside, soon?"

Only then did I remember Lydia's vivid, original description to me of the person to look out for: *"When my father walks into a room you will know him as a horseman straightaway, by his bowed stance and posture, unbowed spirit"*.

If her emotive portrait had faded from my mind over a long journey, it matched Tiro's advice. Perhaps I'd become too preoccupied with envisaging my opponent, letting him grow into something else? Into an ogre more formidable than he'd prove to be in practice. Not some arrogant patrician but a down-to-earth cavalryman, horny-handed son of Moesia. And I could imagine how reluctantly an independent-minded horse warrior with that background might have taken to service with the legions - their massed formations of heavy infantry, inflexible discipline.

But whatever sort of man my opponent had become by now, by the age of eighty, all we needed from him today was simply an appearance. For him to march out into the street before us, to stand and be recognised – even a hobble would do.

Pending his *adventus*, we and Ascanius must stay there till he did. Though the longer we waited, the quicker a pathetic array of caged birds and chickens before us would lose its novelty and the greater the stallholder's impatience at us failing to buy even one. While the longer we blockaded his selling frontage in the face of better customers, the more tense he'd get. Meaning something had to give.

From left to right, another mule train on its way down to the eastgate passed to block our view but, by the time it cleared, the head porter was gone. Had Ascanius taken this opportunity to ask him about his master's location, their agenda for the day?

From our side of the street, we could only guess, but the onus remained on my outdoor clerk's shoulders to confront Firmus and notify him in person of his pending court appearance - the day after tomorrow. But when would this happen, if ever?

Patience, it's said, provides her own reward, but this hackneyed proverb says little about how quickly you should expect its compensation. In our case, it took the passage of half another waterclock's worth of watching – one we wasted in growing frustration - before a new figure stepped out onto the porch. His sudden appearance enthusiastically greeted by the looser gang of rogues still left hanging around it. Disreputable men off the streets who seemingly represent the highest standard of client which even so important a figure as Firmus could assemble for his following in a remote frontier town like this one.

"Surely this time, it's him?" I said to Tiro.

Brown as a berry, skin like old leather - from weather, not sun – and bowed like a rider, exactly how Lydia painted him, but he might have passed for yet another wagon-driver, if not for fancy clothes. All the bowing and scraping now came from the clients - although none from Ascanius, whom we watched step forward through the press, taller than the rest. Tiro and I in our hooded cloaks moved forward at the same time, intending to cross the road and get closer, hear what he'd say – until a military horseman riding-by threatened he'd knock the pair of us down there and then, if we didn't wait while he passed. Which we did.

"Marcus Cocceius Firmus, regional centurion and citizen of Lugvalio, I'm here to announce your summons by the judicial legate, Tiberius Claudius Paulinus, himself. To say that you're required to attend on his honourable court in a hearing to be held in the emperor's camp, at the fourth hour of the next morning following tomorrow...." boomed Ascanius in his best parade-ground voice, crossing the porch as he did so. Alone.

Every other onlooker present seemed to be what I've heard young Rianorix call *'gobsmacked'*, but the ancient barrel of a man subject of his onslaught looked Ascanius coolly up and down like he's only mildly amused. As if receiving a stentorian summons on the threshold of his home came as hardly any surprise, although unwelcome intrusion. Ascanius might have bellowed but the old man responded more gently, in calm and equable tones:

"Don't worry, soldier, I can hear you alright. Am pleased to confirm that I'm not completely deaf - or else not yet anyway. So tell me, my friend, whose dog are you? What's the name on your chain, whose barking do you do?"

By now the centurion's clients had formed an ugly ring around Ascanius while they decided among themselves who should enjoy the privilege of hitting him first. Ascanius remained defiant, rejecting their physical threat and accompanying insults:

"I am a free citizen of Rome, sir, and no-one's dog at all. And if your own hounds strike me, then it will be at your peril."

"Well, at least you've identified me correctly, citizen – as the *regionarius*, Marcus Firmus, which is who I am. So perhaps you could identify yourself now - I think you owe me that courtesy. Say who sent you and what case of theirs this is, on which I'm supposedly summonsed? It smells to me like a try-on, but tell me the name of your claimant all the same, this man who's holding your chain?"

Decimus Ascanius had seen us move across in our cloaks to stand beside him and he looked at us instead. A glance caught by Firmus, who cocked his head in our general direction to ask him the obvious: "The hoods are with you?"

Ascanius nodded: "Yes, sir, they are. As the lawyers in your case. And you should ask them directly if you need to know more. Though your claimant is no man…"

By then the mob of clients had clocked us too, but our additional presence in the street only seemed to confuse them by offering so much choice. Three different targets, any of whom they'd willingly assault – given the nod. But while they worked out an order for themselves, which of us to start with, most deserving of attack, Firmus intervened by calling them off anyway:

Clive Ashman

"Gentlemen, gentlemen! Let's not descend to violence, but let my clients slip away, resume their normal day. I'm sure everyone here has better things to do than debate these things in public - and I won't be a witness to fighting, not in my own town."

It was true that a reasonable-sized crowd had gathered by now, attracted by all this shouting and movement. Like he said, it was hardly an edifying prospect for a man of Firmus's social rank to stand around in the street outside his own home, discussing on what terms he's summonsed to court. Or referee a fight. So I could easily imagine why he'd want our chat transferred to somewhere more private – and the invitation which came:

"Come, gentlemen, please step inside my home. Let us discuss this business like gentlemen. In private, without acrimony or violence. If there are procedures to be followed, then follow them we will. The rule of law must have its way…"

I'll admit that the idea of stepping into the walled confines of my opponent's lair filled me with concern. Made me feel trapped, reflecting on spiders and flies. But this man we're due to face in litigation seemed to be behaving in a civilised fashion, and in my experience you can't run cases of this nature without a modicum of cooperation occurring between both sides. Between the parties and their lawyers, assuming as I did that Firmus would appoint one of his own. On which basis, I was willing to be polite and accept his courteously-put invitation to enter the house.

While Tiro knew the score and could be relied on to play the game, I also recognised that Ascanius was new to all this. That he would need a tighter rein indoors, the stalwart that he is.

"Thank you, centurion" I said. "We're happy to come in with you and make clear what comes next. Agree the court's formal expectations of us both as parties. Though that's all it will be…"

His clients moved off into the street, grumbling and looking daggers – items I'm sure they probably carried - while myself and my own followers passed from Firmus's grand entrance porch into the more private areas of his large, well-furnished home.

Considering that traditional superstition about ill-luck attending those who fail to cross thresholds properly, a belief known to be strongest among northerners, I ensured my companions made this transition correctly. On the 'just-in-case' principle steering them by the shoulder while we did so - for their sake, not mine.

Lining the wide corridor we entered by and leading towards the centre of his house, I immediately noticed numerous stone altars. Variously dedicated to Mars and Apollo, Hercules and Mercury, or Fortuna Redux - to name only a few titles glimpsed while we quickly pass through – they might read like a stonemason's catalogue but were unusual, heavy objects to find kept indoors.

At which it occurred to me that a *regionarius* with the spare money and inclination to commission such a remarkable assembly of large, outdoor altars for the interior of his household must be someone with an unusually well-developed sense of how the gods participate in everyday life. Speaking to degrees of devotion approaching the exceptional, they also match the character of a man sketched-out for me by his daughter.

Born on distant banks of Danube but now becalmed amongst the deep weirdnesses of Outer Britannia, his private collection of altars only confirm her account to me - a superstitious man.

Unduly anxious too, a soul keen to propitiate almost any divinity who's willing to intervene to his benefit, as-or-when required. And if this philosophy is hardly unique, I'm always cheered by any signs of weakness in adversaries. Those vulnerabilities of temperament or character I watch-for in anyone ranged against me - hoping to exploit them, given half the chance.

Firmus led us next through his atrium: into an impressive open space meant to receive visitors and dominated by a rectangular fishpond filled with ornamental carp. Its large back wall stood decorated by a well-executed fresco showing the moon-goddess, Selene, embracing her lover, Endymion. Very tasteful indeed.

Other high-value artworks I mentally catalogued as likely to compose the centurion's eventual estate upon death included several statues with plinths, a collection of dangling terracotta masks, plus three or four original paintings. All could do well at the sales and fetch a good price, further guarantees for my fee.

Clive Ashman

Passing from the atrium and these highlights, we filed into a large reception room beyond. This being October, the warmer weather was gone, and after the time we'd spent out on the street, I was personally grateful for the heat circulating from two charcoal braziers burning at each end of the room.

Firmus gestured expansively towards an assortment of carved chairs and couches, so we sat down on whichever one seemed nearest, but all the time I had this nagging feeling like it's him controlling us and not the other way around. Something with his background I guessed he would be good at - but a method I felt determined to counter, whenever my chance at it came.

The walls of this room we'd gathered in were painted a deep red and those two braziers gave a matching glow, but there was still an indefinable chill in the air once Firmus took command of our agenda by asking - indeed no, by telling us:

"Will you introduce yourselves individually, gentlemen? Tell me who you are, who sent you - for whom do you act?"

"Absolutely, centurion, and I'm very happy to do so. My own name is Gaius Januarius Justinus, the advocate, and here beside me sits my senior clerk - Tiro. Our outdoor process-server you've met with already - his name is Decimus Ascanius."

"Then good morning, gentlemen all, and welcome to Luguvalium. Welcome to our humble, humble home. I'm only sorry we don't meet under happier circumstances, gather here as friends. So tell me, Justinus, about this unknown client of yours – a person so anonymous, they're no man. I think it's high time we heard the name, the nature of their claim, don't you agree…?"

"The client whose instructions I enjoy in this action is a noble lady of Eboracum, by name Lydia Firma. You will know her as your loving daughter, but her reluctant complaint to me is of how you discard her regardless. Cut her out of your will."

Once he'd got over the shock, Firmus's face turned to fury, rapidly reddening under a vinegar tan: "In Mithras' name, is there anything worse than an ingrate? A woman who won't be told?" he thundered to the ceiling, raising a fist before continuing:

Lawyers of Lugvalio

"Because my daughter married well - got herself wed to a very wealthy man - Quintus Aculeo of the *Fiscus*. To a man whose occupation tends to generate riches as easily as a fowl may lay eggs. But it seems she demands more of that yet, only this time from me!" he shouted, like the street outside us should know.

"It's correct to say, centurion..." I inserted "that I find myself instructed in a new suit for patrimony which names you as the father. One to be brought in the name of a client who is your natural daughter. Where she will say in due course - I'm afraid to confirm - that you have failed to make proper provision for her in your will. Shown more preference for others."

"The girl has been difficult, while you're a mere lawyer, sir, and do not know the score."

"My client's instructions, sir, are that she has been dutiful, but very much hurt. She has only just lost her mother when you suddenly remarry, decide to cut her off..."

"Her *mother*, you say? So what could *you* know of *that*, you scrolling fool, Justinus – you cannot even *begin* to guess at it!"

"Guess – to guess at what, centurion?"

"That the woman bringing your client up - my noble Aurelia - was never her true mother. Only a dutiful nurse-maid. *Ha!* Now you hear it, what d'ya say to that, eh? While her birth-mother..."

"Was a minor chieftain's daughter... By name, she was Caria... of the Corionototae, another northern tribe."

"*Jupiter, Best and Greatest, why yes!* But how in Hades Name does a travelling nonentity like you are, Justinus, discover anything so important as that? But damn your eyes, sir, yes - since you do mention it and since it all took place a very long time ago, why shouldn't I admit it to you now? Because, yes, Justinus - as an act of mercy I did once rescue a tribal girl bearing that singular name from the travails of servitude. Only for her to die right in front of me in the equivalents of birth - may the eternal gods guard her darling soul! Oh, the utter pity of it – the world will never know how much I loved that poor, dear, persecuted girl. How it broke me when she died, Justinus, with only Lydia and the sweet shape of her face that's left me, for *any* reminder..."

"Then surely even more reason, centurion, why you should not be disinheriting her now?"

"Ye gods! Whatever has happened to my authority as a man or the laws of *paterfamilias*? Am I no longer to be the master in my own household?" he raged. "Always told what to do by women? Tormented by insatiate madwomen, even at my age – to the very end...?" he railed, pulling at the folds of his tunic like he'd tear it.

The sound of his roaring lament must have resonated upstairs and throughout the whole household, because in no time at all the doors to the red conference room burst open with a clatter. Through them rushed a lithe young woman with long blond hair, dressed in little more than a shift, who seized Firmus by the arm:

"Oh, my dearest Marcus, what is this noise about? What is the matter, lovely, and who are all these men?"

"My wife, Metella..." muttered old man Firmus with reluctance, while we all swung round to greet her politely, as visitors do in houses. If she really was twenty, then it had clearly been a hard life, one involving soldiers – that much we already knew. To which extent her recent union with Firmus must represent some sort of natural progression, although the sixty years between them still looked to me like unbridgeable gulf.

Constructing pontoons across the Danube, under hostile fire...

A more positive appraisal would focus on what lay beneath her traditional woman's *stola*, flimsy as it was. Would acknowledge her legs as long and shapely, ligaments taut and lean. Producing just the one child to date - whoever its father, whichever the cohort – insufficient to detract from a slender belly, some nicely fruitful breasts.

So I could recognise the pleasures of the flesh now available to Firmus, if not liking her persona. An assessment - judging by my colleagues' expressions – in which the rest of us shared.

"It is Metella, indeed?" I questioned.

"Yes, that's me..." said the piece, bouncing with confidence and emboldened by her physical possession of valuable urban property. A possession which, as every lawyer knows, can amount to nine points of the law: "And whose dog are you?"

The canine jibes were close to tiresome now, but I stayed polite:

"My name is Gaius Januarius Justinus, the advocate - and I visit this house with my companions, madam, in order respectfully to advise both you and your eminent husband of certain legal proceedings to be issued against you by his daughter..."

"My new step-daughter? Oh, her - she's barking..."

"Madam may feel related, though I know it's hardly how Lydia Firma views it. While the judicial legate has authorised summonses to be issued, for yourself and your husband. The pair of you are therefore most respectfully requested to present yourselves before him. To attend on his honourable court - inside the emperor's camp, outside this town - for a hearing to be held at the fourth hour of the next morning following tomorrow's."

"Who, me?" she said, puckering-up, as if to a mirror. "What's all that fancy talk and long words got to do with a good girl like me? I know nothing of law..."

Whatever a mirror might make of it, I did not like her look - although from observation of life I could guess how desperate and vulnerable she'd been; if maybe not '*good*'. Facing destitution like so many of her sisters in the camps, the odds stacked against them, what better choice exists for those in that wretched situation? With child by a common soldier - another unreliable male making-off – but then this wealthy widower appears, riding to her rescue. Unfeasibly ancient but craving young flesh, I somehow doubted whether poor Metella would have been the first in this predicament whom Firmus had taken-on or '*rescued*' in that way. Leaving only his daughter disgusted, while the rest of the world acquiesced. Sneers only in private.

And if the only judgement I was interested-in would have to be the court's – one that's based on law, not morality - by now I'd had enough. Wanting to take our leave from the *regionarius* as quickly as possible, I rose from my chair and aimed for his reception-room door.

Clive Ashman

"To the day after tomorrow, then!" I said on turning to go, by the entrance to his atrium. "It will be a Formulary Procedure - do you understand what that means, sir? Where you could decide to deploy a lawyer of your own, if only for technical help..."

"I'm a simple man..." he lied, as if he hadn't yet grasped how much of his story I'd learned. "So why should an honest soul have any need of a lawyer...?" he'd continued, as though his own dubious background - like Caria herself - was another thing lost to history. Like his notorious antics from forty-odd years ago had never made the law reports nor become the stuff of jurists: "Of a man they send into court to tell lies for their client...?"

"That's for you to decide..." I replied, crisply, despite my private belief that any layman who chooses to represent himself in court is hoist with a fool for their client: "But frankly, sir, if there's one thing which having your own lawyer to hand might help you comprehend, it's the serious position you're both in. And your absence of alternatives – why you and your wife must attend on the legate, or at least to start with. No argument."

"What, none?" he replied, almost but not quite suppressing the snarl of an arrogant man. One who resents obligation and dislikes duty in all its forms – whatever the authority, however imposed.

"No, Marcus Firmus, because you and your new wife are legally obliged to attend upon the court the day after tomorrow, as I say. Under ancient Roman law – as old, in fact, as The Law of The Twelve Tables - their very first Table..."

"First table?" he said, as if I spoke of furniture, though I disbelieved his ignorance.

"Yes, sir, that part in the First Table which explicitly states: *'If anyone summonses a man before the magistrates, he must go. If the man summonsed does not go, let the man summonsing him call the bystanders to witness and then take him by force. If he shirks or runs away, let the summonser lay hands on him.'* Though if that's what it actually says, sir, I do most sincerely hope that none of what's written there would be remotely necessary. Not with a highly-respected public official like yourself, sir."

Lawyers of Lugvalio

"I see, Justinus – and, if nothing else, I will thank you at least for explaining it to me so clearly. So graphically. I'm only a layman, you see, but I've got the message and understood everything you told me. And, no, I don't like to see people brawling in public, so Paulinus and his court can rest assured we'll both appear before it, without further compulsion. Nothing so undignified for my dear wife and I… although I don't suppose you'll be too surprised to hear that it will also be my – *our* – intention to fight you every step of the way, Justinus, once we're there. To ensure that you lose. And that you will live to regret having *ever* taken-me on - the centurion Marcus Firmus. But my wife and I will thank you for your considerate advice of today, all the same."

When we arrived outside, back in the street, Firmus gripped my hand so firmly it hurt: "To the day after tomorrow then, Justinus!" he'd said. Like it was something to look forward to - a happy reunion with friends - not that vicious fight to the death he implicitly promised. All his threats had been subliminal, but if I feigned a smile to him despite them, inside I felt frightened.

"That man! I genuinely believe he's the most difficult and dangerous adversary I've faced, in all my practice of law…" I admitted to the others later, as we trudged together in a light drizzle back from town over Eden bridges, towards the High Fort.

"Ha - *"difficult and dangerous"* eh? Then I take it you've not met the young Caesar yet?" blurted Ascanius: "Not heard the latest stories going round town about *him*, eh, boss? Because I think you'd discover some pretty serious competition for good old Firmus to be had there. *'The common enemy of mankind'* what some folk in Lugvalio already call the lad. And I'll bet young Caracalla's somewhere nearby now - in the Green Zone, snug in a tent with his dad. So maybe an encounter with our young prince might help put this bent old gent' into some sort of perspective, eh? Help you feel grateful for small mercies, boss - like maybe what we're up against here could be a damn sight worse…?"

"What on earth are you rabbiting about, Ascanius?" asked Tiro, in a tone of quiet disapproval more stern than if he'd shouted.

"Caracalla, like I said - just thought he'd provide a useful local comparison for us. That's all, Tiro - no offence, eh? A benchmark for whatever we face with old Firmus, before you lock horns in front of Paulinus. One to make the boss feel better, knowing we got off lightly with Firmus for our opponent. Or even Paulinus for the judge, come to that. But it's only a thought, boss, only a thought, eh? Though who knows, who knows – because it feels to me like anything's possible here in the Green Zone, at Lugvalio."

Decimus Ascanius laughed oddly again, like he'd had drink – another issue I wondered about – while Tiro rightly looked shocked at this dangerous frankness voiced in so public a space.

Even between friends, my senior clerk's distate for this whole sequence of stupid remarks issuing out the mouth of our outdoor legman was the response I most agreed with. Making a mental note that I should be rebuking Ascanius about what he'd just said, too - only later, once he and I were in private. And also to wonder - discounting the drink - what on earth possessed him?

Because Rome's great Imperial family may move in other, higher spheres, worlds unimaginable to us plebs. But for so long as they're encamped nearby - fleetingly present within a frontier city and occupying the same patch of earth as mere provincials like us, breathing the same chilly air - then no Roman citizen in his right mind (*even one who thinks he strolls alone with trusted friends; over an unlit river-bridge in the penetrating rain...*) should dream of risking such completely crass pronouncements as my outdoor clerk just aired.

The idiot!

Because Praetorians have ears.

Lawyers of Lugvalio

Chapter XXII

I knew the one day left free after our successful service of the court's summons on Firmus also represented my last chance to prepare properly for tomorrow's appearance beside him before the judicial legate, Tiberius Claudius Paulinus. An appointment where myself and my opponent would, together with the legate, formulate the shape of my client's case, as it's later to be tried.

Cooperate as enemies.

If I intended spending today mainly on my detailed preparations – a process inevitably boosted by the natural nervousness which flows from a pending court appearance, as professional actors also find – my more immediate priority was to cross the flood-plain and visit Lydia in her rural retreat beyond the city. Take this final opportunity to brief the client in person about what we'd encounter tomorrow, facing the *legatus*.

As I so often tell Tiro - in our business, looking after the client must be the first objective. And in this exceptional and unusual patrimony claim where we enjoyed the instructions of Lydia Firma, it's hardly professionally improper for me to admit to you now that never had the process of honouring that laudable priority provided more personal satisfaction in practice.

Lawyers of Lugvalio

With Decimus Ascanius as my security detail escorting me in a carriage driven by Trenico via two bridges to her lodgings in the country, I intended using our later journey back to the High Fort for my opportunity to take him to task over his unwise remarks of yesterday to myself and Tiro. How amenable to that advice he'd prove in practice I soon began to wonder, once it dawned how oddly withdrawn Ascanius became during our outward trip round the edge of the city. Not even an impressive view of the tent-lines for Legio II Parthica extending eastwards and limitless to our left, wreathed in woodsmoke from their many camp fires, appeared sufficient to dislodge his uncharacteristic sulk.

This was hardly the Ascanius I'd grown used to. An ex-soldier, I naively assumed the spectacle of Severus's new boys from the Danube forced to rough it down by the river - digging-in to see out the coming winter inside single-skinned tents, their shelters made from leather - would be a sight to cheer him up. Contrasts in comfort I mistakenly assumed would make him feel happier about his own – if only on the basis that anything looked better than theirs – but I couldn't have been more wrong. Ascanius just looked down at his feet, instead of at a legion out the window.

When our coach arrived at the outlying farm where my client enjoyed the bucolic sanctuary granted by a city magistrate and his lady wife, Lydia was waiting to receive us indoors in some silky robe. She'd never looked lovelier - something else which would have to change, however pleasing it might be for now, as I planned on explaining to her shortly.

But before we got into all that, I chatted briefly on our arrival with the magistrate, Titus Flaminius, who half-lamented, half-rejoiced at the sight of all the empty fields and paddocks around us, his deserted grazing-runs another consequence of the Severan army's insatiable demand for yet more cattle and sheep.

Including every last one of his.

"In twenty years of farming here, I've never made more money from this job…" he boasted. "We've had army quartermasters swarming all over the shop, begging for anything their men can eat, while even our tattiest of hides seem to do them for leather. And once I've met the tithe for taxes, then everything else is straight profit. Wonderful! Though the only problem left to us now is whether I can keep hold of enough breeding stock for the coming winter, get things going again by next spring."

"There's a Big Push coming in the spring…" I parroted, like every soldier says.

"Yes, so I've heard…." said the duovir, wearily. "Why all the main battle groups are pulled-up tight to the Wall - save for the advance guard they've sent to Trimontium. There's thousands of men and horses, assembling to prepare. But wherever they park them, it beats me how they'll manage to feed everyone in camp this winter, pending the advance. Let alone once the invasion proper kicks off next spring and the whole lot heads north."

"Do they buy any beasts in, from people beyond the Wall?"

"Of course they do – lots. Those tribes are our allies – I buy plenty of stock out there myself. No, they've got nothing to fear, and the army couldn't do without them either. It's them what lie beyond who're going to face a reckoning. *Creatures*, they are…"

By now it had become far too late in the season for the luxury of holding client consultations outdoors, so Lydia and I met-up in the farmhouse. The magistrate's kindly wife bustled in with some home-cooked treats and then bustled out again:

"I expect you two will have plenty to discuss, ahead of tomorrow's big day, so I'll leave you in peace!"

Although, as it happened "Where's Tiro?" would be my first question from the client.

"Tiro, eh? Do you miss him already, m'lady?"

"I think he's very capable - you've got good support there, Justinus. I simply wondered if he was alright?"

"Oh, don't worry about Tiro, ma'am. He's absolutely fine. Everyone's fine. I left him back at Uxellodunum, safely writing-up notes. Preparation is everything, you see. But I thought I'd pop across and visit you today. Brief you about what to expect and how to conduct yourself tomorrow – if that's helpful?"

Lawyers of Lugvalio

On representing a person in legal proceedings, I always find there's generally a bit of a dilemma over how much to explain to them. Inevitably, this will vary according to the individual, their intellect or temperament - not to mention how grave the issues are at stake. What risks there are to their fortune.

Some people will want to know the far end of everything, being naturally so worried or concerned over the possible risks or outcomes that they'll quiz me about every eventuality. While there are other clients who simply do not want to know one single thing, leaving the whole show to me while off they go to weep quietly, in an upper room. Or else bitterly complain:

"Costs - always it's about costs, isn't it, Justinus? Why does every move you make have to cost me?" (Like I do all this for free).

In the case of my client, Lydia Firma, I was gratified and not a little surprised to encounter an educated woman wanting to know and understand every technical detail. Not to mention those insightful comments of her own she'd tend to make about their significance. Why I took more pains with Lydia:

"Because law interests me, ma'am, and also because it's my daily bread, I will have to beg your patience, lady. I will do my level best to explain everything clearly – but please don't be afraid to stop me, should I ever become boring…."

"Oh, I'd never shrink from that, Justinus, believe me!"

I believed her.

My account therefore began with a careful explanation to my client of how tomorrow's preliminary hearing before the legate would aim to arrive at a formula to shape our eventual trial.

Since I am a lawyer and therefore rejoice in the law's formal language, I simply could not resist – indeed, it's my honest belief that no proper explanation is complete without them – from making a complete recital to m'lady of those six separate parts or stages involved in the Formulary procedure. Namely: *nominatio, intentio, condemnatio, demonstratio, exceptio* and then, finally, *praescriptio.* Evocative titles which roll off my tongue and fall careless from my lips as softly as post-prandial poetry.

Clive Ashman

My client shifted position uneasily in her wicker chair but politely said nothing, so I felt justified in continuing:

I explained to her how the very first stage, Nominatio, would be the part where Paulinus appointed a specific judge for the trial, so setting a tone for the case - but that she, Lydia, as plaintiff, would be allowed to suggest other names herself, from the official list until the defendant to her claim, the father, could agree one.

"What if there's no agreement?" she asked me. "What if he won't agree to any of the names put forward? My father is a very difficult man, you need to understand that."

"Don't worry..." I said. "If there's no agreement on a name, then the judicial legate will decide on one. He has the casting vote, remember."

She frowned, and I got the distinct impression that her faith in the legate's likely objectivity, in this or any other area of judicial discretion, was not very high, but – absent any further comment from my client – I moved on to the next.

"Now, intentio is the key stage for us, m'lady. Intentio is where we specify the plaintiff's statement of claim, where we must state the question upon which your claim will be based. Where what I am aiming for in your case is something like: "Should his current will be declared void and the testator Marcus Firmus be ordered under civil law to make proper provision in his last will and testament for his natural daughter Lydia Firma?"

"Mmm..." she said, like it's hardly enough - although she didn't enlarge further, stroking a strand of hair from her face.

"The third stage, condemnatio, is not really something I would expect to be applied in your case, my lady. Condemnatio gives the legate or a praetor authority to condemn the defendant in a limited sum of money, or else to absolve him. To my mind it would be an utter disaster were the tribunal to decide to go down this road. Happily, I really don't believe they're going to be an issue for us, as it's not going to arise."

"I very much hope not!" was all she said about that, knitting her eyebrows - almost in fun?

"Then the next stage, demonstratio, is for unliquidated in personam claims. That is where the court will state the alleged facts out of which your claim arose."

"They'd better get that bit right! Go on, Justinus...." she said, leaning-in closer, a heady waft of rose petal drifting-in with her interest. Collecting myself inwardly, I resumed notwithstanding:

"More technical yet, is exceptio and replicatio. Say your father, our defendant, wanted to raise a specific defence - like self-defence, for instance - he would do so through filing an exceptio. As it is, and quite frankly, I can't see any pleading of that nature being relevant or available to him - although you never know. However, if he did try it on, and we on your behalf wanted to refute that defence as entered, then we would file a replicatio - explaining why his defence wasn't valid. I'm afraid that particular process can go backwards and forwards, with the last one whose exceptio or replicatio is proved on the facts ending-up as the overall winner."

"Oh, I don't like the sound of that at all. But he hasn't got a lawyer, has he? Will that make your job more difficult?'

"Not as far as I know but, yes, it most probably does, m'lady. Although when we took our leave of your father the other day at his house, I did suggest he got one."

"That was rather generous of you, Justinus, but never a policy I'd recommend with him. Give my father an inch and he'll definitely take a mile. And so far as I'm aware, he ran his successful case of forty years ago against the government without any legal representation or assistance whatsoever. Or else that's what he always told us."

"Hmmm, well, if that sounds a bit unlikely to me, we'll just have to see. In some ways, yes, I'd certainly find it easier if he did get some proper representation, but sometimes.... well, quite often in fact – especially when the advocate they choose is a total idiot – it can easily ruin the whole case. Including for the unfortunate person they're supposed to be representing. You'd be surprised how often I've seen that happen, m'lady..."

"Seen *what* happen, Justinus?"

"Opponents paying lots of money to a belligerent but foolish lawyer who successfully screws everything up for them. *Everything!* Whereas if they're co-operative, a good lawyer can often achieve an outcome that's fair for everyone. And soon..."

"Well that won't be how my father approaches things - it's death or glory with him. Obdurate to a fault. Now you said there were six phases to tomorrow, but have so far only told me five?"

"Correct, m'lady. Well spotted! The last is praescriptio - which is all about limiting the triable issues involved to the matter in hand. By which I mean avoiding you as a plaintiff needing to bring another case against the same defendant – your father - on a similar or related issue."

"That's fair enough – and why ever would we? But if we can get through these tedious technical stages tomorrow without everyone falling asleep, is it correct that all we'd have actually achieved in my case would be it being adjourned for trial on yet another day?"

"When you put it like that, ma'am, I suppose you're right, though it represents quite a lot of progress in my book - speaking as a lawyer. Although there is another, alternative outcome to tomorrow's proceedings. One I'm not expecting but which, since you've asked me, I suppose I ought to mention. While I don't want to get your hopes up too high, milady, because I don't believe it will happen but - only because it does happen sometimes - for completeness, I'll mention it now..."

'Which is?"

"Only very occasionally, a case like yours can be settled completely on the day of the preliminary hearing. A plaintiff can come along to the hearing and challenge their defendant to take an oath supporting his case – but please don't expect me to ask for that here. On the likely facts of your Dad's case, I'm not sure how this would actually work for either of us anyway..."

She looked expectantly up at me, winding a forehead ringlet round a finger in the hope of clearer exposition.

Lawyers of Lugvalio

"Maybe, for instance, he could be asked to make an oath to the effect that you weren't actually cut out of his will. In these circumstances, ma'am, if a defendant were willing to swear such an oath, then he'd win. And of course, if he won't, then he loses. Nor should we forget the third option, where he turns it all back onto us. Demands the obligation to tender an oath from the plaintiff - who'd similarly win if they took the oath, or lose if they didn't. Because most of the well-known jurists and Roman legal writers advise us that: *"Where a party is sued in any kind of an action, if he makes an oath it will be a benefit to him"*. Which is perfectly true in theory, but I really can't see it happening here or being much use to us either. Why we don't usually bother."

"So you think we are definitely going to trial?"

"We are, m'lady - all the way, just as I promised you. And that I will be there, standing by you to the end."

"Thank you, Justinus, you are a good man. Which makes you the more vulnerable to my father, who is not. Please do not ever underrate what he's capable of, Justinus, however charming you find him. Or venerable. And since he's so old, it seems like he's only got worse, because I know he'll still stop at nothing. Nothing – I warn you! A lifelong policy of utter selfishness has taught him what works. Helped him to survive active service in the army yet come away with his health, fortune, and official status intact, not to mention a nubile young wife. To face down the government. He's never going to change those priorities now – whoever dares stand in his way. Even when it's me, standing behind you…"

I accepted her praise with a quiet inward pleasure, but knew there were several more things I should say. Other incredible facts which I'm deliberately holding back from her at this stage, doubting it for the right moment. Why I changed tack:

"I do appreciate your patience, ma'am – and am sorry if I bored you. At least you cannot say that I never shared these technical mysteries with you. So when the legatus calls them out in court, at least you'll understand which phase it is we've reached."

"Is there anything else I should know?"

Clive Ashman

By all the gods, surely there were, but like a coward I dared not mention one of them – resorting instead to my usual hackneyed comparisons with theatre, no less valid a cliché for me telling every client the self-same story:

"Well, aside from all that boring technical stuff, ma'am, lets not forget the theatrical. When every courtroom's a stage, where first impressions count. Why it's worthwhile you bringing your two sons along, and all of you dressing-down. I'm afraid that today's bright silks must be discarded for a while, milady, and from now on it'll be widow's weeds for you. Attend on the tribunal and your father like you're the bereaved at his funeral, both you and your sons. Black clothes torn, hair long and unkempt. The very picture of grief. Can you do that thing for us?"

"So that's why you told me to let my boys' hair grow-out?"

"Exactly, ma'am, it was indeed. Because you three must swallow your pride together and put on a show. I know you are a proud woman and doing so won't come easy, but I'm afraid that's how it's always been done, in our Roman courts."

I think this was the first piece of advice I'd given her which she'd not initially challenged in some way, but - to her credit - the lady Lydia took everything I'd said immediately on board and we parted on good terms. It had been harder work persuading her about some of it than I'd probably expected, but at least there was comfort in knowing that the client I'd be attending court with would have a pretty good idea of the process, an intelligent understanding. A client who might play a more useful part tomorrow than too many others my experience usually managed.

Unfortunately, as I greeted Trenico then clambered back into our carriage, I found more aggravation awaiting me inside in the shape of my recalcitrant bodyguard, Ascanius, slouched in a corner.

He'd hardly said anything at all, all day today, but my next task would be to tell him off roundly now for some of his dafter remarks of yesterday.

Further hard work.

Lawyers of Lugvalio

Chapter XXIII

Whatever's the matter with you today, Decimus Ascanius?" was my opening gambit as I clambered into the carriage and tapped on its roof, signalling Trenico to move off. Ascanius stirred uncomfortably on his wooden seat and looked lethargically out of the half-open side window across the empty cattle-runs of a city duovir. Lacking an answer, I pressed him again:

"You're usually so sensible, Decimus Ascanius. Until yesterday, when the three of us were walking over these river bridges - don't you remember? Coming out with some truly incredible remarks - dangerous, disrespectful comments about the Caesar. The kind of careless talk which has cost good people their lives and could cost us ours. So what on earth possessed you?"

"I'm sorry, sir, it's difficult..." he sighed.

"Not half as difficult as it would have been for us, if anyone overheard you."

"With respect, sir, who in Hades' name would do? On a bridge in the middle of nowhere – in the middle of a river? No-one else around and it's raining cats and dogs, as usual in Lugvalio – so what's the big problem, boss?"

Lawyers of Lugvalio

"The Praetorian Guard, they could be one problem, for sure. Marching up and down that muddy riverbank night-and-day, Decimus Ascanius, night-and-day. While their official patrol-walk was only a cock-stride away from where we stood at the time."

Even as I scolded him, I watched his crumpled face fall.

"Oh, yes - *them!* Of course - look, I'm really sorry, Gaius Justinus. Honestly - I'll admit I never thought about *them*..."

"No, but the imperial bodyguard do. They think of little else. Spend half their time looking-out and listening for people like you. For people who speak out of turn, might become a threat to their imperial lords and masters. Don't you know the history of our ruling dynasty, Decimus Ascanius? I'll mention it once in the privacy of our carriage and only as a warning, but they're natural-born killers. Say the wrong thing and they'll have you."

"Look, I'm sorry, boss. Admit I should've known better - a lot better. But with everything I've been through myself, you don't need to warn me about the Severans. No, sir, not another word. Because I've witnessed it first hand... seeing I was there."

"*There*, Decimus Ascanius, where's '*there*'? Wherever do you mean?"

"*Ante diem XI Kalendas Martias* - at Lugdunum in Gaul."

"Oh, I see... the eleventh day before the Kalends of March – on the festival of *Parentalia*?"

"That's right, sir – exact date and time. Nearly eleven years ago it was. When Septimius Severus, the man these Praetorians are sent here to guard, our great Emperor himself, defeated the army of the so-called '*usurper*' ...of another Decimus like me ...Decimus Clodius Albinus, at the battle of Ludgdunum in Gaul."

"You're saying you were there?"

"Yes, sir, that's right..." Ascanius put his head in his hands. "And the root of all my problems - including this one. Bad things I shouldn't say. Because it's eating me up, sir, eating me still..."

"Look, we need to bottom this, Ascanius. Can I take it you got up to rather more during your service with the Sixth Victorious Legion than just running a burial club for their fourth cohort? In which case, don't you think it's high time you told me the whole truth? And nothing but the truth. The full story about whatever it was that you didn't admit to, before we appointed you?"

"All right, Justinus – but most of it you'll know anyway. An unfinished business that hangs like a cloud over Britannia - over me, over you, over everyone. Over all of our heads. Leaving this city and every army-base the length and breadth of the Wall full of frightened soldiers. Every man knowing that come spring, once the skies brighten and the days lengthen, their Emperor will order them north - into Caledonia. Into an empty, trackless wilderness that goes on forever, eats half-alive whoever it don't drown."

"A punishment for our British legions, as much as any tribe?"

"I'd say so."

Ascanius was right – we all knew the history. Or at least how it began, during what hindsight and Tiro call the *'Year of the Five Emperors'*. After Marcus Aurelius's appalling son, Commodus, got killed and then - only eighty-seven days later - his upright successor, P. Helvius Pertinax, was murdered too, the Praetorian Guard put the imperial throne up for sale by public auction. Its novel procedures conducted from the walls of their camp, where a rich senator called Marcus Didius Julianus was stupid enough to turn-up and bid, get proclaimed emperor on that shabby basis.

Whether our governor in Britain, Clodius Albinus, was among those encouraging his purchase, I don't know, but Roman armies on the Danube and in Syria didn't like it when they heard. Both provinces straightaway proclaiming their own governors, making Septimius Severus and Pescennius Niger into rival emperors too.

If the assassins of Pertinax were his bodyguard, the Praetorian Guard – holding grudges about austerity, his parsimony with their pay – the main mover was Aemilius Laetus, the Guard's own commander. Elite troops appointed to protect emperors, not to kill them, but now adding professional auctioneer to a portfolio of skills. By June, they'd lost patience with Didius Julianus as well, murdering him just before Severus arrived in Rome as emperor himself. Having force-marched at the head of his legions all the way from the Balkans and been greeted by the Senate, the

Lawyers of Lugvalio

Guard's latest killing left Severus less than impressed. He therefore ordered the Praetorians to parade weaponless outside the Eternal City, where they were immediately disbanded.

So that by force of arms and military daring, Severus had in short order taken physical possession and control of the world's greatest city, *de facto* its empire. Whilst he made sure to refill the Praetorian ranks with his own loyal supporters. Mostly Pannonians, a race famed for strength and bravery but never their intellect. For being *"strong in the arm, and thick in the head"* as Ascanius puts it. These men we encounter daily on the riverbank - safeguarding the Green Zone, its sheets of sodden purple.

Though it took him another two years to consolidate his grip, Severus had marked time with a side-agreement with Albinus, acknowledging him as his ally, an intended Caesar and heir. But it was only after Severus defeated Pescennius Niger at the Battle of the Issus, his further victories in Parthia, that the denarius finally dropped and Britain's insular complacency broke. Once Severus proclaimed his eldest son, Antoninus - otherwise *'Caracalla'* - for his sole Caesar and heir, even a dullard like Albinus could get the message. Left with little choice, Albinus finally allowing himself to be proclaimed emperor by his own troops. Knowing that a reckoning with Severus had become as inevitable for him as it surely was inescapable, the whole Army of Britain was shipped across to Gaul in the prelude to its final act.

"I suppose I can guess what side you were on in all of this, eh, Decimus Ascanius?"

"Serving with the Sixth in Britain, I expect you can, boss…"

Earth-shattering recent events – little more than ten years ago – and still shaping lives today. But since *'forewarned is forearmed'* as they say, I thought it wiser to take a little extra time out in our journey to understand rather more about my Outdoor Clerk's involvement in world events than perhaps we'd established to date. As an exercise, much like interviewing a witness, only this time it's one undertaken for the whole team's mutual protection.

Not only his.

Clive Ashman

"So once Severus defeated Niger and put what's left of the Syrian garrison into the doghouse, I presume that's when he returned his attentions here? Because until then - as I remember it, Decimus - things had felt pretty stable here, hadn't they? Quiet, you might even say - Britannia being out on a bit of a limb?"

"Yeah, boss. Clodius Albinus was still the lawful governor, the emperor's official representative, so what else were we in the Sixth expected to do but swear loyalty to him? Why wouldn't we - and who else? While Severus was busy in the East, even us soldiers out on the parade ground were being told by the higher-ups that Severus was sending Albinus regular messages of goodwill. Promises of a rosy future, signed-off with love and kisses from the wife and kids: '...*love Julia and the boys*'. So, yes, you're right – everything seemed perfectly calm, like it was normal. But you need to realise that nothing's ever normal with Severus, boss. Just because he smiles a lot doesn't mean he's not a devious, lying, murdering bastard. Has blood on his hands..."

"Please try and be more careful, Ascanius – like I've told you before, you can't risk coming out with inflammatory remarks like that in public. Not even in private either, come to that..."

"Don't worry, sir – Trenico's up on the roof and he's as deaf as a post, while no-one will hear anything over the wheels. No, I'm only saying it for your benefit, boss, you know that."

"Maybe so, Ascanius, but complacency was Albinus's greatest failing and I don't want us making the same mistake. So don't risk my own safety, let alone yours and that of your friends."

"No, you're right there, but you asked me for the truth and I speak as I find. Because what happened to Albinus and his mistakes have ruined my life – *fact!* He should never have let Severus finish Niger off separately – *fact!* And that oath we soldiers from the Army of Britain made to Albinus as governor was legal. A proper thing, you see. What turned his fate into my fate, all our fates. Made it our military duty you see, boss, a simple matter of military discipline. That's what the Army teaches you. So we couldn't just swan off and change our minds – if no-one else, sir, you as a proper lawyer should know that."

189

Lawyers of Lugvalio

"Any oath made before the gods is a serious business. Binding."

"Too right, sir, which was fine up to a point, or at least until things started to go pear-shaped the following year. Albinus had been promised the Caesar's job, but once he hears that Caracalla's got it instead, he gets the message. That there's a big party going on elsewhere for which he's no invite. So Albinus gets the army in Britain to declare him Emperor and starts planning a fightback."

"By which time I guess you'd have been serving with the Sixth for quite a while?"

"Yes, sir, I had, right from the age of eighteen. Whatever else I've told you – including that stuff about the burial club and Eboracum for our home base - it's all of it been true."

"Though we never got onto the crucial bits, did we, Decimus, like whatever happened to you next?"

"Sorry for that, Justinus, but I promise you that this time I'll give it to you straight. The works, boss, with nothing missed-out. No lies, no pack drill…"

"Fire away, Decimus Ascanius – just so long as you're careful. And please try to speak more quietly."

"Yeah. So what it is, sir, I think everyone felt sorry for Albinus. Obviously he's not a bit like us, his men, but a cat can look at a king, can't they? I think we respected him for an educated man, come of a good family - a very good family in fact - and dutiful to a fault. Although looking back, a bit tardy on the uptake as well - maybe a bit dim? Too slow at realising others might be less honourable. And I bet he didn't fancy taking on a ferocious operator like Septimius Severus either, sir – but who in their right mind would do? But Albinus had been important here for ages, first appointed by Commodus. What with all the military and naval forces he had at his disposal here in Britain, all of them loyal - and managing to serve three successive emperors to date, without putting one foot wrong - we took it he'd be safe."

"Well forgive me, Ascanius, but he must have been a bit of a mug to think being a good man offers any sort of protection in a wicked world. Against the other type, it only makes you weaker."

Clive Ashman

Ascanius grimaced wryly but I continued: "Even the official histories admit Severus buried Albinus in flattery and promises. Including imperial roles he dangled under his nose. Baubles for good behaviour, for keeping out of trouble while Severus swanned round, finishing off his rivals. Till he got back to him."

"Like you said, sir. Until Albinus finally realised Severus was coming for him next - whatever he did or said, wherever he went. No hiding place. That our man was just another piece on the board. A game of draughts where 'Niger' means Black - and he's dealt with. While 'Albinus' is White – who so far is not. Not yet, but he's next. So if it looked like his turn, what else would you have done in his circumstances, boss, if you were the governor?"

"Strip Britannia of its garrison and every serving soldier – send them south to fight?"

"What you said. So he marches us down to the south coast, to ports like Rutupiae or Dubris, where we piled into a fleet of naval transports. It took them a week of days to get us all over the Narrow Sea to land in northern Gaul, but once me and the lads came ashore, we didn't face one whiff of opposition."

"Sounds like a pretty major effort?"

"Too right it was, boss! All three British legions in the one, expeditionary force - *legiones VI Victrix, II Augusta,* and *XX Valeria Victrix.* Once everyone had arrived in Gaul, I'd say we were as delighted as the governor when a Spanish legion turned up too. The entire garrison of Hispania - *legio VII Gemina* – come across to stand shoulder-to-shoulder with us. Why Albinus and his lieutenants told us, from now on we couldn't lose."

"Though wasn't that Niger's mistake, too? Another contender for the Purple thinking they've got overwhelming force on their side, that it meant Severus must surely be doomed?"

"Yes, though we had more reason. There was this other general on Severus's side - Virius Lupus, he was called. I expect you'll remember him, sir - came over here as replacement governor, once Albinus lost his head. So in Gaul, this Lupus and his legions attacked us, straight from the German frontier. Well, we really sorted them out - they came a real cropper, big-time. Those

191

Lawyers of Lugvalio

Rhineland troops were tough soldiers, but we swept them away! Killing so many of them obviously made us more confident, left Albinus controlling half the western empire and that. We thought Severus was truly on the back foot, would only want to parley."

"But Severus hung on in the East, and of course he still controlled all of Italy, held onto Rome?"

"That's it, sir, and all the time he's building his forces back up - softly, softly, like. Despite that bloody nose we gave Lupus - 'The Wolf' as they called him. Why we felt secure in Gaul, though the gods alone know what you had to cope with, back in Britannia..."

"Well, you've already told us what you think of Brigantes, Decimus Ascanius, so I'm sure you know what *they* got up to. People told you since what we faced at home as civilians - hiding half-starved behind city walls. From the Caledones to the Maetae, it felt like every northern tribe with a grudge against Rome had seen their opportunity. Once your garrisons withdrew, gangs of robbers, thieves, and murderers rushed down to fill a void. Pouring over the Aelian Wall to flood into our province. Wanting to get their own back, tear down the works of Rome."

"I'm sorry, sir, it can't have been good, but our orders took us to Gaul and we had to obey. No argument. What happened back home was hardly our fault. Though even an old sweat like me can get it: why Severus and his gang are back here today. Wanting that thing – the only thing which ever seems to matter for them. Fresh vengeance for older wrongs – payback time, yet again."

"Revenge, revenge! Is this the only instinct of our times? All I ever hear about from anyone, Ascanius – whether it's you, the clients or Brigantes. Like everyone's got a beef about someone, always wants revenge. Where will it end?"

"It's human nature for sure, boss. But back then in Gaul we found Severus and his men reinforcing the Alpine passes. Strongly-enough to hold Albinus at bay, stop our advance on Italy. So we couldn't do a Hannibal - even without elephants! But what with winter and Armilustrium coming, we weren't that bothered. No, if his Pannonians wanted to lean on their spears

192

through the blizzards, then good luck to them, poor bastards. We thought we could polish our armour in the valleys and hunker down safely till spring, sort it all out the following year. Beat up more Germans, get into Italy. Except Severus had secretly been gathering a bigger army along the Danube too, and next thing we knew they burst through the mountains. March into Gaul with snow on their boots to attack at Tinurtium, on the Saone river."

"A winter campaign - surely that's pretty unusual, isn't it? And hardly very sporting, either. So where were you in the middle of all this? Where's Decimus Ascanius when the action happens?"

"It was February, boss, and freezing my nuts off. Because Severus had launched a winter campaign, it took us completely by surprise. Forced us and Albinus to pull back in disarray. Left me and several thousand of my brilliant mates from the Sixth stuck out there, somewhere in the middle of the province. A long line of *'grunts'* slogging across endless frozen flatlands, carrying pounds of kit across our shoulders in Albinus's so-called *'strategic retreat'* towards Lugdunum and safety, the largest city in Gaul."

"Lugdunum, eh, Decimus - an appointment with destiny?"

"You might put it like that, sir, but not how it felt at the time. More like an appointment with frostbite. When we arrived, it was just another big town, and we were only grateful to stop marching. Get out of the cold."

I looked outside the carriage window to realise we were passing the eastern edge of Lugvalio. The outer bank and ditches which mark its civic domain. When I'd thought that travelling up here was a big enough deal for all of us, nine solid days more discomfort than I can usually tolerate, but here I was talking to an ordinary soldier – *well, an ex-soldier* – about events he'd witnessed more like *a thousand* miles away from where we rode now.

A plain enough man, yet he'd seen and fought in one of the worst but most spectacular battles in human history. Contested not between Roman and barbarian, but in what every schoolboy knows for probably the largest and the bloodiest ever to be fought between Romans - to our everlasting shame.

Lawyers of Lugvalio

A surviving combatant from "*Dies Parentalia*" – the Day of the Dead - a festival day where they should have been honouring our ancestors, not slaughtering their living heirs and fellow citizens.

It made me think about how far even the most ordinary person may travel nowadays, and how readily - although it's true I've never gone much further south than Londinium, myself.

There for some citizen's appeal against a death sentence, if I remember it right. Another one of those cases which I, we - or perhaps I should say, more correctly - 'the client' - unfortunately lost. And another unhappy outcome to one of my cases leaving me unpaid and out of pocket...

But if I might never have left my own province, the Emperor Severus came all the way here from Africa and he brought his empress from Syria. While this man I travelled with today had been eyewitness to a massive battle somewhere in Gallia Lugdunensis. And if some think this hyper-mobility for people is what most defines our empire and era, a product of our sophisticated modern road-system, then I still sometimes wonder whether it does more harm than good? When it seems to deliver invaders and usurpers, foul pestilence and exotic disease, more readily than it ever brings us money, goods, and trade?

In my reverie, I realised Ascanius was looking at me expectantly – as well he might, since I'd left him shivering there at Lugdunum, a cold soldier fresh off the road. Like I should say something more sympathetic, so I tried: "The reputation of that terrible day is awful, Decimus, I fear to press you further...?"

"Its reputation's justified, boss, I don't mind admitting it. And look - I'm not making excuses either, sir, not for anything I've done - but I don't think I've been right since. I don't really know why..."

"Listen, Decimus, I'm sorry – I hope I've not been too harsh with you. But let's be clear, you're saying you were actually there – at the Day of the Dead?"

"If that's what they call it, though it ran over two. It was *two* days of hell."

Clive Ashman

"I'm ashamed to admit my own knowledge is restricted to books. To Herodian, say, or Dio Cassius's latest - Tiro's favourite historian. Second-hand sources a mere civilian should hesitate to mention before a time-served veteran - an eyewitness like you are, Decimus. Though I'm always struck by Dio's claim that there were a hundred and fifty thousand soldiers present on both sides. Was such a figure even possible, do you think...?"

"Don't discount it, Justinus. Based on what I saw, I'd say forty thousand of us came from Britain alone. Just getting them there took our British fleet the best part of a week. That's before you add the legions of Gaul and Hispania, the auxiliaries in support. Though I can't vouch for the Severan strength."

"So where were you and the Sixth in the line of battle, this terrible day we discuss?"

"Heavily dug-in on the right wing – not how we'd normally fight. We made a line of deep trenches across the frontage of our camp, and in front of them dug circular pits, disguised with loose earth and bracken on the surface. Each had a sharpened stake in the centre. "*Lilia*' is what the army calls them and it's quite an old idea, but no less effective for that. Attackers who fall into one usually get impaled, or at least they should break something. It's how they're used to this day, in front of the Aelian Wall."

"Nice idea – did they work?"

"Oh, yes, sir, they did – although not everything else did. You see, both sides had been limbering up to each other for the best part of a day. Lots of manoeuvring to no purpose going on for a while, but the first sign things were going badly on our opposite flank came when a few of us saw some Spaniards from our left wing, running back towards their camp. Severus' men chased after them, killing plenty and plundering their tents, but our lads from the British contingent stood fast on the right, knowing that we had trenches and covered pits laid out in front of us. Until the signal to advance, when we deliberately moved forward in formation – slowly, and only so far as to where we knew these secret traps were - before hurling our javelins at extreme range. All of it done carefully as part of the one deliberate plan."

Lawyers of Lugvalio

"Did it work?"

"While we stuck to it, yes, it did. Instead of advancing further, we turned around to make it look like we were frightened men, wanting to retreat. The plan was to draw the enemy after us and it worked a treat, because that's exactly what happened. Severus's men so annoyed by our brief attack, so contemptuous of what appeared a half-hearted advance on them, that they charged us immediately. Attacked in loose formation. Reaching our hidden pits and trenches, they ran like a rabble straight into disaster. All the men in the Severan front rank fell down into our secret excavations. Got stuck on their stakes or tangled in the blackthorn. Made easy meat for archers."

"Amazing – and clever, too!"

"Yeah – so that, whatever was happening to our left flank, me and my mates on the right thought the day was ours. All the while this was going on, the rest of Severus's army were getting caught in our hidden pits and trenches. Going down in lines, annihilated under an endless shower of incoming missiles, fired from our side. That's when I first saw Severus for myself…"

"You saw the emperor himself?"

"Yes, Justinus, I did – looked him right in the eye. Man to man, one soldier to another, if only for a moment. An instance never to be forgotten. But not once in all the years which have passed since did I ever see him again. Not from that day to this, sir, I'll swear it, not once - not even in Eboracum. Not until I get this new job with you, and we stroll through the gates of Luguvalium together and into its marketplace, only last week. And there he was again, sir, large as life…"

"So the first time you actually ever saw him was on the battlefield? That winter's day on the plains of Lugdunum, across the water in Gaul?"

"Yes, sir, it was - like I said. In the very thick of it, we were – and you can't fault his courage, I'll give Severus that. Never forget the sight. When his whole army seemed to be falling apart in front of us, right in front of our lads from the Sixth. And then he called out for his Praetorians to help - pointing at us, waving and bawling so hard at them - that they came up too quick and charged into the same trap without looking. Met the same fate."

Ascanius raised his eyes skywards, whilst making a narrow gap between his forefinger and thumb: "By Mithras and all that's holy – and I know I can share it with you, sir, my words will go no further – I'd say that our brave British legions came *that* close, Justinus – *so very, very close* - to smashing Severus and his Danube army into a million gilded pieces."

"And from what you say, Decimus, far from helping other troops already trapped, he nearly got his replacement bodyguard - those new *'Pannonian'* Praetorians of his - wiped-out too?"

"That's how it looked to us. And if all that didn't seem bad enough, then he lost his horse from under him, only a bowshot away from where I stood in the shield line. I saw that poor beast go straight down myself, sir - riddled with arrows, its eyes rolling white, and his soldiers in flight all around him. But instead of grabbing another horse and getting away, Severus tore off his riding cloak so that *everyone* – and of course that includes us lot opposite - could see *exactly* who he was. See his face and shining armour. Then he drew his Spanish short sword and rushed-in amongst the runaways. Hoping either to shame them into turning back, I guess, or die fighting amongst them..."

"Sounds like our dear emperor could have easily been killed?"

"More's the pity that he wasn't, sir, more's the pity - if you want my private opinion about *'The Butcher of Lugdunum'*. But just at that point when the battle seemed lost to Severus, for want of a horse for him and a bit more resolve in his men, then Aemilius Laetus comes riding up..."

"What, Laetus, that devious lizard who presided over the murder of Pertinax and set all this off? Commander to those original Praetorians who killed the very emperor Severus claims he walked all the way from Pannonia to Rome to avenge? The late, lamented P. Helvius Pertinax himself - last man of integrity left to us standing, till Laetus's men decide to kill him, too...?"

Lawyers of Lugvalio

"Yessir, him - Laetus, the same conniving hypocrite! Me and my mates standing firm in a wall of iron facing Severus - and then this Laetus appears unexpectedly behind us, with all his heavy cavalry."

"What did you do?"

"There wasn't much we could do, boss. I just remember hearing this sound like thunder with my comrades and all of us turning round to see what the hell it was. And there they were: squadrons of charging lancers, attacking us from behind. They completely overwhelmed our line in moments - turning Albinus's victory to dust on the spot. Years later, I met someone in a bar who'd been there as well. He told me that Laetus had been holding his massed horsemen back deliberately, right until that point. Seeing the struggle so closely matched, apparently he just sat there, calmly looking-on. Hoping both generals would perish and that any surviving soldiers - whichever side they're from - would pass the imperial baton to him. The bastard. Except once he realised Severus' side was rallying, thanks to the emperor's bravery, then Laetus finally plays his hand. Sends in the cavalry, enough to decide the whole business against us in a moment..."

"I never realised it was such a near run thing..."

"Oh yes, boss, very close indeed. But finally we were defeated and you never saw such a disaster for Rome and her legions - whatever side you were on. The whole plain covered with bodies. Our men and horses, all dead and dying, mutilated by wounds. Armour and military equipment what took the factories years to produce, scattered around like so much useless junk. I can tell you, Gaius Januarius Justinus, our Roman blood flowed red in the streams and ditches that day, it poured into the rivers."

"Where was your leader?"

"They say Albinus tried to hide with a few companions inside a small, white house beside the River Rhone, but once they were discovered and the place surrounded, I'm told he killed himself."

"Rather than be captured alive by Severus?"

Clive Ashman

"Wouldn't you? And if he did decide to die there and then, sir, I think he was wise. Straightaway, Severus ordered that the dead bodies of any senators who'd supported Albinus, even the non-combatants, should be sought-out and mutilated on the spot - on the field of battle. Punctured and hacked about, just for the sake of it. Severus certainly lived up to his name that day – they say he completely lost it. His fury and vengeance was unstoppable - bloody unspeakable, I'd say - and I think it's all because he knew how very close he'd come to losing it. The battle, I mean…"

"If he could do that to *dead* senators…?"

"When Albinus's body was recovered then dragged-up before him, Severus had it beheaded. The veteran I spoke to claimed that Albinus might still have been half-alive when that bit happened. Anyway, he orders that the head should be put into a separate drawstring bag and sent direct to the Senate in Rome, along with a threatening note. Next thing, Severus remounts and then – repeatedly, in a blinding rage – rides on horseback over Albinus' headless body. Backwards and forwards, backwards and forwards he goes, until it's just a mangled mess. Then he orders its butchered remains be pegged out on the grass right in front of the dead man's home, exposed to public view. Until later on, when Severus changes his mind again and orders Albinus' corpse be thrown into the Rhone - along with the naked bodies of his wife and innocent children, who've also been found and killed."

"This makes for pretty grim listening, Decimus, it's hard to take in. How do we reconcile your horror stories of today with that beaming figure you and I saw in the centre of Lugvalio, only the other? Though what I'm more interested in is what happened *to you* after the battle? Where were *you* while these terrible atrocities ran their course?"

"With a small group of mates from the Sixth, trying to get home. Still crossing Gallia, we heard Septimius Severus was busy executing anyone important in the province known to have supported Albinus. Even been polite to him. We were of no importance at all but still knew we were wanted men, so we kept to the woods and forests, stopped using the roads."

Lawyers of Lugvalio

"Sounds sensible to me, Decimus. Most of the story is public knowledge by now. Anyone can read Dio's latest bestseller - it's not like it's secret. It's true anyone prominent known to have sided with Albinus was rapidly put to death, leading men or distinguished women. To the point anyone who coveted their neighbour's land, even just a corner of it, could get what they wanted by lies - denouncing them as traitors. The rest of their goods confiscated and sent to the public treasury, the *fiscus*. That's how it was that Severus could fund such generous gifts of money to his soldiers, like no emperor before him. And with pay-offs like that, no wonder he's reigned as their unchallenged commander-in-chief ever since - remains the empire's master. They know he's pure gold."

"Yes, boss, and speaking as a soldier, Severus understands how to keep my kind on side. Holds no other priority. Once he knew Lugdunum had surrendered and opened its gates after the battle, Severus gave it over for his surviving legionaries to loot and burn. Rape and pillage at will. Whatever…"

"Well here's another bit I don't understand, Decimus, because I know Severus served as a governor of that province, early on in his career. I'm told it's a nice place. And his elder son – Caracalla – was born there too, during the father's tour of duty. After all that, did he hold no nostalgic fondness for this city? No lingering affection for somewhere he's lived? His children were born? So how could he do it – let his own troops savage the place?"

"Because he's crackers, boss – not a scrap of humanity left in the man. Or his sons. Sentiment means nothing to them, sir, it's only power and blood that interest them. They're butchers."

"Did you see what happened to the city yourself?"

"I did, sir - it was bad. Me and my mates hid in the hedgerows till nightfall, watching from the plain outside while columns of black smoke reached for the sky. As for its poor, tormented citizens – well, may the gods have mercy on their souls. At least by then we were too far away to hear them screaming…. beating our retreat through the surrounding woods. On our way out."

"It sounds like you were lucky to escape the battlefield, Decimus… how come you managed that?"

"Without the funds from our burial club, we'd have never got as far across Gaul as we did. It took us several months, losing friends and money along the way. Often we were starving, or hunted down like outlaws. Some of my comrades disappeared overnight, or got lost in the forest, while others just fell ill - died on the march. One of the last of us got arrested after being denounced to a local magistrate by some villagers he'd begged to sell us food. Me and another hid, then we escaped down the street. Unfortunately, by the time the northern coast comes into sight and it's a case of finding a suitable port, I'm left completely on my own. The only survivor from all of us."

"I'm really sorry, Decimus – it sounds dreadful. But after Lugdunum, I seem to remember a sort of breathing space, once Severus's attention returned to the eastern provinces and war with Parthia. Back in Britannia, stripped of its defenders by Albinus and ravaged by the tribes, we had hard times too. As I know to my cost - surviving a siege with nearly no work or income to speak of, my practice dried up."

"That must have been tough…"

"Look, I'm sorry – it's nothing compared with your experience. Forgive me. But I assume you were still fighting your way back across the Narrow Sea, on your own?"

"Yeah, but what bothered me most, sir, was knowing the unburied bones of my comrades lay scattered about on the Field of Lugdunum, whitening in the sun. Troubling my conscience no end. I'd pray to the gods every night, knowing it was only thanks to my possession of *their* savings, gathered to ensure some proper burials for *them*, that I've enough money in my purse to get me alive to the coast, buy me a passage to Britain in the filthy hold of some Gallic fishing boat. But what else could I do?"

"It's awful, but certainly not theft in my book. And hearing it makes me feel even more embarrassed, Decimus, about some inconsiderate things I said to you earlier about such matters, when we left Cataractonium. I'd no idea of the grim reality behind your stewardship of those monies, and I most sincerely wish to apologise to you right now, Decimus. I feel very strongly that someone should tell you - should put you right about it – because personally, I'm absolutely certain that the shades of your dead comrades would not rebuke you for one moment over the use to which you put their burial fund. Knowing that it kept you alive, if only so you can now tell others their story."

"Thank you, sir, that's very kind, very generous. I'm grateful for how you put it, and just hope you're right. That the dead will prove as forgiving, when we meet again."

"Of course they will - as we will remember them, every *Dies Parentalia*. But technically you're also a deserter, Decimus, are you not? What happened about that, once you got back to Eboracum? Surely it's a legal status only likely to cause you – and maybe even me – yet further danger?"

"It's a yes-and-no, boss. When I got back to town, there weren't very many lads left alive from the original Sixth who I actually needed to hide from, or avoid. Most of my officers had either been killed in battle, murdered afterwards, or sent off to the salt mines. And I reckoned that if I was going to keep a low profile, then a busy city is just about the best place to do it. Rather than out in the country, where everyone knows your business, or else thinks that they do. So, yes, boss, I've survived there ever since, living in a tenement, hiding in plain sight... until you gave me this job."

"This is unfortunately typical of a civil war, Decimus. But turning brave men like you into outcasts, murdering everyone who's seen as a rival, plus their wider families, achieves nothing in the end. It only perpetuates strife: see Dio's new book - it's easy to read between the lines. And Dio should know - he's a serving senator himself. Saw it all first hand, like you have. How - once back in Rome, that summer - Severus next turned against the Senate. Confiscating property and executing twenty-nine of its members before he demanded they deify the unlamented Commodus by senatorial decree. Now that he's achieved all of that – and with Caracalla installed as his junior Caesar, Niger and Albinus both eliminated - it's easy to see how the next job on Severus's endless to-do list would be shipping half an empire's army across to Britain. Making a start on exterminating the Caledones, beginning next spring...."

"I know, sir. That's why he's here, lodged in one of those fancy tents down the hill. And that's why I see him like an old warhorse, one that needs the fresh smell of blood in his nostrils. Regular, too..."

"The way you tell it, Decimus, it's like he's developed a real physical need? An actual thirst for blood-letting, but on a massive scale. Like he's restless, can't give it up, it's become his whole way of life. Expecting the next instalment what gives some purpose to his days?"

"You've got it in one, boss. Demonic, some say. And exactly what bothers me most. Why you and I need to talk about it."

"Like we're doing now?"

"Yeah, 'cos this is it, boss - the whole point. Because his trail of blood is what led us *both* here. Right here to him. To Luguvalium today - like it must mean something? Like it's Fate what's working things out – whether she's Fortuna, or a nemesis..."

No wonder Ascanius hated our ruling family – both the father and his two, awful sons. And no wonder he hadn't produced a metal discharge diploma on appointment either - because he didn't have one to produce, having never properly left. Yet another military malefactor in my orbit to deal with - a man risking execution on arrest, but forced to seek employment with a penniless lawyer to keep other wolves from his door. One way or another, it's the type I seem to attract - like trouble itself. His mention of Fortuna or Nemesis was tasteless - though it made me shudder inside, I was determined not to let it show. As if I didn't have enough problems or obstacles to overcome in this case already, without him adding *them*. But despite my private feelings of irritation, I made one more effort to be kind:

Lawyers of Lugvalio

"Well, thank you for being so honest, Decimus, it's quite a story and no mistake. One to tell your grandchildren about, should you live to be old. But if it helps explain your dangerous indiscretions of the other day, it doesn't excuse them. And, no, I won't leave everything to the gods - we should run a tighter ship than that. Because I still need to stress the dangers, both for us and our case. When our professional duty to the client *especially* includes not making things worse for her - never mind ourselves. So your making rude comments about Caracalla in a public location will always run the risk that someone unfriendly overhears it and then denounces you. Or even me, or all of us - tells the relevant authorities. But this time, all I'll say is: *"Be a lot more careful in future, for your sake and ours - please keep it to yourself."* Because we don't want your private grudge against the ruling dynasty to land us all in jail. Put us to the rack..."

"I understand and accept what you say, Justinus, although nothing I've told you about was meant as an excuse. And it's also accepted that you need to know my background, although I trust it goes no further. As I place my trust in you. Because, sir, even if I'm sorry, I'll admit I'm also scared…"

"What, you, Decimus Ascanius, scared? No - I don't employ you to be scared. I employ you to provide our party with private security, not go around feeling scared!"

"I know, sir, you're absolutely right, and please don't get me wrong - I'll do my level best. But I'm scared for you, for all of us. For you and Tiro, for your client – even for myself. I came along to provide protection for a professional gentleman, a bit of muscle in a tight corner. Maybe sort some minor argy-bargy outside the law-courts, not expecting anything worse. Because I never expected a job like this could bring me face to face with Severus and his mob again, or the brutal Caracalla!"

"Who's to say that it will - and why should it anyway, Decimus Ascanius? We've come here to find a suitable judge, not bump into the emperor - there's nothing special about us. We're just an ordinary set of private litigants, come along quietly to plead our minor case in a local court, then as quietly slip away. So what is it that you're saying? It's not like we travelled across here to confront them – to overthrow an emperor or foment unrest against his son - perish the thought!"

"No, but what it is, boss – whatever we intend, I'm worried we've put our head into a real hornet's nest here. By choosing to bring Lydia Firma's case across here, instead of Eboracum, that somehow we're delivering ourselves to within a dragon's-breath of the beast itself. And, yes sir, it's true I'm also worried that someone here might denounce me. Identify me as a missing soldier of the Sixth – someone escaping the field of Lugdunum who never rejoined his legion. Needs bringing to justice himself."

"Who would do that?"

"I've got to admit it, sir - seeing Severus in the Forum last week has really unsettled me. *Really* unsettled me. I mean - what would we do if *he* recognised *me*? When I took on this job, none of these were situations I ever thought to encounter. Never in a thousand years. No disrespect, sir, but with me thinking you're just a boring, harmless lawyer stuck in limited lines of work, it meant that when I agreed to join you I thought we'd only be safe…"

"Well thanks a lot for that. So you're asking to be released?"

"No, Gaius Januarius Justinus, nothing of the sort. So please don't get me wrong - I won't desert you and I won't let you down. Not the client neither. But I don't think it clashes with my latest role to warn you of danger. To say that you need to think twice…"

Enough was enough and my staff were making me edgy.

Running a litigation my chief clerk thought we would lose before a court which had doubted my right to be heard. In the homicidal presence of a ruling dynasty my bodyguard believes to be so obsessed with butchery, on a global scale, that it never can be sated. Might as easily pick on us next, as anyone else.

Whilst at the same time confronting our powerful defendant – a man who's ex-military himself and making similar threats – all of it for the sake of a beautiful client, who won't pay us if we lose.

Lawyers of Lugvalio

So is it any wonder that I felt increasingly nervous myself about how this whole damn thing might end?

Because, no - it's not what I'd joined for, either. Never mind anyone else, I'm just as ordinary. A hack practitioner in wills and deceased estates, a quiet man more used to administering their legal affairs for the kind of client who's more usually dead – less like to answer back. The kind of legal business that can be resolved peaceably and slowly, in a state of funereal calm.

Never once in all my career – mediocre as it may seem - had I ever found myself involved in another case to remotely resemble this one. Nor so freighted with danger, whether real or imagined.

When the quiet life had always been - by and large, save the odd difficult beneficiary – such a welcome feature of my normal daily practice, a key part of its gentle appeal. Until this particular one came along to upset the apple cart.

But if everyone around me seems so frightened or pessimistic about my latest case, its likely or possible outcomes - their suggested list of the potential risks we're all running only growing by the day - then maybe I'm the one who's too slow?

Missing out the most over issues more vital. Including that personal, singular question which no-one else can answer but me. This one I'm finally asking – belatedly at least, but better late than never: *"Should I be scared for myself?"*

Chapter XXIV

When the day of the Formulary Hearing arrived, and supported by my senior clerk along with his outdoor equivalent, the three of us attended at the agreed time and place to join with my current client and her two young sons. Assembling by arrangement and in a collective sense of nervous anticipation outside the main entrance to the panelled tent of the judicial legate, within that unusual deep hollow which Praetorians call *'The Green Zone'*.

Finding myself once more at a unique location girdled on three sides by a rushing river (or else Uxellodunum) - upon its fourth by the Aelian Wall - and disregarding whatever physical safety we gain from its bowl as a cockpit for litigation, an odd mood overcame me. My normal professional confidence in the justice of our cause suddenly draining away - completely.

Firstly, I suppose, at the oppressive sight of yet more sentries from the sinister Praetorian Guard, promenading in their peacock finery along the riverside path. And secondly, from a growing awareness of our incredible proximity to the Imperial Family themselves, encamped in luxury nearby. Then thirdly, from the wretched litany of pessimistic fears and uncertainties about our overall prospects for success with which my client, friends or colleagues, in a whole succession of ever-more depressing conversations, had worked to weigh-me down. Of which it was Ascanius, who probably finished me off...

Lawyers of Lugvalio

So it was with a heavy heart, and these sensations of imminent doom or failure now beginning to consume me, that I re-entered the judicial legate's leather pavilion. Just in time to find Tiberius Claudius Paulinus taking his seat in a carved chair on a raised dais; rolling back the folds of his toga to a weathered elbow and getting ready to tackle that morning's list of pleas, trials, and adjournments. Clearly keen to get cracking.

In the diffused gloom of the tent, I spotted our aged respondent and his new wife - that brassy blonde, Metella, sitting with her legs inelegantly crossed while jiggling the left foot to illustrate perpetual mental turmoil. And no wonder.

At least our service of the summons had won the intended outcome: both of our defendants entering a personal appearance before the court in response, their very first in our case. Immediately demanding out loud that - since everyone summonsed to answer our accusations was now here – then we on the other side should be *forced* to go on with our action this day, to take it to trial, or the two of them be allowed to withdraw.

Like we lacked in resolve!

My client seated decorously beside me in her darkest cloth of mourning, I rose to my feet and spoke with great gravity and moderation to introduce ourselves and our case more formally. Expressing my sorrowful regret that there seemed no sign of competent representation present to achieve an equality of arms between these warring parties – a line of argument I knew from last time would flatter Paulinus's professed sensibility to fairness, ingratiate me further with the court.

Paulinus, as expected, agreed these sentiments at once and turned to Firmus to ask whether he'd anyone acting for him - at which precise moment the leather flap down the far end lifted and an undernourished advocate whom the court-clerk announced as '*Eurythmus*' hopped into the tent.

Paulinus looking this new arrival up and down like he's what the proverbial cat's brought in, while I – on instinct – thought I detected the rare but delicious sensation of a difficult case that's already turning our way?

This Eurythmus for his part did no more and offered no more by way of apology for disrespectful lateness than to plonk himself down on a chair before the dais. Nor did he bother introducing himself properly either, let alone his unfortunate clients: whether by name, status, or otherwise. Though he then bobbed-up (from having just sat-down) to complain that: *"Both of my defendants are being placed in an impossible and unacceptable position, one that needs remedying immediately…"*

Apparently indifferent to increased fidgeting and bridling up on the bench, Eurythmus continued by pointing out – with some justice, I'd be first to concede – that they'd only had two days' notice of our proceedings, and hence little chance to prepare. That his clients would be left open to popular suspicion and ridicule ever thereafter, if it all went against them. Unless they were given a proper chance to be heard in their own behalf, that is. For which he's demanding an immediate adjournment by the legate as their minimum entitlement, during which recess he could take their instructions and arrange a coherent defence.

To which spectacular opening, and before he'd even sat down again, Paulinus as crossly replied: "I don't care whether your two clients are left open to suspicion and ridicule or not, advocate, but I do care about timewasting. This is my court and the defendant side are summonsed here on a formal suit for patrimony, but – thanks to your unannounced intervention – they appear to be running away with all sorts of side-issues and irrelevancies already, with no idea of procedure. So can we please stop wasting time, gentlemen, get a grip and get on with it? Today!"

Paulinus had got the measure of Eurythmus straightaway – we all had – and identified him for a skinny windbag, one whose bullying style hadn't worked, because he turned to face Firmus and mock-seriously confided: " Do you see now, centurion, how useful it can be to have a proper lawyer speak-up for you, explaining your case?"

209

Lawyers of Lugvalio

Firmus' face was like Olympic thunder, his square white beard evoking Zeus, but Eurythmus was oblivious, beaming like he'd just received a massive compliment. Wordlessly bowing in thanks, so steeply he nearly banged his forehead on the wooden table in front – how I wished that he had! While Paulinus turned drily back to me:

"Consider what in fairness we ought to do, Justinus, for these people are complaining to me that they are not being allowed to prosecute an effective defence…"

I dropped my head meekly and said it was a decision I was happy to leave to him, but after some whispered advice from the Clerk to the Lists, Paulinus ordered that the testator and his heir should be instructed either to get on with our case today, and deal with the administrative process of agreeing the necessary formulations. Or else each defendant should come in front of him individually, and state sufficient reasons why our proceedings against them should be adjourned at their request.

Warning them that unless they either did that - or else got on with the case today - he would go so far as to pronounce immediate sentence against them both for bringing false witness, by ordering the sequestration and sale of the testator Firmus' estate, there and then.

This was a seriously shocking threat and an unexpected turn of the tide, especially so early in a case. Not surprisingly, it seemed to rock the other side to their foundations, and who could blame them?

As the writer Pliny says, the first duty of a conscientious judge is to show patience, but Paulinus had quite obviously become so irritated by Eurythmus and his hectoring style already - not to mention by how these petty interruptions from Firmus' side prevented matters getting underway - that he'd decided to get awkward. While I only felt relieved that any lingering suspicions Ascanius might have fostered in me, about how unspoken loyalties among former officers of *Legio II Augusta* might prompt a partisan bias in the court against us, were as clearly misplaced.

Clive Ashman

For a properly-trained advocate like myself, this early reverse for Firmus represented a crucial development: *'captatio benevolentiae'* as it's called. Cicero's classic stratagem for winning points and approval from a judge and jurors when the trial is barely underway. *"Get the court on-side, early doors..."* as my old tutors used to exhort me. And from our side's perspective, so long as Eurythmus appears for the other lot, then it looks like milady's still in the game with more than a fighting chance?

Although on philosophical questions about law and morality - his attitude to young women, say, or family obligation - Firmus might seem no better than an old fool, lacking in remorse, I also saw a cunning type, one dangerous to cross - as his daughter took pains to warn me. This veteran soldier finding himself publicly humiliated by an opponent in law he'd probably never thought capable - before a fellow former-soldier to boot. Even at its worst, not how I imagine he'd have expected today's proceedings against him to kick-off. And whilst I knew Firmus would hold Eurythmus responsible for this early humiliation to start with, my sudden flash of optimism came bracketed with other fears - about what else an old soldier might do, when he wants revenge?

There was the sound of a sudden squall outside and a fusillade of raindrops swept across the outer surface of the tent. It looked like the wind was getting up again, but so too was Eurythmus. After another bout of whispered conferring, Firmus's advocate rose to a crouch and looked sheepishly towards the tribunal:

"Having heard what the court has to say, both my clients now instruct me, sir, that they are willing to follow those limited procedures you've set down for resolution today. But they will insist on reserving their right not to test the evidence yet, nor anything else which the claimants may purport to say of them, until the time of trial. Where they will fight it out to the death."

"Excellent, that's good to hear" said Paulinus, seemingly undismayed to hear such extremes of language being voiced in his court - I suppose there's worse said in barracks?

211

Lawyers of Lugvalio

"So let's get this show on the road, starting with *Nominatio...*" he added. "And to my mind, gentlemen, there are a number of eminent possibilities available in the vicinity, any one of whom could provide an excellent chairman for your case."

"Possibilities, sir?"

"Yes, Justinus, by which I mean our new *praefectus* of Praetorians, the learned Aemilius Papinianus, for instance. Or perhaps Gnaeus Ulpianus, whom I understand is also available? Happy to hear a few extra cases, if only to keep his hand in..."

Eurythmus was still standing, but before offering us his next contribution tugged thoughtfully upon a scrawny beard floating forlornly towards the outer extremity of his shortish chin. Its sparse fuzz another possible pointer to moral or physical weakness, before he stated to the court - out loud, if you please, not one hint of embarrassment - that he'd never heard of either.

As one way of announcing a spectacular ignorance of both Roman law and lawyers, this surely took the biscuit. Nor was mine the only jaw dropping. When nothing could more vividly illustrate the paucity of skill and understanding that was then available at the Lugvalio bar - but from whose parochial corps of advocates poor Firmus must still appoint a lawyer - than this petty discounting by his chosen representative of two of the finest Roman legal minds in a generation. Generations, even.

Hearing this cretinous dismissal, Paulinus simply rolled his eyes at me and chose to change the subject: "Well, there it is. I've given you a few names to be going on with, gentlemen – think carefully about them, but I've got another suggestion anyway, if these two won't do. Meanwhile, aside from the chairman, we also need to select a panel of judges to be your jurors at trial, from an approved list of local citizens. Shall we deal with that point instead?"

"My client, Lydia Firma, is the plaintiff and it is my respectful submission, sir, that she should be allowed to suggest some names from the official list herself, and then the defendants to her claim given an opportunity to agree them, or not, in turn."

Clive Ashman

Eurythmus rose again, drawing his toga around him: "I cannot promise the court - or indeed my learned friend, Justinus – that there'll be much agreement around here. My client reserves his right to reject any or all of these names, and so does his wife."

Paulinus leaned forward from a raised dais and knotted his brow: "I'd much prefer to see some co-operation between the advocates, gentlemen, but if there's no agreement forthcoming from the parties on any names, indeed on any other issue, then you can rest assured I will make my decision anyway. Like it or not. And the same goes for the matter of a chairman. Where I'll have the casting vote, remember, so I hope neither advocate will waste their opportunity to influence me... it won't come again."

"We will try and agree a list of names, sir, and then return it to the court..." I said.

"Very good, that's the spirit, so let's turn to *Intentio* – the point where we finalise your statement of claim. What do the representatives have to say to me about that?"

"My suggestion, sir, would be along the lines of: *"Should his current will be declared null and void and the testator Marcus Firmus ordered under civil law to make proper provision in his last will and testament for his natural daughter Lydia Firma?"* I added quickly.

Eurythmus let out a guffaw, while Firmus and Metella both chuntered away in the background.

"Do the defence have anything more formal to say about that particular suggestion?" asked Paulinus, his voice heavy with irony. If the respondents and their lawyer could manage to provoke the chairman at trial as thoroughly as they were currently managing it with Paulinus, I doubted we could lose - whatever the Younger Pliny might say.

"Or should the respondent beneficiary Metella be allowed under civil law to receive it all instead?" Eurythmus chipped-in, like it's the first thing that's come into his head: "After all, as the tribunal knows, if this marriage with my client's new wife, the second respondent, lasts for a calendar year, then she'll be acquiring the same legal status as his first daughter presently enjoys. By law, anyway..."

213

Lawyers of Lugvalio

"This is what you'll get…. interrupted Paulinus, as if he hadn't heard him: *"The agreed question for this court is whether the testator Marcus Firmus's present will should be declared null and void, and the testator ordered, under compulsion, to show adequate provision is made in his current will for his natural daughter, Lydia Firma, to an extent specified by the court?"*

The wind outside had grown stronger and seemed to take hold of the wooden framework to the tent, shaking it bodily. A loose flap by the entrance porch broke away and had to be grabbed then secured by a slave to stop more weather getting in. Metella put her arms around Firmus, who shook her off angrily. Another storm was building, and not just in the heavens.

"On the basis we've got an agreed form of words and the parties co-operate that much, then I'm prepared to reciprocate by omitting the third stage - *condemnatio*." Paulinus announced. "So I won't be fining these defendants money, but neither will I absolve them – their case must go to trial. And turning to the next stage, *demonstratio*, it's now for me to state the alleged facts out of which this lady's claims arise, which shall form the basis of trial."

Eurythmus rose to his feet, pulling again at that beard: "I do hope those facts will be limited?"

This was my chance: "The clerks are noting everything, sir, and what I'll suggest runs like this. My claimant client, the lady Lydia, is sole surviving natural progeny of the first respondent, the centurion Marcus Firmus, himself recently widowed. Remarrying within eleven days, he has cut the claimant off from her inheritance in favour of his new wife, the second respondent. Your court is invited to rule."

"I'm happy with that…" said Paulinus "It sounds short and sweet, quite enough for trial. Any technical points – will the defendants be raising any more-specific defences?"

"Meaning *exceptio* and *replicatio*?" piped Eurythmus, more to show his clients that he understood a tiny bit of what's going on

214

here, the nature of these terms, than to notify they had any serious grounds to file them – when we all knew they didn't.

"Correct, advocate, correct! And if they don't apply, it brings the court to *praescriptio* next – us limiting the triable issues involved to this singular matter in hand. Which means that you, Justinus, must formally confirm to me that your plaintiff won't be bringing any similar case against these two defendants – whether on similar or related issues."

"An undertaking my client is happy to give…" I said, bowing, but only from the neck, while Goatface snorted again in the background, having failed to think of any defence.

"Excellent – well, I think that's this case sorted, gentlemen, and thank you both for your valuable help" Paulinus said with heavy sarcasm as he turned towards his nearest scribe, who stopped writing at once.

That was when Eurythmus struck: "It seems you've forgotten one thing…" he says. "What about *Nominatio* – have you decided yet, who will chair this case at trial?"

Paulinus paused and turned back. "I mentioned a few well-known names to you earlier, advocate, some pretty well-known lawyers, but you seemed less than impressed. Though there's another famous jurist who's currently in town and available…"

"Famous, you say…" gulped Eurythmus "and available, too?"

"Oh, yes, it's quite a *curriculum vitae* - I think you'll agree. Brilliant enough, I'd hope, to satisfy even our friend for the defence. Because the gentleman I've in mind has earned his stripes, been a proper lawyer in his time. After studying law under Scaevola he practised as an advocate himself, you know, just like you two do. In the reign of Marcus Aurelius he became our youngest-ever state attorney - as *advocatus fisci* appearing for the government in defence of suits brought against the Treasury, its *fiscus*. And I've reason to suspect that someone special here once won a little fleeting fame there by besting that department? A minor defeat in litigation which my suggested judge happily left behind him upon becoming *quaestor*. That senior appointment for which he travelled back to Rome, became enrolled in the Senate before rising through a whole sequence of government posts in quick-fire succession. Such were his merits. So that by the time the senatorial ranks became depleted by another Antonine Plague, I'd suspect that capable men like him were in pretty short supply. Because the brilliant career of Lucius Septimius Severus has advanced ever-more rapidily since... to that glorious conclusion in which we all rejoice."

My right eyelid started to twitch uncontrollably and I had to brace my left leg against the wooden table to stop it from quivering. *Was this real, did he really say that?*

An outcome beyond my control and our very worst nightmare, but surely it couldn't be happening to me.... to have the Butcher of Lugdunum sitting in judgement on my own little case? I would never be able to go before him without thinking of Clodius Albinus – his head put into a sack, wife and children into the Rhone. Even the thought of Severus was enough to make me ill...

Tiro looked sadly across at me over the width of the table, the desperate expression on his face that of a man who knows he'll never win his freedom - while I looked bleakly back, like the man who's just lost it.

'*Fiat justitia...!*" said Paulinus, with a malicious twinkle in his eye. "Next case!"

Ascanius had been right about him after all.

Chapter XXV

I've commented before on that superstitious belief among the uneducated - that you must cross a threshold properly or else bad luck will befall you. But in the case of my own return from the court to our billet in the converted stables at Uxellodunum, it was me who had to be carried bodily out of the carriage and over its threshold by Trenico and Ascanius - such was my state of despair.

Hardly a hero's return.

Or as the dead poet, Martialis, puts it: *"Lis numquam, toga rara, mens quieta"* – 'It's lawsuits never, the toga but rarely, if you'd keep a quiet mind'. Another mantra I've too often breached and now must reap the consequence - akin to nervous breakdown.

My staff were very kind.

Ascanius went down to '*The Retiarius*' and returned with a jug of white, while Tiro sent Rianorix off to town in search of decent food. They and the driver put me onto a couch and then fussed around, in an obvious attempt to improve my mood, pull me out of the doldrums.

I could see that it upset them all mightily to see me so upset, and I also knew that it was my professional duty to pull myself together, restore the morale of my team.

In addition, I felt ashamed and concerned about the effect of my obvious adverse reaction on the client herself, who'd been left to

217

ride back alone with her children to the *duovir*'s farm in the country without those words of encouragement and reassurance which in truth I knew I owed her.

We had three days to prepare for the trial, and here I was - out of it, done. Tiro folded his arms and looked down at me sternly:

"What was it you always said?"

I lifted my chin up from my chest to confront his unrelenting gaze: "Uh? No, Tiro, I don't know what you're on about – what did I always say?"

"*Our first responsibility is to keep the client happy...*' what you always used to tell *me*."

I knew what he meant and felt very guilty: it was the old story of '*Do As I Say, Not As I Do*'. I had to pull myself out of a very deep hole, that's certain, but found it easier said than done. But for Tiro's sake, for my client's, and everyone else's, I knew I needed to manage it. With a superhuman effort, I therefore managed to say: "Yes, I'm sorry, Tiro, and you're absolutely right. I need to see the client. So get Trenico and the driver to bring the carriage-team up. I'll go after her now, follow her back to the farm...."

"What about the food that's coming, Master? Will what's ordered go to waste?"

"No, get Rianorix to plate-it up. I'll eat mine cold once we're back, you lot carry on."

On our way to the farm, we traversed the eastern edge of the city walls, in the usual way, along the usual route. Since Trenico needed us to divert to get some extra supplies, we perforce entered briefly.

This was unfortunate.

Once again the streets were crammed, but this time for a different reason - Samhain was finally upon us and all the native peoples whose festival it was - along with their fattest beasts, whose sale-time it was – were pouring into town to drink and sell stock, clog up the roads. Get more drunk and then fight.

Samhain is - for these coarse gangs of Celtic people who throng the alleyways at Lugvalio - their own special festival, much older than Rome. Framed to celebrate the end of their harvest and the beginning of winter, it marks the coming of that dark time whose onset I most dread, if only for the weather. When the souls of the dead return to old haunts in search of human hospitality, wandering free from their tombs for offerings of food and drink left out for them. When feasts are held to which these souls of the dead are each invited, an empty place left at table.

Even here, inside the cold heart of a Roman frontier metropolis, this festival of the wilder nations felt to me like a weird and liminal time. Where the boundaries or borders between our world and this strange '*Otherworld*' of theirs can so easily weaken, are more easily traversed. A time when it's believed that malign spirits – demons even - exploit the lengthening shadows of dusk to cross unnoticed into ours. When there could be no season darker, no atmosphere more appropriate to mirror my own current mood or else this great battle against evil and its agents which we've come such a long way, cross-country, to fight.

The formalised combat forced upon us by the death of a Roman matron, the virtuous Aurelia. Her period of mourning not even over but the husband already remarried, her ashes laid in a garden only to be trodden by some shameless replacement.

At the roadside, we watched army quartermasters and native cattle-breeders compete in impromptu street-corner auctions to buy cattle for slaughter or saving. Striving to ensure that both the common people and their legions, plus sufficient livestock, can survive a coming winter. And now there's an entire army encamped outside, many times the usual population, I could guess that everyone living within and around this little city would be holding serious concerns of their own about the food supply running out. Or who'll be left to starve?

Knowing there's always that risk, when treating with the army, that - failing an acceptable deal - the soldiers will cut up rough and decide to help themselves. Take it away anyway.

Though the sight to bother me most was unexpected for its resemblance to another livestock market recently seen. Its reminder of Stanwick, as I saw several lines of grim-faced, tattooed men in woollen plaid lope through Lugvalio streets. What Ascanius would probably call a *'hunting party'* – only here there were more of them and quite clearly arrived, if happily unarmed. At least Trenico would know the answer, so I pointed them out and asked him directly: "Are any of these Brigantes?"

"Of course they are, boss, or some of them will be. Britannia's stuffed with mongrel tribes and look, it's Samhain, after all…"

"Not Carvetii, then?"

"Yes, we're in Carvetii heartlands, of course – there'll be loads of *them*. But beyond armed checkpoints on the Wall, there's little else to stop visitors. In from adjoining tribes - come to trade and drink, sell at market, have a bloody good time. *'Up Samhain!'* like local folk say. Don't forget these Brigantes believe themselves a nation and their territory's massive. Vast swathes of it, sitting on both sides of the Wall. And you know their goddess Brigantia ain't fussy, either - she'll accept worship from anyone, even the Roman troops. Why you'll see her image everywhere. So yes, boss, I do think it's likely you'll see plenty of Brigantes round here too - come through for the festival and let loose in the lanes."

"Then we should be giving thanks to the gods, that our army is here in such strength!" my only response to that piece of news.

As a result I felt nearly as glad to exit the walls of Lugvalio as I'd been that strange day at Stanwick, and it was good to be out in the country. We rolled up a long trackway lined with leafless trees towards the farmstead, to find my client reading in a wooden garden-room, tacked onto the side of its house.

The intelligent and educated woman wearing a long robe and wrapped in a mantle who put down her book and rose from a bench to greet me there was willowy and tall.

A stature so unlike her father's that it must have come from the mother but, when she hailed me, my heart seemed to lift to a height, just at the sight of her:

"Ah, Justinus! Whatever happened to you this morning, eh… *advocate*?"

Clive Ashman

There was nothing better I could do than to throw myself on her mercy, apologise if I'd let her down. So I sat down next to her and told her all about Ascanius, his story of survival - what horrors he'd witnessed on Lugdunum Field. And I was equally frank about what terrors his account now wrought in me - discovering only this morning that the Great Malefactor in these terrible atrocities was to be the very judge allocated to hearing our case.

The idea of me... of us, standing-up before Him... maybe even standing-up to Him? I'll admit that it scared me – and she knew.

Her response epitomised kindness. She opened her hand, which was warmer to the touch than you might expect for an autumn day, and placed it straight onto my jawline. Although the weather was hardly that cold, a secret shiver ran through me as she gazed into my eyes with those piercing blue orbs of hers:

"Do not blame yourself, Justinus, this reaction of yours is perfectly understandable. And you're right – it's certainly a grave situation. We've come a long way and it's frustrating to find so many obstacles put before us. Or else to think that justice might be denied because her outcomes are entrusted to an emperor. Or a mass-murderer. But if you ask me, Justinus, I still think we should not let this natural fear rule our judgements, or force us to lose a sense of common purpose. Now Samhain is come, I think that you – me, the whole team – must confront our *'demons'* together. Including this Great One, who is sent here to try us."

I agreed and thanked her for her consideration and encouragement. Advising of my professional view we were still in with a chance – that I retained a viable plan for how to run her case at trial. I also admitted to a ready awareness of how the fear of fear can itself be self-defeating, which was why I was so determined to master these doubts, if only for her sake. To stand up to the demons – even her *'Great Demon'*, as she so wryly put it.

Lydia smiled and gracefully withdrew her comforter's hand from my face - my shudder imperceptible, I'm sure - and said how pleased she was to see how quickly I'd rallied.

"You and I, the people who help us, together we're a team... " she sighed. "Once we cease to think with one heart, we risk

221

everything falling apart. We must never let our determination crumble, because I'm only the latest in a long line of litigators. Like my father did in his day, I want to be able to say to my sons on another that I too fought the law, but this time the law lost."

"We go on, m'lady?"

"We go on, Justinus – whatever it takes!"

Seated together on the bench, I therefore produced the lengthy written witness statement which Tiro had compiled for my client, capturing her discussions with me in the coach during our long journey over the mountains. I handed it over and gave her enough time to read it carefully through first. Then we followed a process of discussing and rehearsing its contents - as I usually do with any client shortly to appear in court. I also provided some additional hints on self-presentation - including how she and her sons should dress, what mannerisms and responses I would want each of them to display at different stages of the trial, when I gave the sign. Plus all the other coaching-tips and hints thought necessary for her to have a persuasive impact on a watching judge and jurors, to achieve a successful outcome in her cause.

"Is there anything else you need to know?" I concluded.

"Yes, Gaius Januarius Justinus, there is." she replied, firmly. "Because I remember earlier conversations where I felt you were holding something back. Aspects to my case you weren't prepared to share with me then – for whatever reason. The same discussions, if you remember, where I made it clear how I'm no longer prepared to spend the rest of my life in subjection to my father. Refuse to be treated as a weaker spirit any longer - just because I'm a woman. But now that you and I are brought to the time of trial – required to confront this *'Great Demon'* together - then it seems to me that, if you want me to do a good job for you as your witness, then it's about time you were more open with me as my lawyer. Shared what you know."

"Very well, m'lady, if you insist on it, then of course I will – and perhaps the right time for full disclosure has arrived, exactly as you say. Though perhaps it won't be what you imagined, more of a shock than you expect – take a deep breath, m'lady!"

She looked at me in understandable alarm but I continued:

"Based on information received from an important witness I intend to use in your case – he was a contemporary of your father's, a close associate at the time – I need to say a little bit more, m'lady, about this notorious litigation your father won against the government, around the time you were born."

"A little bit more? Why's that, Justinus, when you told me before, it's only history now?"

"You asked me something about the woman involved, and why she wasn't executed."

"The one who killed the soldier, got sent to the mines?"

"Yes, you'd asked me why not, and at the time I didn't answer, because it's a question of law."

"Relating to our case?"

"Not here and now, no. Not really, not as such…. "

"So why should it matter to me, Justinus?"

"Well, because - as I think you've already realised, ma'am - if a low status woman like she was – what the law classifies as a *mulier* – if she commits a capital offence like murder, then it's true that the only appropriate punishment has got to be death. Their execution. An outcome which must be right, after all - only fair. Or at the very least, if there were mitigating circumstances in their case, a woman like that might be sentenced to hard labour. The sort of work which will kill you pretty soon anyway."

"Yes, that seems fairly obvious to me, even as a non-lawyer. What else should killers expect – and if that's right, which it must be, then why wasn't she done to death?"

"You see, m'lady, although she was sentenced to a form of hard labour, it…."

"It was only to the salt-works, which has always sounded like a bit of a cop-out to me. So what exactly did she do once she got there?"

"I'm told she worked as a cook…"

"A cook, Justinus… *as a cook*?"

223

"Yes, a cook. Because she couldn't do hard labour."

"She couldn't do hard labour... what sort of a regime is this? Have the authorities gone soft?"

"No, it's the law, ma'am. There's a legal exception."

"An exception, Justinus – so where is all this heading?"

"A *mulier* committing a capital offence can only avoid execution or hard labour, as the prescribed penalties for a serious offence like murder, if she's with child..."

"*With child*? Why do you lawyers always use two words when one will do? You simply mean pregnant, don't you, Justinus?"

"Yes, ma'am, of course I do... pregnant."

Lydia looked at me with her mouth open – not the most attractive I've seen her, I'll admit - but she did not say another word. We sat there in silence for a little while longer like this and I personally thought it better to let her absorb everything I'd said already, before adding to the story. Loading yet more woe.

Eventually, but without more from me, she took the wooden-bound book she'd kept latched on her lap till now and threw it – out through the door of the garden room and onto the lawn outside. Her aim was excellent because it went straight between the door-frame to bounce off a sundial, then fall into the long grass around it. This was also the first time I'd heard Lydia swear, but it took another expletive before she gathered herself to add:

"So this girl of his was expecting. The one he went to so much trouble to rescue?"

"Yes, ma'am, that's correct. She was."

"And so who was the father? No - please don't tell me...!"

"I think you've worked it out."

"This case of ours, Justinus – it's led to so much more than I ever thought..."

"Don't say I didn't warn you, milady. When we started."

"No, you did, and I don't blame you for it. And nor, I suppose, should I blame a lonely soldier, marooned at the ends of the earth – almost *Ultima Thule*. Awaiting an inevitable death."

"Like his presiding gods deserted him?"

"Indeed, Justinus, indeed. I do know that's how he saw it, because he often said so himself. One desertion leading to another and all those hints he'd drop about briefly leaving his post on the *limes*. Like he eventually did with my mother too, I suspect."

"I'm sorry."

"No, it's not your fault, Justinus, so don't apologise. Like he's been a deserter all his life. Is that what you wanted to tell me?"

"Not exactly, milady."

"What else is left to say? Do we know what happened to the slave girl? Or else to this child she was carrying – did either of them survive? Ever live to tell the tale?"

"One of them did, milady."

"*One?* Which one, Justinus, and how? Where are they now?"

I couldn't bring myself to say anymore. I turned and looked into those bright blue eyes of hers and thought I could cry for her myself, but since she'll be doing it soon, I decided that now was the time and - since it's a messy job – one best left to her:

"She's right here in front of me, m'lady."

"*In front...!*" she croaked. "Oh, merciful heavens, Justinus, not the child...?"

"Because it appears your true birth-mother was not the noble Aurelia, this loving person you describe as bringing you up..."

"Not Aurelia...?" she gasped, suddenly grabbing my arm. "Ohhh, no, surely, not...?"

"No, m'lady, I'm afraid not. Your natural mother was in fact a woman of the tribes – known to her people as Caria. A short name that signifies a native Briton, drawn from well beyond the Wall. From a remote, obscure tribe – an upland folk known as the Corionototae. What her people would call a free princess of the blood; we Romans, a chieftain's daughter – and a minor one at that. At least until later, when she became captured by raiders then delivered to your father, sold-on to be his slave..."

"What... my mother was a slave? No, Justinus, you cannot be serious, it would be a scandal! How can you know that – how can you be sure of this, anyway?" she wept inconsolably.

Lawyers of Lugvalio

"I have interviewed the witness who says this in person, ma'am, and consider him a most reliable source. An elderly soldier who served in the north with your father, a long time ago. Whose word is so reliable, in fact, I intend to rely on him at trial."

Without another word, I saw Lydia stand up, dry her eyes, draw her mantle and robe tighter around herself, then sweep out of the reading room into a walled garden without one backward glance.

I reluctantly watched her go but thought it wiser not to follow.

By anyone's standards, this was bitter news to swallow. That morning she'd woken as a patrician but here she was already, by the forenoon a common slave's daughter. Of barbarian stock, but with the blue eyes of Thracia. Consequences and catastrophes borne of some sins of the father, this man who cuts her off now. No wonder they hurt. I knew she'd need some time to come to terms with it - if ever - though I'll admit to my own surprise she never guessed it earlier.

I walked out onto the lawn and picked up that book she'd been carefully reading from and then as wildly thrown away. Wiping loose blades of wet grass off varnished wood, I unlatched its cover to find Marcus Aurelius's *'Meditations'* – collected words and thoughts written down by a philosopher-emperor out in the field. Campaigning with his legions in the forests of Germany. Living in a tent and slaughtering Rome's enemies, even as he contemplates what minor acts of kindness a decent man might manage, within the course of one short life.

Unlocked by a latch, it opened at once where she'd inserted a pheasant feather: *"What are the children of men but as the leaves that drop at the wind's breath?"* her selected section said.

Since it was not intended for me, I shut it at once - carrying the book indoors and back into the garden room as a precious object not deserving to lie outside in wet grass. Replacing the book on a side-table where sunlight could dry it, I turned back towards the doorway to see a small boy standing within the frame looking hard at me. It was Flavius, one of her sons, or maybe Julianus - I'd never quite established which one was which.

"Hullo" I said.

"You've upset my mother" he replied, holding a wooden sword point-upwards in sharp rebuke. More children of men than a warrior, but his mother's fighting spirit.

"I'm sorry, son, she's had some bad news, that's all. Which one are you?"

"I am Flavius - my brother's in the stable, looking at the horses."

"Oh, that's good. Do you like staying here on the farm?"

"I liked it at my grandfather's better - it was better in the town" he said. "But he doesn't seem to want to see us anymore. "

"Oh, I don't know about that... "

"I don't like that woman he's got there. She's silly."

"Grown-ups can be stupid, it's true. Where's your mother gone?"

"She went to the end of the lane, where you see the walls of the city. I think she was crying." He brushed a thick mop of hair away from his eyes using the point of his sword.

"Careful, you wouldn't do that with a real sword!" I commented. "You'd blind yourself."

"Huh!" he said. "You're no soldier – what would someone like you know about any of that? But I know you've upset my mother - I saw her go off, running away from you."

"Don't worry, Flavius, I'll go and find her. Check she's alright. And if I do that, will you go and check on your brother. Make sure he's not been kicked by the horses?"

"Alright" he said and turned on his heel, while I set off down the drive. I followed the track and its skeletal treeline back towards the public road to find her standing by a pair of gateposts at the end, her eyes red-rimmed from weeping. I said nothing at first, just stood next to her, looking silently towards the silhouette of Lugvalio's rooftops in the foreground. White smoke rose lazily from the distant barrack-blocks of Uxellodunum, there on its cliff to our right, and appeared to have her full attention.

Lawyers of Lugvalio

If our situations had been different, indeed in any other circumstance, I might well have put an arm around her – but I understood how doing so could be nothing short of disastrous.

What I practice is law, which is a cold and heartless thing that requires you keep emotions separate. She was my client after all, and it was important not to confuse things. Things were confusing enough already, without me involving her.

So we stood there by the roadside in silence, her designated advocate waiting patiently for a suitable point to arrive where she might thaw and I could break the ice. Which, eventually, she did:

"Oh, Justinus, whatever can I say? What am I to think, whatever can I do? My whole world seems to be falling apart!" she gestured, despairingly.

"I'm really sorry, ma'am, I can see it will be an awful shock. Why I waited such a long time to tell you. Hung back from doing so, until you gave me no choice."

"And, yes, you're right, it's absolutely awful news - a terrible, terrible shock. One I wish I'd never pushed you into sharing…"

"You never knew?"

"No, Justinus, I didn't. Not a clue. So to be told something like this, right out of the blue - that the Aurelia who brought me up was not the mother who gave me life… how could I believe it? Although now that you've told me, it does put me in mind of some strange sensations I remember sometimes having as a child. Half-forgotten ideas I probably suppressed - that things were somehow not how they seemed. I don't know what made me think like that, but I do remember the thought. Some childish sense of anomaly, irregularities I suppose. Something wrong about my father, how I guessed it - if only in dreams. And now I've been proved right, because he's been an utter scoundrel!"

"There is no easy way to deliver news like this…" I said, as a man who's had some practice.

"No, you can say that again. Oh, my word, and for all the Immortal Gods, such a dreadful thing to take in. Though it's a lovely name, I suppose, there's that…"

Clive Ashman

"What is, ma'am - hers or the tribe's?"

"Both, I'd say - and *'lovely'*? Yes, Justinus, I do think you might claim that for *'Caria of the Corionototae'*..." she said bravely, briefly brightening-up. "It has a certain ring to it - princess too, you say? Well if compensation's to be had, then I suppose there's romance in the sound of it. In her whole tragic story, sad as it might be."

"Yes, there was something about her for sure, ma'am. And I'm only glad to hear you see it like that..." I forced a rictus smile.

"Though it's still such a shock for me, Justinus – believing I was Roman, only to discover that I'm not. Not what I thought. Does this make me a half-Celt, into more of *'The Other'*?"

That was a possibility to interest me, help explain some of my more personal reactions to her, but the response I offered was tactful. More rueful, instead: "To be honest, do any of us know what *'Roman'* really means anymore, m'lady? Nowadays... and weren't you half-Pannonian or else a bit Thracian, already?"

"Oh, I don't know. Whatever it means, I'm still beside myself, Justinus. It's far too much to take in..." and she started off crying all over again. (*So this last bit from me clearly didn't help*). Pulling at her clothing in a way I'd hoped to see her later do in court, except that here we've no audience and it's no grist to the mill. Keen to placate her, I tried a different tack instead:

"Take your time..." I hushed: "They say time can be a great healer..." sounding hopelessly weak, straightaway.

"Time, Justinus, time? Huh, what use is that? When the names of Caria and her people – or her tragic, wretched fate - are just history themselves. As ours will soon become. When we all turn into nothing more than history, mere ashes and dust - in time."

"If it's history, ma'am, it's a story integral to your claim. One we need to tell. How your father rescued her from the salt works, then sued the government for her price. Brought her back to Isca after, where I'm sad to say she died. Died in childbirth, died producing you. Where tragedy met kindness, kindness and forgiveness, because your dear Aurelia still took you on, right from a baby. Kept your family secret to the grave."

Lawyers of Lugvalio

"My father used to boast that once, when he was in the Army, he'd abandoned his post and got clean away with it – but he never explained to us the the whys or the wherefores. Even then. But now I suspect we've found the actual answer. Oh, the infamy of it! And as for my poor, dear, dead Aurelia - and forgiveness – well, I think '*loyal*' must have been her middle name. Now that she's gone - you won't desert me, will you, Justinus?"

"Of course not, m'lady – here till our journey's end. Like I always say, you and I will go down with this ship - if need be. That I'll see you through, still be here for you even if we lose. Though I genuinely doubt it will really come to that - not when we've got right on our side and a story to tell which I know your father won't want to hear us telling. Especially not in front of an emperor. No – you can trust me on that score, at least."

Later, when we got home from the farm – thanks to the passion of our encounter and the pleasure I took in her company – I felt oddly enlivened. Despite her distress, more at ease about our whole case and its prospects - invigorated and encouraged by these conversations with a lady, her fierce femininity.

So I walked whistling into our billet back at the stables where, even though it was late, the daylight long-gone, I found Tiro there all alone, writing at his desk with the aid of one, single oil lamp.

"Where's that Rianorix gone, and what about our food?"

I asked him, pretending to be cross. "I'm hungry enough to eat a horse."

Tiro put down his stylus and shrugged his shoulders, like he didn't know. "We could get one from the *Ala*...?" he suggested, straight-faced.

"Maybe he's absconded?" I said, continuing the joke: "Scarpered somewhere to snaffle it, hiding for a feast. What do you think, Tiro, has the ungrateful child simply run away - gone off to scoff the lot?"

"I sincerely hope not, Master..." sighed Tiro "...although with young men today, there's nothing would surprise me."

The particular lad in question would be missing all night.

Chapter XXVI

It was the Praetorians who found him.

Floating in the river, his small body caught amongst the usual raft of autumnal flood-debris which collects beneath the bridge-abutments. Trapped there among the bits of tree and fallen branches, his red hair still shining.

One of their soldiers – who'd got to know us by now and knew where we lodged – had sprinted in full armour up the hill to our billet in Uxellodunum to warn us. Arriving out of breath at the old stable we occupy, he was almost incoherent at first. Once he got his breath back and we got the message, Tiro and I ran frantically back downhill with him. Down to the riverbank where they could point him out.

I've said what I've said about the emperor's bodyguard, but those guys were good to us. Did everything they could to help.

The Praetorians had a light skiff, rowed by eight men, which they use to patrol the river. Moored downstream, nearer the city, they sent a messenger to call it and soon it came up. Once it had been manoeuvred into position beside the cutwaters of the northernmost bridge, an anchor put out, the soldiers onboard used the shafts of their javelins to try and fish him out.

Lawyers of Lugvalio

When the skiff returned to the bank where we waited for them, Rianorix was curled-up amongst the rowers like he's asleep. Two of the Praetorians lifted him out with an ineffable gentleness and care, before delivering him into the arms of Ascanius.

"He's only a kid!" said my bodyguard, silently weeping. Young Rianorix had gone a deathly grey with patches of mottling already, his tunic soaked from the river, though his reddish, curly hair gleamed the more for its water.

There was nothing left we could do.

"What's happened to my boy? Did nobody see anything?" I implored them.

The Praetorians discussed it amongst themselves, and one in their number - who'd been on duty yesterday afternoon - said he thought he'd heard shouting, seen a gang of men chasing another, smaller individual along the far side of the river, before they disappeared into the trees. Nothing more, and beyond his body, we held no other clue. Nor did we need one.

There might have been no direct evidence, no better account of his murder than this, but I still knew who it was who'd been responsible. We'd heard enough threats: Firmus and his supporters club, those louts who congregate at his door every morning. City thugs and toughs who do their master's bidding.

Done for a warning to us.

As soon as we'd got his little body back to the stables, wrapped in a soldier's cloak, I turned to Ascanius:

"Bring me Longinus Matigus!" I croaked in a hoarse voice and then I said it again, once I'd got my breath back better:

"Bring me Longinus Matigus. Go straight to Voreda, Ascanius, Ride with all speed with a full team and bring him back to us alive! We must get him to shelter and then keep him safely, hidden here until the time of trial."

I suppose out of habit, Ascanius stood up from the child's crumpled body and saluted me like it had been a proper military order. I laid my ring-bedecked hand on his shoulder, like it was:

"Go from here, Decimus Ascanius, go at once to Voreda in a closed carriage without another moment's delay. Escort the veteran Longinus Matigus safely back to Uxellodunum without one of our opponents – let alone their tame thugs in the city – noticing the pair of you. Not even guessing for one glimmer that we've got him on our side. Because I want to know he's alive."

"I go…." he said, turning to the door with tears in his eyes.

"Do not waste another moment getting there, Ascanius…" I said, repeating myself, so great was my grief and inner agitation:

"Because if I am to win this case for m'lady - whether she knows it or not – the outcome of this whole wretched affair depends on us keeping Longinus Matigus alive. Safely hidden in a total state of secrecy. So that he can survive alive to appear before a court as our one key witness, come the time of trial. Because now we really know! After all this, after what they've done to Rianorix, then we know for certain that we cannot allow this so-called centurion, this brute Marcus Firmus - or any of his hounds – to get near to any one of us again. Nor let them get their hands on another of our comrades, not one. No, Ascanius - not ever again – so go!"

"I go…." he repeated, and went.

A sword unsheathed in his hand.

A flagrant breach of the law on its way.

Lawyers of Lugvalio

Chapter XXVII

Without realising at the time what I was doing - or that this was where Destiny and the Fates would take me; such separate worlds collide - I had spent almost my whole adult life in reading, writing, and studying our codes of Roman law. In order to equip me - for better or worse – to withstand those terrifying demands it would make of me in one momentous trial. Where I would stand up inside an impromptu northern courtroom before the Master of The World, sole emperor of Rome, to argue - against every odd - for mine and my client's cause, our future very existence.

My senior clerk's freedom.

Why it is, from that standpoint of exquisite terror in which we found ourselves that day, I exhort you young people for whom life seems interminable - the lures of love, lust and idleness irresistible - to write and study all you can. So that you may speak sense when you need to and it's become vital - speak-out when you must. If only to save your own life - or another's by your efforts - come the testing time of trial.

This trial we had come for. Beyond the bridges, we used a corrugated track to access the Green Zone, usually joining it where the land dips steeply on entering the bowl. Seeing its familiar arena before us once again, we already understood how the courtroom convened for our hearing was not today a tent.

Lawyers of Lugvalio

Because the Emperor Lucius Septimius Severus Pertinax Parthica Augustus Maximus might have been about to enter Caledonia, bring terror to the savages, but he was not a well man.

Gout and the northern weather had together seen to that.

So the judicial legate's draughty, leather pavilion had been dispensed-with and their new heated bathhouse requisitioned from the *Ala Petriana* instead. Cleaned out inside.

I marched into the bathhouse at the head of my team, under a red sandstone lintel crowned with elaborate inscriptions, one of them dedicated to an emperor's remarkable wife. Its *'Julia Domna, Mother of The Empire'* adding her touch of inimitable grandeur to the hallway of a functional military building. And my hope that the impact of certain live evidence I intended calling might contribute a not-dissimilar effect towards my client's cause.

Make no mistake, a proper entrance is important – and, no, I don't mean the architecture, because every courtroom is theatre. Since if you'd do trials, you've got to be a showman. Where eloquence won't work, if it turns up in rags.

Why, apart from a better toga - but against my usual habit - I'd also spent some time improving my appearance and to shed the smell of horses. Fully-bathed and freshly-barbered only that morning, my hair slicked-back and beard shaved away, I'd paraded through the Praetorian's checkpoint like an incoming ambassador. Wearing every expensive ring I possess, and a few that were less so, in the hope they would add to impressions.

Because if you'd win at court, then it's important to look like a winner – and I meant to paint that picture from the outset.

Tiro and Ascanius preceded me, clearing a way through the crowd – followed by myself, then our attendants marching in line. Sennovarus and Sulio were come along to take notes, while Aulus Equitius – who without his beloved mules feels bereft, has no role - was only included to increase our total number. Though so well-dressed you might think him a jurist, but never a farrier.

Finally, and bringing up the rear, trotted Tocitanus and Trenico, porting my trial-gear in wooden trunks upon their shoulders.

Clive Ashman

"Oh, Justinus, you look wonderful!" said my lady, when we met outside the building. Which was pleasing to hear but ironic, because today she most definitely didn't. Following my express instructions of the day before to the letter, she'd worked very hard against it - looking like a ruin.

"My champion!" she added, gripping my arm till it hurt.

All of the benches in the hall were taken, while there was an additional ring of people standing many bodies deep around the walls of what was a fairly-spacious interior anyway. Portable screens had been set up in an attempt to shield the intended courtroom area from other, less-salubrious aspects to its normal daily usage, like the soldiers' graffiti down its walls, bad air from their latrines. The tribunal itself stood as tightly-filled, what with the emperor reclining in a litter, ministers and bodyguards clustering closely round its dais. Even the upper galleries marking each end of the hall were packed-out with men and women leaning over the rails to see and hear whatever went on.

With all their chattering, doing the first was easy, the second more difficult already.

Every category of society was here, talking loudly and excitedly to each other: every class and age - from soldiers and civilians to courtiers and princes. Freedmen, tribesmen, citizens and slaves; fathers and mothers, sons and daughters. Standing together on tip-toe in excited expectation, awaiting a unique spectacle for these parts. Come to watch the *'Emperor of All The World'* condescend, if only from boredom, to try a local case himself. Contentious in nature, brimful of scandal - of titillating titbits - and save only the arrival of the Imperial host, its army of soldiers or courtiers, the biggest thing to happen in Luguvalium *for years*?

Forty-five lay jurors – what we jurists call *'judges'* – would sit to hear the case, for that was the correct number to be appointed from an agreed list of Lugvalio citizens. I say *'agreed'*, when the likely reality would be that my client and I – not being local – could not recognise one single name from their official voter's list we should object to. Leaving the majority chosen likely to be yet more placemen of Firmus, unbenonced to us.

237

Lawyers of Lugvalio

Biased against us to a man - like that grim-faced one at the end, who crossed his arms and splayed his knees the moment we came in. Fixing me with such a steely stare and glare of defiance, I should know from the outset that whatever fact I mentioned, whatever laws we cited or evidence adduced, there was nothing we could ever say or do to persuade a man like he was. And if my suspicions were right about him, then here's another increment in steepness to this vertical ice-cliff we'd set ourselves to climb.

Aside from the jurymen, but in front of the tribunal itself, a large crowd of advocates gathered on both sides, with only myself and Eurythmus actually attending as actors. The rest being a cloud of unemployed Lugvalio lawyers, milling around in tatty togas worn for show. There simply to be seen - or see how it's done.

The Emperor Severus looked down at me from where he reclined full-length on a luxurious litter, carried into the hall by his bearers then placed onto the raised dais from which he'll shortly hear our case. I knew this autumn would be his sixty-third on the surface of this earth, but I'll never forget looking-up into those limpid, melancholy, soulful brown eyes of his.

So ageless, yet so puzzlingly incompatible with the countless piles of Roman dead over which, during those years of inexorable ascent from Pannonia to the imperial throne, I knew he'd clawed his way. From the banks of the Issus to Lugdunum or Lugvalio. Those heaps of corpses which were to him no more than convenient ramps. A useful *glacis* of butchered remains over which he and his dreadful sons are forever condemned to clamber, creating only more. Bred for strife and chaos, the three of them, but answerable to no-one. Not even God?

I looked up at him and he looked down at me, then I thought he gave me the nod - like a gladiator licensed to kill. So I rose to my feet, drawing my freshly-laundered toga around me and taking a slow, steady breath in standard orator's style. To my amazement, my eyelid didn't twitch and my leg didn't quiver - I felt as cold as ice. Although inside me I still cried for Rianorix, I felt oddly, coolly, cruelly determined to win, but would never let it show.

Clive Ashman

Though my fear had been silenced, it still lived.

The room fell silent too.

"This case is brought on behalf of Lydia Firma, and I hope this most honourable and fair-minded of tribunals will find it worthy of their distinguished attention - if only because of my lady client's high position, the singular character and merits of our case, and the importance of the outcome of this trial which you are about to hear for her future financial well-being, not to mention her two fine sons, Flavius and Julianus, continuations of the line. The lady Lydia is herself a person of high birth, married to a man of praetorian rank, a distinguished servant of the state, but - as a woman - owning nothing. And unfortunately, as the gravamen of our complaint will state and the court will shortly hear, also recently disinherited of the whole family estate by her octogenarian father. By the man you see before you today - our first respondent, your regional centurion, Marcus C. Firmus. A lamentable decision by him which represents his to my mind, unconscionable, final act in what may seem – or as you members of the jury may assess them to be - an impetuous, if not utterly-demented series of actions by him. Primitive impulses to which he as respondent reverted in the course of senile turmoil, following the death of his faithful first wife – the noble and much-missed Aurelia, my claimant client's late but loving mother."

A sentimental sigh and another ripple of arm-crossing went around the walls and a few jurors as they digested that much for a start, and then I resumed: "Within eleven days after the death of the noble Aurelia, our defendant of today, Marcus C. Firmus, the grieving widower, had in one fell stroke – as he will say and I regret to report - fallen violently in love, married a second time as a result, and granted Lydia Firma a step-mother half her age. At the same time, and for good measure – *'by bronze and scales'* as the legal phrase has it – making that bogus new will disinheriting her which we've come here to challenge today. My client therefore suing for her father's effects in the Courts instead - against both him and the new stepmother, our second-named respondent."

Lawyers of Lugvalio

At this natural pause, Eurythmus leapt to his feet, only to assume a half-bowing, half-cringing posture before the bench, while offering his snide suggestion:

"Before my friend goes on any longer, will your Majesty be wanting to impose a time limit on the length of our speeches? To mitigate any unnecessary prolixity, his exuberant verbosity. Will you want water-clocks, my lord?"

Ouch. It seemed that what Eurythmus was really trying to do was sap the momentum from my opening, whatever early traction I'd be gaining with the jury, but it's certainly true that a custom has developed in the courts for counsel to request, and judges to grant, an individual time-limit for advocates' speeches of only two water-clocks. Or even one apiece. With a really grumpy judge, you might only get half-a-clock. Reactions to this rule vary, as those who plead prefer to get their speeches over and done with, rather than go on pleading; while those on high, obliged to listen to them, just want to survive that bit as quickly as possible, concentrate on reaching the right decision by its end.

Severus turned to me with the pleasantest of smiles, a man without conscience: "We've heard a brief summary in opening from you already, Justinus. Do you expect to be much longer – or will we need the clocks?"

"Not for my opening, no, my lord, I very much hope you won't. And the position is neatly summarised in a set of facts already agreed with the legate: namely that my client, the lady Lydia, is sole surviving natural progeny of our first respondent, the centurion Marcus Firmus, a man recently widowed. Remarrying within eleven days of his loss, he cuts our claimant client off from her inheritance in favour of his new wife, the second respondent. These are the outline facts exactly as agreed - while our pleadings will say that it's wrong, why your court is invited to rule."

"So how does this set of agreed facts translate to your final question for trial as the legate, Paulinus, chose to formulate that item?"

Clive Ashman

"His actual question, Majesty, as it was framed by your judicial legate for this jury of citizens to try, is equally concise. It runs along these lines: *"The agreed question for this court is whether the testator Marcus Firmus's present will should be declared null and void, and the testator ordered, under compulsion, to show adequate provision is made in his current will for his natural daughter, Lydia Firma, to an extent specified by the court?"*

"I see. A question which seems factually clear enough, but allows me some discretion. So what might be the technical legal issues, invoked along the way?"

"From the point of view of my client, lord, and this question recited, not many. The main argument is practical. About whether the present form of Firmus's will makes sufficient provision - in this case, for his only surviving offspring, his daughter, and the two young grandsons. We say that it doesn't. While from a jurist's viewpoint, you might argue that it's also about what we lawyers would call *'testamentary capacity'*..."

"A concept I understand, but - for the sake of helping the jurors - would you like to define it for them?' Severus enquired.

Another pleasant, reasonable request, delivered politely - though not to be argued with anyway, coming from someone so used to getting his way. From this courteous man my Lydia dubbed *'The Great Demon'* during conversations at the farm and, per Ascanius, was his *'Butcher of Lugdunum'*. For that one fleeting moment neither felt right, so seductive the power of his aura.

"Yes, Majesty – can I respectfully suggest the jurors might ask themselves this extra question also, in light of the evidence: *'Did he know what he was doing, when he made and signed-off the will?"*

"Yes, I agree that sounds right – did you hear that, members of the jury, hear what he said? Because I think that question will suit us, too. So tell me, Justinus - to address it, how do you intend to present the rest of your case, because I haven't got all day."

Born in Leptis Magna, that day's judge might be known to some as *'The African'* but if his complexion was darker than poorer people like me - forced to live in northern climes and so rarely seeing sun - it remained hard to say whence his own bloodline had sprung. (Despite that forked beard). Whether Punic, Phoenician, Syrian or Berber, Severus could be a mix of all four - or of many other peoples - maybe of none? Was he even Roman?

Enough to make him more 'Other' than the Corionototae, then? Oh, no, I doubt anyone could be that...

So I looked upon his composed, equable features and as calmly replied: "If it please you, my lord, and the court will consent, then the way I'd hope to tackle it is this. Beginning with my client, I will rely on her testimony, given in person, to acquaint the court with her and her family's history, detail our grounds for her claim."

"You intend to call her?" he said, like it mattered not to him – as it probably wouldn't.

"Of course, sir. In fact, my lord, I must. Or rather I ought - if your court will grant her a voice..."

"Any other testimony we should expect?" he asked me, gently again, with that faintly Punic lisp. Pleasantly soft.

"Just one more person, my lord - called to establish a few elements of historical background which I'll contend to be relevant." *When half an advocate's role is to throw dust in the eyes of the jury, here's some grit I'd keep in my pocket for later.*

"Military history, perhaps? If so, Justinus, I'd look forward to that. Since the first-named respondent was a soldier once, was he not...?"

"Some of it will be - and, yes, indeed he was, my lord... a veteran."

"I do enjoy hearing about things like that you know, Justinus. Being a bit of a soldier myself."

"Majesty, indeed, though I fear there will be nothing to compare remotely with your own illustrious achievements. Though you are correct, lord, since it will concern the respondent's...."

"My first client will object..." whined a hunched figure to my right, hardly daring to look the tribunal in the eye. "May it please Your Imperial Majesty...!"

Clive Ashman

For himself, Severus barely acknowledged Goatface - only remarking: "Well, we'll cross that bridge when we get to it...."

While I thought to myself how unwise Eurythmus would be, in attempting any sort of argument before a man with thirty legions at his back. Ready at his beck and call, and enough to frighten anyone. Anywhere.

Firmus's equivalent would be his paid-for supporters club, rammed in a body down the rear of the gallery. His *claque*, who misunderstood and compounded their advocate's error - announcing themselves into the bargain - by cheering coarsely at this point. Punching the air like Eurythmus had scored. An ill-judged intervention which - very visibly, I'd say - displeased our presiding officer not a little, an emperor as it happens. Their crass ululation reminding me of Rianorix: prompting me to wonder who among this *claque* behind us was directly responsible, if not active in his death - aside from their patron, himself?

Under normal rules, I would have made a longer speech – and then the defence likewise, followed by the evidence of witnesses – but this was hardly a normal case.

Our procedures were made-up, invented. Obliged to follow the random whims of an emperor instead – to concentrate on keeping him entertained, field his interruptions. If the jury got convinced of anything along the way, then all to the good, so much the better, but that was incidental. It certainly made my job much harder, because this was a trial like no other - one whose conventional structures and sequenced submissions had been abandoned already to humour a uniquely-powerful judge.

Nearly a God.

"Do you wish me to continue, my lord?" I asked him.

"Yes, I do – but for one other little question, before we get going. About the effects of inheritance tax..."

"*Vicesima Hereditarum*, lord?"

"Correct, Justinus, because I imagine that you, as a practitioner in estates, will be intensely aware – as I find all the officers of my *fiscus* are - that the inheritance tax on death, as levied by our government, comes in at fifty per-cent of the total value of any inheritance?"

"It does, my lord, but only if and when the bequest is made to persons other than the testator's direct descendants. In our case, *not* if it's made to a lineal daughter."

"Correct. But if your first respondent, Firmus, leaves it all to your second, to Metella on death, then half of his estate would be lost to the family straightaway anyway. Given over to the state?"

"That would become true, my lord."

"You realise where I'm driving… and that I've soldiers to pay?"

"I do, my lord, and thank you for your great frankness. There's no doubt it must add extra poignancy to my poor efforts at persuasion, if my client's cause is to be argued before the state's most senior guardian of a limited public purse. But just like poor Sysiphus, that is the boulder I'm obliged to push uphill in your imperial presence, my lord."

When he let me continue, I got on with the case – whatever the odds stacked against us. To which by now should be added another, in the form of a greedy exchequer.

I will not stretch your patience further by repeating here everything which I said then, because by now you will have heard every relevant fact from me already. Only to state that - fired-up by all the promises I'd made to my client, and the lamentable sight of her down there in the well of the court, her mourning rags torn as she clutched them, stained by the outflow of tears - I gave free play to my indignation, to my anger, and to so many other resentments on her behalf, that the whole audience fell utterly silent. Even their emperor.

That silence into which she bravely stepped next, primed to give evidence before them as our principal witness. Tutored so thoroughly in her tragic demeanour that - when called-on to testify and (*in answer to my question*) mentions her late mother - she can produce without prompting, hold-up for the jury, an artist's framed portrait of a much older woman. *I cannot vouch for its likeness to Aurelia but the effect was deeply moving - onlookers wept.*

Clive Ashman

Whilst when I asked about her sons – young Flavius or Julianus - she would take each one of them in her arms and force their tousled heads (*gratifyingly tousled by now, so long without a trim*) deep into her bosom. To an extent which - and in another, private context - I might easily have envied; although it served only to mortify both of her boys, whatever else it did for the jury.

All of it powerful stuff, and I was pleased to see that we were making some headway, signs of jurors starting to crack. To the point there were already a few among the jury - grown men indeed - who were weeping while I paced up and down right in front of them. Tearing at my own clothes like she'd done at hers, disordering my hair. Piling on the agony for everyone because I knew we dare not lose - as I invoked every precedent, called down every law, implored every God. Gave it all I'd got.

Like that metaphorical ship of refuge I'd promised for Lydia, this speech of mine sailed along with a favourable wind in its sails, an audience rapt in the palm of my hand. And as was said of Demosthenes' speech on behalf of Ctesiphon, so it is admitted by those close friends and supporters able to witness my performance, that damp October day in a bathhouse of the Ala Petriana, this speech I gave there transcends *almost everything* I ever attained in a courtroom. From that day to this.

Its flow not even stemmed when, in the midst of my most eloquent and highfaluting passages, I was obliged to divert into cold calculation instead. To illustrate how cruelly reduced and bitterly straitened my client and her two, fine sons would become, without the modest proceeds of her father's estate to sustain them over the storm-tossed seas of life. Its onerous expenses.

Or as my client put it herself, in her main evidence to the jury:

"My greatest fear in life is that should I end up with no money. My boys and I left with nowhere safe to live…"

I could not have put it better myself, so that as I called to my clerks for counters and they cleared a space on the table to deploy them, for one passing moment this court of law became translated into a kind of private counting-house.

Lawyers of Lugvalio

Leaving a jury watching-on finally to understand that this claim of hers was about much more than sentiment or those traditional duties owed by a *paterfamilias* to his most dutiful of daughters. Its theme more about survival – not to mention cold, hard cash.

"Tell me, Justinus, do you consider this is a case likely to fall into that special class described by Thrasea, the kind of decision suitable to set precedent?" asked Severus.

Precedent! How my heart leapt at the thought. As I expect it did for Firmus, who'd won that trophy before. But the one heart whose reaction I could never expect to guess - assuming he even had one - was that of Severus himself.

I knew I would have to think quickly, calculate on my feet, because an emperor with armies to feed, Praetorians to garland with gold, needs every penny. Why, he'd had senators murdered for the sake of their estates, just to confiscate wealth, and I didn't want him thinking that Lydia getting her hands on her father's might be thought by us lawyers to set any sort of trend.

To win glory with lawyers be damned, what I most wanted with Lydia was for me to win it *with her*. So my answer was instinctive but - even as I gave it - I knew I never did anything finer. Cutting myself off forever from any chance of professional immortality, I flung my counters down onto the table:

"No, my lord - of course not. And it won't!" I thundered. So much for glory and fame. Tiro watched me sit down, his face a picture of disbelief, but I only winked secretly back.

"Well, I think that's quite enough for one day" said Severus.

"Court rise!"

Everyone present leapt to their feet and bowed as his bearers raised the emperor's litter, before it and his glittering cortege filed through the hall and out of the entrance, followed by an entourage of soldiers and ministers, the jury dispersing after.

Clive Ashman

While my staff packed our effects away for Tocitanus and Trenico to uplift, Goatface came across to me with a supercilious expression fit to rearrange his few tufts of grey hair with:

"You know you're going to lose, don't you, Justinus? The emperor can't let you win, and – even on the facts – you haven't got a prayer. My client, the regional centurion, is entitled to do what he wants with his own property and no court is going to allow a mere *woman* to interfere with that basic right."

"Sorry, Eurythmus, but it's you who'll be the loser. I'll give you fair warning – if you let this case continue, if Marcus Firmus does not settle tomorrow, if he won't agree his daughter's entitlement, then I'm going to take him apart. Destroy his reputation."

"Ha, that's complete rubbish! What can *you* do? My client is a very distinguished man - you've nothing on him. How could you? So why don't you and your client just go home, Justinus - get back to Eboracum where you belong? Before it's too late…"

That evening, I walked with Tiro along the top of the high cliff at Uxellodunum and past the southern gate to the fort, to beyond the ditches. It had recently rained and the ground was still damp, but a fresh westerly cleared the air.

We stood in silence beside the small, square mound of beaten earth now marking the place where we buried Rianorix last night, in as close an approximation to the rituals of his people as we could reasonably imagine or devise. From up here he would always enjoy a unique panorama - through tall pine trees and southwards towards that distant tail of spinal mountains we'd crossed together on the way from Eboracum, what seemed ages ago. That same remembered range of rolling blue hills over which - or so we hoped - we'd soon be returning in safety, ourselves.

"You close our case tomorrow, Master" he asked. "How will it end?"

"I honestly do not know, Tiro. It rests with the gods."

"Have we been dutiful enough for them – observed enough ritual, sacrificed when we ought?"

Lawyers of Lugvalio

"I'm no sacerdoter, Tiro, only a lawyer. The only ritual I really know. Though they do say the gods love a trier, and surely we've done enough between us, at least to claim that badge? Once Silenus and Rianorix became our sacrifice, I don't think there's any god going could ask us for more. The gods will surely know it, but we've nothing left to give. We're through."

Over the river meadows spread out below the cliff, we had a marvellous birds-eye view. Eastwards over the leather tents of Severus's newest legion, laid out in regular rows and interspersed with roadways. Hundreds of men swarming around and over them like so many ants, taking down tents and carrying their equipment to long lines of waiting mules.

"What's going on down there?" I asked him.

"Those men we see below are a detachment of Legio II Parthica. I'm told they're moving-out soon, starting from tomorrow. Going up to find the rest of their legion in a new forward base at Trimontium. Getting ready for Spring."

"But why leave now, so late in the year – when they looked pretty settled?"

"Haven't you heard, Master? Apparently there's been another outbreak of the sweating sickness, in the camp below. Their commander blames the low-lying location, saying it's unhealthy - too damp at night. Mist off the marshes. So now everyone's moving out, just to get away from the river. Marching further north to rejoin the rest of their battle-group. Once they've packed-up their tents, I suppose they might as well."

"It'll be cold up at Trimontium."

"Have you not noticed, Master? It's getting colder for us here."

Chapter XXVIII

When we returned in strength to the Green Zone for the second day of our trial, the crowds had grown even bigger, allowing fewer ordinary citizens to access the bathhouse and watch us. The balance inside would be taken-up by privilege, major figures from court - once word got around that here's a bit of a show, a more entertaining way to spend another wet day in Lugvalio than by pacing-out pavilions.

Two lines of Praetorians formed a walkway for us through the centre of this mob, using the shaft and butt of their javelins to keep spectators back, while myself and my contingent marched in a stone-faced, single-file procession straight through their middle.

Heading towards the main entrance of the Ala's red sandstone bathhouse and always facing forward, never looking to left nor to right for fear of a fight, we aim directly for the door. And if we would claim sanctuary beneath its inscribed '*Julia Domna*', then first we are obliged to endure a closer inspection by the crowd.

Run the unpredictable gauntlet of their pity, ire, or ordure:

Lawyers of Lugvalio

"That's the prosecution that is, you can tell by his rings… Gold, that one - judging by the size of it."

"Oh, just look at her, poor soul – and you should have seen how she looked yesterday. Even worse…"

"What a mess she's got herself into! Such a state and no wonder… cast adrift by her father, the dirty old dog…"

"There you are – that's him. Her lawyer, Gaius Justinus. They say he's supposed to be good…"

"No wonder her dad wrote her out, she looks a right ruin… Really let herself go…"

"What a bunch, the whole lot of them. Fighting with family! Swanning around with fancy lawyers, more money than sense…"

"Are those her boys? Proper young men – but, oh, to see them now! Dressed only in rags, lank locks to their shoulder…"

"Who'd have thought it was their own gran'pa what would write them out – I mean, how could he do it? I just hope he rots in Hades, him and his strumpet…"

"There's that lying bastard Justinus. Chuck something at him, will you, lads? The smug bastard, should've got him last night…"

Happily no missiles came but my client disliked the scrutiny, whether for herself or her sons, though worse would surely follow, once we got inside. Our case for the disinherited resuming that morning, a continuing ordeal for my client which would include the other side and their speech in defence. But first we must stand for the arrival of the emperor – an elaborate set piece.

A protective screen of Praetorians filed into the hall first, then formed a ring of armour round the dais, followed by the emperor himself on his litter, carried by eight muscular slaves - Ethiopians, I guessed them. Once they'd set him down in his presiding position atop the tribunal, then members of his immediate family; his ministers and courtiers, the eunuchs and clerks; could process in order of seniority into the courtroom to take up preordained positions around him. Where the closer an individual stood, the higher would be their place and status in these complex hierarchies of the Imperial Household - that much was clear.

Clive Ashman

This would be a memorable day for us anyway, but - aside from the case – it will stay imprinted in my memory forever, because it was on this wet October day in Lugvalio, the second of our trial, that I first saw the Empress Julia Domna in person.

Come along with her son, the Augustus Antoninus – *'Caracalla'*, as he likes to be known - though he's not yet arrived at this party.

The Empress herself I knew only from her head and shoulders, as shown on coins – but I can certainly confirm that all those elaborate hairstyles stamped out by the Mint are authentic. Though I cannot offer you any more useful technical description of how exactly she wore it that day in Lugvalio, suffice to say that she looked undeniably lovely, and dripping with jewels.

Leaving my client beside herself with awe and pleasure just to be *'In Her Radiant Presence'* - whatever other jeopardy Lydia and I might find ourselves facing later-on, as the day unfurled.

Beside Julia Domna's role as a fashion trend-setter for ladies everywhere, across our whole empire, everyone in that room would know of her fabled background as a Syrian-born aristocrat, born of a long line of priests. Officiates in yet another of those peculiar eastern cults you know I don't approve of – Baal, I think, was hers.

By the time she married him, Septimius Severus was already a middle-aged widower, his empress-to-be only sixteen. An outcome that wasn't by chance, because Severus had gone out of his way and out to the east, specifically seeking her hand - after hearing how a fortune-teller told Julia she'd one day marry a king. Highly superstitious himself but not yet anything of the sort – a mere provincial governor - this was just the sort of thing to fascinate someone like Severus, the fish that bit on her bait.

Once he'd hunted her down to Syria, become rapidly entranced, it was just a matter of bringing her back to Rome to be married - where they say her appearance, wit, and intelligence charmed everyone else just as much. Undeniable personal qualities equally useful for keeping her alive throughout the murderous politics which characterised her husband's subsequent rise to the purple.

251

Lawyers of Lugvalio

Not least of which was her beauty - as apparent inside this impromptu courtroom of Lugvalio, on that day of our trial.

Entering the main hall of the *Ala*'s bathhouse, converted for our temporary benefit, Julia Domna went immediately to where the emperor reclined on a dais at its end. Straightaway showing herself most attentive, plumping-up his cushions and stroking his grey, curly hair. Together they made such an affectionate picture of devoted married bliss, it looked good enough to paint - and we'd all seen similar on walls. Official portraits of Severus and family - all smiles (if not his boys) and so serene, you'd think them equals in innocence.

That was when the door at the far end of the bathhouse opened again and a burly figure dressed in the arms and armour of a general swaggered into the room, all eyes pivoting to him. A response which clearly gratified him but would be required anyway, because this was Caracalla. His progress to the dais marked by a shimmering sequence of abject genuflection from every courtier and civil servant he encountered on the way. And once he arrived before the tribunal itself, all the Praetorians presented arms and stood to attention, their eyes on the ceiling.

The other thing that happened in the hall was how the temperature plummeted, but I didn't believe this was just because he'd left a door open. No, I would say there was always a definite chill to accompany Caracalla – that followed him round the room like a ghost, would hang around in his presence like miasma.

The temperature of terror.

Never was youth born into more privileged circumstance, his whole life spent in luxurious expectation of that ultimate power which – even from childhood – he knew would come his father's way. Yet never was there living person upon whose countenance was seen more clearly carved - as if in written words - those extreme cruelties and hatreds; all-consuming resentments; spiteful unpredictability, so fundamental to his nature. That beast which raged within, settling his brow into one permanent snarl.

Truly, the face of a predator - even a demon?

Clive Ashman

"The common enemy of mankind" is what Ascanius had called him, that time we crossed the Eden. And in fairness to my veteran of the Sixth, I understood this dangerous indiscretion for the product of older hurts – hatreds for which it's hard to blame him.

Although I doubt so unwieldy a description out the mouth of a common soldier could be his own invention? But wherever he got it from, that's certainly how he put it. And if I told Ascanius off for it later, we all knew exactly what he meant. Understood it precisely – would not demur. Because there was not a man, woman, nor child present in that hall on that morning for whom Caracalla might not present an immediate personal threat – prove actively lethal. Exactly how it felt, from that very moment when he burst into the room, for everyone else who was there.

Why we all froze.

As if to prove my prejudice, I watched the young prince saunter late onto the dais, red leather strips on his shoulders bouncing off a shiny cuirass, where he went at once to stand by his father. For one fleeting, happy moment comprising the perfect family group. A tableau – the empress standing there to one side, just to the emperor's right. Her son behind his father, our senior Augustus, right there to his left. Leaving all that we missed from the set being Geta himself - his brother's hated sibling.

Severus must have realised what an attractive composition they created – like I say, there are always plenty of copies available on canvas or board, commissioned by the state for distribution around a loyal empire. Hung in the tax-office and how usually captioned: *"Our Dear Imperial Family - Duty and Devotion."*

That's when Severus made his miscalculation, tried to reinforce this effect. Reclining awkwardly on an elevated litter but with his eldest son standing directly behind him, the emperor raised his left arm and moved it towards him. Sending a hand back to his son's shoulder or forearm, but what it met with was armour. As a gesture, one I'd imagine honestly intended for a father's statement of paternal affection, perhaps imperial approval, but the point in this manoeuvre where things went so horribly wrong.

Lawyers of Lugvalio

Maybe youth felt embarrassed by age but, whatever the excuse, Caracalla brusquely pushed the emperor's hand away and then - forming his own hands into one circle – applied them to his father's neck, grimacing while he did. Whether it was intended as horseplay or not, here was shocking spectacle. For us mere mortals to witness '*The Master of All The World*' suffering his own beloved son and heir to place both of his hands around the father's neck, as if in mock strangulation... Was it even meant?

The silence which descended upon the hall at this dreadful prospect was total – everyone stunned, but no-one daring to breathe. Curling our toes.

Its chill became ice, but then that awful moment was gone. A treasonous tableau disintegrating before us almost as quickly as created – once Caracalla let go, his father withdrew the arm, and our beautiful '*Mother of the Empire*', Julia Domna, herself had intervened, by tapping her son playfully on his bronze breastplate, making a gentle report.

"Family, eh?" she trilled lightly, laughing soundlessly as if this sort of thing went on all the time, in the Imperial Household at least. Which - as we more cynical suspect - it very probably does.

"You're only being provocative, I know you don't mean it!" she added. *While speaking for myself, I thought that he probably did.*

The technical lawyer's term for proceedings held before an imperial magistrate is '*cognito extraordinem*', but these had turned into extraordinary proceedings in every other sense as well. From the nature of my client's claim to the unique choice of judge imposed on us. Or our remarkable venue for trial: in this converted military bathhouse on the rim of a natural arena, at the outer edge of empire. And that's even without counting this latest intervention – by an out-of-control, not-so-sweet prince.

But it seemed to me then that the more bizarre and incredible, difficult and unfavourable, each element to our little struggle became, the more determined myself and my team, my noble and courageous client, would together grow. The more we would pick ourselves up and buckle-down afresh, to that point where I could not have asked any one of them to do any more.

And so it went on – as we returned to the case. Because I'd spoken last yesterday, it became Eurythmus's turn. Goatface got up on his hind legs and began the peroration:

"By way of introduction, Majesty, I will say that although this speech of mine will be a long one, I rise in the hope it will meet with as kind a reception from Your Imperial Majesty as might have done a short one. Because in this delicate matter of my client's daughter's unprincipled challenge against that settled authority and legal possession over which any citizen, and this gentleman in particular, should expect their entitlements to stand assured under our law - in this challenge to the rights of a *paterfamilias* in particular; someone who is both a distinguished veteran, an officer ranked as regional centurion, but also a man stricken with the wisdom of years - then I may be confident, my lord, in how conscientiously your honourable court and this jury will weigh her claim and those issues. Just as I also trust this tribunal will surely conclude, Majesty, by thoroughly rejecting each and every one of his vindictive and disgruntled daughter's worthless arguments as being contentions unfit for a sensible court's further toleration. For you may rest assured, Majesty, that – however far my opponent may have strayed - I shall myself remain diligent in how closely my own response to the claimant advocate's flimsy opening will adhere to the Athenian model. Since I may sincerely promise you, my lord, how gratified you will feel at discovering your interest renewed by the fullness and history of my subject-matter and the neat way in which you will find it divided-up. By my limited collection of only the most necessary digressions, and your undoubted pleasure as a general in hearing about my client's long military service and well-deserved honours. Satisfactions I can promise this court, when it encounters only those categories of eloquence most necessary to an orator. And whilst I've no intention of criticising my opponent here, I expect your court's approval of my own professional techniques to grow greater, if only for their contrast with his..."

Lawyers of Lugvalio

Sucking-in breath, he continued: "Just as mine are employed – but rightly - in support of my client's resistance to so unworthy and feminised a challenge. In refuting a daughter's impudent and contrived claims made against a father's natural authority. When so much of what I assert – but could not venture to invoke before any tribunal more appropriate than Your Majesty's – concerns those paternal dignities which he shares with this, *most august of courts*. And if a few of my contentions are controversial, I can still promise you, my lord - they shall *all* be closely-argued…"

"Water clocks, my lord?" I enquired politely, rising to my feet.

"I think I've got the picture, Eurythmus. Now what I'd like most, and in that I think I also speak for the jury, is to hear from your client directly…" said the emperor.

It was his right as the judge or presiding officer, inclination as ruler. Now that Severus had taken control of our case, it would be shaped to his wish – not the jury's. Right from day one, I'd taken the precaution of placing Lydia in her widow's weeds beside two weeping sons, in front of their wooden seating. Intending a maximum appeal to these embanked jurors' pity, I believe we'd achieved it before the emperor addressed my client and family:

"What happens next is I'm going to ask your father, you boys' grandfather, to come and stand in front of the jury and make his explanations to the court. If that makes any of you uncomfortable, can I suggest another seat…?"

Coming from the Butcher of Lugdunum, who threw Albinus's children into the Rhone, these kind words felt so unlikely as to be actively creepy - though I confirm it's what he said. As they returned to sit beside me, Firmus took his turn, stepping awkwardly up and taking the boys' places at the centre of the courtroom. His legs were bowed but his back was straight, his bearded chin up and bald head polished like a chestnut, but his demeanour stayed a soldier's, pride still unbroken. Leaving Eurythmus so out of it and so ignored that his client's main evidence would have to be led from the bench:

"You hold the office of centurio regionarius hereabouts?"

"I do, lord, I do..."

"And what does that involve?"

"I hope Your Imperial Majesty will forgive me if I admit that what might pass for a city council in Luguvalium has earned an unenviable reputation for ineptitude. Thanks to the usual quality of their membership, I regret to report to this court that its council has successfully established - over a long period - a consistent tradition of civic incompetence. Why my main focus since appointment as your regional centurion has been to mitigate their ill-thought-out decisions' worst effects, in the town and district. Whether it's a hare-brained street scheme meant to control wagon-movements in the centre - or that statue of our dear emperor they commissioned hardly matching your magnificent likeness, Majesty; now that we're blessed with your presence, lord, stand better placed to compare. No, I'd say it's been one continuous job for me ever since, shepherding them back onto the right track, sorting out the mess..."

"I imagine you're quite indispensible. And tell me, Marcus Firmus, before that, am I right in thinking that you served as a soldier? Became raised to the centurionate?"

"Indeed lord, I was – lastly in the Second Augusta..."

"Ah, yes, the Second - a British legion I've got to know well. One way or another."

"It was a long time ago, lord – I've been retired for many years. Many years."

"That's probably as well for you. But you served on the Caledonian *limes* once – on the line I intend to reclaim?"

"I did, lord, I did, in the days of the Deified Pius. So, yes, I had that privilege – in command of cavalry. Thracians, they were, yes - Thracians. Like me..."

"That's good, it does you credit. You know I praise our veterans?"

"I do, lord, I do, and we thank you most earnestly for that."

There was a bang, then a crash, and the Praetorians leapt to attention - Caracalla left the building. As he swept out through the main doors, a cold draught blew back in the room, though his father didn't seem to notice. The most powerful man in the world, a man who had everything, yet – only moments ago – nearly strangled by his son in full public view. I nearly felt sorry for him, then, but Severus seemed more interested in our defendants' dysfunctional family arrangements than his own:

"So how old are you now, Marcus Firmus?"

"Eighty, lord, I have seen eighty summers."

"Remarkable, quite remarkable - well done you!"

"Thank you, lord, most kind…"

"And this is your new wife…?"

"She is, lord, she is – absolutely. Mother to my new family."

"Will she stand up?"

Metella bounded energetically to her feet, parts of her body continuing to move after the rest had arrived, while the emperor inspected her gravely from his litter.

"And you, lady, are the second respondent, I take it?"

"I am, lord, I am…" she said, taking her cue from her husband's breathless repetition, and so emphasising the effect.

"Remarkable!" said the emperor again, while she looked around the room, blushing.

I'll grant this to Severus – he knew how to humiliate people. Even without them ever realising it - though I knew him capable of very much worse. So used to getting his own way, it meant nothing to him when he did. We could be chopped to pieces right in front of him and I don't think his expression would even change: benevolent, beneficent, and vague. No, I bet he wouldn't blink - inscrutable and heartless, but charming.

A military dictator pretending to be our First Citizen of the Republic in a republic that didn't exist; his pretence thinner and more superficial than anyone before him. Because it's all about the soldiers – and nothing else matters. Least of all, the people – mere civilians like ourselves.

Clive Ashman

"Quite a gap in years between you, centurion, I'd venture to suggest?" added Severus.

"There may be, my lord, there may be – but I've still got so much love to give…" agreed the proud husband, oblivious, while a snigger ran round the jury.

Even without his son present, Severus on his own remained enough to terrify me, to terrify anyone. Even just to speak to; make a speech before - but I knew I couldn't let it show.

Confidence, or the appearance of it, is everything in advocacy, while the show must go on. And I'm proud to say that it did. Knowing, after Caracalla's gone, that no-one else could seem as bad or as mad – not even his dad – I finally struck:

"My lord…" I interrupted, still surprised by my own daring as I stood up again to make a formal request long rehearsed in my head: "I mentioned yesterday about us establishing certain elements from the defendant's background. Additional aspects I'd like to commend to your court as relevant – to be admitted into evidence, today."

"My client will object!" rebounded Goatface, his long face turning puce under whispy bits of beard. "When the daughter's had her say already… She's said more than enough!"

"Relevant, you say, Justinus?"

"Yes, my lord, in terms of evidence in rebuttal. Because if - as my friend, Eurythmus says he does - if he wishes to tell you more about his client's honourable military service and well-deserved awards, thinking they'll add credit to his cause before the jury, then I will seek the right to call other evidence in rebuttal. To show you otherwise."

Firmus stood there, perplexed and bewildered. Quite alone in the middle of the court and, I've got to admit it, still a tough old bird for his age – while legal argument raged all around him. Though I felt few scraps of pity - in fact none, since Rianorix.

However Eurythmus did, approaching his client and aiming to show solidarity by standing right beside him. Placing a reassuring arm around his client's bony shoulder in an unfortunate echo of that recent episode with Caracalla - moments before and still fresh to general recollection - but also so furious that now he's tripping over his words, turning them into spittle before they are sprayed into the air, towards an astonished bench:

"I must object, Majesty, object most *firmly*…. but begging Your Highness' great pardon. Surely this man…. who's a nobody….a civilian….a travelling wordsmith, no better a man than that! This… this….this *so-called* Gaius Januarius Justinus. Surely he cannot be permitted to come over here…… to Luguvalium, where he's not even registered at the bar… Setting himself up as some kind of military *detractor*, my lord… as if to act like some self-proclaimed *critic*? Daring to damage or deny your majestic words of praise for the veterans, my lord… brave men like my client! No, surely, lord, he *cannot*…?"

"Eurythmus has a point there, Justinus, though I'm intrigued by your line. Why on earth should we let you?"

"Because, my lord, if the centurion Firmus insists on introducing the circumstances of his military service into evidence to the jury, with the intention of showing honourable service and good character… on the basis the jury could be misled into thinking those circumstances provide good grounds - in their own right - for him freezing his only daughter out of any will…. then there's another witness I'd like to call. In rebuttal, another picture I could paint. Provided and of course, that this court will consent to it. That you'll allow me, my lord…"

I sensed how all this could wet his taste buds, intrigue a military-minded emperor. That he only needed to be given one more good, legal reason why he should say '*yes*' to my tantalising request, then he'd gladly get to hear the worst. So that after a longer conversation with his wife, standing right behind him, Severus leaned forward and crooked a be-ringed finger towards the Clerk of the Lists, who bustled over to the side of his litter.

It was a rather shorter consultation they had between them – whispered so we couldn't hear, but one I'd guess ran something along the lines of '*It's up to you, my lord….*" before the emperor turned to look back at us, his face brightening at the prospect:

"Well as you can see, I've given careful consideration to this application, taken advice, and you can call your unknown witness, Justinus. Though, I warn you, they'd better be good...."

I stood up and spoke to the Clerk to the Lists: "Could you bring him in from outside, please – you'll find him standing beside the main door, next to my bodyguard."

"Of course I can, Justinus, and what name should I say?"

"Please ask at the door for Longinus Matigus. Call-out for the veteran, Longinus Matigus, and tell him the time has come for him to enter this court as our witness."

From the corner of my eye I caught the centurion, Marcus C. Firmus. His mouth was clearly moving but no words came.

Only signals of distress.

With his back to the client, Eurythmus hadn't even noticed and was edging slowly away, although I could guess already what would likely happen next. Nor was I the only one – Lydia, thinking so much faster, had reacted in a flash.

Once his eyes went back into his head and his thin, brown knees folded-up beneath him, Firmus would be heading for the floor, but his daughter got there to catch him before he'd even struck, the elderly centurion crumpling into her arms like a child.

As family tableaux go, this one should win first prize - so much better than the Severans. Acting judicially but disliking competition, the emperor took one look and promptly decided an adjournment was in order - the only useful thing he could do.

"Court rise!" he announced. "You've got the space of one water-clock to sort things out between you – let me know through the Clerk how it goes. We can only hope the defendant makes a full and rapid recovery in time..." he added, then signalled for his bearers to go.

"All rise!" shouted the Clerk to the Lists, as the emperor and his litter were conveyed quickly to the door.

Everyone else in the hall leapt to their feet, bowing and scraping while the Imperial column swept past them at speed. Forty-five jury men adding to this chaos when they mostly left their seats, while Lydia remained on her knees in the middle. Still supporting her father while he reclined in her lap, the black drapes of her courtwear suggestive of shrouds. All in all, a most affecting scene – one of filial devotion personified. Provided you did not know - or maybe could forget – about their shared, unhappy history.

A background of betrayal, secret murders and lies.

Could they sweep it all now under the one convenient carpet, like feuding families do? Which – if they did - might be all very well, but what would it mean for our claim? Would Firmus survive, the emperor even let us proceed?

As the crowd swirled madly around us, left her this space in the middle, I looked up towards the ceiling in search of inspiration, any escape from this madness. Saw the domed roof of the bathhouse studded with terracotta tiles, its conduits for warmth. One in three stamped with just three letters: '*IMP*" what they say. Their concise logos of power make our shorthand for '*imperator*' – meaning an emperor, '*The Father of His People*'.

And if that's so, then what should I be doing about my client's?

After Lydia, it was Tiro who was next, or rather the first in my team, who did something useful - pushing past me with a beaker full of water to kneel down beside her, raising its rim up to Firmus' blue lips. That and his daughter's support seemed to help bring the old man round, because I saw his red-rimmed eyes flick open and a frail, transparent hand go up towards the cup.

After what happened to Rianorix, I don't think I could have brought myself to offer my aged adversary any help whatsoever, but Tiro - being Tiro, and wiser - had seen our way through to a much longer game. After all, if our client was to be provided-for in her father's new will, then it was important that our defendant testator didn't die on us now. Or at least not here, in this place - and not yet. Not till he'd changed his will - recognising this harsh reality what reminded me to get on with chasing the same objective. To play my own part.

So off I went looking for Goatface – who I found standing alone just outside the front door, getting a breath of fresh air while his client fought for his own, inside the hall.

"Now look what you've done, Justinus. It'll be your fault if he dies" he said coldly.

"And no thanks to you if he lives, which he will, by the way...." was my reply. "He's an old man, but it's only a faint. He'll be back on his feet before long. But there've been enough lives lost already, and I think the best advice for your client is to reassess his position. Reconcile with his daughter."

"What are you talking about, Justinus? Lives lost? And who's this Longinus Matigus, anyway, what's he to do with all this?"

"I warned you yesterday, Eurythmus, that if Marcus Firmus does not settle with us soon, if he won't agree his daughter's entitlement, then I'm going to take him apart. Destroy his military reputation today, before our commander-in-chief."

"What's this Matigus character got to do with all that?"

"He's a Thracian, one of your father's lieutenants, back in the day. Served with him on the *limes* of Antoninus Pius, before we pulled-out. Soon, once that water-clock's run-out, I'm going to prop him up in front of the emperor – sorry, the judge, our imperial magistrate – and ask him to share some old war stories with the jury. Adventures he shared with your client we now plan to share with this court. Because whether you and Firmus intend to be present or not, I'm sure Matigus giving his proof in your absence will be more than enough to satisfy Severus. No, not to satisfy, but actively annoy him, in fact."

"Adventures... what in the Name of Jupiter, Justinus, could this ancient joker's so-called '*adventures*' have to do with the Doctrine of Reasonable Provision, as made under a will? When all I need to do is cross-examine him, ridicule him as thoroughly as you and the rest of your client's irrelevant and unmeritorious case deserves, and her claim will be thrown out on the spot. There and then. You know Severus holds little sympathy for women."

"Saving Julia Domna, who sits behind him in court and enjoys the ear of our judge. So much brighter than the pair of us, as I think you'll shortly find. No wonder her name's written over the door – you underrate her contribution at your peril. But if you really must descend to abuse between advocates, Eurythmus –

263

well, the more fool you. Haven't you noticed that already – because it hasn't done your client much good so far, has it? Like Hyperides said to Philippides, in his second speech: '*If you think your usual vulgarity and joking will win your acquittal in court, or obtain from the jury an indulgence or sympathy to which you're not entitled, then you're a fool who's very wide of the mark.*' "

"Hah! You think you're so clever, Justinus, but I hardly need to take your advice on how to run a case. Not from an unregistered offcomer like you are. Or to stand here and listen to you twining, tediously quoting the classics. But more important than that, what evidence can this ignorant Thracian of yours offer us today that's of any practical use or relevance to anyone, anywhere?"

We'd begun our acrimonious outdoor confrontation just outside the Ala's new bathhouse on an elevated grassy terrace, the river and its bridges behind us. Directly below us stretched the Imperial encampment, on low-lying flatlands crossed by the Aelian Wall. So I gestured Goatface to follow me, so we could move further away from the front-door or any idlers who might overhear, to a more private spot overlooking this wonderful view.

He'd complied reluctantly, looking warily round like it might be a trap. Which of course it was, of a sort. One I'd worked on for weeks – only mental, not physical, and he doesn't realise it yet.

"Apart from your client, Marcus Firmus himself, we will say that the witness as to fact I've brought along to give evidence today - this Thracian veteran, Longinus Matigus - is the only survivor from a criminal gang of military deserters left alive. He will tell this court that - about forty-five years ago in Caledonia, on the *limes* of the Deified Pius and at the direction of your client, then his superior officer - the members of this gang abandoned their posts and their duties. Operating through a network of Hibernian pirates and Greek slave-traders, they organised a night attack on some government salt-works by the coast. And the sole reason for this outrageous illegal raid, orchestrated by your client, was to extract a common slave girl of his. The young woman with whom he'd become infatuated, despite being found guilty by a magistrate of murdering one of his own cavalry troopers in cold blood inside his fort. Whether she's guilty in fact is quite another story, one that only aggravates the tale, but the reason in law why she got sent to the saltworks. Then, following this raid, where several other innocent people were incidentally killed or enslaved - including a works manager, I should mention – but once the girl's been rescued and restored to her owner and lover – to Matigus' commander, the centurion Firmus – your client has the effrontery and gall to issue his by-now notorious litigation against the state. His fraudulent suit for compensation over a so-called ransom to pirates which he claimed he'd been forced to pay."

"Mmm... I'll admit he told me about that bit. That he sued the *Fiscus* and won. Over the price of a girl."

"Too right, he did, yes. Firmus using the courts to sue the government for its careless neglect of his property. Getting back whatever he'd paid out to the pirates as if they were necessary expenses, reasonably incurred restoring an owner's lawful rights. His fraudulent claim, waged by an officer and deserter."

"Yes, it might not look good, I can see that. Assuming the Thracian's story were true, the court agrees to believe him."

"Oh, yes, it's true, alright. And from a credible witness. One who'll happily come before this court, won't hesitate to report how the centurion Firmus abandoned his own post, then required his subordinates to do likewise, just so they could ruin a public saltworks, get others killed. All of it for the sake of releasing one convict, his singular criminal. Not to mention robbing the Treasury afterwards and stealing public money under the convenient mantle of law. Winning himself a mention in the law reports, creating legal precedent. Yes, it's quite a catalogue of offences for the one indictment and Severus won't like it one bit."

"Alright, Justinus, I've got you - so where does this leave us lawyers?" groaned Eurythmus, indecently quick to abandon his client no sooner than I'd finished. Implying we're mates after all.

"Well, I'd suggest, with a set text derived from the second book in Arrius Menander's '*Of Military Matters*'."

Lawyers of Lugvalio

"Err… which says…?" Ignorance and incipient alarm turning his weak face more craven than usual.

"When a deserter is found in a city, it is usual for him to be punished with death." I recited, having learnt it by heart on the road.

"Mmm, if you choose to put it like that, Justinus, I realise things don't look too good. But what do you suggest that we do?"

Eurythmus had changed his tune completely now, wanting only escape. For himself, if not his client, so he falls on my mercy.

"The water-clock's nearly out, and the emperor's coming back. Does Firmus really want to have his back story shared with our current commander-in chief? This judge who's sitting today? Because if he does, then I could foresee your client's execution easily completed by sunset. Tidily crucified along the walls of Lugvalio to encourage all the others. We know Lucius Septimius Severus Pertinax is famously keen on military discipline and that he loves a good example, but never the bad. Not a man to upset either, but I fear this particular example would only provoke him, tip him over the edge. Demand the cruellest punishments, like he dished out to Albinus. Even at eighty, your client won't want to be crucified, will he? I'm told it's no way to go."

"Look, I'll pop inside and have a quiet word with my client, see if he'll come round. I just hope he's feeling more receptive, although none of this will help…" Eurythmus said, self-pityingly.

"But that's precisely why Firmus collapsed. He recognised the name, knew exactly what it meant for him."

"What *does* it mean, Justinus? Just tell me what you want."

"That your client pulls himself together and goes before the court when it reconvenes this afternoon, Eurythmus. Where he publicly agrees to its formal order that he makes a new will immediately. One which he executes publicly with bronze and scales in front of witnesses, leaving his estate to his daughter."

"Is that all…?"

"No, because you will also confirm to the emperor that - on the basis of the new will he executes - Firmus is conceding our claim and the parties are ending this trial. By mutual consent, done-with here and now. Though what I accept you may not wish to mention is how it also leaves your client - the fraudulent centurion and secret deserter, Marcus C. Firmus - escaping not only inheritance tax, but another type of execution altogether."

"His execution, Justinus – is that what you're really after?"

"The judicial torture followed by a nailed death which myself and quite a few other people present here today might think he richly deserves? No, of course not. All my client wants is to receive her just entitlements. She is not a vengeful person, not a bit of it, though there might be others here who are. And you more than anyone, Eurythmus, should know the wisdom in that old saying *"A good settlement is better than a good lawsuit"*. So that what I'm offering Firmus seems like a very fair bargain to me."

"You dare to call it a bargain, Justinus?"

"Yes, brother, I do. Where the only useful role left for you as his advocate is to explain to your instructing client how – if he wants to stay alive, hopes to avoid a painful and shameful exit from this cruel world of ours – then following the procedures I specify represents the only way he'll be leaving this courtroom alive, as a free man. His only options for escape - possibly also yours! And, as a fellow lawyer, I can only wish you the very best of luck in getting a positive result from that particular brief, *my friend…*"

Lawyers of Lugvalio

Chapter XXIX

The *regionarius* had no choice, and very little time left him in which to comply with my requirements, either. So everything else following, that afternoon at the bathhouse, necessarily happened very quickly indeed - starting from the moment he crumbled.

Adopting the pathways to compliance I demanded from him and his Lugvalio lawyer, Firmus made the will as required and duly swore it. There and then in front of witnesses, in favour of his daughter like I asked. Face expressionless and stoney, a statue.

Meaning our trial proceedings could be ended the very moment he'd done it, and with the format of his new will meeting my client's entire needs and satisfaction, everything else happening afterwards felt like anti-climax. Though this avoidance by Firmus of justice - the whole basis for how Eurythmus and I had persuaded him to cooperate, after all – his evasion of a punishment which some thought he'd earned, remained something that always would irk me. Even if I'd never wish a crucifixion on anyone: no, not ever – so don't get me wrong.

As for our judge - well, Severus had bigger fish to fry: a family to control, legions to marshal, an empire to run, Caledonia to invade. Once his litter left the building, the emperor's interest in our little case disappeared as quickly as he did, and I was only grateful.

Lawyers of Lugvalio

Not wishing to encounter *'The Butcher of Lugdunum'* face-to-face again, or at least not in my lifetime – and not really wanting this cruel autocrat to hear old Matigus' story either, to be frank. If only for fear of my elderly, Thracian star-witness getting arrested himself - or indeed anyone else younger, for that matter.

Including Ascanius, the Sixth's oldest deserter.

Leaving the outcome of our case as a private triumph, instead - one my client and I, along with our team, could celebrate privately at leisure. In safety, and more how I preferred it - that quiet victory we'd travelled so far for, working so hard for to win.

In my own case, I spent that day's evening down at the sign of *'The Retiarius'* along with Tiro and Ascanius, where between us we drank rather more of the landlord's excellent Falernian than was probably good for us - but who in the circumstances could blame us? We felt that we'd earned it, while the wine got added to an ever-growing slate.

So it's no wonder I slept badly on my wood and straw truckle inside that stable at Uxellodunum, woke unexpectedly early. It's the Falernian I should blame - or my lingering worries about receiving payment. Even our most grateful clients sometimes change their tune, once the money gets called in. Would milady?

Unable to sleep longer, I dragged on a tunic and doused my face from a water-jug, then went out for a walk on my own, into the dawn. One that took me to the cliff.

Standing there beside the unmarked grave of Rianorix, its mound of beaten earth, I surveyed the river-meadows below. Regular rows of rectangular imprints in yellow grass left for our only reminder that the massed tent-lines of *Legio II Parthica* ever rested here, just a few days before. That Severus's crack new legion once passed through Lugvalio, before marching off to Trimontium and into Caledonia, maybe never to return?

Like Rianorix himself, another reminder of how transient we are, even empires and legions, when so formidable a fighting force can leave so little trace. Once the yellow grass grew back, their churned *intervallum* lanes returned to pasture, future generations would be oblivious to the history of these meadows. What epic scenes and lives they'd hosted. Likewise that grassy bowl behind me, where - for now - an emperor still resides.

"You did your best, lad, so thank you for that. We won in the end, you should know..." I told him, looking out on mountains.

If a later Praetorian report might implicate Firmus and his tame hoodlums as the principal suspects - culpable culprits for young Rianorix' discovery in the Eden - we hardly needed further confirmation and I still blame myself. Knowing he need never have faced their malice if the poor wee boy hadn't been dragged all the way over here as part of my retinue, at my insistence.

Turning with a sigh from his melancholy mound and its meaning, a river and its flatlands, I looked away to my right. Across towards the waking city, where wispy spirals of browney-grey smoke rose from its walls beside an eastern gate.

The house of Firmus adjacent, it happens. And since that's mere coincidence, the smoke of hearth-fires typical of autumn, I conceded it no attention. Walking back towards our billet without these seasonal signs of morning deserving further thought. Where, upon arrival, I discover all three of our 'T's – that's Tiro, Tocitanus, and Trenico - up bright and early together. Me telling them to rouse Ascanius - the one you'd expect to be first - and then to harness our carriage-team, get things ready to leave.

Because I planned on going to see milady up at the farm, with the chance of being fed by the *duovir*'s generous wife my extra incentive, one possible bonus from making our calls in the morning. With an extended slate I'd managed to run-up for food and drink at *'The Retiarius'* among a list of other closing issues to be discussed with Lydia Firma before our role was seen as over.

On our way there, we went across the bridges and traversed the eastern edge of the city walls in the usual way. A route so familiar by now that these mules of ours had learnt it. As we passed the eastern gatehouse, we could see through its twin arches and directly into the town, where it looked like something was up.

Lawyers of Lugvalio

People and shouting, beside those columns of smoke. Against my better judgement, I authorised our driver to go in. Just like the last time, a decision I'd come to regret – or at least up to a point.

Inside the city and uphill from the gate was a familiar location – the caged-birds seller in his usual spot, there on the left, our opponent's mansion on the right. Smoke spiralled from its centre.

In the street outside his door, the same crowd of thugs and toughs – probably the very gang which killed Rianorix, or else terrorised him into a river – but leavened this time by the forces of law and order, such as they were in Lugvalio. A pair of *vigiles* from the town watch guarding his porch – two military pensioners, greybeards in antique helmets clutching equally theatrical spears, both nearly as old as Firmus. Symbolic sentries perhaps, but contributing little else that's useful otherwise towards the public peace.

Whilst all around them swirled mayhem: a mob out of control. What I mistook at first for *harpastum*, that traditional game of urban football played by the poor, as they kick an inflated bladder from one end of a city to the other, break a few of their bones in the process. Because half the town's population seemed to have gathered outside the House of Firmus and everyone present was shouting. Until a man in a white toga to their centre climbed onto a stone mounting-block at the roadside and tried to calm them all down. But since his preferred method was also by shouting - only louder still – these efforts hardly met with any success that I saw, as we unwittingly entered this volatile scene.

Once our carriage had stopped outside the entrance porch, I asked Ascanius, Tocitanus, and Trenico to disembark first, then to make an outer ring against the mob before Tiro and I could follow. I was glad to see all three of them carrying long wooden staves taken from our carriage roof, where they're usually kept for defence upon the highway but seemed as necessary here.

Once down in the street, it was difficult to make ourselves heard or find out what was happening, because the shouting and yelling continued unabated. Including also a - not unfamiliar -

refrain of "*That bastard, Justinus*...." which could be heard from time to time. Maybe I was wrong to intervene, but it had been curiousity which overcame me and - now we'd actually arrived - I was determined we were going to see this thing through.

So what in the Name of Jupiter *was* going on? The particular man in a red tunic by the front door who seemed the main source of unpleasant remarks about me was presumably one of Firmus's clients, among his senior hitmen, and might otherwise – apart from all his abuse – have been the best to tell us, him being staff.

Ascanius clearly thought so too, because he went straight for him – grabbing him by the throat and jamming him hard against the back wall of the centurion's porch to ask. Not nicely, either.

In the past and only in jest, I'll admit I might – perhaps originally – have referred to my brave Outdoor Clerk as "*late ornament of the Sixth Victorious legion...*" Even as a joke, it's now another remembered remark which only makes me squirm, feel thoroughly ashamed. Because Decimus Ascanius has nothing of the ornament about him, and is probably the most courageous and determined man I've ever had the privilege to meet.

And I can only imagine how fiercely he and his comrades from the Sixth must have stood up to Severus, that bitter winter's day on the plain beyond Lugdunum, because this loud man in the red tunic of Firmus' gang of louts would not have known what hit him. Though we soon got an answer, once our Decimus did:

"It's the boss... old man Firmus... *owwfff... ooogh*... Stop, stop, you're hurting me, *please!*"

"What about your boss? What's happened to him?" said Ascanius, winding red tunic's neckerchief into a rope to throttle him with: "Tell me, and maybe I'll let go."

"Something bad... *urgghh*... just let me breathe and I'll... *Ow!* He's been attacked... we thought it was you lot... then I saw... *urgghh*... I thought...*oh!*"

"Thought what? Talk sense to me, man!"

"*Owww!* You'd better see for yourself... just put me down, *pllease!*"

Lawyers of Lugvalio

Ascanius obliged by throwing him down, very hard, onto the brick floor of the porch and gestured towards the open front door.

With the way now clear and with Tocitanus and Trenico screening us, both of them armed with staves, Tiro and I burst in through the scattering crowd and a pair of bronze doors.

We scrambled, almost ran, down that long corridor I clearly remembered from our last visit, so oddly-lined with a fearful owner's lifetime collection of upright stone altars. Their aligned dedications, made to many gods. From which we pass into the impressive atrium, designed to receive visitors formally before an equally-memorable fishpond. While the further we left the outside world behind us, the more a mob's shouting out in the street became replaced by that awful, ritual keening and strange screams we heard, emanating from his house's very centre.

And still that smell of smoke, as if from scented wood.

Just like we'd noticed on our last time in the atrium - and forming a backdrop fit to frame its fishpond - rose the spectacular centrepiece to his house. That multi-coloured, high-quality fresco of his which so elegantly captures the moon-goddess, Selene: caught forever in sentimental gestures and a frozen affection. Endlessly embracing her tragic lover, Endymion, while below them the centurion's Danubian carp will zig-and-zag forever. Backwards and forwards they go, forwards-and-back across the *piscina*, his fishpond. Criss-crossing its tranquil waters and tiled, acqua-blue floor as they pass untroubled lifetimes in these slow, pointless, perpetual, peregrinations of theirs.

Only, this time, the carp didn't wander alone.

They entertained an interloper - come to swim with the fishes. His name was Marcus Cocceius Firmus and he seemed pinioned by a thicket of thrown hunting-spears to the painted fresco behind. Viciously impaled. On his knees in the water, but with chest, arms and shoulders tightly pinned to Selene on the wall.

No wonder her red lips hung open, aghast – the painted goddess as stunned by this atrocity as we felt it ourselves.

Another domestic tableau, only this one unspeakable.

Clive Ashman

His head hung low-down as if in crucifixion – a white, venerable beard stained with dark red and resting deep in his chest. Leaving his final expression concealed and mysterious beneath a beetling brow, although I for one did not care to check how he might have looked, what a death mask might reveal. However unlikely; whether it's contrite regret or even rhapsodic euphoria; either way, these were things I preferred not to witness. To judge.

And whatever it was, I couldn't see, although I suspect he hadn't been left like this for too long. It had been cold overnight and the blood seemed fairly fresh. Semi-liquid, where it poured down through his tunic from nine mortal wounds, then into his pond. Though neither these globules nor the knees of their owner seemed much to bother his carp, which had easily and already found some alternative routes for their daily routine.

Devising new paths, they swim on regardless, ornamental to the end. Unlike their owner, the centurion Firmus - who's definitely dead, in no way ornamental, and would never swim again.

The fire was in the garden and came from two almond trees, producing that smoke. Such lovely, dainty trees – so who would do such a thing, and why? Chopped-down and burnt in so senseless an act, no one understands it - if not done as a signal?

We were also agreed that this awful screaming still coming from the middle of the house was most definitely Metella's, so Ascanius searched the row of adjoining rooms upstairs to find her quivering in a bedroom. Describing her condition there as unhurt but hysterical, making little sense – her understandable reaction to this one, appalling crime.

Although hardly so hysterical as to have overlooked the sensible precaution of first gathering together several valuable bronze statues with plinths, a rare collection of terracotta masks, and four original paintings, which she then hid inside a large wardrobe.

"*In case of looters, opportunists or arsonists - another visit by the killers....*" how she explains it, Ascanius reporting back. As my client's legal representative, equally the reason why I seized them.

275

Lawyers of Lugvalio

Although rather more important - and the most obvious question for everyone present - was who it was had been responsible for this most shocking of crimes? The more shocking answer being that it might well be obvious...

Even intended to be so.

Because the deceased had died there in a fusillade of spears, a torrent - delivered together, at once. So there must have been more than one killer, while those nine points employed look like nothing you'll see in the army.

Match possession in the eyes of the law.

No, these were sporting spears - from the butts of their home-made, ashen shafts to the tips of their bronze or iron spearheads. Like their heron-feather decorations, they spoke of tribal work. Nothing of Rome, reminiscent of huntsmen. Of natives, at that.

And in case they thought these instruments weren't explicit enough for telling us the truth, then the wicked people responsible had vandalised his fresco with a centurion's blood.

Like it's important we knew.

Yes, you could still see Selene, make out Endymion, but above the centurion's sagging head and shoulders - across a faultless, painted blue sky - they'd written the most important part out using only one word. That one single name which someone's crudely drawn, in wavering capitals but bloody big letters:

NECTOVIL - what it said.

No clearer message imaginable – that this was Brigantian work. In a world obsessed with revenge, here's yet another example. Another score settled, if only but slowly. Their trooper Nectovilius, nearly fifty years late.

My only surprise, that it took them so long.

Clive Ashman

Seated quietly on the stone edge of the pool and absorbing this scene, I heard hobnailed sandals scrape a mosaic floor and saw that man in the white toga come in from the street, unannounced.

He was followed slowly by those two *vigiles* I'd seen at the door, holding their spears like they're walking sticks. Equally useless.

And with me thinking him some sort of civic official, he turned out to be another magistrate, the city's second *duovir*.

"Is it safe to come in?" he'd asked me, breathlessly, as the *vigiles* accompanying looked warily round the rest of the room. Tiptoed cautiously into view.

The three of them directing their gaze anywhere, anywhere. Other than directly at this bloodied, impaled corpse which is slumped right there in front of them, occupying the very focus of his fishpond. Of our minds.

The *vigiles* most nervous of all, fidgeting and adjusting their ridiculous helmets awhile, like they expect another attack.

"Oh, yes, it will be…" I answered calmly, stroking a fish.

"Perfectly safe. It's all over now."

Lawyers of Lugvalio

Chapter XXX

You say my father died on a fresco? I cannot believe it – on a beautiful work of art? That one I remember at the centre of our house showing the moon-goddess, Selene, embracing her lover? Oh, it sounds simply awful - did no-one hear *anything*?" she cried.

Pinioned to his fresco by nine hunting-spears in a painful crucifixion, I dared not estimate how much noise Marcus Firmus might have made. Nor how quickly he died. Maybe he did linger a little, if only in deference to Arrius Menander - wanting to stay at his post a little longer; one last time? Show he could in fact remain - reversing a lifetime's reputation for retreat, making-off?

Either way, the centurion died alone. Enjoyed no protection, despite so many clients – that *claque*, his supporters club. Those street thugs and bullies who raised not one finger to protect him, yet would murder Rianorix on his order. By now, all his friends had deserted him – even Metella. As once with his soldiers - left to hold the Ochre Fort in the last days of Pius, while he's off to the coast. Whether it's comrades or family, always much the same story – one of reckless desertions, defaults done in favour of new.

"Whoever they were, m'lady, they'd have moved in total silence. As skilled hunters naturally do."

"And that writing on the wall?"

Lawyers of Lugvalio

"A crude abbreviation – de-latinised, it was - from the Roman name for that cavalry trooper who died. Murdered in your father's fort on the old *limes* of Antoninus Pius. Forty-five years ago in Caledonia, it was, before you were born. Nectovilius, his name. The records say he served Rome faithfully for nine long years, until something bad happened, in the Ochre Fort... "

"It's the name of that soldier who got killed by the girl they sent to the saltworks – by Caria herself. That girl from my father's law-case you believe was my birth-mother?"

"Well, his was certainly the name on the wall, though who it was who killed *him* might be a different story – I don't want to distress you further, at a difficult time."

"But that's what you're saying – that my father's past finally caught up with him?"

"I'm afraid so, m'lady – or that's how it seems. That its roots are tribal – rest with Brigantes. A primitive act of revenge for their loss of one clansman. Though I don't know if anyone around here will investigate more closely, want to take it any further."

"But what about the emperor? My father was the regional centurion and got killed while in office. Unlawfully, too - I can't see *any* emperor being pleased about that."

"No, ma'am, you might be right there. Though he was a very old man who's lucky to have lasted this long. And at least it was quick. So we'll have to see what the authorities choose to do about it, if anything. But in the meantime, how do *you* feel?"

"It's been enough of a battle for everyone, just getting ourselves out here and then winning the case. Getting this far. Everyone's completely exhausted, Justinus, and that includes me. Plus my own personal trauma from this latest horror - not to mention everything else you managed to uncover. Not all of that was welcome either, as you well know. Not to mention the good people we lost along the way – poor Silenus, or little Rianorix. So even if we had money and energy enough between us, Justinus, to take-up the cudgels afresh, this time over what happened to my father – what good would it really achieve? What chance would we even have of identifying the group of individuals who were responsible for his death, let alone bringing them to justice?"

"Like I say, I'd suspect a group of indigenous people, m'lady - a party of Brigantes. Savages, to be frank. An untraceable gang of native hunters who would have crept down from their lawless uplands under the cloak of Samhain, then as quickly melted away. Beyond the reach of Roman justice."

"Whatever *that* amounts to, Justinus! Because I have to say, my recent experience has taught me no respect for the law. Only to recognise it all for a game. A game that's played-out by men with no scruples. Though when I say that, excepting only *you*…"

"As a gentleman of the law, I suppose I should regret hearing you speak like this, m'lady. Left with so little respect for our ways, though I appreciate you excepting me. But this time, you're probably right - I don't think we'll ever catch the culprits."

"Regrettably, we won't. While for me, there's a particular remark of yours, Justinus, which always sticks in my memory. What you once said to me about those northern tribesmen, sometime we were out on the road: '*Kick one and they all limp.*' A vulgar phrase, I think, you learned from a soldier. When it looks very much like – a great many years ago - my poor, arrogant father made the same mistake. Fell foul of the whole Brigantian nation - not realising they'd never forget. Never, ever forgive him. Just that one, impulsive error of judgement, he made so long ago. A mistake and a lesson which I think none of us should even dream of repeating - don't you agree, Justinus?"

"Yes, m'lady, I do. Not if we don't want to reap the same whirlwind - whether you call it Nemesis or The Fates. And if we're agreed on that, then what will you do now?"

"I will sell my late father's house and property as soon as I can. Pay-off his creditors and harlot, see she's provided-for, and then return to Eboracum alone. Where I feel like I'm finally going to be allowed to be myself, stop being haunted by the past. A proper Roman matron - self-reliant, thanks to the independent means you've won me. Providing for my two young sons and myself, but not beholden to anyone – not even a husband in the *Fiscus* - I can give my sons a future without having to ask. Because whatever my father did wrong, however selfishly and meanly he's behaved, I know I'll always miss him. Or the father he might have been, if only he'd tried…"

"You know, m'lady, when I was outside the courthouse twisting his lawyer's arm, I did wonder about what you were all doing together inside it. While you cradled him there, in that pitiful pose. So may I ask you, ma'am, did you confront him then? Was there any reconciliation – did your father even try?"

"No, Justinus, I did not, and neither did he. I could not bring myself – what would be the point?"

"The point?"

"My father is – or rather he was – a very old man. Unwilling to acknowledge even the half of what he's done, been responsible for. Those things he selectively chooses to forget – events that don't suit. Usually waving them away with: *'Oh, time is a great healer…'* Or other platitudes like that. Those feeble homilies to which he always seemed partial."

"You did not take the opportunity to challenge him?"

"Not as such, no, Justinus. Yes, I had this pathetic person present in my arms but, no, I could not bring myself to berate him about whatever's happened in the past. Not there, not now he's so helpless. I couldn't bring myself to say what maybe I should have once said - something like: *'Look what you've come to, pater…. what a pretty pass you've reduced us all to…'* No, it just wasn't worth it, Justinus – they're his problems, not mine. He was the one who's got to live – and die – with whatever he's done. Did."

"So you said nothing at all?"

"No, because I'm not a vindictive person, Gaius Januarius Justinus. Because when I said I came here wanting justice – it was never anything like that I was after. No, not at all."

"The Brigantes clearly were…"

"Well, they're a different story. Nothing like me. All I ever wanted from my father was for me to receive proper provision from him, when he eventually died. My just entitlements, not a punishment for him. That's all – both for me and my boys. Just in case Aculeo ever abandons me…. and, no, I'm not saying that he would, Justinus, but we women hold nothing at all in this world. While you men have no idea…"

"So what did you say to him, to your father, while you held him in your arms like that? Did he offer or say anything useful to you himself, some crumb of contrition? Words helpful for you?"

"No, I'm sorry to say he did not. Or else nothing I'd prefer to have heard. Yet another opportunity missed – and his last."

"But where did that leave you, milady? What other matters could you resolve while all this to-do went on around you?"

"After Severus stormed out, I asked my father if he could breathe and then Tiro – ever-faithful Tiro - came up quickly with some water, thank goodness, and we both gave him that. Which seemed to do the trick - because my father looked up, straight into my eyes, where I cradled him in the centre of the courtroom, and he said to me: *'You've always been such a good girl, Lydia, such a good girl. I was always so proud of you – always so like your mother'*…"

"Not what he said at the house, that day we served the summonses…" I muttered under my breath, but fortunately I don't think she heard me, because Lydia continued apace:

"To which my reply was: *'Why did you never tell me the truth about HER…?'* Because I'd always guessed there was something wrong, that something wasn't right in the family. Something I could never put my finger on, even while Aurelia still lived."

"That thing which came as such a shock, when it fell to me to be the one who told you, up at the farm?"

"Of course, Justinus, because whatever else I'd imagined, I'd genuinely never thought of anything like that. That thanks to him, I'm borne of native woman, even a slave…"

"You know there's still more to it than that?"

"What, Justinus, would you test me further? Like one of those poor witnesses you lot love to torture at court? Cruelly tormenting them, just for mentioning truth?"

"Madam, there's nothing I would far less do than ever cause you pain. Don't forget whatever we did over here was done in fighting for your rights. But you know there's another aspect to your father's wrongdoing it doesn't feel like we've squared…"

"Would you lade me with yet more woe, Justinus? When I've already learned how brittle his military reputation was - this *'brave veteran'* we had always honoured as a family. This same centurion who abandoned his post and his men, all of it for sake of selfish passion…"

"Only because, when you mentioned the case of Nectovilius to me a few moments earlier, m'lady, I heard you refer to him as: *'that soldier who got killed by the girl they sent to the saltworks….'*"

"By Caria?"

"Yes, except of course that Nectovilius wasn't…. "

"Not killed, Justinus?"

"No, not that. Yes, of course he was killed, but not by Caria - that's what I meant. Not killed by your birth-mother."

"So I presume your next Jovian thunderbolt, Justinus, will be to tell me exactly who did?"

"I'm afraid so, milady. And please remember, ma'am, I did not come all this way here to cause you any grief. No, I travelled to Lugvalio only for you, and only to defend."

"You are the most honourable lawyer I know, Justinus. Although I'll admit life has been kind in that respect and I've only met a few. But, no, you needn't fret over this latest disclosure – I think I worked that issue out for myself, quite a while ago."

"That it was your father who killed Nectovilius?"

"Oh, yes, Justinus, that's a realisation I reached some time ago. Without you or anyone else needing to spell it out for me, thank you. Me and the Brigantes likewise, around the same time."

"I'm sorry…"

"There's no need, Justinus. It's news I can live with. My father will have killed many men in the course of a long military career. Directly or indirectly, in his service of the state. Even as a child I understood that. I've seen enough die in the arena not to become exercised by the sight of wrongdoers executed. And by the sound of Caria's experience, this Brigantian trooper certainly had it coming, whatever his people back home might want to believe."

"Which, to be fair, matches how old Longinus tells it."

"Yes, but - either way - none of that matters very much to me now, Justinus, because it's the fraud and deceit I most hate. Those repeated derelictions of duty by a parent who was always presented to us as such an honourable man, a paragon of duty."

"Because he left his post?"

"Yes, now I realise something resembling that seems to have become his defining failure. And a recurring one, too - it becomes emblematic. First he left his post at the fort, and then my mother – both of my 'mothers', in fact. One way or another. Because I cannot help still seeing Aurelia as my mother, whatever 'facts' you say you've unearthed about this lost woman of the tribes…"

"Caria gave life to you. And submitted to hard labour in the mines out of love for your father. Someone else whose unselfish sacrifices were only made to save a centurion's reputation."

"She did, and I honour and bless her memory for it, believe me. But from the moment he arrived in Britannia, it appears that my father's reputation came to be built on nothing better than perjury. Those lies which either the law or else you lawyers have helped him construct into a great tower of deceit. Lies he must have gone into court only the other day, fully intending to tell - or else relying upon a creature like Eurythmus to tell them on his behalf. That's what upsets me most about all this, Justinus, and why any apology from him would have probably come too late. All that fraud and deceit – I feel it's shameful to his memory."

"Like you put it before, ma'am, and I'm forced to admit to you now, you're probably right. Maybe our practice of law too often amounts to little better than a game. And if an old man of means hires an expensive lawyer to tell lies for him in court, it doesn't make those false claims of his any more honest. Any more valid."

"Yes, Justinus, that's the whole trouble, precisely what I loathe! Because I really dislike thinking about my father winning his famous victory against the *Fiscus* by lying in court about the hows-and-whys of Caria's rescue. That was dishonourable, too."

Lawyers of Lugvalio

"I hope you don't feel the same way about how we conducted your own case? Fought your corner against him?"

"No, Justinus, you've done a wonderful job. Ethical and honest, I'd say. I'm only sorry about all the pain and loss your discovering the truth about my father for me - and then dragging it out before a court – has caused us. Each and every one of us."

"It's the price of success – there always is one. Though you are going to be rich, ma'am, and we all carry regrets. At least you will be able to reflect upon yours in comfort..." I added.

"Yes, it looks like it, Gaius Januarius Justinus, and you've been simply amazing. I really don't know how I'd have managed it without you, or how I can ever thank you?"

"Well, paying our bill would be nice. Especially important for Tiro, but I think it should please Ascanius, too."

"Yes, of course I will, Justinus - no question. And in full – you've all worked so hard. No, I'll never forget what you and your team have done for me, you know. Not ever."

"No, and I'll never forget you... *my lady.*"

Clive Ashman

AUTHORS NOTE

As historical fiction tends to, this tale weaves random invention with recent archaeological discoveries; a few textual survivals and the occasional fact - plus a series of flukes - into one thread. So here's my explanation for where some of these ideas originate:

It was the great Eric Birley who, in 1936, analysing inscriptions on a set of five Roman altars discovered in Scotland (**RIB 2174-77**) made an unexpected link with Roman law. Altars found back in 1771 by the Antonine Wall fort of Auchendavy - my *"Ochre Fort"* – and now displayed at the Hunterian Museum in Glasgow.

What four of the five altars from Auchendavy have in common is their same commissioning author: the Centurion Marcus Cocceius Firmus - he of the Second Augustan legion. That senior soldier for whom Professor Birley made a direct link with what he suggests is the only surviving piece of Roman case law attributable to Roman Britain. The reported case whose unusual facts survive only through a fluke – through their later recital in the Sixth Century *'Institutes of Justinian'* at Byzantium.

From AD 537, Justinian was Emperor of the Eastern Roman empire, and a Byzantine codifier-of-laws whose retrospective digest aimed to cover a thousand years of Roman jurisprudence. Assembling his compilation, Justinian's scribes repeated a much-older case which was originally reported by the Roman jurist, Sextus Pomponius. A case whose facts Professor Birley links with the same M.C. Firmus commissioning a set of Scottish altars.

The man whose precedent - so far as that concept exists in Roman law - established how their (*to our mind grotesque*) concept of the legal ownership of a slave (*their status as 'property'*) could continue despite the slave in question having been condemned to the mines for an unknown offence. Kidnapped later by pirates from the government enterprise where she's being held, Firmus somehow got her back - and then sued the government for whatever price he'd had to pay to do so, by way of compensation.

Brilliant as Birley's epigraphic detective work remains, as he tracks Firmus from Moesia to Rome, and then up to Scotland -

287

and repellent as the everyday cruelties of Roman slavery could be - what most inspired me were a few unanswered questions.

Like: why did this centurion mentioned by Pomponius go to so much trouble to get one woman back? How did he make contact with the gang of pirates who took her - and on what basis did their negotiations proceed? (*All of this even before he set about the government later, to claim back her price*). So what was her crime – and, most pertinent of all, why was she so important to him?

Also on display in the Hunterian is a gravestone dedicated to another Roman soldier, this one known as Nectovilius. A Brigantian from northern England who served for nine years with the Second Cohort of Thracians, though he'd never seen Bulgaria.

Unfortunately but not unusually, his memorial stone is incomplete - omitting cause of death. Meaning no-one can say that I'm wrong or deny he was murdered. Although his memorial was actually found at Mumrills, further east along the Antonine Wall from Auchendavy, no-one can say either, that it wasn't there – back at 'The Ochre Fort', I mean - where this son of Brigantia, servant of Rome, finally met his end?

Caria and her people, the Corionototae, feel more elusive yet. Were it not for another fluke, they and their melodic name might be lost forever. An illiterate northern British tribe, overlooked if not ignored by every geographer, chronicler, or historian of their age; those following on. Maybe seen as *'The Other'* and so obliterated from the record - just another small clan absorbed or overwhelmed by Caledones, by Picti or Maetae - who knows?

Their fluke arrived in 1725, when an inscribed stone (**RIB 1142**: *unfortunately since lost*) was found in the Anglo-Saxon crypt under Hexham Abbey, then copied by the draughtsman who captures its wording forever. On a stone originally commissioned by a prefect of Caesarian cavalry, Quintus Calpurnius Concessinus, to fulfil the vow he'd made earlier to a god of *'most efficacious power'*, it expresses the professional satisfaction of Concessinus at having, as he deftly puts it, *'slaughtered a party of Corionototae.'*

Clive Ashman

His massacre assuring the survival - if only in writing - for these Corionototae themselves, who otherwise disappear without trace. For unless the Roman town of *Coria* or *Corstopitum* – modern day Corbridge - is etymologically-linked, their cultural erasure stands almost complete. *'Ethnically-cleansed'* as the modern idiom has it.

A lost, indigenous people who – like the Brigantes or Carvetii themselves – once comprised the spirit of these remote, northern uplands. Made their presence felt against Rome's ultimate power.

Whilst it would be the invading English and their passion for cricket – tennis, less so – plus a series of climatic events, that led to the discovery of another major element in this story. When Carlisle Cricket Club responded to repeated floodings of their clubhouse at Edenside in Stanwix (a suburb of the city) by planning for a replacement higher-up, on a nearby tennis court. Its level terrace overlooks the flat, low-lying bowl which provides a natural amphitheatre for the club's pavilion and cricket pitch, a meadow which in Roman times was crossed by Hadrian's Wall.

The location where, in May 2017, a team of archaeologists led by Frank Giecco and Kevin Mounsey from Messrs. Wardell Armstrong Ltd. arrived to undertake a pre-build evaluation of the tennis court. Their initial discoveries naturally included the usual Georgian and Medieval debris expected of Carlisle, an ancient city whose role during centuries of Border Warfare is well known. Less expected maybe were some Roman features appearing, although Carlisle's strategic importance during that era means that traces of Roman activity can appear just about anywhere in a town whose recorded history began with the timber fort founded there by Petilius Cerialis, around AD 71. Developments later followed by the large cavalry fort of Uxellodunum constructed across the river at Stanwix as part of Hadrian's frontier system. *(As the largest fort on the Wall system, containing its most prestigious unit, often suspected for the Wall's operational command HQ?)*

Occupying the opposite side of the River Eden, Luguvalium's original civilian settlement was itself promoted in prestige about eighty years after Hadrian, when Septimius Severus granted it the formal status of a tribal capital – as *civitas* to the Carvetii tribe.

Lawyers of Lugvalio

Even so, and eighteen hundred years later, it still surprised more than a few historians when the disused tennis court at Edenside began to reveal the footprint of a substantial Roman building.

Perhaps the most notable amongst many finds eventually made there was among the very first, when the Wardell Armstrong team unearthed floor pillars from a single heated room and, beside them, a triangle of inscribed sandstone. A stone whose incomplete Latin dedication possibly matches - as Frank Giecco has suggested - the abbreviation for one of several honorific titles bestowed on a third century Roman empress called Julia Domna by her powerful husband, Septimius Severus himself.

But before we get into all that, it should be conceded how many others got here first. Since dressed stone comes at a premium around Carlisle - indeed anywhere west of the Irthing Gap, where most stone quarries run out - then builders of the city's castle, cathedral, and defensive walls had throughout the Middle Ages sourced their raw material from a ruined Roman city, one thousand years older. Why this re-discovered Roman building has not only been 'robbed' of stone, it has also been systematically trenched, tunnelled, and mined of it - so determined were the mediaeval masons to extract every last piece.

Today, what's left of the Edenside building looks like it's been bombed, although it's true to say that almost every particle of Hadrian's Wall hereabouts went much the same way – recycling is hardly a modern virtue. Yet despite these centuries of stone-robbing, eight separate rooms were eventually identified by the archaeologists, part of one Roman building. At least three of whose rooms, and quite possibly five, could boast underfloor heating - the classic Roman hypocaust, beneath flagstoned floors.

And if this number of heated rooms plus a smoke-blackened stoke-hole together tend to confirm that this was indeed a bathhouse, then for whose benefit was it built and run, for so long? One candidate seems obvious. Near to the riverbank and also the important cavalry fort of Uxellodunum, garrisoned by the Ala Petriana, the discovered building's proximity and lack of adornment meant it seems a fair bet that if - it were a bathhouse - then it would have been a military bathhouse. A wager becoming bolstered on the very last day of the dig, when a soldier's tombstone was found carrying this less than mysterious endorsement: "…ETRIANA."

Mediaeval stone-robbers might have removed almost everything, but what they clearly didn't care for was the brick they left behind. What archaeologists call 'CBM' – 'Ceramic Building Material'. Red tile from floors or the brick pillars (*pilae*) once holding them up, or pipework nozzles which archaeologists think slotted together to direct warm air into the domed, vaulted ceilings and roofs typifying Roman bathhouses from this period.

More tantalising yet, but in the same ceramic, were those square tiles neatly imprinted with an 'IMP' of sharp precision and meaning. Mainly found on the floor – I assume they fell from the ceiling - more of these logoed tiles were discovered at Edenside than the rest of Carlisle. More indeed (*I'm told*) than in the rest of Britain put together. If that's correct - and I helped-out on site at the time, saw or handled plenty myself – then their blunt message must be important. Why, for the purposes of my novel, I've dared take it further – to claim their corroboration for my fictional case.

If the archaeological context suggests (early) Third Century AD; their three-letter stamp is no acronym but in fact another abbreviation: 'IMP' being 'IMPERATOR' in full. "*Emperor*" is what it says in Latin, although "*This is Imperial Property – Hands Off!*" more what it means. Or else "*Here's an Emperor's Work!*"

Tiled texts that explicitly evoke an emperor's power over this remote northern town and - if a soldier's tombstone can corroborate Edenside's links with the glorious Ala Petriana, shock-troops of the Wall - then what about Julia Domna herself?

The inscription possibly referencing her was discovered early on, in May 2017, and Frank Giecco – who's described this site as being the highlight of his professional career – suggests that it probably decorated the main entrance door into the bathhouse.

(*On the basis it was indeed a bathhouse, that is. Rather than, say, a mansio, a government inn for official travellers - another possibility?*)

Lawyers of Lugvalio

Leading his published introductory report about the dig at Edenside to suggest that this large stone building, with its suite of heated rooms, might have been constructed (*or indeed used?*) during an Imperial visit, whatever else was done with it later. And if that assessment helps in turn to corroborate a direct historical link between Carlisle and Septimius Severus - his immediate family, too - then imagining Julia Domna's name emblazoned over its stone-framed doorway serves to remind those seeing its wording of a significant woman herself.

That Julia was willing to travel all the way to Britain from Rome, accompanying Severus during three hard years of military campaigning in the north, speaks volumes for her remarkable fortitude and the strength of that firm relationship she enjoyed with her husband. Sharing the hardships with him until he died at York in AD 211; where we know that their two adult sons, Caracalla and Geta, travelled with their parents on the same expedition. And whilst there's still a debate to be had about whether her inscription from Edenside dates from AD 208, or else postdates the death of Severus, three years later (*or even relates to her sister?*) you'll understand why, for the purposes of plot and timelines, I've taken it as being Julia and choose that earlier date.

Julia Domna herself was born about the same time as my character Lydia Firma was, or perhaps a few years earlier - around AD 160 at Emesa (modern day Homs) in the Roman province of Syria. The youngest daughter of Julius Bassianus, a High Priest of Baal, Julia came from a powerful dynasty of priestly kings who ruled Emesa as a client state of Rome.

When Severus heard how she was subject of a prophecy that she'd marry a king, this superstitious older widower beat a path to her Syrian door and soon they were married. A union of minds later helping to propel her husband's remorseless path to power.

Throughout his lifetime, Septimius Severus would shower Julia Domna, his beloved wife and empress, with many titles and dignities. Titles which range from *'Mater Castrorum'* (Mother of the Camp) *'Mater Senatus et Patriae'* (Mother of the Senate and the

Clive Ashman

Country) to *'Mater Augustus'* (Mother of the Augustus) but it's the latter honorific historians suspect for the fragment from Edenside.

Strictly, his reign began at Carnuntum in Austria on 14th April, AD 193, during the *'Year of The Five Emperors'* when he was governor of Pannonia and Legio XIV Gemina reacted to the current crisis by proclaimed him Emperor. By then 48 years-old, Severus would begin his march to power via a bloody civil war in which he would separately defeat the governors and garrisons of two separate Imperial provinces – first Syria, then Britannia.

Hence it was not until AD 208 that Severus and his entourage finally arrived in Britain on their *'expeditio felicissima britannica'* - where his first priority was to restore Hadrian's Wall, which had suffered serious enemy damage while governor Albinus was abroad with the British army in Gaul. Major repair works probably both a precaution and the prelude to punitive invasions of Caledonia which Severus planned to launch from AD 209-11.

The northern Maetae and Caledones had repeatedly breached a succession of peace treaties with Rome, and Severus's revenge would be terrible – the human silence in Scotland resulting can be detected archaeologically for over a century. However, even his biographer concedes that Roman casualites were heavy, too, as their legions chased an elusive enemy deeper into the glens.

On 4th February AD 211, his job still only half done, Severus died exhausted at York, where he was cremated on a mound just off the Tadcaster road and the Imperial Court soon reverted to strife.

Upon death, both sons succeeded; an arrangement which could not last long due to the pathological antipathy between them. Back in Rome, Caracalla, the fratricide, soon murdering his brother, Geta, in their mother's lap.

No wonder sight of any of his scowling statues is enough to reveal Caracalla for the psychopath he was. And, as history records, a son hardly averse to making similar physical attacks directly on his father, even in public and during his lifetime – something which I've also imagined occurring right here in the Green Zone. (*While I'm sure any reader of Edward Gibbon will easily*

*recognise where Decimus Ascanius's 'Common Enemy of Mankind...'
jibe came from).*

Once Frank Giecco, Kevin Mounsey and their team had struck
gold with the 'Julia Domna' stone in May, a much larger
excavation of the Roman building at Edenside ran between
August and November 2017. Supported by nearly 150
professional or volunteer archaeologists and helpers (*including the
writer*) it represents a superb example of community archaeology.
This second phase identified all eight rooms mentioned above,
which remain preserved *in situ* under sand - where the hope is
that one day you will be able to view them again, displayed in the
basement of Carlisle Cricket Club's projected new pavilion.

Knowing the structures unearthed so far coincide in date with
Severus and his wife's known presence in York and northern
Britain; and acknowledging the increased construction activity in
Carlisle around this same time, including Severus's grant of civic
status – not to mention all those '*IMP*' tiles, littering the
bathhouse floor - then it's hardly unreasonable to envisage the
Imperial family and court of Severus visiting in person, as Frank
Giecco also points out. (*Maybe even resident for a while?*)

Enough to set me imagining how this large, heated building
beside the river at Edenside - decorated as it is with a dedication
to the Empress Julia Domna - might on the bases of its location,
proximity, and vintage (*but assuming it's better fitted-out?*) have
operated as more than just a local bathhouse for the resident Ala?

Based on the practicalities of the time, it's true that northern
Roman Britain presented a pretty bleak environment for any
contemporary visitor more accustomed to facilities available on
the continent of Europe. Eighteen hundred years ago, that was
Britain's reputation, which poets like Florus confirm when they
moan about our weather – something else that hasn't improved.

While the itinerary which Justinus and his party follow and the
time that it takes them to do so are equally authentic, if you chose
to use the known route and way-stations which I've described.

Clive Ashman

So too are that impressive bridgehead at Cataractonium, its tombs and wayside *thermopolia,* or else the young, self-castrated cross-dressing priest of Cybele: equally-recent discoveries during Highways Agency road-widening works to the A1(M) motorway.

Even for a restless, soldier-emperor to visit and obtain shelter, let alone his feisty wife and attendant court, there would still have been a pretty limited choice of suitable billets available to them along the Wall-line - even fewer you'd call urban. So we can only really imagine Carlisle, Corbridge, South Shields and Vindolanda as comprising a short list of the barely-tolerable few.

But if you were a tough, militaristic emperor like Severus – used to being on the go and with three, long years to spend in this province before dying, exhausted at York – and provided you also bear in mind that three out of the four locations listed above were Roman supply-depots, then it's reasonable to imagine him wanting to visit each in turn, at some point during his stay.

And if - in Roman times - you stood outside the *Ala's* bathhouse at Edenside, looking down into a natural, grassed arena formed by two rivers, the Eden and Caldew, you'd have seen Hadrian's Wall running across the middle distance before you. Stanwix (*Uxellodunum* or *Petriana*) and the Roman Stanegate, their main road into Caledonia, are close-by to your right - while the River Eden and whatever extent of bridges or bridging the Romans thought necessary to carry their Stanegate over it (*I've suggested two*) are immediately behind you. Mixing my eras, Carlisle Castle and the River Caldew can be seen to your left, in a landscape which includes the adjacent flat area where a captive Mary Queen of Scots once watched her courtiers and jailors play football.

So it was this assembly of important historical terrain and known archaeology which inspired me to imagine its charming grassy bowl as a providing a uniquely-secure location where the peripatetic Imperial Court of Third Century Rome might have chosen to pitch its luxurious tents with some confidence of safety.

Because if Henry VIII could manage his *'Field of the Cloth of Gold'* at Calais, then I've no doubt that - with his track record and the limitless resources available to him – then an adaptable Roman emperor like Septimius Severus could manage a *'Green Zone'* at Carlisle, run the business of empire well enough from here. While incidentally and along the way also providing her lawyers with a temporary venue for Lydia's litigation.

Truth is lost in the mist of ages, but need not trouble a writer of fiction aiming to tie historical circumstance and archaeology together in a case that's fit to plead. If doing that involves pushing the envelopes of age and era; the lifespans of known individuals or installations to fit their extremities; then I hope a kinder reader will tolerate it - I can justify each in more detail.

As the poet Byron puts it: *"A man has to serve his time in every trade. Save censure – critics all are ready made."*

So before any critic rushes to dismiss my plot as far-fetched for a Roman period where average life expectancy was only twenty-five – then chooses to mention that particular bit where a newly-widowed eighty year-old, eleven days after bereavement disinherits his daughter in favour of the twenty year-old female he's as promptly married - let me point out these facts are a direct lift from the successful patrimony claim which Gaius Plinius Caecilius Secundus (*'Pliny The Younger', d. AD 113*) considered his finest victory as a practising advocate in the Roman courts.

Wills create trouble in families as frequently as lawyers' speeches turn out too long – which is why a Roman hour needs three water-clocks and their judges would use them in court.

I once did a trial myself – some wounding or assault – where the complainant became so overwrought while giving their evidence that he collapsed in the well of the court. Fainting outright - only to be caught and held before landing by the person standing nearest. Since this was also our defendant in the dock, charged with his brutal attack, their tender tableau together bore an uncanny resemblance to a real-life 'Death of Nelson'.

Left his prosecution doomed from the start.

As with Lydia holding onto her father, unexpected episodes like this do happen in court - it's true. And similarly, whilst Ascanius's description of Lugdunum Field derives from Cassius

Clive Ashman

Dio, it also draws on authentic veterans' accounts of waging war, across the water in France:

Like the old guy I sat beside in the Blacksmith's Arms at Talkin, one evening. Retelling the occasion when he and his mates in the Border Regiment from Carlisle were defending a ring around Dunkirk in Northern France, June 1940. Successfully holding its perimeter and German panzer divisions at bay, until a clanking noise from tracked vehicles rolling-up behind him gave them notice that, for he & his comrades, their war would now be over.

As the cavalry of Aemilius Laetus once did for men of the Sixth.

So whether it's based on eyewitness accounts or historical record; on physical topography or the latest in archaeological discoveries - and disregarding whether any of this actually ever happened in Lugvalio... or else if it did; maybe in a different order... or perhaps at different locations, some of them spelled differently... in other subtly-different ways - I'd still claim there's very little of what's been attempted here lacks any basis in fact. Not least since half of the characters mentioned are real and stand known to the record: can be found listed at the back. Or as Robert Graves puts it rather better, in an introduction to 'I, CLAUDIUS', his peerless novel of imperial Roman politics:

"Few incidents here given are wholly unsupported by historical authority of some sort or another, and I hope none are historically incredible."

Much like the Corionototae.

Clive Ashman, 4th February 2021   *(in lockdown)*

Lawyers of Lugvalio

DRAMATIS PERSONAE:

[1] Historically-recorded characters:

Lucius Septimius Severus Pertinax Augustus - as a Roman emperor, reigned from AD 193-211 (*A man living up to his name*).

Julia Domna – wife of Septimius Severus, and Roman empress: AD 193-217. (*Committed suicide upon the death of Caracalla*).

Caracalla – Antoninus, eldest son of Severus and Julia Domna: sole Roman emperor from AD 211-17. (*A psychopath and fratricide*).

Cartimandua - as Queen of the Brigantes tribe in northern England, reigned c. AD 43-69. ("*Cleopatra of the North*").

Geta – the youngest son of Severus and then joint Roman emperor with Caracalla: AD 211 (*until murdered by his brother*).

Gaius Calpurnius Agricola - Governor of Britannia under Domitian: AD 79-84. (*Subject of Tacitus's eponymous biography*).

Lucius Alfenius Senecio – Governor of Britannia under Severus: AD 197-208. (*Appears on inscriptions as repairing Hadrian's Wall*).

Decimus Clodius Albinus - Governor of Britannia, defeated and killed at Lyons (*Lugdunum*) AD 197 (*His head was sent to the Senate*)

Didius Julianus – briefly a Roman emperor after buying the empire at auction, AD 193. (*Murdered by the Praetorian Guard*).

Marcus Cocceius Firmus – recorded as a Centurion of Legio II Augusta on the Antonine Wall. (*Other roles, as the father to Lydia Firma and a regional centurion at Lugvalio, are my own invention*).

Claudius Pescennius Niger – a Roman governor of Syria, defeated by Severus at the Battle of the River Issus.

Antoninus Pius – a Roman emperor, and possibly their best (AD 141-162) who ordered the Antonine Wall be built across Scotland.

Marcus Aurelius – a philosopher and soldier; he reigned as Roman emperor AD 162-180 and was the father of Commodus.

Marcus Fabius Quintilianus – '*Quintilian*' – considered among the very greatest of Roman jurists.

Quintus Calpurnius Concessinus – a prefect of Caesarian cavalry, Britannia. (*Notorious for his <u>not</u> taking prisoners*).

298

Clive Ashman

Tacitus – an important Roman historian and senator - full name: Publius Cornelius Tacitus, who lived c. AD 55-120.

Cassius Dio – another, rather later but important, Roman historian and senator: as C. (or L.) Cassius Dio: AD 155-235.

Tiberius Claudius Paulinus – an officer who commanded Legio II Augusta in Britain and was also a governor. (*My judicial legate*).

Venutius – the consort of Cartimandua and a king of Brigantes, reigned AD 43-70 approx. (*A cuckold and a rebel, neither ended well*).

[2] Fictional characters:

Gaius Januarius Justinus – a noted advocate of Eboracum and – or so he claims – generally considered to be: '*The Man on Wills*'.

Decimus Ascanius – once a soldier in the Sixth Victorious legion, but now taken on as Justinus's '*Outdoor Clerk*' - his bodyguard.

Tiro – as a slave once purchased by Justinus, but now his senior Managing Clerk and therefore indispensible. Hopes to be freed.

Lydia Firma – the daughter of Firmus, wife of Aculeo: "*milady*".

Flavius & Julianus – the two young sons of Lydia Firma with Aculeo - equally embarrassed by their parents, of course.

Aurelia – the recently-deceased, loyal first wife of Firmus.

Caria – a slave, convict, concubine and chieftain's daughter; princess of the Corionototae people, later dying in childbirth.

Epiclitus – an entrepreneurial Greek slave-trader, active across northern Britannia, c. 160s AD. Pops up all over, only takes cash.

Eurythmus – a lawyer of Lugvalio and useless: '*Goatface*' as here.

Aulus Equitius – an experienced farrier and horse-coper, employed in running Lydia's mule teams. Probably ex-army, too.

Longinus Matigus – aged Thracian veteran of their Second Cohort under Firmus. Hoping for a quiet retirement at Voreda.

Metella – lately a camp-follower, now Firmus's second wife, she also appears as a named respondent in the current litgation.

Namatobogius, son of Colinagius, from the Votadini tribe - Tiro's original name on the record, before he became enslaved.

Lawyers of Lugvalio

Quintus Curius Aculeo – a wealthy accountant in the *fiscus* at Eboracum. Lydia's miserly husband, he dislikes spending money.

Probius Agendus – a cohort commander at Verteris fort, dubbed '*The Collector*' thanks to both his public role and private tendency.

Rianorix – a native Celt newly employed in Justinus's *officium*, almost certainly also a slave. Conscientious & keen: his undoing.

Rufus Sita - standard-bearer to the First Cohort of Thracians based at Lavatris fort, he also does payroll. Self-effacing to a fault.

Sennovarus & Sulio – two slaves owned by Tiro himself, as his inseparable clerical assistants. Used to taking notes.

Silenus – an elderly household slave from Eboracum, the property of Lydia & Aculeo, he suffers from a shortage of breath.

Titus Flaminius – a farmer and *duovir* of Luguvalium, one of two city magistrates and a successful cattle-breeder. Or he was.

Tocitanus & Trenico – employed as baggage handlers & coach drivers, for lifting and carrying, they are both household slaves.

Valerius Restitutus – an embittered cohort commander at Maglona fort. With round shoulders & too few troops to mention; but a shiny row of the very latest in mechanical, bolt-firing guns.

Clive Ashman

Glossary of place names:

'The Ochre Fort' * - a fort on the Antonine Wall, at Auchendavy (*now a farm*) near Kirkintilloch in East Dunbartonshire, Scotland.

Arbeia – *'The Fort of the Arabs'* - a coastal military depot at South Shields, Tyne & Wear, in northern England.

Bravoniacum – a Roman fort & civil settlement at Kirby Thore, Cumbria, in northern England.

Brocavum – a Roman fort at Brougham, near Penrith, Cumbria, in northern England.

Caledonia – the Roman name for most of what we would nowadays call Scotland. (*Rome's Afghanistan?*)

Cataractonium – a Roman town, bridgehead, and roadside fort at Catterick-on-Swale in North Yorkshire, northern England.

Coria - or *'Corstopitum'* - the military depot at Corbridge, Northumberland, northern England. (*In Corionototae territory?*)

Colonia Eboracensis – a part of the Roman city at York which was reserved for retired military veterans.

Clota – The Firth of Clyde, Scotland – a west coast, tidal estuary.

Dubris – Roman port at Dover, Kent, England (or *Portus Dubris*).

Eboracum – the Roman city & legionary base at York, North Yorkshire, in northern England. Capital of *Britannia Inferior*.

Epiacum – Whitley Castle: an isolated Roman fort guarding important lead-mines up in the hills near Alston, Cumbria.

Hibernia – the Roman name for Ireland - nearly, but never invaded by them. (*"One legion should do it…"* claimed Agricola).

Isca Silurum – the large, legionary base for Legio II Augusta at Caerleon, Gwent, in South Wales.

Isurium Brigantum – an official Roman tribal centre and town at Aldbrough, North Yorkshire, in northern England.

Lavatris – *'The Summit Fort'* - a Roman cohort fort at Bowes, County Durham, in northern England. An elevated spot.

Londinium – the city of London, largest Roman city north of the Alps, and later their provincial capital to *Britannia Superior*.

Lugdunum – the Roman city of Lyons, in France, and site of a major battle in AD 197.

301

Lawyers of Lugvalio

Luguvalium Civitas Carvetiorum – the official Roman title for their city of Carlisle in modern Cumbria, as a tribal capital.

Lugvalos – '*Walls of Lugh*' – one alternative (*Britthonic*) name for Carlisle and its pre-Roman settlements.

Lugvalio * – another name for the Roman city at Carlisle.

(As preferred by Justinus, if only because he finds it easier to say...)

Maglona – a Roman cohort fort, *mansio*, and river-crossing at Greta Bridge in North Yorkshire, northern England.

Moesia – a large Roman province, south of the Danube and covering several modern Balkan countries.

Pannonia – the Roman province including parts of Austria, Hungary and Serbia, of which Severus was governor in AD 193.

Parthia – an independent desert kingdom of infamous horse-archers, at war with Rome for centuries.

Rutupiae – the principal Roman port of entry to their British province, at Richborough, Kent - on England's south-east coast.

Stanwick, North Yorkshire – a royal '*oppidum*' and foremost tribal centre for Brigantes, before the Romans turned up...

Trimontium – an important expeditionary base at Newstead in Scotland, for the Roman military. (*Rome's 'Camp Bastion'....?*)

Uxellodunum – '*The High Fort*' - at Stanwix, Carlisle. Home to Ala Petriana: an elite, double-strength cavalry regiment of 1,000.

Vallum Aelium – '*Hadrian's Wall*' - the famous defensive system.

Verterae – or *Verteris* - a Roman fort at Brough-under–Stainmore, Cumbria, and central to their military communications network.

Vindolanda - '*White Lawns*' - the Stanegate fort at Chesterholm, Northumberland, excavated by generations of the Birley family.

Vinovia – the large and important Roman fort at Binchester, near Bishop Auckland in County Durham, northern England.

Virosidum – a Roman outpost fort at Bainbridge in Wensleydale, North Yorkshire, northern England.

Voreda - 'Old Penrith' - a Roman fort at Plumpton, in Cumbria.

[*Author's invented name, or an alternative spelling = artistic licence].

Clive Ashman

<u>Glossary of Latin terms:</u>

Ala – literally, *'a wing'* – the term applied to cavalry units, since that's where they were usually deployed on the battlefield.

Ala Gallorum Petriana milliaria civium Romanorum bis torquata – which is to say: *"The Petriana cavalry wing of Gauls, one thousand-strong - awarded Roman citizenship and bracelets twice, for gallantry"*. A fast-moving strike force – Rome's elite of the Wall.

Attacotti – a notoriously-fierce tribe living in what we nowadays call Ireland, often raiding Later Roman Britain.

Auxilia – meaning, literally *'help'*: their second-rate auxiliary troops. Not yet Roman citizens & expendable first-line in battle.

Centurio regionarius – a regional centurion: therefore administrative, and more of a local government role.

Cognitio extraordinem – extra-ordinary legal proceedings.

Cohors – a cohort or military unit: usually five hundred men.

Corionototae – a notoriously-unknown tribe who lived in northern Britain; now almost lost to history, but for a lost stone.

Civitas – the official designation of an urban settlement's civic status: e.g. *'Luguvalium Civitas Carvetiorum'*.

De Officii – *'On Duties'*: Cicero's classic essay about legal ethics and the proper role of an advocate in court.

Equites singulares augusti – elite cavalry, mounted bodyguards to the emperor. Distinct from Praetorian Guard.

Fiat justitia – a legal exhortation: *"let justice be done!"*

Fiscus – the Roman state Treasury, as was successfully sued by the centurion M.C. Firmus in fact.

Harpastum – a form of Roman football, as played by the mob.

Intervallum – *'between the walls'* – i.e. roads in a military camp.

Lares – the personal, family gods of a Roman household, usually in the form of small statuettes, normally kept indoors.

Legatus juridicus – non-military: a judicial legate, senior judge.

Legatus legionis – legionary legate: the commander of a legion.

Legio – a legion of 5-6,000 heavily-armoured infantry, to be recruited from Roman citizens only. Shock troops of empire.

Officium – an administrative office or chambers.

303

Lawyers of Lugvalio

Praefectus – Prefect: the commander of Roman auxiliary infantry or cavalry. A three-year posting on the career ladder.
Pugio – the distinctive military dagger carried by all soldiers in addition to a sword.
Retiarius – a specific type of very lightly-armed gladiator who fought with a weighted net and trident, only. Still dangerous.
Scotti – another Irish tribe, who (c.5th-6th centuries AD) migrated from Ireland (Hibernia) to occupy Scotland for the first time.
Thermopolia – the type of heated fast-food shops found from Pompeii to Cataractonium. (*See A1(M) highway-widening works*)
Vicus – the lowest civic grade, for villages or the settlements which sprang up around most Roman forts in northern England.
Vero – Yes, or indeed: "*It's true!*"
Vigiles – With no police in Roman cities, these Town Watchmen were the nearest thing.

BIBLIOGRAPHY:

(i) *'The Roman Histories'* Books 76-77: Cassius Dio
- C. (or L.) Dio Cassius (AD 155-235)
(ii) *'Digest of Roman Law'* 49th Book, Ch. XV:
- Emperor Justinian (AD 527-533)
(iii) *'Marcus Cocceius Firmus: An Epigraphic Study'*
- Eric Birley MA FSA FSA Scott. (AD 1936)
  (publ.) The Society of Antiquaries of Scotland.
(iv) *'The Carvetii'*
- Nicholas Higham & Barri Jones (1991) (publ.) Alan Sutton
(v) *'Handbook to Hadrian's Wall'*
- J. Collingwood Bruce (14th edition by David Breeze)
  The Society of Antiquaries of Newcastle upon Tyne (2006).
(vi) *'Land at Carlisle Cricket Club, Stanwix, Carlisle – Draft Phase 2 Archaeological Evaluation Report'* **(CL12406)**
- Frank Giecco, Technical Director,
  Wardell Armstrong Limited, Burgh Road, Carlisle (Jan. 2018)

Clive Ashman

Timeline of Roman *'BRITANNIA'* in the north:

AD 43 – Emperor Claudius orders four Roman legions to invade and conquer Britain. They successfully land on the south coast, in Kent.

AD 51 – After seven years of fighting, the main British resistance leader, Caratacus, flees north to seek sanctuary with Cartimandua, queen of the Brigantes tribe, but she hands him over to her Roman allies, instead.

AD 57 – Cartimandua divorces her consort, Venutius (*who, per Tacitus, had possibly also revolted against the Romans then - 'though defeated*) to marry Vellocatus. Later, in AD 69 - after the death of Nero & right in the middle of another Roman civil war - Venutius' (*second?*) rebellion overthrows Cartimandua, who is narrowly rescued by a squad of Roman cavalry.

AD 71 – With the Brigantes still in open revolt under Venutius, the new Emperor Vespasian orders the final conquest of northern England. After Cartimandua's rescue, his recently-appointed Roman governor, Quintus Petilius Cerialis, restores order & defeats Venutius, before moving north.

AD 74 - By the end of Cerialis' governorship, he's successfully conquered all of northern England; founding Eboracum (York) and then Luguvalium (Carlisle) where he establishes large, permanent garrisons.

AD 84 – As governor from AD 79, Gnaeus Julius Agricola campaigns against the Caledonians: finally defeating them in pitched battle at Mons Graupius, somewhere in north-east Scotland. (*The exact location remains uncertain, but is thought to be Perthshire or Aberdeenshire*). After his final victory, Agricola is recalled by a jealous emperor, Domitian, to enter quiet retirement in Rome and be written about by his son-in-law, Tacitus.

AD 122 – After another uprising in the north, the new Emperor Hadrian visits the province in person and orders the construction of a fortified wall to divide Roman Britannia from *'the barbarians'*.

AD 141 - Emperor Hadrian dies and is succeeded by his heir, Antoninus Pius, who reigns until AD 162. During his reign a new frontier line, much further north, is constructed and garrisoned for 20-25 years.

AD 145 - Septimius Severus is born at the city of Leptis Magna on the Mediterranean coast of Libya. Moving to Rome, he begins a legal career.

AD 162 - Antoninus Pius dies, possibly from plague, to be succeeded by the thoughtful Marcus Aurelius, so continuing the Antonine dynasty.

AD 163 – Roman troops abandon the Antonine Wall - pulling back to re-commission and permanently re-occupy Hadrian's Wall for the remaining two-and-a-half centuries of Roman rule in Britain. (*Movements and reorganisations perhaps related to another uprising by the Brigantes?*)

Lawyers of Lugvalio

AD 180 – Emperor Marcus Aurelius dies; possibly from the same plague he'd consulted the oracle of the Clarian Apollo over; and his appalling son, Commodus, succeeds to the imperial throne.

AD 182 – The Brigantes, along with other tribes of northern England & southern Scotland, are apparently in revolt against Rome, yet again. Fighting reoccurs along Hadrian's Wall, with Roman towns much further south raising walls and defences for the first time against this new threat.

AD 193 – *'Year of the Five Emperors'*: Commodus is murdered by his wrestling tutor; then his disciplinarian successor, Pertinax, is killed by Praetorians. The Roman Empire is put up for auction by the Praetorian Guard and bought by Didius Julianus, whom they murder next, once Septimius Severus is declared emperor by his troops at Carnuntum in Pannonia. Pescennius Niger declares likewise in Syria and Clodius Albinus follows suit later, in Britannia. Niger is first to be destroyed.

AD 197 – The civil war resulting ends with the largest known example of Roman fighting against Roman: the Battle of Lugdunum (Lyon, 19th February, AD 197) where Septimius Severus defeats Albinus, the governor of Britannia. Severus sends new governors to Britain, who purge any supporters of Albinus and begin rebuilding/restoring Hadrian's Wall. They are joined by Severus in person (**AD 208**) when he arrives with reinforcements to take command of the British campaign.

AD 209 – Following years of raids & attacks, Severus leads his armies beyond Hadrian's Wall & into Caledonia to live up to his name and punish the tribes. Roman armies rely on meeting an enemy in pitched battle, but the Caledonians adopt guerrilla-warfare tactics instead, causing heavy Roman casualties. Roman revenge amounts to genocide, but a peace of sorts is achieved and their legions suddenly withdraw.

AD 211 – Septimius Severus dies at York, on 4th February. Once cremated, he's succeeded by both sons, one of whom soon kills the other.

AD 208-211 – By now Britain has been divided into two separate provinces: the south is called *"Britannia Superior"* (Upper Britain) and the north *"Britannia Inferior"* (Lower Britain). For the next two hundred years, London remains as capital of the south, with York administering those northern parts of the island still considered an imperial possession.

AD 410 – The Romans finally abandon Britain, according to some sources advising the native Britons to *'look to their own defences'*.

Drawing of a Roman four-wheeled carriage, based on sculpture.

(Illustration © The Author - 2020)

Lawyers of Lugvalio

Follow the latest adventures – legal or illegal –
of the Eboracum brief, Justinus, and his lady Lydia
as their newest casebooks become launched on:

www.voredabooks.com

Clive Ashman

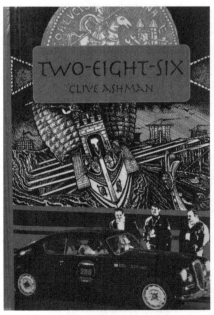

Signed copies available from: **www.voredabooks.com**

Lawyers of Lugvalio